W9-AES-435

THE DEVIL STONE

THE DEVIL STONE

Caro Ramsay

SEVERN
HOUSE

First world edition published in Great Britain and the USA in 2022
by Severn House, an imprint of Canongate Books Ltd,
14 High Street, Edinburgh EH1 1TE.

Trade paperback edition first published in Great Britain and the USA in 2023
by Severn House, an imprint of Canongate Books Ltd.

severnhouse.com

British Library Cataloguing-in-Publication Data
A CIP catalogue record for this title is available from the British Library.

ISBN-13: 978-1-4483-0974-0 (cased)
ISBN-13: 978-1-4483-0976-4 (trade paper)
ISBN-13: 978-1-4483-0975-7 (e-book)

All Severn House titles are printed on acid-free paper.

Typeset by Palimpsest Book Production Ltd.,
Falkirk, Stirlingshire, Scotland.
Printed and bound in Great Britain by
TJ Books, Padstow, Cornwall.

PROLOGUE

He was on top of the world. He ran and ran, blood pumping with sheer exhilaration, on through the woods, over the top of the hill, then up the stairs, two at a time.

Flying.

At the bottom of the monument, amongst the old beer cans and the discarded syringes, he started to scramble up. His trainers slipping on the smooth marble, his toes catching in the angles of the statue, his bloodied hand grasping, leaving red feathered traces on the stone, scarlet teardrops on the steps below. At the top, face to face with the soldier, he hugged his unyielding friend, telling him that he loved him before swinging out on an outstretched arm, looking across the night cityscape. He was beguiled by the twinkling lights, the deep dark scar of the Clyde and the unhurried fireflies of red and amber on the motorway. He breathed in deep, taking in the sight of all that was below him, knowing that he was a hawk, and that all this was his.

He could dive if he wanted.

He could fly if he wanted.

He regarded the little people, the rooftops and the dear green city.

He closed his eyes, feeling the energy in the air, let go and launched himself into space. For an eternity, all he could see were the trees swirling below him, the clouds dancing above him, and the grass, the green sweet grass that welcomed him so warmly.

He wasn't sure when he hit the ground. He was just there. No longer flying. Now embraced by Mother Earth, a small stone cutting

1

into the skin of his cheek. One leg was twisted to the side. His shoulder wasn't where it should be.

A comforting hand was on his arm, giving him a reassuring pat, then fingers slipping his iPhone from his pocket and a voice asking him for his PIN number, telling him that help was on the way.

ONE

The day was dying. Long shadows followed the two lads creeping round the outer walls of Otterburn House, their silhouettes echoing furtive movement before being absorbed by the ivy on the bricks of the old mansion. Once through the arch at the walled garden, they dropped their hoods and started to swagger.

They moved in silence though they knew no one was home to overhear. Their only companions were their shadows, and they weren't much for talking.

Scotto gave the cars the once-over: the Lexus, the Jaguar, the Land Rover and the Audi. They'd turn a pretty penny if only he had the right contacts. He saw Bainsy pointing to the lower window – a single pane, wide enough for them to get through easily; they were skinny wee guys, built for speed. Scotto fixed some duct tape to the leaded glass before knocking it gently with his favourite mallet. A lightning bolt cracked across the pane, and the accompanying snap echoed around the darkening garden, caught by the high hedges. The rooks took flight and headed for the cover of the trees.

They waited. No alarm, no lights. No shouts, no slippered footsteps rushing across the hall, no barking dogs. No response to the noise. Just the angry cawing of the circling birds.

Scotto tapped round the edges of the frame, easing the larger shards of glass on to the tape before lifting them clear of the wooden casing and settling them against the ivy. He lifted the remaining jagged pieces with his gloved fingers, chucking them over his shoulder where they nestled amongst the cream-coloured stones of the driveway. He hefted himself up, sitting on the edge and swung his legs over, the soles of his trainers squeaking as he landed on the tiled floor.

Bainsy, the shorter of the two, took a running jump at it.

They flicked their phones on, swiped to torch and flitted the beams across the white tiles of the kitchen, the rugs, the eight-burner cooker and the copper pans hanging from the ceiling. The glimmer from Scotto's phone halted for a moment as it highlighted the wine rack. He'd heard there was a whisky collection here as well. That'd be worth a few bob if he could get it to the right guys in Glasgow.

Bainsy nudged him, telling him to get a move on, reminding him what they were here for. They sneaked through to the older part of the house where the hall's wooden panelling was festooned with weapons and armour, three storeys rising above them. The staircase circled all four walls to the top landing in the apex of the eaves, the clouded sky clearly visible through the roof window, as were the gyrating birds. Scotto looked up and felt uneasy; he'd never seen anything like it. The McGregor family had lived here for generations. They were minted.

And they were here for a bit of rock? It didn't make sense.

All around him he could see small valuables, easily disposable for cash. But Bainsy was only after the stone, the Devil Stone. He was obsessed with it.

The gossip around the village was that the McGregor family were away on a cruise, and Otterburn House, with its treasures and secrets, had been sitting empty, alone behind the wrought iron gates. It would be rude not to pay it a visit.

Scotto looked at the panelled walls with the stag's head trophies, the long drapes of tapestry portraying the family crest above, and below, the wide carpet, blood red and fastened by bright brass rods. He leaned on the newel post, sniffing, jerked his hood up a little higher, pulling a face at Bainsy. 'Something's crawled in here and fuckin' died. It's mingin'.'

'It's an old hoose, of course it stinks. There'll be deid rats an' folk's grannies up the chimney. Come oan, the old yin keeps it oan her fireplace. Find her bedroom and we find the . . . Jesus!' He pulled back at the sight of a giant stag's head on the half-landing, fourteen-point antlers, the beam of the torch catching its glassy eye. 'Ohhh, Ah nearly shat masel.' Bainsy sat down on the red carpet, his cuff gathered in his hand, jamming it in his mouth as tears streamed from his eyes, trying to stop laughing.

The stag regarded them with disapproval.

'Oh deer,' said Scotto, joining in with the laughter. 'Get it? Oh deer.'

'Fuck's sake, man, come oan.' Bainsy got to his feet, unsteady, farted and yanked up the waist of his jeans that had dropped down his hips to bare the legend Dolce & Gabbana on the waistband of his counterfeit boxers.

They started up the stairs again. Scotto looked at the figure in the window, wondering who the guy with the beard and doleful eyes was. Moses? Noah? Jesus? Some bloke in an amber tunic and burgundy robe, a lamb at his feet. He wished those brown eyes would stop following him.

Thou shalt not steal.

Bainsy was made of stronger stuff. He didn't give a toss about Jesus or the cross or what it all stood for. The faith of lambs right enough. He followed the master of the fire. And he was reclaiming the stone.

The smell was stronger here, thick enough to chew, causing Bainsy to cough and flip up his hoodie again. 'Ah think they fucked off oan holiday and left the dug, and it's crawled intae a corner and died.'

'Smells like it crawled up your arse and died. That's rotten, pure rank, by the way.'

'Why's it so fucking dark?'

'The tint't windae. Ma pals got a motor like tha', cannae see a fuckin' thing. And naw, yer naw puttin' a light oan.'

Something, some feral sense of self-preservation, stopped them at the top of the stairs. A little pause to steady the nerves, yet they knew there was nobody in the house.

Bainsy turned to take a last look at Jesus, checking he was still immortalised in glass and not following them to remind them of the way of the light as they continued up and along into the valley of darkness.

Scotto stepped onto the first-floor landing. The beam of light over the ornate ceiling showed it was bigger than his flat back in Glasgow. The old woman, old McGregor, would have her bedroom up here. According to Bainsy, she was worth millions; she had diamonds, necklaces. She might even have a bloody tiara. And she had the Deilstane, resting on velvet in a glass display case, sitting on the marble hearth, fire and brimstone bleeding together. Bainsy had been telling him some shite about a stone that bled real blood. Too much of the old Mary Jane, that was Bainsy's trouble. Scotto had his own plan to steal anything small enough to pocket and get it back to Glasgow, get it sold and make some dosh. He'd keep that from Bainsy, who was insisting a blood-stained bit of rock was going back to its rightful owner.

At the moment, Bainsy was standing still, merely tilting his wrist as he shone the soft beam of his phone round the walls of the landing, the light moving over an oil painting of a few skinny horses before pausing on a large picture of some blonde bint in a long white frock. She looked a bit of all right, probably an ancestor of the McGregor family. Then the light picked up the slashes on the canvas. One horizontal, one vertical, the shape of an inverted cross. A feeling of faint pleasure grew somewhere in the back of his mind. He shone the beam from side to side seeing the shelves of leather books that lined every wall, the four archways that led off to different parts of the house and, in front of the banister, a grand piano.

'A fuckin' piano in the hall, eh?' Bainsy got a nudge from Scotto, a jerk of the head. 'What's that worth? How much d'ya think?'

'Aye right, Ah'll just stick it up ma jumper and away we go. Ya dick.'

But Scotto was looking at the candlestick on the piano lid, highly polished silver, worth a few bob but too big. More interesting were the silver and gold trinket boxes, small enough to lift right now: eight of one, ten of the other.

Bainsy dropped the light beam towards his feet to see the blood-red carpet bordering the dusty wooden floor. The stink was worse here, bad enough to gag a ferret.

He looked down at the toe of his trainers as he kicked something soft; instead of the wooden floor, there was a patterned duvet, lying all fankled up, covering something.

Scotto's torch homed in. 'Some bastard's been here afore us. That wis ma plan – get the stone, get some good stuff, aw' oot oan a sheet, wrap it a' up then drag the whole shebang doon the stair. Looks like some bugger's done the job a'ready.' He scanned the light around, seeing the line of peaks in the duvet, in a row, like toes in a bed.

'Hey, look.' Bainsy shone the light across the floor, catching a maggot-ridden goat's head perched on a red velvet chaise longue; from it ran a trickle of dried liquid, two bright goblets on either side. Two daggers, their blades dull and stained, were arranged between. There was a black figurine, goat-headed, winged and forked-tailed as a centrepiece, and as the beam of light dropped, he saw the inverted cross and the charred book. Even he could guess, from its feather-thin pages, that it was a bible.

He started saying something that Scotto couldn't make out, then his eyes closed, opened again, and he smiled before moving the light down, giggling a little, jerking the phone, causing the beam to drop suddenly where it caught the ghostly white face staring at the ceiling with nacreous clouded eyes. Unable to stop himself, he looked along. Another face. Then another. Five of them in a row, cheek to cheek. Dried white skin clinging to thin cheekbones, mouths open, teeth bared. A single black slug was weaving its slippery trail across the grey forehead of a girl he recognised, a girl he had quite fancied in fact, Catriona McGregor.

In panic, he dropped the torch and darkness fell on them.

Scotto pointed to the archway through to the bedroom and screamed.

Bainsy saw two red eyes in the darkness, staring right back at him.

SCOTTISH BALLET'S PRODUCTION OF *La fille mal gardée* at the Theatre Royal in Glasgow had been hailed a triumph; the clog dance had been reimagined, the maypole sequence re-choreographed and the finale sent a crescendo of joy and praise echoing around the auditorium. The curtain dropped, and the pain, the sweat, the exhaustion of the dancers were forgotten in the euphoria.

Kate Miller sat beside her mother's wheelchair, eating a bar of Fruit & Nut, waiting for it to be over. Her own interest in dance began and ended with *Strictly*. Ballet was not Kate's thing, too much jumping around in silly tights for her liking, but her mother had loved every minute of the performance, no doubt rolling back the years to when she used to dance. Being a 'solidly built girl', Kate had never tried ballet.

And it cost a fortune. Just as these tickets had. Much more than Kate could afford with three kids living off her single wage.

As the principals took their curtain calls, tears softened her mother's eyes. Kate gave her a clean hanky before joining in with the standing ovation. Her mother raised her hands as far as her arthritic shoulders would allow, clapping with enthusiasm.

They waited, her mother rabbiting about the performance and the new principal male dancer, Borshov, as the other patrons filtered out the theatre. Her mother tapped his picture in the programme, as she explained some technical points. Kate nodded mechanically and risked a look at her watch, keeping an eye on the front doors and judging it was still too busy for the chair to exit easily. She sat back and waited as her mother droned on. Kate had parked in the Cambridge Street car park and, while dancing had kept her mother sylphlike in her youth, she was now a fair weight to push up that hill.

An usher came to chat to them, enquiring if they needed any assistance, which was shorthand for asking them to leave. The name 'Anna' was scripted in black on the bronze badge pinned to her red waistcoat. *Had they enjoyed it?* Of course they had. Kate listened as her mother prattled on, taking Anna's slim hand, forcing the usher to crouch down to speak to her eye to eye. This was going to take some time; her mum enjoyed a good blether.

But Anna was well rehearsed in these situations. She gradually straightened up, releasing her hand from the old lady's grasp. It was a cue that their conversation was over.

Kate nodded in gratitude, stood up and released the brake with her toe and slowly rolled the chair down the slope of red carpet as her mother kept up her incessant chatter, not noticing the folded programme slip from her lap. Anna walked alongside, nodding, saying, *Oh, you were a dancer, were you? Did you ever perform here?* By the time they reached the main doors Kate knew that Anna was engaged, studied pharmacy at Strathclyde University and had a rescue dog called Peanut. As they reached the foyer, somebody called for Anna's assistance, no doubt another part of the familiar routine, thought Kate, as the usher said goodbye and that she hoped to see them again before being swallowed by the darkening auditorium. A tall woman glided towards them, must have been an ex-dancer from the way her black hair was pulled back into a classic chignon. She handed the programme to Kate's mother, with a shy smile.

'You'd miss that when you got home,' she said, her voice low and melodious. Then she was gone, the eye-catching yellow of her dress disappearing into the crowd milling on the pavement.

'You hold on to that,' Kate told her mother; the programme had cost a hard-earned tenner. She began pushing her mum towards the multi-storey. It was twenty to ten, a quiet summer evening in the city. The air was still warm with a gentle hint that the chill of the night wasn't far away. The street was emptying, pub doors were open, but most of the drinking now was in back alleys, backcourts, under gazebos and makeshift marquees that evidenced the recent pandemic. Glasgow had, on nights like this, morphed into Paris. Kate thought it was lovely to see. Two young men came round the corner, their jaunty stride bouncing them along, looking as if they had no intention of getting out the way.

Kate felt her mother tense in the chair, gnarled knuckles gripping tighter on her handbag. She subtly looked round, trying not to appear nervous, but the only people in sight were two women in front. One was dressed in blue, her neat bob swaying as she laughed at something, linking arms with her companion, the tall lady in yellow. They were chattering as they walked, slowly, probably recalling the performance. The two young men came close to the wheelchair then sidestepped, saying hello. The taller one, who was slightly more sober, blew her mother a kiss, to which the old lady responded, 'I wouldn't kick you out of bed.'

Near the car park Kate spun the chair, pulling her mother up the kerb rather than pushing. As she turned the chair back round on its rear wheels, a young woman, her long floral dress winding round her legs, totally absorbed in undoing the buttons of her light summer coat, almost bumped into them.

'Oh, sorry, wasn't looking where I was going.' She swiped her purple corkscrew hair from her smiling face, seemed to notice where they had come from. 'Excuse me, but have you walked up from the Theatre Royal?'

Kate opened her mouth to answer but her mum was too quick.

'Oh, yes, it was—'

'You didn't see a set of keys, did you? As you walked up? I think I've dropped them somewhere between here and the theatre.'

'Oh, dearie me,' said Kate's mum. 'No, we didn't see anything, did we?'

The young woman pulled her phone from her pocket. 'I've already called the theatre. I'd better nip back and see if anybody's found them.

The trouble is, I'm sure they were in my hand when I left.' She shrugged, like it was hopeless. 'Well, I thought, I was sure.'

'The staff are still there – they were closing the doors when we left,' said Kate, wishing the woman would get out their way.

'I really need to get a move on.'

Kate murmured under her breath, *yes, why don't you.*

'Did you enjoy the ballet?' asked the old lady, sensing a gap in the conversation that she needed to fill.

Kate placed her hand on her mother's shoulder, sensing something off about the disparity of the young woman's stillness and her anxious words.

There was a slow beat before the summer coat flapped as the woman nimbly sidestepped to their right and Kate felt her handbag being jerked from her left shoulder, breaking the soft contact between her hand and her mother. The handbag was away, tucked under the arm of a skinny lad on a bike, pedalling quickly up Cambridge Street. Kate must have shouted as the two women in front turned to see the thief travelling towards them. They parted company, seemingly moving out of the way to give the bike a clear path. Kate saw the one in the yellow dress step out, right into the path of the bike. The boy raised both his arms like he was celebrating victory, the bike jackknifed, and he was in mid-air. Kate saw her handbag catapulting along the gutter, her phone and purse erupting from the open clasp.

'Oh, good God,' cried her mother, her hand on her chest, but the words were stuttered, her breathing laboured. A grey pallor rose in the old woman's face, her lips turning purple and her hands clamped on the arms of her chair as she fought for breath. Kate immediately reached for the mobile phone in the bag that was no longer there. Along the road the woman in the yellow dress was on her mobile, kneeling down beside the young man writhing on the ground.

Kate took another look at her mother and shouted, 'Can you call an ambulance?'

⋆   ⋆   ⋆

POPPY THE LABRADOR BOUNCED to her feet, snarling before Betty and Doug heard the battering at the front door. It was too late at night for a casual visit; Betty Knox was already in her housecoat, thinking about going to bed. She held the dog by the collar and looked through the spyhole.

Wee Billy McBain and his daft cousin, the one with the stupid hair, were standing in the front garden. Bainsy was the bad boy of the village, always off his head on something or other, on the lookout to nick anything that wasn't nailed down. Rumours were that he had started carrying a knife. She didn't open the door but dragged the reluctant dog back into the living room where her husband was snoring again, the news muted on the television. She nudged his knee.

'Doug? Get the door, it's that McBain waster and his wee pal. Get rid of them.'

He muttered, 'Whit?' But she shooed him from his sleep.

She was too tired to be mugged, and certainly not by the likes of Billy McBain. 'Tell them to get to France. Whatever they're wanting they're not getting.'

Doug Knox was nothing if not obedient; he padded his way to the front door and opened it, still in torpor, and had no resistance when the skinhead rushed past him, knocking him against the wall.

'Jesus, gonnae get the polis.' The cousin's thick Glasgow accent came through loud and strong from the front garden. 'Get the polis, will youse?'

Bainsy looked close to tears. Knox could smell vomit on his breath, could see the fear and the tremor.

. Was this a scam they were trying to pull? Knox was wary, but he doubted it. The cousin stayed out in the garden, staring blankly. He was so unsteady on his feet, Knox went out to give him some assistance, horrified to see the teenager's bleeding hands, the blood smears on his face.

Betty was at the door now. She knew shock when she saw it – the pale face, the rapid breathing – and there was blood dripping from his fingertips. 'Oh, son, what's happened to you?' She put her arm out, and the teenager began to cry, sobbing and holding onto her as if for dear life itself.

'There's something fair amiss here, Doug,' Betty said, taking the cousin by the shoulders and marching him into the kitchen, where she sat him down on a chair and wrapped his hand in a clean towel. She could see a sliver of glass was embedded deep in the skin. She held onto him, looking straight into his eyes, asking him what his name was.

'Scotto.'

She asked him what the problem was. Had there been an accident? Was somebody hurt?

Scotto shook his head.

He was in a state: his big blue eyes red-rimmed, the flattened waxed peaks of peroxide hair, snot running from his nose, the blood-smeared face, two skinny bloodied hands of scarred skin and bitten nails. 'They're a' deid, all on the flair wi' slugs and stuff everywhere. We thought it wis a deid dog but it wisnae. It wis a deid goat, oan the wall, wi' its eyes hingin' oot . . .'

'William McBain, what have you been smoking?' shouted Betty over her shoulder.

Scotto pulled her back to face him. 'Up at the hoose, they're a' deid. Call the polis, Ah'm telling you, at the big hoose.' His head jerked on his scrawny neck. 'Up the hill, they're a' deid.'

'Otterburn House? What do you mean they're all dead?'

'A' deid and rottin' on the flair, Jesus! A' puffy. Stinkin'. There wis a deid dug and a deid goat and . . . oh God!'

'They were supposed to be on a cruise,' muttered Betty to her husband. 'I'll phone up, make sure everything's okay.' She walked to the hall, while her husband tried to piece together what the two young men were saying. What had they seen? Had they imagined it? Bainsy had a reputation for smoking all sorts. Betty came back in and shook her head. 'No answer on the landline, and Barbara's mobile's not connecting.'

'They must be away. I'm calling the cops,' said Knox, looking at Scott who was still shaking, knee pumping like a piston, his face grey. The white towel round his hand was slowly turning crimson. He didn't trust these two one bit, but something had happened and it had scared them. At the end of the day, they were just daft lads, not even in their twenties. Knox's boys were the same age. There but for the grace of God . . .

'Get yer finger oot! They're a' up at the hoose, deid on the fuckin' flair. Fur Christ's sake . . . Oh, man . . .' Scotto was wailing now.

'You mind your language, son. Doug? Go next door and get Moira and Jim. I'm no' getting left with these two. You get the police.'

'Ah'm telling you, they're a' deid.' Scotto started sobbing. 'Ah'm telling you, the Devil wis right there, starin' at us wi' big red eyes.'

Betty rushed him to the sink as he began to retch again.

Knox got on the phone. 'I'm Douglas Knox, I live in the last bungalow in the village before the road turns up to Otterburn House. Billy McBain and his pal, Scotto somebody, knocked on our door tonight They're in shock, I mean, deep shock. One has shards of glass in his hand, and they say they broke into the house and found bodies on the landing. And no, I don't know if it's true. From what they're saying I think it's the McGregor family. I think they may have come to some harm. The boys keep saying they're all dead.'

'All of them?' asked Constable Whyte.

Knox nodded. 'All of them.'

TWO

Christine Caplan finally put her key in the lock, turned it and stepped into the twilight world of her family home, number 27 Abington Drive: a soulless house where curtains never opened and nobody ever laughed. Seven years they had lived here, having had to downsize after Aklen left his job, and although she had accepted the need to move, this house had never felt like home.

The Drive was asleep. Middle-class suburbia at one o'clock in the morning. The neighbours' cat strutted out from behind the hedge and tiptoed over to her. Seven years, and she still didn't know the daft thing's name; she didn't know the neighbours' name either, just knew them from their constant complaining about the uncut grass or Emma's car being parked on the street. And, Caplan suspected, they left their cat outside on long wintery nights. The cat arched his back against her leg while mewling at her, wanting in and looking for food.

Caplan walked through the hall without putting the light on, the cat trotting in front of her to the kitchen, straight to the cupboard where she kept a secret store of Dreamies. She called the cat Pas de Chat; it was their own little joke. She tinkled some of the dry biscuits into a saucer and placed it on the floor, then gave the cat some water which he took one sniff at before walking away, tail twitching dismissively. The house was silent. The heat of the summer day had gone and the overgrown plants in the garden were alive with clouds of insects. A dark flash went past, a bat sensing a meal in the still air.

She examined her yellow dress under the fluorescent light of the

15

kitchen. And swore. Two long streaks of bloody vomit, a present from the daft boy on the bike as she had knelt beside him. The dress was ruined, and it would be a long time before she could afford another. All thanks to that kid. She had knelt down, stopping his head from hitting the corner of the pavement while she called the paramedics for both him and the old lady in the wheelchair. Her night out at the ballet ended with a two-hour wait in A&E while Kate Miller's mother had her cardiac rhythm stabilised. Her daughter had performed CPR when the old girl's heart arrested fully before the arrival of the emergency services. The woman, Mary Prior, had a well-documented history of heart trouble and the casualty doctor had said it was very fortuitous that they had been present at the scene.

Caplan looked at the staining again, the red seeping into the yellow, thinking about the boy, the mugger, who could have cycled past them on the opposite pavement, through the lane and away through the city streets.

But he had cycled straight for her.

It seemed to her he had leapt off his bike when the front wheel had hit the kerb and his face was bleeding before he had the seizure and started vomiting. But to quote many witnesses she had interviewed in her career: *it all happened so fast.*

Her ruined dress seemed an apposite end to a terrible day that had started with her hearing for professional misconduct, then the incident with Danny Doran, ending with Emma pulling Mary from her wheelchair to the ground for CPR.

Caplan took another look at the dress. She had put it on that evening with such anticipation. The ballet had been good though. Like the old joke, 'Apart from that, Mrs Lincoln, did you enjoy the play?'

She walked into the living room, hoping that her husband might have stayed awake to find out how the hearing had gone, if she still had a job, if they could still afford the mortgage on this house; to celebrate if it had gone well, to offer solace if not. But Aklen was fast asleep on the sofa, curled like a child, knees pulled up, hands together under his chin. He was wearing the same joggers and T-shirt that he had been wearing when she had left this morning, when he had been lying in the same position but on his bed upstairs. Funnily, as he had slept more and more, she had needed less sleep, working overtime to earn more money. It did have the added advantage of keeping him out her way. And vice versa no doubt.

She closed the door quietly, in the knowledge that she could have played 'The Dance of the Sugar Plum Fairy' at full volume and the other end of the Drive would have heard it before it woke him up. Climbing the stairs, the noise of Kenny's fingers tapping a keyboard got slightly louder. He was playing some video game, talking to another lonely boy while shooting people in an alternate universe. There was no point in letting Kenny know that she was home; he would have never noticed she had left.

In the bathroom, she got undressed, dumping her dress in the bin, reminding herself that she was lucky. She could be Danny Doran's mother. A young man with a future ripe to be wasted. Maybe if this house wasn't so comfortable, Kenny might go in search of succour out on the streets with a needle in his arm, mugging old ladies near multi-storey car parks.

She took a quick shower, turning the water to cold for the last few minutes, then dressed in her leggings and a warm pullover. Brushing her long hair from its chignon, she went downstairs, picked up her mobile and checked her messages while the kettle boiled. The house was still deathly quiet. Pas de Chat sat at the back door, washing his white face with his paw, looking cute.

A weak decaf then outside, Pas winding round her legs, onto the decking at the patio doors, where she took her chair overlooking the garden.

She closed her eyes, savouring the coffee, gathering the strength to process the events of the evening in more detail.

Such a lovely evening at the ballet. She smiled at the memory of when, in her youth, she had danced one of the villagers in the clog dance, the one the widow kicks. She had been more than a background dancer. Her career had shown much promise when she was that age. She stretched her bare feet out in front of her, seeing the evidence of knurled, misshapen toes. Years of abuse, to dance. That was all she ever wanted to do.

Then she grew two inches too tall.

Her first career had failed. Her second wasn't looking too secure either.

Pas de Chat, watching her wriggle her toes, decided to jump on her feet, claws out.

It had been good to see Emma. She had the best of both her parents, she was a caring young woman who would take no nonsense from anybody. They had spent time together that evening, having dinner and going to the ballet, talking about each other rather than family crisis management. The cheaper tickets that Caplan was entitled to as a lifelong supporter of the Conservatoire came in useful on these occasions, teasing Emma out from her student flat near the university which she preferred to her large bedroom up in the attic of the family house. Who could blame her?

With the stress of the day, the long hours, she began to doze, comfortable in the dark, watching the bats dart back and forth; almost too quick to register before they were gone. She woke up when Pas clawed her knee, jumping at the sound of her phone buzzing. A text from her friend Lizzie, asking if she was okay. It was half past two; Lizzie must be late coming off a back shift.

'I'm good.'

'You still got a job?'

'Tell you tomorrow.'

'Ballet?'

'Great.'

'Coffee, usual place and time?'

Caplan smiled and texted back a thumbs-up emoji.

She closed her eyes again, considering getting a blanket from the house and sleeping out here for the couple of hours the night had left. The dawn would wake her. She could do some stretches on the decking before meeting Lizzie.

She must have dozed off with Pas on her lap and her mobile on the arm of the chair as it woke her when it rang at four in the morning.

The voice at the other end was uncertain, 'DCI Christine Caplan?' She didn't inform him it was DI now. 'Can you come to Stewart Street? We need to interview you.'

'Me?'

'You witnessed an assault, Cambridge Street, at 21.49 yesterday. I'm afraid there's been a fatality.' The voice sounded young and rather nervous. 'We need a statement from you as you were at the scene, albeit in a civilian role.'

'No problem,' said Caplan. 'So, Mary Prior passed away?'

There was a pause at the end of the phone. 'No, the deceased is male, a nineteen-year-old called Daniel Francis Doran.' His tone drifted upward at the end of the name as if he was seeking confirmation.

Another bat flew across the garden, swallowed by the shadow of the trees. 'Yes, of course. I'll be in at seven.'

'OH DEAR.' DCI BOB Oswald eased his large frame up the last step and onto the landing of Otterburn House, growing redder by the minute. He had rested halfway up the stairs to consider the image depicted in the glass, quoting quietly, '"Who came before Me are thieves and robbers, but the sheep did not hear them."' Turning to the scene, he saw the drawn, whitened faces, the shining tracks of the slugs, the frayed tattered skin where lesions had been nibbled by rats, trapped in the bright beams of six torches.

'God knows, I've seen enough,' said DI Garry Kinsella, his hands clamping his mask to his face, studying the bodies.

'God knows everything,' corrected Oswald mildly. 'Lights?' he asked, looking up to the high window.

'We've sent Whyte down to find the fuse box. The electric's off all over the house.'

'Aye, because this couldn't get creepier. That's rather alarming.' Oswald shone his own torch around, picking out the rotting goat's head on the red velvet cushion, in the same state of decomposition as the bodies. Two knives were lying in the sign of the cross, dark staining still visible on the blades. Old leaves, dried and withered, were scattered around and something mouldy was adding to the smell that Oswald could not easily identify over the stink of decomposing flesh. Two brass goblets lay on their side, revealing a crimson residue, a small trickle meandering onto the wooden floor. 'Am I seeing right? Has somebody been drinking blood? Is that a statue of Lucifer himself?' He glanced over his shoulder at the stained-glass window, looking for reassurance.

'Yes. Don't ignore the inverted cross on the floor and, er . . . that.' Kinsella shone his torch up to catch the curling canvas of the portrait. The subject looked as though she had been disembowelled. 'But there's no human blood from the victims here.' He moved the beam across the floor to the bodies. 'I'd say they've been strangled. Look at how fine the damage is on the men's necks. There's not enough blood to suggest that anything was sacrificed when it had a pulse, certainly not that goat.'

Oswald had noticed that the victims' heads were in perfect alignment, indicating that the bodies had been dragged and positioned precisely. 'Can we pull back the covers, just to ensure there's no more surprises underneath?'

'Let me get a few more of' – the crime scene recorder hesitated, nodding at the line of bodies, reluctant to give voice to the horror – 'of . . . them. I've already got the video.'

Oswald steeled himself, still a little unsure that it was good practice to move a victim. There was much about this scene that didn't make sense. The horror of it was overwhelming. At first. But he had an inkling it had been staged to shock, to overpower them emotionally and put them off their game. Apart from that the scene was almost tranquil. The victims looked like they had been put to sleep.

Somebody was guilty of murder and misdirection.

Oswald was from Cronchie originally, a town ten miles along the coast. The McGregor family were local royalty, here round Otterburn and up to Cronchie and the islands out in the sound. He vaguely knew two of the people who lay dead in front of them and he knew of the other three. He'd met Stan and Barbara McGregor on a few occasions, but that was it. They were older than him, maybe late fifties. The heartbreaker was the body nearest the stairs, the subject of the slashed portrait: the old lady, Charlotte. Looking forward to her eightieth birthday, and here she was, lying rotting on the floor, in her gardening clothes with her seed pearls still round her slender neck. Undignified. Inhumane. The police officer in him noted, instinctively, that these pearls were vintage and of extreme value. With his track record, Billy McBain should have ripped those from the putrid neck of her corpse when he had the chance. Oswald had spoken to Douglas Knox briefly at his house and heard first-hand that Bainsy and his cousin had both been hospitalised for shock.

These bodies had been here for days, weeks even. It was the usual story: the pathologist from Inverness was busy, so they were sending one up from Glasgow instead.

Oswald, Kinsella and Gourlay, the DS, tiptoed around the bodies, chatting quietly, while various crime scene techs stood in clusters getting organised. A thankful cheer went up from downstairs when the lights reluctantly flickered on. The loud crunching of gravel in the driveway announced the arrival of more technical support. They all jumped when 'Onward, Christian Soldiers' sounded out over the deceased. Oswald's ringtone. He pulled his phone from his pocket with a gloved hand and listened, taking a few steps down the stairs. 'Yes, it looks like the entire family except one . . . one of the sons? The youngest one I think, Adam? Or we haven't found him yet. I can vouch that it's the old matriarch, Charlotte. And Barbara and

Stan McGregor, their daughter Catriona. The other young male could be either the son or a boyfriend of Catriona. So, no confirmed ID on him as yet . . . No, we can't look for ID, the bodies, they're, well . . . too close together, and we want as little disruption as possible . . . Yes, laid out like sardines and left to their endless sleep. Strangulation would be my guess.' He listened for a while, glancing at his watch under the cuff of his nitrile glove. Nodding, he swiped his phone off then turned to the increasing number of officers and tech staff on the landing. 'The family were gathered together for the old girl's eightieth birthday. Most folk in the village knew they were all going on holiday, a cruise, on Tuesday the fourteenth, which they did for her seventy-fifth and her seventieth. Bainsy would know that. The three dogs were put in kennels that Tuesday morning. We'll get confirmation of times and dates as soon as the world wakes up. Could these bodies have been here, undisturbed for three weeks? Is that possible?'

'Probable from the smell of it,' muttered Kinsella, looking into the high eaves, wishing the daylight upon them.

Oswald sighed heavily, speaking directly to his inspector. 'Looks to me like somebody wanted the McGregors dead, not just access to the premises, otherwise they would've done what the boys did and waited until the family were away. All these satanic artefacts might be there to unsettle us. It doesn't look right. It's a mishmash of unconnected concepts. I mean, how does that slashing of the portrait fit in?'

'Maybe one of the satanists went off the rails, was offended by the angelic blonde woman, you know, the way she's portrayed like an icon. Or he was just a wee hooligan who couldn't help himself,' said Gourlay, regarding the painting. 'The cross is inverted – could that mean something?'

'How many people does it take to keep control of five victims?' asked Oswald, assessing the two men lying in front of him. Both were fit and healthy, strong, difficult to control if they hadn't been quite so dead.

'You can pull the cover back now,' said the recorder, moving behind the powerful figure of Kinsella, using him as a barrier to the odour.

Oswald nodded. 'Be careful, Garry.'

Kinsella tugged at the thighs of his crime scene suit and knelt down, pulling back the corner of the duvet over the nearest body, Catriona's. He did it with care, folding the material back on itself to catch any evidence that might be dislodged. His other hand clamped his mask hard to his nose and mouth. He guessed this victim, the daughter, was between twenty and thirty, parchment face, sclera turned blue, rictus smile. The light summer blouse, the gold heart on a chain round her slim neck both testament to the day she had got dressed to run last-minute errands for their holiday. The lace collar of the blouse, lying like a choker over the damaged tissue, had a garland of slug trails which glistened in the lights from overhead. 'Rodent scavenger activity here, at her ears.'

'That's definitely Catriona – you can see the family likeness in the portrait.' Oswald held his torch closer and leaned over to see, suppressing feelings of revulsion. Catriona McGregor lay staring up with alien eyes, her mouth slightly open, white teeth framed by ragged brown lips. *Almost beautiful*, thought Oswald, feeling terrible for thinking that, but no . . . she did look like a work of art. There was something very still and very disturbing about her. Her soul had departed, leaving this atrocity. He noticed that behind her browned lips, her tongue seemed very pale. 'Is there something in there?'

Kinsella repositioned himself, twisting slightly on the balls of his feet, the shoe covers squeaking. 'Here? In the mouth?' He looked at Oswald for agreement to go ahead.

Oswald nodded, bending over to get a better view. 'There's something there?'

'I remember this bit in *Silence of the Lambs*,' said Gourlay lightly, a ripple of amusement breaking the tension, and Kinsella muttered the words 'sick bastard' under his breath.

'For once I'm glad you stink like a Turkish brothel – it's slightly better than Eau Decomposition.'

'Chanel Turkish brothel,' corrected Gourlay with a wink.

The DI took the plastic tweezers proffered by the double gloved hand of a crime tech. He placed them carefully in the mouth after easing the jaw open. Slowly, he prised out a pyramid of stiff white card that tried to revert to its original flat form once free from the constriction of the mouth. He eased it out before dropping it into the evidence bag that was being held open, ready.

The gloved hand appeared again, took the bag and closed the seal before holding it up to the light, shaking it free so that the contents sprang completely flat, and handed it back to Kinsella, eyes furrowed in disbelief. 'It's a Polaroid, faded but recognisable.'

'Recognisable as what?' asked Oswald.

'Recognisable as who. It's Catriona. She's lying where she is now. You can see the light blue shirt of the adjacent victim. What kind of a sick fuck did this?' He passed the bag to Oswald, who pulled the polythene tighter, holding it close to his face and peering. 'These lesions look fresh. This was taken at the time of strangulation, or close to it.'

'This is the work of one unhealthy mind,' said Kinsella, kneeling to look at the body of the man next to Catriona.

'Do they all have this souvenir of their passing?' asked Oswald.

They stood in silence, except for the gentle footfall of the other crime scene staff moving around the ground floor, on the stairs and in the rooms off the landing, as Kinsella opened the mouth enough to see the edge of the folded Polaroid within.

'Oh dear,' said Oswald again. 'Okay, I've seen and heard enough.' He jerked his head at Kinsella. 'Outside, five minutes?' he said, before heading down the stairs, pausing for a moment to meet the dark eyes of Jesus.

*   *   *

THE DRIVE OF OTTERBURN House was now full of cars. The gates had been crowbarred open and lay twisted on their hinges. Kinsella stood beside Oswald's Audi Q3, waiting for his boss to finish a phone conversation that nobody else was privy to. From his end it sounded like Oswald was gaining intel on the McGregor family, informal but invaluable in an investigation like this. What Kinsella couldn't figure out was who his boss was talking to at half one in the morning. Oswald's voice was almost a whisper as he paced up and down at the far end of the wide sweep of light grey gravel. The night had seemed endless, the sky above indigo, the stars incredibly bright.

Kinsella strolled up to the gates, relishing a moment's peace as he considered the odds of the two teenagers breaking into a house with five dead bodies inside. From the snatches of conversation he could hear, this was what his boss was discussing, and it sounded like he was talking to a civilian. He heard the date, the ninth of July, twice and glanced at his watch, this Saturday. His eyes caught a movement at the top of the gate. Something fluttering, snagged in the wrought iron spearheads, a fragment of triangular cloth caught and ripped from somebody's trousers as they climbed over. He picked his phone from his jacket pocket and called his colleagues back at the house, asking for SOCO to come down. He was thinking about climbing up to get it himself when his boss finally came off the phone.

Oswald yawned. 'Is there anywhere round here I can get a coffee?'

'Brodie's garage has a machine.'

'Good, I'm heading home. Tomorrow's going to be hectic. I'm pretty sure it's Adam McGregor who's not there.' He swiped to the photograph that had just been messaged to his phone. 'That's Gordon, the eldest brother. What do you think?'

'Yes, that looks like the body next to Catriona.'

'Okay, so we have Gordon deceased on the premises and wee brother Adam missing. Gordon was a banker or a stockbroker, up from London. Adam is the black sheep, a New Age hippie. I've just phoned the wife's cousin; he runs the Clachan Pub. He says Adam came back for his granny's birthday, uninvited, but he hasn't been around the village recently.'

'Interesting,' said Kinsella.

'But the damaged portrait is a bit personal. Seemingly, the old girl doted on her youngest grandchild. It was the rest of them who had issues with him.'

'Why? No good at polo? Is that cause to strangle your entire family? Mind you, if you met my in-laws, you might be tempted. One of the blessings of my wife leaving me.'

Oswald chuckled. 'Adam was more tree hugger than hedge fund manager. He might be absent because he's lying dead in the woods somewhere. Get a search team on the grounds round the house.'

'And one on Skone?' asked Kinsella.

'Why?'

'He might be out there with the Allanachs.'

'Get onto the grounds search as soon as the sun comes up. Then we'll think about Skone. Number one priority is to find him. At this point, he is missing, no more than that.'

'Of course, guv.' Kinsella looked out to sea, to the vague shadows of the three islands sleeping out in the bay. 'Skone, the one with Honeybogg Hill?'

'Indeed, famous for the honey, amongst other things.'

Kinsella nodded. 'You think they worship Satan over there, at the commune?'

Oswald tutted. 'Oh, behave yourself, Garry. It's not a commune. The Allanach Foundation at Rune is an ecologically sound society. The brochure didn't say anything about worshipping the Lord of Darkness.' He too looked seaward, watching the haar drifting over the water. 'A bunch of burnt-out professionals, growing their own veg, home-schooling their kids. Every second one of them went to the LSE or has a PhD. If that's where Adam is, he might not know about his family. The Foundation doesn't have internet or TV for general use, so he might not find out until we tell him.'

'Unless he did it and scarpered back to Skone to hide,' said Kinsella thoughtfully. 'I thought they had orgies out there at the summer solstice, which is a bugger. We've missed that by a fortnight.'

Oswald turned to look at the towering darkness of the house with the stained-glass window over the front door, illuminated now by the light behind. 'Aye, all burning fires on the beach and skinny-dipping, that's what I've heard. Don't know if it's true, don't care. Find out when each member of the McGregor family was last seen, exactly. Prioritise finding Adam. The family's not home until the ninth so that alarm would have been set and it goes through to Cronchie nick. Who turned it off? Same for the electricity. Find out who picked up the mail. And send somebody nice to talk to Bainsy and his pal in the hospital, if the doc consents. Get Douglas Knox's statement on record. He knows the McGregors, come to think of it. Might be up for a formal ID. And keep the chat of satanists to a minimum – distraction like that can derail an investigation.'

'You think it's a load of bollocks?'

'Well, that depends on what you believe in. Good and Evil, both powerful forces. Without darkness there can be no light.' They stood leaning against the Audi, watching the fog bank advance across the sea. 'God, look at that. There'll be bloody photographers all down the coast tonight.' He looked at his watch and corrected himself. 'This morning.'

'The Polaroids? What was the point of that, guv?'

Oswald shrugged. 'We'll ask when we find the sod who did it. Who are the local boys on the team? I know you have Mackie.'

'Craig, McPhee and Whyte are all local. One DC and two uniforms. Mackie's intel,' said Kinsella. 'What about Polaroid film? That's not easy to buy these days, surely? I can get onto that.'

'Good thinking. I want everybody in Otterburn interviewed. This is a close-knit community, a stranger stands out; even those who live on Skone are known here. I'm not having the press going off on the satanic angle; the country can do without devil-worship slaughter with their cornflakes.' Oswald released a slow, steady breath. 'Make sure counselling's available for anybody who needs it. Those bodies have been there for weeks. Another few hours won't hurt.

'I'll get an incident room opened up in Otterburn – be good to have a street presence – but obviously we'll be at Cronchie in the interim.' Oswald heaved himself into his car. 'You're in charge now, Garry. This case will be a huge boost to your career and a fine swansong for me. I'll call media liaison before anybody starts the weird rumours.'

'Weirder than what's in there?'

'Never be amazed about how depraved humans can be, Garry. I'm heading home. I'll see you at seven. You take care now.' Oswald asked the sat nav to take him to Brodie's garage and switched on his dashcam. He looked in the rear-view mirror; Kinsella was pulling his phone from his jacket pocket, pressing once and holding it to his ear. The inspector had already finished the call when Oswald drove off. The last vision of him in the mirror was neatly framed by the sloping gates before being swallowed by distance and darkness.

Oswald was soon on the narrow road that hugged the waterside. He knew this shortcut well, but the sat nav didn't recognise it. He drove carefully; the route went close to the water at points. No nice beaches here, the land three or four feet above water level, the tufts of wild grass clinging on the overhang. Huge, dirty-looking sheep with impressive horns stood and challenged the headlights, the same beams catching jet-black lambs scuttling away.

He linked the Bluetooth on his phone, left messages for his wife that he was on his way back, then left a few more at Fort William and Cronchie so they'd be ready for the morning shift coming on duty. Mentally, he was putting a team together. Kinsella was capable but lacked confidence. He was reserving his judgement on Gourlay. Harris was clever but kept himself to himself. After this case his team would be somebody else's problem.

Oswald switched off the Bluetooth and relaxed, concentrating on his driving and nothing else. He put his foot down, the Audi's powerful engine responded immediately, and he began to enjoy the challenge of driving on the twisting road, seeing the low-lying haar creeping closer. Real driving: fields on one side with a deep ditch separating them from the road, and the narrow inlet of the firth on the other. It was dangerous and thrilling. He felt young again. No kids in the car, no wife telling him to slow down. He was exhausted, but the adrenaline of the drive was waking him up fast. He was on top of his game.

THREE

After the seven o'clock briefing was over, Kinsella walked out into the early morning sunshine of Cronchie Station car park, jacket over his shoulder, and checked his phone. Nobody had heard from Oswald, not a word. Leaning back against the bonnet of his new Merc, Kinsella sighed, already exhausted with the stress of it all. Every fibre of his body wanted caffeine. The activity at Otterburn House was gradually scaling down after the hours of frenetic sampling, brushing, staining, photographing, swearing and getting in each other's way. The pathologist had finally arrived and pronounced that the deceased, on first examination, had all been strangled: the men by ligature, the females by pressure of the human hand on the neck, a difference she found interesting. Dr Ryce had specifically requested that the bodies remain in situ until the Eviscan examination had taken place, in case there were fingermarks embedded in the skin. It was a chance in a million, but as evidence went, it was a golden cherry they would only get one bite at. Ryce had also requested that the Polaroids remain in place until the bodies were taken down to the mortuary in Glasgow, which had been chosen as it could accommodate them all in one locale. The Fiscal agreed to the move. A search of the house had yielded no other areas of interest: no signs of a struggle, no blood spatter, no disruption of any kind. Catriona and Gordon's old bedrooms had small overnight bags unpacked. Larger suitcases for the cruise were still packed and stored behind the back door. Adam's bedroom was bare, the mattress uncovered, the duvet folded up at the bottom. As there were no more members of the McGregor family who lived on the premises left alive, the investigation team could lock the door and walk away. Kinsella had made sure the necessary security was placed round the house.

The searches for Adam McGregor in the grounds and out on Skone island were already well under way.

The time gap between the murders and the discovery of the bodies – maybe three weeks from what their initial enquiries had uncovered – was working both for them and against them. It certainly made the case unique.

The sedate progression of the crime scene had taken on the chilling stillness and grandeur of the house. Oswald had made a few good points about the killings but nothing that couldn't be easily explained. Five people were difficult to contain and there was no evidence of a struggle. The perpetrators could easily gain access if known to the family, or if their visit was expected in some way. DC Whyte's mum worked on reception at the local surgery; it was known that Charlotte rarely went out. The order the cars in the rear drive were parked in and their registered owners – Barbara's Jaguar, Stan's Lexus, Gordon's Range Rover and Catriona's Audi TT – suggested that the wife had either not gone out or had been the first back. Her husband's Lexus was drawn in behind her Jaguar. Ryce had offered more evidence to that effect: only Catriona had outdoors shoes on, killed before she had even the chance to change. From the shoe racks at the back door, this was a house where you changed your footwear. At the scene, Oswald had instructed him to task DC Toni Mackie to build a timeline for the family that day: the precise time that the dogs had been taken out the house, the last time the gates had been closed behind a homecoming car as the family prepared for a cruise they'd never take, and so on.

And there was Oswald's question about the neat pile of mail. It showed somebody was around so why had they not reacted to the stench that was obvious to every officer who had entered the premises. The two boys who broke in had remarked that they thought there was a dead dog rotting somewhere. Kinsella doubted that anybody could have missed it.

The murder wall was going to be busy.

The mobile in his jacket pocket rang. He listened to the news then closed his eyes and took a deep breath, before carefully replacing the phone He nodded. The case was on, the case of a lifetime, as Oswald had said.

LIZZIE FERGUSSON SAT AT one of Epicure's outside tables, looking at the breakfast menu, considering if she'd treat herself to the healthy avocado smash on toast, then reconsidering. The fattening croissants were so much cheaper. And tastier. She was waiting for Christine to appear. Her friend was never late; she ran her life like clockwork, like her hair: nothing out of place, nothing to show that, behind the scenes, it was all slowly unravelling.

And some of that, maybe a lot of it, was Lizzie's fault.

And that made her feel like shit.

DCI Caplan always followed procedure to the letter, so it was doubly odd that she had got herself into so much bother recently. She could have lost her job yesterday, but Lizzie doubted it. The hearing couldn't have gone that badly, or Lizzie herself would have already heard through the cop shop grapevine. Instead, she had caught a whisper that Christine had been questioned concerning an incident in Cambridge Street last night. An attempted mugging had been stopped by an off-duty police officer and that was always a legal minefield. That plus the disciplinary might push her to the dark side; maybe she'd join her in a frothy coffee and a chocolate croissant to cheer herself up rather than her habitual green tea and slice of unbuttered toast.

Lizzie doubted it.

There was no chance of Christine eating anything much here. She never ate much anyway, a remnant from her dancing days. Looking up from the menu, she saw her friend walking round the corner, as elegant as ever. Lizzie was glad to see the dark navy suit, the collarless cream top and the dark blue leather rucksack were all in place. She was ready for work, so still had a job.

They hugged, two strong women ready to put the world to rights.

Lizzie waved the waitress over and ordered a cappuccino, a green tea and the chocolate croissant she decided she couldn't live without. Caplan asked for a plain French roll. No butter of course.

'You ever work out of Stewart Street? I've been in that bloody place since seven. God, you'd think *I'd* stabbed somebody,' said Caplan, straining the teabag. 'By the time I got out I was thinking stabbing might be quicker.'

'I heard. Back to the main story though – what happened yesterday at the hearing?'

'Oh, that,' Caplan said, sitting upright, straight-backed and legs crossed at the ankle like the Queen. She paused as the croissant was put down in front of her friend. 'I was asked if I'd like to spend some time as DI.'

'No!' They were quiet again as Lizzie tapped her Visa against the proffered card machine.

'Oh, yes.'

'Except you didn't lose that evidence intentionally,' Lizzie said, letting her intonation drift up to a question.

Caplan ignored her. 'What's it all for? We still got the conviction; the lost sample had no critical evidentiary value. To top it all, they said – and I could see the smirk on their faces as they said it – they "felt they needed to support me".'

'Not that old shite again.'

'"With all that I was going through, they wouldn't give out the full disciplinary action" that they could. They didn't want to sack me. Just requested that I move to a less stressful role. And a pay drop. The Federation will take a look at it, but I'm tired of the whole bloody thing. I want to leave it.'

'But all somebody did was lose a bagged sample?'

'Exactly. It shouldn't happen these days.'

Lizzie dabbed her forefinger on the plate, picking up the flakes of pastry. 'What did you say?'

'That I trusted somebody with it that I shouldn't have trusted. I was the boss; I was responsible.'

'I guess that's true,' said Lizzie carefully, looking at her friend over the top of the cup, trying to catch her eye, but her gaze was focused elsewhere, on the traffic on Hyndland Road.

'They could have looked at it in context. It was a trying case. It was very early in the morning after a long, difficult night. Not twenty-four hours I want to revisit, certainly not in front of those soft arses.'

Lizzie blew the top of her coffee, causing ripples in the froth, and stared at her friend, knowing that not a word of that was true. She was amazed Christine had been believed. She was *never* careless. Never left anything to be second-guessed. She could work thirty-six hours straight without a single hair from her chignon escaping. The minute Lizzie left the house she looked like she'd fallen over in a wind tunnel. She knew her friend had had only three hours' sleep, yet she still looked as if she'd just stepped out of the shower. It always needled Lizzie slightly, that perfect exterior. But there was something Christine was not saying, so she prompted her: 'Yeah, work your backside off, and at the first slip-up, they dump you in it. Policing these days? It's a tightrope. It's not fair.'

'Who said life was fair?' muttered Caplan. She sighed. 'They were so keen to say the demoted post would be less stressful for me "at this moment in time".'

'At this moment in time? Until when?'

'Exactly. I'm not sure when they think Aklen will get better.'

They watched the traffic for a few minutes, content in their silence.

'When did I first meet Aklen? Was it a dinner party? At my house, I think. I remember burning the fondue. We got pissed instead,' said Lizzie. 'Or was that another party? Because Sarah and I already knew each other, and she wanted eight round the table. It must have been at her house then. But she invited that stuck-up DC she'd been landed with. Sarah was married to Dave at the time.'

'She was married to Keith,' said Caplan, ever attentive to detail.

'Was she?'

'Yes. And you hadn't even met John, forever to be known as The Bastard.'

Lizzie giggled. 'Weird that. You ended up sleeping with my husband while, at that moment, every woman in the room wanted to sleep with yours. Aklen was so beautiful. I remember you saying he could be mistaken for Alain Delon. We thought you were joking. You weren't.'

'He was very handsome back in the day.'

'And when you walked in, we all thought how the hell did that skinny bitch land him? We were well impressed.'

'Those were the days, eh? Long gone now.'

'Did they say where you'd be stationed?' asked Lizzie, thinking that she'd hate to have Christine at her office.

'Knowing my luck, it'll be The Bastard's new team.'

'Mmm, that'll be a situation I'd like to witness. He's SCD at the moment, pulling together a big drug operation, Jackdaw. So I hear down the grapevine anyway; he never tells me anything.'

For a moment both women fell silent, thinking about The Bastard, a man they had both loved once, until they had found out about each other: unlikely friends, united in his treachery.

Lizzie took a bite of her croissant, cupping her hand underneath to catch the flakes.

'I was involved in an incident last night. A nineteen-year-old boy died.'

'What?' asked Lizzie. 'Dead? I thought it was a mugging.'

Caplan's head turned slowly. 'It's out on local radio, is it?'

'Just heard something in passing,' muttered Lizzie.

'He was off his face, I don't know what on. And the woman in the wheelchair, the victim of the mugging, had a cardiac arrest, and poor Emma had to run down the road, get her out her chair and do CPR while her daughter stood there and cried. As the old girl and the mugger were removed from the scene by two ambulances, I ended up driving her daughter to the hospital.' Caplan looked down the street. The morning rush hour was building, the air was already turning hot and muggy. She leaned forward, forehead creased. 'But it was strange. He had his hands in the air, lost control of his bike and fell off. He started having a fit. I was trying to keep his head from hitting the kerb while he coughed blood all over me. Ruined my yellow dress. All because I took Emma to the ballet.'

'A good deed never goes unpunished. Do you mind if I light up?'

'They're your lungs.'

'I know, I'll chuck it when life is easier.' Lizzie took a deep drag on her cigarette and released it back to the air through pursed lips. 'That will be the day after hell freezes over.'

'How are you doing?'

'Same shit, different day.'

'Kids?'

'Still alive. Missing their dad. The Bastard.'

A small Jeep drove past, the sound of rap pulsing out from behind the blackened glass. 'Do you? Miss him?'

'Nope. I miss the maintenance he's supposed to pay me. I heard he's bought a new sporty Audi and took his new floozy to Paris for the weekend.'

'Nice of him.'

'Did he ever take you to Paris while you were his floozy?'

'No, not Paris,' Caplan considered. 'There was a supposedly romantic weekend at Gleneagles, but I recall paying for that, obviously so you wouldn't see it on the credit card.'

'The Bastard.'

'Indeed.' They toasted the object of their scorn, joined in sisterhood.

'Why did it take so long for me to see it? But in the end, you did me a favour. Now I don't have to suffer him growing old, bald, fat and farting like a trooper while watching *Match of the Day*.'

Caplan turned her head to look down the street. Lizzie realised she had been less than tactful. Aklen was growing old before his time, asleep for hours on end, too sick to work for years. He was ageing rapidly, while Caplan, the serene beauty of her, was becalmed in the progression of time. She'd looked like that when she was nineteen and she still would when she was sixty. Not for the first time she realised how striking a woman her friend was in profile. How preternaturally calm she could stay.

'I'm going to see Sarah this morning. Not by choice. I think I feel a bit sorry for her, pulling me over the coals for stuff I'm not guilty of.'

'Why does she want to see you? Surely they punished you enough this morning?'

'No idea. Maybe I'll be shunted off to Tulliallen to explain to the new recruits what happens when you step out of line, just to ramp up my humiliation.'

'She wouldn't do that.'

'She would if she was told to. Assistant Chief Constable? She didn't get that by not being the fox in the henhouse.'

Lizzie sighed. 'And we're going nowhere. I'm stuck at the bottom of the ladder because of childcare, and you've been practically demoted. You might enjoy working as DI, you never know.'

'In my first action as an off-duty DI, a guy dies.'

'That's shit.'

'That's my life.'

Lizzie smoked. Caplan sipped her green tea. Looking at the traffic. Thinking.

After a while Lizzie said, 'Do you recall Oswald, Bob Oswald? He was at Glasgow Central for a while around 2013, 2014?'

Caplan shook her head. 'He doesn't come to mind.'

'Big guy, always laughing. Married a young nurse he met when he was bitten on the bum by a police dog.'

Caplan smiled. 'The things you remember about folk.'

'Well, he was transferred back home to Fort William around 2015. He'd done his thirty, was looking to collect his pension, when he lands a mass murder, five bodies in the same house. It was on the wire this morning.'

'Five?' Caplan's eyes narrowed. 'What happened?'

Lizzie shrugged. 'I'll keep an ear out for further details, but there's something they're keeping quiet. All the same family? My money's on murder suicide; there'll be a body swinging from a tree somewhere. Those wee villages up north, the midges alone would affect anybody's mental health.' A motorbike thundered past, only to be caught at the lights where the rider revved the engine in frustration. 'I remember when he requested a return to his old stomping ground. Can't think why anybody would volunteer to go up there to work with the sheep shaggers and the thistles. All that quiet and open space. It'd drive you nuts.'

'Yes,' said Caplan, looking up at the beeping of a lorry reversing, holding up the traffic, a car horn blared in impatience. The noise of a city coming to life. 'Must be hell.'

THE ASSISTANT CHIEF CONSTABLE'S office was scented with a heady mix of cleaning fluid and stale coffee, the aroma of the latter floating down from the machine in the corridor. The boss's workspace was bright, the glass bricks allowing the refracted sunshine to bounce around, leaving rainbow geometry on the blue carpet. It was very warm, which was more than ex-DCI Christine Caplan could say about her welcome.

ACC Sarah Linden had come up through the ranks with Christine Caplan and Lizzie Fergusson, and gone further than both of them. The three women had always enjoyed a good working relationship; at times close colleagues, at other times professional adversaries, they had always respected each other. Linden had been disappointed in Caplan's sudden fall from favour; there were few enough women in the higher ranks of Police Scotland without the ones who got there getting themselves into trouble. She had always believed that there was something of the star about Caplan, and Sarah Linden never liked to be proved wrong.

She got up at the crisp knock on her door, and crossed her office, stepping over the piles of paperwork on the carpet; her friend deserved more than an 'Enter'. There were times they would hug, times they would shake hands, but today there was neither. Some days were a Christine/Sarah day, others were ACC Linden/DCI Caplan day. Today was a 'Hello, take a seat, Christine' day, with the seat in question an island in the middle of the room. Linden took her place behind her huge, very clean desk and her nameplate, then placed her palms together on the file, as if she was thinking about praying. 'I'm not going to talk about it, Christine – enough has been said at every level.'

'Thank you, ma'am. I think I've heard everybody's opinion on it,' Caplan said quietly, sitting down with that perfect poise, her dark hair pulled back in her trademark chignon.

'Tea?'

'No, thank you.'

'Okay . . .' Linden hesitated. 'It's been left to me to decide what happens to you, in the wake of this disciplinary incident.'

'I'm sorry about the loss of the evidence in the Brindley case. I know it can't have been easy for you to deal with.'

'I'm glad you appreciate that. Anything we do with you will be wrong in somebody's eyes. May as well do something that's wrong in every-body's eyes. Give you a chance to redeem yourself. Fuck this up as well, and there's bugger all anybody can do. You'll sit at DI. Young men with degrees will get promoted over you. Women with attitude. All reminding you of who you used to be. You'll get a pension. And obese after years of watching CCTV in the basement eating ginger nuts.'

'What a lovely picture of my future.'

'It's not uncommon. You're going to assist in the Otterburn murders.'

Caplan didn't think she had heard right. 'I'm sorry?'

Linden gave her a moment to digest it. 'Highland Division. DCI Bob Oswald appears to have gone AWOL.'

'Lizzie was just talking about him.' Caplan frowned. 'What do you mean AWOL?'

'Exactly that. Left the crime scene in the early hours. Nobody's set eyes on him since. DI Kinsella thinks he wasn't himself but is keeping that quiet. So will you. He's concerned about Oswald's mental state. Oswald had let it be known to a select few that he was seeking retirement, that this should have been his last hurrah, but he might have had a coronary at the wheel.'

'Bloody hell.'

'Yes. Oswald has a wife and two young kids, so use tact. He's a popular officer. Get up there. If he reappears, fit and healthy, you're his Girl Friday. Kinsella is assuming temporary command. We have no other DCIs available.'

Caplan tutted. 'Really. Well, I'm not a DCI now so I can't help.'

'Don't start. There's a hole, and you're the plug.' Linden looked at the other woman over the top of her turquoise-framed glasses. 'And you're a good fall guy if it all goes tits up.' She smiled. 'But you're used to that. However, the McGregor name equals money, privilege and power. Even if Oswald manages to return on form, he'll have a lot on his plate. At his stage, cops can zone out. Frankly, I don't think he should be working at this level. With his condition.'

'Condition?'

'Very slight issue with his heart. Kinsella's good but lacks experience. DS Iain Gourlay's the highflyer. Good cop. He'll be promoted next. He'll be Kinsella's boss in two years and probably mine in five. For now, stand three feet behind Kinsella, guide his investigation and make sure he's not swamped by Gourlay.'

'I've had enough of internecine conflict,' sighed Caplan.

'Oh, they're good pals. It's just that Kinsella can lean on Gourlay a bit and that's not always a good thing. You've had years in major incident. He has three months.'

'You want me to act like a DCI but not get paid or get the support?'

'DCIs do not lose evidence, do they, Christine?' She shook her head. 'There's already a lead. The two lads who found the bodies at Otterburn have more than a passing interest in devil-worship. Satanic artefacts were found at the scene.'

Caplan nodded. 'Well, I guess there's not a lot to do up there.'

'One of the lads is a vicious little bastard, local. The file's been emailed to you. He plays Black Sabbath backwards, drinks blood, has sex with goats, that kind of thing.'

'Like I say, not a lot to do.'

'Kinsella's interviewing for a confession and mental-health assessment to make it pretty. Work up the tree. See who's pulling strings. Fling the book at them.'

'Okay.'

'The murders took place three weeks ago. At least.'

There was silence as Caplan digested the information. 'And nobody wondered where they were?'

'Some big holiday or other. One member of the family is untraced. Adam McGregor. Youngest child, and by young I mean passed driving test, not Farley's rusks. Search teams are out in the grounds and on an island looking for him today. The bodies remain in situ awaiting an Eviscan exam.'

Caplan nodded slowly, saying with heavy sarcasm, 'So, those boys murdered the family then went back a few weeks later, got a fright that the deceased were still there and went for help?'

'Hence the psych report to that effect.'

'If I find evidence to the contrary, that one of the family was involved? This Adam? A murder suicide pact?'

'Adam and his granny were close. Her portrait was slashed. Nothing else was damaged. Might be something there.'

'She must really have turned against him to cause that degree of outrage.'

'If you find evidence to support that, please, don't lose it, DI Caplan.' Linden stood up, hand extended out to the tall, slim woman sitting opposite her. 'It's a big case. I'm going to Cronchie to keep the press happy. Get up there ASAP. You can't be as unpopular there as you are down here.'

'It would be hard,' agreed Caplan, getting to her feet, shaking her friend's proffered hand, holding it rather more firmly than she intended.

'Look, none of this is your fault.'

Caplan shrugged.

'It might help you to get away. You've been under such strain. It might help to put a bit of distance in the situation.'

'Thank you, ma'am,' said Caplan, emphasising her friend's rank, reminding her that this was a professional conversation, and her home life had nothing to do with it.

But it did.

Because she was a woman.

'Nobody in any position of power has a doubt about your integrity.'

Caplan raised an eyebrow.

'Well, nobody with any brains.' Linden got up and opened the door of her office, paused, closed it over again. Her voice low, she said, 'You know, Christine, I've known you a long time. Police officer. Colleague. Friend. I read the report of the Brindley case closely, I read what happened to that evidence that you . . . lost. Didn't much sound like the woman I know.'

'Unfortunate series of events, ma'am.'

Linden gave a single little nod of her head. 'The woman I know might take the heat for another. For a close friend, maybe. Can't think who that might be.'

The two women stared at each other. Linden looked down first.

'Can I go now? I need to pack,' said Caplan.

The door did not reopen; it stayed as it was.

'I'd never be brave enough to put my career on the line. I'm far too selfish,' said Linden.

'As your rank bears out.'

'My door is always open.'

'Well, it's not at the moment, is it, ma'am?' said Caplan coldly.

FOUR

Kinsella had thought about grabbing himself a coffee, but decided he was wired enough and settled for an orange juice and a tuna sandwich. The scale of this operation was huge, it was all such a balancing act, and in the car park at Cronchie, he had suffered a wobble, thinking about the speed the case was moving at now.

He had felt physically sick when faced with the images of the McGregor family on the wall, one coloured A4 photograph after another, each with their name underneath, their date of birth, the same date of death: the fourteenth of June. Or thereabouts.

The victims looked happy in life. The old lady sipping a sherry. Stan and Barbara sitting on a fence, some glossy-coated horses grazing behind them. Gordon's portrait was an 'informal yet formal' head shot from work. Catriona's was taken in a pub, drink in hand, a huge smile across her face, a younger version of her mother.

Kinsella had looked at those for a long time before walking into the DCI's office, his thumb scrolling his mobile, miles away, when he realised that the door had opened and somebody was talking to him.

'Pardon?' he said.

DS Harris had been there for a while, reading out a forensic report, talking so quietly that Kinsella could barely hear.

'Can you just summarise that for me please, Happy? It's been a very long night.' He slipped his phone back into his jacket pocket.

'The material on the top of the gate—'

'McBain and Frew climbed over to gain access, we know that.'

'The sample is older, weathered, might relate more to the date of death rather than date of discovery.' Harris tugged the knee of his trousers up and sat on the desk. 'The fabric is used as a lining for waterproof jackets, higher-end goods. Do you want me to track it down?'

'Yes,' Kinsella didn't want to appear too keen. 'Yes, do that, but don't spend too much time or money. Look at that end of the market then get back to me, so we know the garment if we see it.'

'You okay, boss?'

'Yes, I'm fine.' Kinsella coughed slightly, sticking the printout underneath his arm as he carefully rolled up his shirt sleeves.

'Billy McBain's in interview room one, hospital discharged him as fit. Frew has an infected cut on his hand. He's been hallucinating, so he's on the back burner for now.'

'Okay,' Kinsella nodded to himself. 'We'll go in, have a chat about what happened last night, the housebreaking. See what the wee shit says.'

'You heard anything from the boss?'

'No, not yet. Lorna's not heard from him either.' Kinsella took a deep breath, made a decision. 'He'd want us to focus on this. Do you not think it's really odd that those boys went to that house, at that time, and found what they found?'

'Of course it's odd. But that's exactly what happened. The minister's wife – Christ I've forgotten her name already – is waiting outside. Joyce? She's happy to be the responsible adult for McBain in case we need one. The duty solicitor is here. Garry, we're good to go.'

'Right.' Kinsella wiped his bald head, smoothed out his goatee and slipped his jacket on. 'Why do I feel shit about this? Why? He's an evil wee bastard, but I've interviewed much worse.'

'Well, we don't want to let the boss down. It's unsettling, him going off like that.' Harris sighed as if the air was being sucked out of him. 'Toni did a great job on the last sightings of the McGregor family.'

'Remind me. Fourteenth of June?' Kinsella closed his eyes, recalling the briefing. 'Something about the chemist? My mobile rang halfway through.'

Harris took out a notebook and flicked over a few pages. 'Catriona went to the village pharmacy to collect all the meds for the old dear on the afternoon of Tuesday, the fourteenth of June. That's definite. The guys in the chemist knew Catriona. The fourteenth was the last day that the housekeeper, Ina Faulds, was working at the house.'

'What's she been doing since? Does she get all that as paid holiday?'

'No, no. She's been in and out the house a few times in the last two weeks. She was away from the fifteenth to the twenty-second herself, and then was popping in and out. She was the one who moved the mail and—'

'Oh yeah, she's the one who never noticed where that bloody stink was coming from?' said Kinsella sarcastically.

Gourlay strode into the office without knocking, a drift of Bleu de Chanel following him. Harris immediately stood up. 'How are you doing, Garry?'

'Out of my depth,' Kinsella admitted. 'Iain, can you get hold of that Mrs Faulds. Davie, let's go and see what William McBain esquire has to say.' He stood up, gathering his phone, his tablet and his good pen. 'The worst bit of this morning was leaving the bodies, locking the place up and walking away. That was what got to me. Felt I was being watched every step.' He looked at Harris. 'You ready?'

'All you need to know, guv, is that he's small potatoes. Odd spells in young offenders, but the last eight months he's been clean. Maybe gearing up for something. Maybe this. He's stayed below our radar because he's making moves to run Cronchie, trying to forge links with organised crime, playing the big man,' said Gourlay.

Kinsella slammed a drawer closed with his knee. 'Okay, casual chat first to get a feel for his mental state.'

'Wish to God Bob would put in a bloody appearance.'

'Remind me to call the hospital again when we come out.'

Gourlay saw Kinsella's fingers tremble as he picked up the folder. 'You're interviewing him as a witness, guv – that's all you're doing.'

'Yes. Of course. He's a violent wee psycho, but he has a lawyer, an adult. If he's one kangaroo short of a picnic, they'll say.'

'Bloody sure they will. And the hospital discharged him as fit. Why are you so edgy?'

Kinsella furrowed his brow. 'That satanic stuff, it creeps me out.'

They left the office and walked along the corridor and into the room where a man in a smart suit, a woman in a floral dress and light cardigan, and a very slim young man, who looked about twelve although they knew he was nineteen, waited. They introduced themselves and sat down; the lawyer and the minister's wife both said hello and settled themselves in their seats.

Billy McBain sat with his forearms on the table, his tattoos showing. He stared at them with an air of superiority that went further than normal bravado. Not the shivering mass of nerves that Harris was expecting. Slowly, McBain raised his right fist and extended his index and pinkie. He lowered his left fist and did the same before extending both his thumbs. He continued to sit like that, saying nothing, just staring at the two men opposite him.

Kinsella knew perfectly well what the gesture meant but still couldn't control the sliver of fear that cut through him.

CAPLAN THREW HER CASE on the bed, opened it and started flicking through her wardrobe, thinking of what she might need in Otterburn and how easily this hot spell could turn nasty. The reservation at the Empire Hotel in Cronchie had been pinged through to her; three nights only, so they must be banking on a quick resolution to the McGregor murders, which suggested they had clear lines of enquiry that were already proving fruitful. Or that they wanted rid of her quickly.

When she had arrived home, Aklen had got out of his bed and had appeared at the bedroom door, yawning. He had looked at her suit and then at the clock, not realising how late it was and why she was wearing her work clothes. He had that confused expression as if he had been parachuted into a situation he knew nothing about. She told him to have a shower as she was heading back out and needed to talk to him. It was very telling that he didn't ask her where she was going; he simply nodded and shuffled into the hall, to the bottom of the stairs, and paused there, summoning the energy to go up. He had lost so much weight. She suspected that if she wasn't there, he would never eat anything and would waste away completely, such was the self-loathing of his illness, the shattered confidence, the breaking of a strong man.

Seven years.

Caplan had put the kettle on and stuck some bread in the toaster, got the jam and butter out, then followed Aklen upstairs to find her small suitcase, starting with her clean clothes that were in the ironing basket. Of the three adults living in the house, she was the only one who knew how to work the washing machine seemingly; a small irritation in the grand scheme of things, but it was the one that rankled her most. Listening to the hum of the shower, she folded in two suits, five shirts that were all variations on the same theme: no collars, different tones of cream, all short-sleeved. She put her walking boots and some outdoor gear, her anorak and thick socks into a separate bag and placed that on top of the case, reminding herself to get her toiletries when Aklen came out of the shower. She went to Kenny's room, knocked on the door, then opened it a little, calling his name gently in an attempt to waken him.

'Kenny, time to get up and have some breakfast.'

The figure under the duvet stirred a little, but not much. 'But, Mum, I'm tired.'

'Well, that's what happens when you go to bed at three in the morning. Get up.' She walked over to the window, kicking dirty clothes out of her way, then opening the curtains with a loud rattle allowing light to flood the room. Swearing emanated from the bed.

'Don't talk to your mother like that and get up. Now,' she chided gently.

'Aw, Mum.'

'Aw, Mum, nothing. Get up, you lazy wee shite.' She pulled the duvet off his lanky frame as she walked past, leaving the room to get on with her preparations to go north. Her laptop, her own tablet that she preferred, the chargers, all those things that could make her life impossible if she forgot them. It'd be a two-hour drive up to Otterburn, and she needed to pop into her office, clear up a few loose ends beforehand. Actually, she was clearing her desk for the incoming DCI, a stark thought. She was no longer operating at that rank; it would take a bit of getting used to. She needed to empty her drawers of all personal items, then carry them through the office, winding through the workstations of her colleagues like some walk of shame. She'd say a few words to them to stop the gossip about the outcome of the disciplinary. Not that it would help. Those who were important to her already knew the whys and wherefores. The rest could say what they liked. But she'd sound enthusiastic about landing the McGregor case and relate the true story that she was acting as back-up for a busy DCI on a mass murder.

They could choose to believe it or not.

She went back downstairs, leaving her bags at the front door, put some coffee into the cafetière and pulled the lever down on the toaster, getting out plates, pouring bleach down the sink, gathering the knives from the dishwasher and rinsing them, thinking about how she was going to say what she had to say. When Aklen came in from the shower, wet-haired but looking more awake, she started, not even giving him time to sit down.

'I need to go away for a few days. There's a big incident up north, near Cronchie. Near where you grew up, isn't it?'

Aklen collapsed into the chair at the top of the table, the effort of the shower having exhausted him. He put his hand out to hold hers. 'Yes, yes, but I thought you weren't doing that anymore.'

'It was suggested that I step down. I wasn't sacked.' She slipped her hand from his, turning away from him, ignoring the suspicion that he would have been happier if she had lost her job. Then she'd stay here, looking after him, making sure that he remained incapable of ever doing anything for himself.

'Do you have to go?'

'Yes, I do.' She wasn't getting into that old argument again. 'I really do.' She closed the fridge door with more of a bang than she intended, but bit her tongue on the subject of the magic money fairy who put a salary in the bank every month.

'What'll happen to me? I'm not well enough to be on my own.'

'But you won't be on your own. Kenny'll be here. You're better than you were, and one day, when that lazy squirt finally goes back to university, you'll find you function . . .' She paused, not keen to add *properly*. 'I mean, it may as well be now than later.'

'I'm not sure you should go.' He screwed his face up, pained by the very thought.

She was scared he was going to cry, that face that used to be so handsome, now haggard and worn.

'Is your job that important to you?'

'Oh, are we having that argument again?' She poured him a cup of coffee. 'Yes, my job is important to me, but so are you. Emma'll stay with the two of you to make sure you don't run out of clean clothes or get diseased by eating rotting leftovers. And I'll be on the end of the phone. I'm an hour and a half up the road – don't get stressed about it, Aklen. Just don't, as there's nothing to be stressed about. You don't have the energy for it.'

He smiled. 'I know, I know, but it all seems scary to me.'

'Nobody is asking you to go outside.' She dropped a kiss on his forehead.

He placed his arm round her slim waist, reaching out to her. 'Well, you know I'll get stressed. It's horrible. I hate it when you're not here. I hate it when you go out late at night. It's not safe. What happened last night, that boy? He died and that could have been you. What would happen if you weren't here?'

'You'd get your own bloody coffee.' She turned away, cleaning the sink while she waited for another round of bread to toast, not daring to ask how he knew about Daniel Doran. The brain fog varied with how interested he was. She squeezed a sponge dry. 'And who told you what went on last night? You know I can't talk about work.'

'An off-duty police officer stopping a mugging? The kid dying? Of course it was on the news.'

'And you shouldn't believe what you read in the paper. You of all people should know that.' She squirted more bleach down the sinkhole with vengeance. 'I get stressed too, you know, Aklen. I get stressed when I look at the bank account and there's more going out than in. I get stressed when I come in from a long shift and you're slumped in front of the telly watching *Homes Under the Hammer*. Again. And there's Kenny, still in his bed, not been to uni for months. He needs to come out of hibernation, and you need to do what your doctor says and set yourself a little goal every day. Would you have had a shower today if I hadn't told you to? No. Oh, here's Kenny down to forage for food.' The toaster popped, and Caplan put four slices in the middle of the table, not forcing Aklen to eat anything. 'Do you want some, Kenny?'

'No, I'll just have Frosties.' He reached for the cupboard, only wearing his pants, to annoy his mum. 'Oh, there's none left.'

'Well, only you eat them. Just before you finish the previous box, put it on the reorder; that way you'll never run out. I refuse to think for you, Kenny. I'm not coming to uni to sit in your lectures for you. I've been there, done that. You're eighteen – it's your life, get on with it.'

'I'm nineteen.'

'Well, organise your own Frosties then.' Caplan watched as Kenny took a chair and turned it round, straddling it as he picked up a dry slice of toast, jamming it in his mouth and munching noisily, trying her patience. She was arguing about Frosties. She was about to tell her son not to sit like a three-year-old. The McGregor family probably had a morning as normal as this, planning their cruise. Did they have any idea what was about to happen to them? Could something so awful happen with no forewarning at all? Of course it could. It happened every day.

'She's going away, she's leaving us,' said Aklen, going for some comedy melodrama.

He couldn't cope with Kenny, not in their relative mind states: Aklen exhausted and distant, Kenny firing on all cylinders one moment then going to his bed for days on end.

'I don't mind her going away,' said Kenny, pinching some toast from his mother's plate. 'As long as bloody Emma's not coming round to do her Nurse Ratched.'

'She is.'

'Ah, please don't go.' Kenny batted his eyelids, his hands clasped in supplication.

Caplan ruffled his hair. He was still her wee boy.

And it continued, the chatter over a midday breakfast. She clattered the dishes into the clean sink when they were finished, knowing that they would stay there soaking until Emma came and put them in the dishwasher. Kenny announced that he was going to the gym. Aklen asked if she needed any help with packing. Did she want him to go out and see how much petrol was in the Duster?

At least Aklen was trying. She could have asked him to take it down to the garage and fill it up, but she was used to him being too ill to do anything. 'I'm fine, love.' She cleared away the rest of the dishes. 'I filled it on my way home, I have it under control.'

'You usually do,' Aklen mumbled, heading out the door and into the front room from where she heard the familiar theme tune to *Homes Under the Hammer.*

FIVE

The two police officers stationed at the broken gates climbed out their car as soon as they saw the blue Duster. A tall, slim dark-haired woman got out and proffered her ID and her warrant card, saying, in an educated Glasgow accent that she was DI Christine Caplan and that she had driven up from Glasgow and wanted a look at the house. And yes, she was perfectly aware how late it was, but she had a good torch with her. She asked them if it was okay to leave her car near the driveway wall, underneath the ornate plaque that read 'Otterburn House 1897'.

She asked if Oswald had reappeared yet. And waited for an answer.

The two cops looked at each other. PC Whyte introduced himself, then said there was no news yet, shrugged and walked away, talking into either his radio or his phone. The other, PC McPhee, slowly pointed through the gate and had the good grace to add that they'd be here if she needed anything.

Caplan regarded them carefully. Whyte needed a haircut. McPhee needed a bomb under him.

She turned her attention to the dark, solitary house, foreboding in the dying light. Three storeys, tall narrow windows, an elaborate portico with pillars. It was a building of symmetrical beauty, over a hundred years old and well maintained, surrounded by a lawn that was a little overgrown, with areas of ragged shrubs and bushes. The larger gardens surrounded the house on all sides, except for the strip of road that dropped down the hill to the village.

On the way up from Glasgow, she had stopped at the Real Food Café for a vegan sandwich and a green tea, and read the reports about the case on her tablet. She'd thought about Oswald, the man whose reins she'd be taking. Why should he go now? At this moment? Something had pushed him over the edge; she'd witnessed that with Aklen. The final straw could be so mundane; it was the tsunami before that did the damage. She wouldn't wish it on her worst enemy.

What had driven him to go? Was she about to inherit it?

Caplan looked down the road. The distance between the Knoxes' bungalow and Otterburn House was more than a mile. The outer perimeter was high pine trees, Douglas firs and an eight-foot stone wall. Nobody would know this house was here: no passer-by, no passing traffic. It meant nothing as everybody in the village knew exactly where the house was, who lived there and when they were going on holiday.

She took a deep breath of cool night air, feeling tired yet invigorated to be released from her duties at the house, away from the gossip and the shit storm back in Glasgow. Caplan knew that she was an embarrassment to her colleagues. They were glad to see the back of her. They'd welcome her return if she closed this case quickly. If not, she may as well resign now.

She had read every word of Kinsella's report on the scene, as it had been when they had attended at one o'clock in the morning. Five bodies, the entire McGregor family.

Minus Adam.

She walked up the drive, her shoes crunching on the gravel, hurting her ankle. She sidestepped to the grass instead and continued, silently, towards the house. She sensed PC Whyte watching her, the one who needed a haircut. He'd be sloppy, she sensed it off him. He was talking on his phone rather than his radio, keeping an eye on her. Walking on, she thought how the missing son would feel when he found out. How would he rebuild his life after this? How would Kenny react if it had been them? She smiled a grim smile; would he even notice? Then there was Scott Frew and Billy McBain, the two young men who had found the bodies. They had been so distressed by the scene that faced them at the top of the stairs, they had needed hospitalisation. Hardly the mentality of those who had strangled an entire family. And yet, Billy McBain had been reported as calm in the interview hours later. Lots of thoughts tumbled round her head as she walked, but she kept coming back to Adam McGregor. As far as she knew, they had found no activity on his phone in the last three weeks. Nobody had seen him either. That was ominous.

The garden at the side of the house was bordered by high hedges and trees. Its seclusion was barely penetrated by the moonlight. Caplan thought there should be another two uniformed officers on the front door of the residence; there was no point in securing the front gate when the outer perimeter was so vast. Rubberneckers and reporters could walk across the fields, climb the outer wall and trudge through the forest to get an exclusive photograph of the house of death. Kinsella had better knowledge of the house and may have thought differently, but the bodies were still in situ, the crime scene ongoing.

There was a crackling in the undergrowth. She turned; the noise had emanated from the trees to her left. She weighed the torch in her hand. PC Whyte or his colleague might have gone that way, maybe having heard something themselves. She stood for a while, listening, hearing nothing else. She was fifty metres, maybe a bit less, from the house. Surely there should have been officers here?

A chill crept up her spine as she sensed she was being watched by unseen eyes from behind the trees. She kept moving, going back to the path, torch in one hand, phone in the other, rucksack over her shoulder.

The house was more impressive close up. Light sandstone, the key and corner stones a contrasting lighter blond that caught the beam of her torch. She waved her hand in front of her face, battering the cloud of midges, while catching sight of a darting object in the darkness – soprano pipistrelles probably. They'd add to the atmosphere of the place, fitting for the manner of death of the McGregor family. Gothic horror, vampires and satanism. Could it be some cult? A tune ran through her mind – 'Helter Skelter'.

The report said the two housebreakers had seen no sign of forced entry before they had broken the window. Caplan wondered how reliable that was.

She knew that Billy McBain was Kinsella's main suspect. He was one of the teenagers who had raised the alarm. If he hadn't, nobody would have been any the wiser. Maybe they needed the bodies to be found? Had he deliberately brought Frew along as a witness? That might explain how he got over the trauma so easily, when the friend had nearly lost his mind.

Caplan had been a detective for a long time. She had worked nights in some of the roughest areas Glasgow had to offer and could sense when something was ready to kick off. Continuing to edge her way round the house, she watched for any movement in the trees. She walked through the arch to the back garden, dipping under the tape, looking across the three lawns, still troubled by the lack of police presence. They were understaffed and undermanned, but the murder of five people deserved better than this. Maybe Whyte's pals had sneaked off to the pub and he'd got the short straw. Maybe Kinsella was sloppy, or maybe the disappearance of their superior put the entire team into temporary disarray. A simple message might have got lost.

More questions than answers.

Who was in the trees? Were they there, watching, wondering who the hell she was?

She got to the corner, keeping in the shadows, noting the line of cars, the double garage and did a quick tally. The Land Rover looked old and functional; the newest car was the Audi TT, and that was about five years old, quality but not flash. There was a barbecue folded up and covered, and some very expensive garden furniture in front of a Victorian wrought iron greenhouse. Caplan could imagine the old lady deadheading her roses, caressing rare orchids. There was some serious gardening going on here. But she couldn't see the old dear, pearls and cashmere, out on a quad bike keeping the rear lawn to a regulation length of an inch and a quarter. She bent down to touch it: real grass, bowling-green smooth, impressive. Unlike the front of the house, the care and management were here in the private space they used and enjoyed.

They had dogs and a working security system. They wouldn't have opened their door to Billy McBain; they'd know him as the local troublemaker and be more likely to shoot him before he got halfway up the drive.

She had no doubt that Kinsella and Oswald had thought exactly the same.

There had been no movement in the tree line, no noises apart from the cawing of the crows and the breeze rustling the leaves, but now she heard footfall on the gravel, moving away from the rear of the property, coming her way. Flattening herself against the wall, she waited. Somebody was walking, very slowly.

A bright light blinded her. She heard a voice, polite but firm, telling her to keep still and move no further.

'Can you get that light away from my face right now?' she snapped. They were a cop. She knew by the way they held the torch. A very quiet cop.

'Can I help you?' said the voice in front of her, male, gentle, enquiring. Another crunch on the gravel as her new companion took a tentative step forward.

'Please shine your torch downwards,' she asked politely, her hand on her bag, ready to pull out her warrant card as she sidestepped the light. A small man stood in front of her, chunky, older than her by a few years and regarding her with nervous disapproval. His shirt, tie and jacket were creased. Her mother would have classed his trousers as casual chinos, but they had a knife-edge crease down the front.

'Sorry about the light, but I heard noises.' The beam gravitated back to her face.

'The torch, can you shine it elsewhere, please?'

'Yes, indeed.' The light did not move. 'But if you're a journalist, you'll have to leave. There'll be a press briefing tomorrow at ten at . . . well, they haven't decided where yet, but they will announce that'

– he nodded sagely – 'in good time.' His outstretched arm was guiding her out of the garden, back through the arch, and she walked as he indicated, her heart still thumping but rather charmed by his politeness.

'Are you here on your own?' she asked. 'Apart from the two officers at the front gate?'

'No.'

'Oh yes, you are. There should be more of you. This is a large property, not easy to keep secure.' She stopped walking.

'I knew you were here,' he responded simply, waving his hand to move her on, like he was shooing a dirty dog from a clean kitchen.

'Are you here on your own?' She turned to face him. He took a step closer. She realised how much taller she was.

'My partner was called in. He'll be back in a moment. I can alert the gate by radio,' he said, uncomfortable. He was lying.

Caplan wondered who he was protecting. 'That's a serious breach of investigative procedure.'

'My colleague said he'd be ten minutes. He was needed.'

'When was that?'

His eyes flicked up to the dark sky then to the ground. He was deciding how to answer. 'About two hours ago,' he admitted, bristling up to his full five feet five.

Caplan continued her walk round the house to the boarded-up window, her companion jogging to keep up. Recent new wood scented the air along with the wild garlic and foxgloves – it was almost magical.

'You're not a journalist, are you?'

'Nope,' said Caplan, still looking at the house. She pulled out her warrant card, presenting it to him.

'Oh,' said her companion.

'You have a key, I presume?'

'Yes.'

'And your name?'

'DC Craigo.'

'Let's have a look round together, for corroboration, DC Craigo. You shouldn't ever have been here on your own. Leaves you wide open to all kinds of allegations in court. Could jeopardise the entire case.'

'Yes, I know,' he said, eyes closing with a slow blink.

'So, who left you here on your own?'

He hesitated.

'Who called your partner away?' she asked sharply.

'DI Kinsella, ma'am.'

'Well, I'll be having words with him about that. There's a briefing tomorrow at nine?'

'Yes.'

'Good. Let's have a look round here and you can get me up to speed.' She was wondering if he was the best they could do. No wonder she'd been sent here to assist.

Craigo found a key, in a tagged evidence bag in one of the many pockets of his jacket. Caplan wasn't sure if her companion was confused, tired, uncertain about where she stood in the place of things, or if she was witnessing the benign sloppiness of a small local force.

He opened the back door for her, revealing a thick mat, boot removers, wellies, shoes, a row of waxed jackets hanging on wooden panelling. Above that, a rack of hooks held a line of keys, each one labelled with italic writing. Craigo reached round and put the light on, illuminating an expensive and modern kitchen, minimalistic, black and white with grey tiles on the floor that probably needed mopped twice a day with dogs in the house. But when they walked into the lower hall, she felt she had entered a museum. There was that same sense of dust and solitude; even her light footsteps echoed up and around, over her head.

They walked up the stairs, in silence, on the agreed access, the plates on every stair, to where the deceased were lying, waiting. She saw the duvet spread out.

And the bodies.

It was deathly quiet. The scent of decomposition mixed with that familiar lemony aroma of a crime scene. The last body, that of a young woman, was half exposed by the lowered duvet, her clothes unruffled.

'Are the crime scene techs finished?' she asked quietly, noting the numbered yellow flags scattered over the room.

'Yes . . . well, no. I think they're coming back. The female victims were strangled manually, and in Edinburgh they have a machine —'

'The Eviscan. Comes from the word evanesce, to fade.'

'. . . that might be able to lift fingerprints from the . . . er . . .'

'Necks of the victims?' offered Caplan. She moved onto the landing; he walked closely behind. The scene was much worse than she had imagined. Somehow, she'd expected blood, signs of violence and a struggle – evidence that they had fought to their last.

But they looked serene. They had simply gone to sleep on the floor.

Caplan left the bodies to their eternal rest, looking up to the portrait above, then down to the altar below. No artistic director of the National Theatre could have designed a crime scene better. Staged to catch the eye of whoever came up the stairs. Had the local bad boy got such artistry? She doubted it.

The piano, the chaise longue, the inverted cross slashed on the portrait of a lady in a cream dress. A faint sprinkling of light floated in from the moon behind the stained-glass window, and rainbow-coloured diamonds danced over the faces of the deceased, giving the impression that there was still some life within. And the goat's head, the goblets and the stains on the floor that may or may not be blood. The daggers were a bit too much. In the middle, was Satan himself, carved in ebony, doing a little jig with his wings out.

She'd read in the file that there had been a Polaroid photograph placed in the mouth of each of the victims. That might have some significance in the occult, keeping the image of the dead in this world as the soul of the victim had flown. It may be three weeks since the murders, and the McGregor family, uncovered, would not look as if they were merely waiting the loving embrace from the heavenly Father, welcomed by a chorus of angels.

They had decayed. The stink of the bacteria escaping from their bowel to invade the neighbouring abdominal tissues overwhelmed the entire house, plus the stench of bodily fluids, external and internal. Caplan had a strong stomach. But her companion loitered on the stairs, staring out of the stained-glass window. Maybe he was less used to violent death here in this idyllic village, a million miles away from the streets of Glasgow where brutality was a common occurrence. Caplan knew better than anybody that people died in the most mundane of circumstances: wondering what they'd be making for the tea, should they pop into Tesco's, had they left the gas on? Death stole you when you weren't looking. Like that boy on the bike, Daniel Doran. Everybody thought they had tomorrow. Nobody got up thinking that this day would be the one: the last time they'd leave the house, feed the cat, say cheerio to the kids as they picked up the car keys.

Anybody who thought like that would never put a foot over the front door.

She took two gloves from her bag and pulled them over her hands, wriggling her fingers for a good fit while studying the portrait hanging high on the wood-panelled wall. A brass light ran the full width of the painting, highlighting its importance. The subject had been targeted by the perpetrators – the image of her body slashed while her actual body had been strangled. The youthful lady of the house, Mrs McGregor, was standing, probably on this very spot, sixty years previously, posed beside the same grand piano. She had the demeanour of a grand duchess of a small European principality. The creamy-white folds of the long, pearled gown were so beautifully painted they looked translucent, shone like silk. The toes of her diamanté-encrusted shoes were visible, sparkled, beneath the hem of the dress, whereas, under the piano was a small dog, a Border Terrier almost obscured by the dark shadows.

'She was a lovely lady,' said the voice behind her, making her jump. She had totally forgotten Craigo was there. 'Lady Charlotte Victoria Kerr McGregor.'

Caplan was impressed. 'You remembered her full title?'

'It's written on the frame.'

'Well spotted,' she muttered.

'I met her twice. My mum knew Barbara McGregor, the daughter-in-law.' He nodded in the direction of the second body without actually looking at it. 'They were on the flower show committee in Otterburn. Charlotte bred a rose and named it after the house. They always had the show here in a marquee on the main lawn. The family let them use the kitchen, more or less opened bits of the ground floor of the house for it. She was our Grace Kelly, really.'

Caplan nodded slowly, seeing the likeness, maybe not so much in the face but in the style, the posture. 'Was the flower show held here last year? Or was it pre-COVID?'

Her companion looked up into the eaves of the house and wrinkled his nose. 'I think it would have been the summer of nineteen.'

'So, we could surmise that many people would know the gardens and the rough layout of the house?'

'I suppose so.' He sniffed and turned his head away to look out the window again, watching the small traces of moonlight filtering through. It was very dark outside now. Caplan gave him his moment, but, good God, he really shouldn't be on the team at all; he knew the bloody victims.

Caplan looked down to the deceased, the babes sleeping in the woods. So much care in the staging. Care and time. And who would know that the light from the window struck the floor there. Somebody who had grown up here. She looked up to the window. *But Jesus called them unto him, and said, Suffer little children to come unto me, and forbid them not: for of such is the kingdom of God.*

'They said they saw the eyes of Satan,' said her companion, noticing the change in her focus. 'The two kids. Up there on the landing. Makes you think, doesn't it?'

She smiled at him. 'You think evil was trapped here on the landing by the power of Jesus on the stairs. What do you think of this? All this satanic stuff. It seems a little out of place in this scene. It doesn't fit with the portrait . . .' She shrugged. 'I mean, why slash that? Because it was her? Or because it was there?'

'That struck me, ma'am. It's not in keeping, is it?' He was alert now, looking helpful.

'And did you know the missing boy, Adam? How old was he?'

'Knew of him. He'd be in his early twenties by now, I think.'

'Did he live here?'

'He has a room on the next floor. Bare, looks like a monk's cell. Not been used for months, judging from the dust. Only the old girl, her son and the daughter-in-law lived here. The three kids had moved on, the two deceased to London, I think. Kinsella was looking for Adam out on the island, on Skone today. They didn't find him.'

'So, he lived locally? Skone is out on the bay, right?'

He blinked, slowly and deliberately. 'He preferred to be out on Skone, ma'am. He went away, he bounced back. The black sheep, every family has one. The other two children were more McGregor, shall we say. Oh, and one thing, ma'am, that you might not know. The only obvious thing stolen is an old stone, a bleeding Devil Stone that the family had.'

'A bleeding Devil Stone?' asked Caplan, barely keeping the disbelief from her voice.

'Yes, there may be other items missing, but that's the only obvious thing.'

'There's a thousand pounds' worth of valuables lying on top of the piano, and somebody killed the entire family to get their hands on a bit of rock. How can something, anything, be that important?'

'Well, that depends on what you believe. It was on the *Antiques Roadshow*, got a bit famous after that. If you think the stone gives its owners great power and riches, why not? Many have died in pursuit of the Holy Grail. Like I say, if you think it has power, then it has power.' He blinked in that slow way that Caplan was starting to find very irritating.

Her silence forced him to continue.

'It was kept in Charlotte's bedroom. It's along there with the sitting room and study. DCI Oswald had a good look round earlier.'

'Shall we?' She turned to face him. 'And where are you from, DC Craigo? You sound local.'

'Yes, ma'am.' Another slow blink. 'From down the road. Well, up the road. Along it, really, to be precise.'

WALKING SLOWLY, CAPLAN FIRST and Craigo four feet behind her, both went through the archway into a long hall, carpeted in deep red, the walls adorned with more oil paintings and gilt-framed mirrors. Two of the mirrors were angled, Caplan presumed, so somebody in bed could see who was coming onto the landing, now that there were no servants to escort visitors. The heavy door was already open to show a large mahogany sleigh bed with a frame at the head to afford the old lady some leverage with getting up. The room was a riot of red and crimson. The bed itself was covered with bolster cushions and thick silken quilts. Tassels and braiding, embroidery and tapestry, everywhere a love of dogs and horses, hounds and hunters, Highland and Shetland ponies, and always a little Border Terrier. It was a lovely room.

At the far side, amongst the chests of drawers and the wardrobes was a high-based chair, a commode, Caplan presumed. It'd be a long walk from here to the nearest toilet.

She glanced at the contents of the bedside table: a digital alarm clock incongruous with the feel of the room, a collection of books, *The Devil Rides Out* on the top, a copy of the Bible tucked underneath, a ribbon marking a page. A small dish with two pearl earrings and a matching necklace nestled in folds of green velvet, a coiled white serpent in the grass. She lifted the clock and looked underneath it, checking the time with that on her phone.

'Am I right in saying that the power was out when the bodies were discovered?'

'Yes, it was off at the mains.'

Caplan gave a little nod as she looked at two photographs: a picture of Charlotte as she had been in the big portrait, with her husband on their wedding day, and then a picture of a young man, jeans, white shirt, sitting on a fence. The similarity in their features was easy to see.

'DC Craigo, this photograph here?'

'Yes, ma'am.' He walked over in his shoe covers, a short stride on the carpet. 'Adam McGregor. Must have been taken before the big fall-out.'

'The favourite grandson or merely the absent grandson?'

'I think he was her favourite. He was very like his grandfather to look at.' He pulled off his spectacles, indicating two pictures. 'As you can see, ma'am.'

She pointed at another two photographs on the sideboard. 'We have Stanley and Barbara, we have Catriona and Gordon.'

Craigo nodded to a few more images, silver-framed. 'And this lady here is Gordon's fiancée, Fiona – no, Finola. They were due to get married later this summer.'

'Was she invited on the cruise?'

'No.'

'Was Adam?'

'No.'

Caplan turned round, tired and irritated. 'Where was this stone you were talking about? Let's have a look at that.'

'It's missing, ma'am.' There was a do-si-do halfway across the room. 'The Deilstane or Devil Stone was kept in this glass case. And as you can see, ma'am, it's empty.' He indicated the display case, wooden-framed, lined in purple silk, sitting above the fire, like a cradle for an ostrich egg.

Caplan shook her head. 'There's a fortune lying around here, and they steal a piece of rock. Have I wandered into a 1950s' horror movie? And who keeps a stone in a presentation case?'

Craigo said nothing.

Caplan walked away. Still a DC at what age? Early fifties? Mid-fifties? He couldn't be far off retirement, surely. No wonder Kinsella had left him at the scene; he was a doughball. Had Craigo's colleague wandered away, the penalty of that being preferable to being bored to death by this irritating little git?

She looked at the portrait above the bed, an older version of Charlotte. 'This family were very keen to immortalise themselves in oil.'

'I don't see any sense in it, ma'am.'

'Neither do I.'

'Yes, ma'am.'

'You don't need to keep saying that.'

'No, ma'am,' he said, poker-faced.

The next room along was the sitting room. Three settees, an open fire, the logs neatly stacked in the grate and a basket at the side. There were easy chairs and matching footstools. A long sideboard covered with more photographs, a silver tea service on a heavily engraved tray, brightly polished, and a dog bed in front of the fire with another beside the chair where Charlotte McGregor probably sat. Some neatly folded clothes lay on the smaller settee. Craigo was chattering as they went, random mutterings about the family getting ready for a holiday, how most people thought that they had gone, and that they had gathered here from their various homes before their flight down to Heathrow on Tuesday evening.

'DC Craigo, this is a big house, and it's all clean and dusted, so they must have had help of some kind?'

'Yes, indeed, the cleaner, Ina Faulds. Nice woman. She's been popping in to collect the mail and store it elsewhere, for safekeeping.'

'I'm sorry?'

'She saved it, just in case.'

'In case of what? In case the house was broken into? And she didn't notice the five bodies lying on the upper landing?'

'Well, you can't see them when you come in the door, can you?' he argued, his light-coloured eyes staring at her.

'No. But you can smell them.'

Craigo looked slightly confused and nodded. 'Oh yes . . . oh no . . . I see what you mean. Toni Mackie knows Whyte's mother; she works at the surgery. It's common knowledge that since Ina had COVID she's had no sense of smell, ma'am.'

'Does she know about the alarm?'

'She does.'

'So, she'd know if the alarm was switched off? You agreed the electricity was off?'

'Now, that's a real conundrum, ma'am.' He actually scratched the top of his head, like Stan Laurel.

'Okay.' Caplan took a deep breath. 'Maybe, at some point, we can go through who knows what. It seems to me that those who committed this terrible crime were in possession of a high degree of knowledge about the house. Would you agree with that?'

'Oh yes, ma'am.' He nodded, on sure ground now.

'And that would point to a member of the family in general and to Adam in particular. Certainly, somebody who had been in the house before. Doesn't it?' Caplan turned her back to him. Bloody drawing teeth. 'And the two boys, the ones who broke in, they did all the damage that was found. Just a broken pane of glass? No other signs of forced entry?'

'No, ma'am.' Craigo looked slightly confused. 'But the Deilstane has gone. If the stone leaves Otterburn House, or if it starts to bleed, death and disaster are sure to follow.'

'So, the entire family have been killed because the stone has left the house?'

'Probably, ma'am.'

'Case solved then,' muttered Caplan.

SIX

It was two o'clock in the morning when Caplan opened the door of her room at the Empire Hotel. It was clean, if slightly worn, with an accent on all shades of cream and brown. She hung her clothes up in the single wardrobe, then placed her tablet on the small desk at the wall, immediately hitting her head on the overhanging TV screen. Swearing quietly, she decided to place it on the bedside table alongside the plastic folder of local attractions.

The air in the bedroom was warm and stuffy, so she took a cold shower and, after some stretching, went to bed. But sleep never came easy. She put the bedside light back on and flicked through the restaurant brochures, flyers for boat trips and coach trips, fishing permit information and a history of the Allanach Foundation and Skone, with old pictures of sheep, beaches, caves, ferries and crofts. It all looked so boring she gave up and fell asleep immediately.

Caplan slept fitfully through the intermittent noise of life within the hotel: the doors opening and closing, snatches of drunken conversation and laughter. It was a stark contrast to the silence of home.

In the Prince Edward dining room, she placed her tablet on the clean, starched, slightly worn tablecloth and perused the laminated, badly typed menu. Variations on the theme of bacon, haggis, sausage and black pudding. Most of it served on a roll or on fried bread. The heart attack special. At the very bottom of the menu, was the complete Scottish breakfast. Served on a white roll.

Caplan called the waitress over, a sleek Ukrainian girl, it turned out, called Erika, and asked for a yoghurt and some fruit. Erika gave her a look that suggested she empathised with her guest's plight, but many others had made a similar request and been disappointed. She went away and was busy for a good fifteen minutes, giving Caplan time to switch on her tablet to pick up any documentation she had been emailed overnight, using her mobile as a hotspot. It didn't look like Erika would be back anytime soon to spy over her shoulder. A couple of emails had come to direct her to the station where she had to report. A local incident room was being set up, but she had to go to Cronchie for 9 a.m., for a briefing with Oswald.

Had he returned from whoever or whatever had been keeping him from his job? She would be his second-in-command, sandwiched between him and Kinsella. She hoped it wouldn't be too confrontational. But if it was, she didn't really care. She'd do what she had to do, get it sorted, return to Glasgow, get her rank back and try to spend more time at home.

She checked her phone. There was an update from Emma: *Dad and Kenny both still in bed.* Emma was leaving for a shift at work, then meeting a pal for an early dinner to discuss their dissertation. Caplan felt guilty; she tried to remember exactly what her daughter's essay was about. Something to do with commercial exploitation of the eco market? Maybe she'd been paying more attention than she thought.

She blanked the tablet screen as Erika returned, looking apologetic, with a pyramid of yoghurt pots and some fruit on a side plate, with a cheese knife impersonating a fruit knife. The yoghurts still had the price label from the local supermarket on the foil top.

From the fruit teas on the cold buffet table, she chose an apple and cinnamon, and sipped it, listening to the soft chatter of the other guests with their ferry timetables and weather forecasts.

She looked out the window at the island lying in the sound, ignoring the headlines in the papers being read at the other tables, having already skimmed the electronic versions, grateful for the skilful manipulation of the truth: the 'bodies found' and 'investigations ongoing'. There had followed a brief summary of the family, respectful but not hugely informative. It suggested to her that ACC Linden, or her superiors, had made a few phone calls to newspaper editors, asking them to tread carefully now for a bigger prize later.

Caplan heard a soft cough behind her, and thought it was Erika, maybe back with a banana to whet her appetite. Turning, she saw Craigo, waiting. He had been home and changed, but his shirt had remained out of reach of the iron, while his chinos had received too much attention. His limp mousey hair was stuck to the side of his head with sweat. The rucksack was still hanging off his shoulder, aiming for the floor.

She hoped the irritation didn't show in her face as she turned off the hotspot, then smiled at him. A grown-up boy scout with his summer jerkin half unzipped. When he spoke, his soft Highland accent was almost inaudible against the increasing chatter in the dining room.

'I've some documentation that may be of interest to you, ma'am.'

'Why don't you sit down and join me?'

He looked round, nervously. 'Really, ma'am, I could just leave it here' – he patted the top of the tablecloth, already thinking of a way out of the situation – 'and you could look at it while eating your . . . er . . .' He looked at the yoghurt and the sliced apple on the side of Caplan's plate, and wrinkled his nose, then he did that thing that really irritated her, the slow blink. '. . . your breakfast.'

'Sit down, Craigo,' she said quietly. 'You're giving me a crick in my neck. And don't call me ma'am in a public place.'

'Sorry, ma'am.' He sat down with startling enthusiasm.

'You look really tired. You have been home for a sleep, haven't you?' she asked, considering it a safe question.

'Only for a shower, then I was back at the station. No time for sleep. We've all been told that we're on this twenty-four seven. It's a big case, ma'am.' He nodded. 'There was a briefing at seven this morning. I thought you might've been there.'

'I thought it was nine.' She checked her phone. 'It says nine.'

His eyes, small and weaselly, their strange sandy irises with the darkest pupils she had ever seen, flicked to the floor then up to meet hers. 'DI Kinsella changed it, ma'am. I don't think Bob Oswald got the memo either as he wasn't there and that's not like him at all. I hope he's okay.'

'We should get down there and join them.' She glanced at her watch, reaching to pour the rest of her tea down her throat.

'Meeting's over. DI Kinsella told me to collect you.'

She had noted the undertone in Craigo's voice; he was not saying what he was thinking. He looked across at another guest, taking delivery of their full Scottish breakfast.

'Have you had anything to eat?' she asked.

'No, ma'am, had no time. You see, I was . . .'

'Well, choose what you like. I'm sure Police Scotland owes you for your time.'

She called Erika, who brought a menu which Craigo looked at, examining the slightly out-of-synch typing. He rammed his glasses back up his nose and said softly, 'Can I have a roll on bacon, please?'

'Of course?'

'And a roll on fried egg and potato scone.'

'Yes, of course.'

'And can you put a wee bit of haggis on that?'

'Yes, and to drink?'

'A coffee.'

'Okay.'

'Plenty of milk and three sugars, please.'

Erika marched off, with an eye roll to Caplan when she requested it be added to her bill.

'When was the last time you ate something?'

'That would be last night.' He leaned forward.

Caplan stirred her yoghurt, searching for any recognisable fruit, suspecting that it would all taste the same anyway. 'Now, what did you really want to tell me?'

'Well, ma'am, have you been sent here after being demoted?'

'It was suggested I step down a rank for the moment. The last person demoted was Dixon of Dock Green.'

'Who?'

'Never mind. Was my incompetence announced at the briefing this morning?' she asked sarcastically.

'Yes, and what could legally be described as a death in custody, though you never touched the boy.'

Caplan had to swallow hard. 'You're all very well informed.'

The coffee arrived, and he sipped at it, making a slurping sound like a small drain clearing. 'DCI Bob Oswald has gone missing, I'm sure of it.' He looked left, right, eyes wide, like a kid with a conspiracy theory.

'Missing? Missing rather than ill?'

'That's the gossip round the station.' He pulled a slight face, considering the problem as he looked out the window. 'He was a devoted Christian so we're worried the . . . stuff at Otterburn, might have . . . unsettled him. It might affect him more than your average cop.'

She recognised his genuine concern and didn't say what was going through her mind. How could a grown man be unnerved by a goat's head and an ornament of Old Nick when there were five bodies less than ten feet away? 'He must have been up most of the night at the house?' She took a mouthful of yoghurt; it tasted of the plastic tub.

'Lorna says he's not been home for two nights. And . . .' Craigo raised a finger for emphasis. 'Toni said that Jenny at Brodie's garage didn't see him although he said he was going there for coffee.' The rolls arrived in front of him. More calories on that plate than Caplan would eat in a week. 'It's more than a little weird, ma'am.'

'Weird?'

'Yes. He leaves the crime scene. He disappears.'

'I'm sure he'll turn up. You know what coppers are like? Some of us succumb to pressure, to drink, drop off the radar for a while.'

'Oh, and are you better now, ma'am? It's an illness like everything else, nothing to be ashamed of.'

'I was talking about Oswald. Not me,' she snapped.

He rolled his eyes. 'Oh, I see what you mean, ma'am, but not Bob, ma'am. He's not cut from that cloth. He follows the ways of the Lord.' Craigo nodded, that wise look in his eyes again.

Caplan took a sip of her apple and cinnamon tea to stifle a smile. Thinking that DC Craigo probably went to church every week to keep on top of the gossip. A case like this, working late into the early hours, was an adulterer's dream.

She knew that better than anyone.

CRONCHIE POLICE STATION WAS a neat little grey-bricked building with the standard navy-blue logo on a dark wooden door. Driving through the town centre, Caplan could see some media activity. The reporters from the bigger papers were gathering outside. The hold on the press could only last so long.

She parked on the street and walked into the station car park, which was only indicated by a tiny sign on a long wall, three or four buildings down from the station itself. She saw the space designated for the DCI. There was a new metallic-red C-Class Merc parked there, standing out like a rose in a sea of white cars.

Had Oswald finally turned up to his work?

After a quick look in the wing mirror of a Volkswagen to make sure her hair was neat, she turned to see a uniformed officer walking towards her. She flashed her warrant card at him.

'Is DCI Oswald in the building at the moment?' she asked, nodding at the Mercedes in the parking space.

'Nope.' He put his hand on his hips as if she had disrupted his tea break and he wasn't happy about it. 'He's not here yet.'

'Ma'am,' she reminded him while nodding over to the car in the space marked DCI.

'That's DI Kinsella's Merc.'

Interesting. She started walking.

He followed her towards the back door of the station. 'Can you hang on a moment, please, ma'am?' He pulled out his phone, got somebody on speed-dial. 'Hi, darlin', is Garry up there? I've got a DI Caplan for him. I think she's the one we're expecting.' He turned round to look at her, his eyes going up and down as he listened to a description. 'Aye, that'll be her.'

Caplan heard the other voice rattle out something.

'But I'm not sending her up if she can't get in the door.' He turned back to her. 'DC Mackie'll be down in a jiffy.' He rang off. 'Through you come, ma'am.'

Caplan thanked him and nodded, chatting about the lovely weather and the issues of policing a tourist town as they walked into the small reception. She recognised the smell immediately; floor polish and coffee, most police stations smelled the same, except the Glasgow city centre ones that had the added aroma of stale urine with a top note of vomit. The strength of each scent varied as the day went on, or what day of the week it was, but it was always present.

'She'll be down in a moment.'

'And you are?' she asked.

'Constable Jackson, Mattie Jackson.'

She held his gaze.

'Ma'am.'

'Thank you, Jackson. Have you been at the McGregor scene?'

'No, ma'am, but I did come in earlier this morning, helped prepare for the briefing. It's a terrible thing.'

Caplan looked round at the double doors that led through to the working parts of the station. They stayed closed, and Jackson showed no sign of opening them for her. She had a vague suspicion that she was being kept here while things were being concealed in drawers or hidden behind screens. 'Are you familiar with the two boys who found the bodies?'

'Oh God, aye.' He rolled his eyes. 'We all know wee Bainsy. I've arrested him a few times, his dad too when he was here.' He went through his locked door to reappear behind the glass partition, leaving her standing at reception.

Caplan smiled at him. 'Are we talking petty theft or the ability to ruthlessly kill every member of the same family?'

'Sometimes a troubled lad is just that, but young Bainsy is a very nasty bit of work. Nothing would surprise me about him. One of those lads – born evil, you might say.' Jackson sniffed, 'It's sad, but it does happen. If you want any background reports on him, let me know. There's plenty. And, with the way it was up there . . .'

'Yes?'

'Well, we've had lads, Bainsy included, going into the woods up round Otterburn at the Bodie Neuk . . .'

'The where?'

'It's a wee waterfall in the Otterburn woods, attracts all kinds of unruly nonsense. Skinny-dipping, drinking, drugs, devil-worship. They sacrifice animals too – we've had reports of pets going missing, ma'am. The McGregors themselves have complained. There was a big party in the woods on Monday thirteenth. We sent Whyte and Gourlay to break it up.'

'The day before the murders?'

'They call themselves Deilmen. I saw that Bainsy gave the Horned Hand when Kinsella interviewed him. It gave him the heebie-jeebies. It's a satanic sign – all the Deilmen do it.'

Caplan nodded; it was a good lead. 'These Deilmen? Are there many of them?'

'A core of four or five at least, can be twelve or more.'

'Does that have something to do with the theft of this bleeding stone?' She remained vague.

'Well, they're braver than me if they took it. The stone has been there for generations.'

Caplan nodded her acknowledgement that this polite, middle-aged man held the stone in some degree of awe. 'Thank you, PC Jackson.'

He looked past her, to the double doors, hearing the thud-thud-thud of heavy approaching feet. The doors burst open. A rather large woman, skin the tawny brown of a good tan, a halo of bushy blonde hair, crashed through them.

'Where is she? Jackson, ma boy, how are you doing?' Then she turned to Caplan without waiting for an answer to either question.

'Jesus, hen, you're awfy skinny. Craigo said if you turned sideways, we'd miss you. Are you the new DI? Right, I'm me.' She pointed to the lanyard that sloped over her ample chest to dangle in mid-air. 'DC Toni Mackie, how the hell are you?'

'Toni! It's ma'am,' said Jackson. 'It's how the hell are you, ma'am.' He nodded at Caplan from behind his glass barricade, an eyebrow raised, a small smile on his face.

Caplan smiled too. Now was the moment to show that she wasn't a stuck-up cow. 'Thank you, Jackson, indeed it is. I'm well.'

Mackie shook her head. 'Garry Kinsella's up there, the DI, like you. He nicked the DCI spot on the car park so that you could get the DI space. Turns out he's not such a spudbucket as we thought. Oh, sorry, ma'am.' She didn't appear at all apologetic; there had been an unsubtle message there.

'She didn't park in the DI space, she parked in the street,' said Jackson from behind his screen.

'Oh, that's nice. One of the guys, eh?' said Mackie, punching in a number and opening the door, causing Caplan to recoil at the sight and smell of a hairy armpit.

As they went upstairs, she tried to ignore the Crocs that revealed thick, cracked skin round the back of her heels, darkly veined with tanning lotion. Caplan noticed people's feet; she couldn't help it. She had already clocked the low-cut sleeveless top, the denim skirt, and wondered about the station's dress code. But it was not her enquiry. While Caplan herself was in bed, Mackie might well have been up most of the night collating intel for the briefing, intending to go home and . . . *get dressed properly* were the words that floated into her mind.

Caplan climbed the stairs behind Mackie, tuning out the constant chatter coming out her mouth; as with Craigo, she paid just enough attention to recognise anything of use. At the top was another set of locked doors. Mackie swiped the card on her lanyard and the door clicked open.

'I'll sort you out with one of these,' she said, holding up the keycard then turned. She looked down at Caplan. 'That's if you feel like staying.'

Caplan stepped up another two stairs, drawing herself level with Mackie, who was smaller than her by a good six inches. 'DC Mackie, I'll be staying here for as long as it takes.'

WHEN CAPLAN ENTERED THE incident room, all chattering keyboards and multiple monitors, it could have been any busy office. Craigo gave an imperceptible wave, not drawing attention to the fact that they were already acquainted. Nobody looked up as they walked in, Caplan following Mackie. The constable nodded to a well-built, bald man with a ginger goatee beard sitting in a glass-fronted office, looking hot and very stressed.

'DI Garry Kinsella. That's Iain Gourlay and Happy Harris with him. Happy is the misery guts and Gourlay is the hot one with the nice arse and expensive aftershave. Kinsella's more designer beards and biceps.' She winked.

'I'll bear that in mind,' said Caplan, looking round to check. Sure enough, Kinsella's white shirt, with the pinstriped cuffs carefully folded up, was a little too tight. Gourlay, slightly shorter, tanned, a handsome man, was turning each page of the file he was reading with slow deliberation. That left the one with the lugubrious expression as Happy. They looked busy, efficient, still working in the oppressive heat, without the sweat dripping off them the way it was running off Mackie, adding to her pungent aroma.

Five whiteboards spanned the front of the incident room, from the eldest victim, Charlotte, to the youngest, her granddaughter Catriona. Caplan blocked out the noise in the room and looked intently at the people they had once been, not the swollen, stinking amorphous blobs that still lay on the landing floor. There was a timeline of sorts scribbled at the side: Charlotte last seen at eleven thirty, Tuesday fourteenth, Catriona at three when she had left the chemist. On the wall was a photograph of Adam, last seen at two thirty on Saturday the eleventh, with a note that said *Wavedancer* above a picture of a white speedboat, its hull decorated with orange flames. The name Jack Innes was written over the photograph of a peroxide-blond young man taken aboard the same boat, judging from the look of intense pride and the paternal way his hand rested on the wheel.

Overarching it all were the words 'Operation Capulet'. That was fitting – all the main players dead at the end of the act.

'We're moving the incident room up to Otterburn, into the old primary school gym hall. It's a judo place now but closed for the summer. The heid bummers are keen to be seen to have soldiers on the ground. Craigo said you missed the briefing? It was all about the last movements. What enemies they had. None. Probable suspects. None.' Mackie stole a quick glance round the room. 'I can email you my notes,' she said quietly, out the corner of her mouth.

'Thanks, that would be useful,' Caplan replied in a similar vein, looking at the roster on the wall, seeing who should have been on the outer cordon at Otterburn House. There were only three names: Whyte, McPhee and Craigo.

Mackie glanced through the glass. 'He'll soon be finished with his pals in there. Put your stuff on my desk for the mo, fucked if I ever get a chance to sit down.'

'Thanks.' Caplan placed her bag beside Mackie's chair, and took a seat, looking at the three men. The squad had shown no reaction when she had walked in, so they had been expecting her. She eyed them carefully, a team picked by Oswald, his legacy if he was retiring. She could sense their energy. Kinsella hadn't been a DI for more than a few months which meant Caplan, with her years at DCI level, could legitimately march into that office and claim it as her own until Oswald returned.

Or she could offer her experience. Whatever way round, they could resent her, a situation which could only be aggravated if she walked into their room now. But, as everybody seemed to be taking a dislike to her at the moment anyway, she may as well give them good reason. She stood up, smoothed down her jacket and took two steps towards the office just as Happy Harris came out the door, carrying a file, nearly bumping into her as he went. She caught a muttered apology. Gourlay, the dark-haired one, followed closely behind but had the good grace to say 'excuse me', a flash of recognition of the senior officer who had not been invited to the briefing registering in his face as she walked past to knock on the glass of the office.

Kinsella was already back on the phone. He looked up, waved her in. As she entered, Caplan noticed how comfortable he looked behind the desk that bore the name plate *DCI R. Oswald*. She nodded to show that he could carry on with the call and that she'd wait.

For the moment.

She sat down, smiling, acknowledging that he was trying to end the conversation quickly. She deduced he was arranging an interview at the hospital. He put the caller on speakerphone, mouthing at her if she'd like to speak to Scott Frew, while saying down the phone phrases like 'as long as an adult can be there', 'not vulnerable as such' and 'requiring an independent person present'.

Caplan glanced at her own mobile as she waited, watching him out the corner of her eye. Younger than her – ten years, maybe more. Didn't sound local, more like a Glasgow accent. No wedding ring. The pictures on the desk were of Oswald's family, a young wife and children for a man of his age.

Kinsella read her impatience and tried to finish the call again, saying, 'Yes . . . yes . . . yes . . . as soon as I know, you'll know . . . I've no idea where he is. Look, I have to go. The cavalry's arrived, thank God.' This was said with a smile to Caplan. 'Yes, keep me posted . . .

leave it to me, yes . . . Goodbye.' He swiped off and closed his eyes in mock exhaustion. When she offered her hand, he shook it gratefully.

'DCI Caplan, I presume. I'm glad to see you.'

'DI,' she corrected.

'On paper but not by experience.'

'I'm judging by that phone call that Bob Oswald hasn't turned up yet.'

'No. I'm getting a little concerned.'

'When was he last seen?'

'I saw him drive through the gates of Otterburn House at half one in the morning. Hasn't been seen since. It's been over thirty hours.' Kinsella ran his hands over his bald head, leaning back so the sunlight streaming in from the window held him in silhouette. 'Initially I thought he might have stolen a wee snooze in the car. He'd worked a forty-eight-hour shift and said he was heading back, well, getting a coffee at the garage on the way to keep him awake. But he didn't even reach the garage. He's disappeared into thin air.'

'Not the type to walk off a major enquiry?'

'Nope. He's the DCI who can go forty-eight hours on black coffee and a ham sandwich. I've heard you're of a similar type.'

Caplan nodded at the compliment. 'Do you think his disappearance could be connected with the case? If he's not been seen since he drove away from Otterburn House . . . You do look worried.'

A frown crossed his face. He rubbed at his beard. 'No. Not anything like that. There's a few in here I might think that of, but not him.' He looked out at the incident room.

Caplan followed his line of sight to DC Craigo, sitting in his crumpled shirt sleeves, endlessly stirring a cup of something while looking at the faces of the victims.

'Anyway, DI Caplan, you've headed up a few murder squads before. You have a hundred per cent record, I see. You solve them fast, and cheaply.'

'Much of that was luck.'

'But you were forced into a demoted post because of mishandling evidence. And the fatal incident before they put you on this enquiry?'

She said nothing, waiting to see the way he would jump.

'And they punish you by sending you up here?'

'The fatal incident was a mugger who lost his balance and fell off his bike. There was no more to it than that.'

Kinsella readjusted his posture in his chair. 'Was he on drugs?'

'No PM as yet.'

'Interesting.' He pushed his chair out and started to swing on it, tapping his pen off the side of the desk. 'Was there a burst of manic energy just before he died? Bleeding?'

'Exactly.' Caplan was intrigued.

Kinsella nodded. 'A new street drug, do you think? There's a rumour that Operation Jackdaw's working on it.'

'Why do you think I'd be privy to anything that lot were working on?'

'Just thought with your friends in high places . . .' Kinsella smiled at her knowingly.

Caplan stared him out. He might know about her affair with the head of the drug squad – he'd done his homework on her and the gossip grapevine was rife – but he might not. 'That lot sit in cars for hours. They eat doughnuts and get piles,' she retorted, smiling.

'Okay, okay. Any ideas about these killings at Otterburn House?' he asked, rubbing his ginger beard again. 'We know it was Tuesday the fourteenth of June. God, it was awful. I remember sitting through a meeting on rural policing that day. What a waste of time.'

The date was in Caplan's mind too; she'd taken Aklen to the hospital for yet another tweak in a stream of endless tweaks of medication.

'What happened at the briefing this morning?' she asked quickly.

He didn't flinch. 'Oh, sorry about that, communication breakdown. Mackie set that up late yesterday.' He moved some papers around on

Oswald's desk nervously, not as sure of her as he had first seemed. 'We sent Craig out to get you when we realised you'd been left off the contact list. Apologies.'

'He caught up with me at breakfast. I was at the scene last night, and your DC was very helpful.'

'Was he now?' Kinsella sounded bemused. 'He didn't mention he'd met you.'

'He said something about a bleeding stone – a Deilstane? That if it ever leaves the house, then disaster will follow?'

'Local folklore. You know about the Deilmen?'

'I heard.'

'I think they might have had some interest in it. The stone was missing when the bodies were discovered.'

'And where is it? I doubt the boys took it, hid it, then appeared at the Knoxes' house with that degree of distress.'

'I agree. But the story is that the Devil Stone can summon up Beelzebub. That's an attraction for our local satanists. Mattie downstairs has a file on them: taking Class A, playing loud music, stripping off, and generally upsetting people, pretending to drink the blood of lambs – probably vodka and Red Bull.' He shrugged.

'Very late last night Craigo was there – alone,' she emphasised. 'There were two officers on the outer cordon, but at the locus he was on his own.'

'Oh, please don't let that fact become public knowledge.' Kinsella pulled a face and looked angelic. 'Please.'

Caplan was glad to see that it bothered him. 'He shouldn't have been left alone in any circumstances.'

'Oh, I'm well aware of that. There were two officers walking around. It's a big property, and it was just a breakdown in communication, but it was six hours, and, well, you'd think that Craig might have had the sense to tell us he was on his own. All he said to me was that he thought there was somebody about; he never mentioned you.' He threw his pen on the desk. 'DI . . .?'

'Christine.'

'Garry. Craig's an odd wee guy. We inherited him. He's not really experienced. He's a whale being dragged by our wee boat, and he holds us back.' He shook his head. 'Anyway, can you go to the hospital to talk to Scott Frew? It's not my job to tell you what to do, but—'

'No, it's not. But I'm happy to interview him. You have to admit that McBain, charming young gentleman that he is, is never going to be on *Mastermind*, is he? The crime scene is evidence of planning and a very clear head. It was staged, don't you think? That doesn't add up.'

He sighed. 'The evidence is there.'

'You might be reading it wrong, that's all I'm saying. While it's good you're keen to push forward, don't close down any other avenues of investigation. Think what a good defence counsel would do with this. We – not you, not I, *we* – have to account for these two lads pulling off five murders.'

'We got a fabric sample from the top of the gates, which might lead us somewhere. Are your thoughts drifting to Adam McGregor? The damage to the painting suggests that.'

'It's an inverted cross; it could be consistent with satanic activity. It might be both as she supported him against the family. He was her favourite. Maybe she was changing her allegiance. It would explain the fact that the killer was apparently invited in. You follow where the evidence goes. We're here to find the truth. It's not a popularity competition,' Caplan said.

'Okay, what aspect do you want?' He looked out at the manpower he had available to him. 'I've a feeling that without Bob I'm in danger of losing focus.'

'Better than having tunnel vision.' She smiled at him. 'I'll keep you right. If Frew is still in the hospital, I'll interview him later today.'

'His foster mother, well, one of them, is on a train from Glasgow. She should be here this afternoon. But he's still having hallucinations about the Devil, still psychologically unstable.'

'Any friends of Adam we could talk to?'

Kinsella looked past her, through the glass to the wall beyond. 'We have a girlfriend, Sandra Leivesley? Mackie'll let you know the address.' He swung on his chair. 'But don't be fooled by Frew: he's close to Bainsy, and Bainsy is a very dangerous young man. Everybody knows him. He won't be able to spit in the village without somebody telling us about it. What if we let him go but keep him under observation? His mental health assessment was fine.'

'Okay, okay. As long as you're comfortable with that.' Caplan considered. 'I was thinking there might be a Charles Manson to his Tex Watson.'

'Who?'

'Every charismatic leader needs a follower to do the dirty work. Charles Manson never killed anybody; he got his followers to do it for him. There could be somebody pulling Bainsy's strings. Looking at the evidence, I don't think you can keep him in custody for just house-breaking. He merely found the bodies. Any official observation of him would deplete valuable manpower. I doubt you'd get anywhere arguing for a surveillance budget, and we're nowhere near the threshold for a warrant to track his phone at the moment.'

'Even though he could have escalated to this atrocity?'

'Do you have any proof? That fabric sample is still at forensics, isn't it?' She shook her head. 'Release him, but keep him pertinent to further enquiries. Ask him not to leave town. He doesn't have a car, does he?'

'Nope. If Toni Mackie got the word out, he wouldn't be able to go for a pish without somebody knowing. Yes, I'll do that. One favour?'

'Of course.'

'Can you take Craig with you today?'

'Yes.'

'But please don't rely on him. Just a warning.'

Caplan nodded.

'He was rejected from another squad, and you can see why. He doesn't play the team game. He didn't tell me that he'd met you last night, but it's all in his wee notebook instead of getting logged in the system.'

'Don't worry, I logged it. And there was somebody in the trees, moving around the perimeter. They backed off when I didn't. I thought it might be the press, so be wary of questions on the protection around Otterburn House. If it was another officer, he was a bloody fast walker as he got there quicker than I did.'

'Noted.' He smiled. 'Anyway, let's introduce you to the guys as Senior Investigating Officer DI Caplan, just until Bob resurfaces. I'm glad to have you on board.'

He was trying, but he was not that good a liar.

SEVEN

As she walked back into the main incident room, Caplan was aware of boxes being packed, labelled and numbered, the familiar signs of a major investigation on the move. It looked well organised and the correct procedures were being followed.

Once he started talking, Caplan realised that no matter his rank, no matter how careless he was on locus security, Kinsella was very good at summarising findings and motivating the squad. It was clear where the main avenue of the investigation was focused: Billy McBain. The nineteen-year-old had been quiet in the last few months after a lifetime of escalating behaviour but was now attached to the gang going around calling themselves the Deilmen. The DI went on to say that Scotland's leading expert, Dr Felix McGarrick, had said that satanism was the fastest-growing faith in the country at the moment; more boys had been registered with the name Lucifer than the name Nigel, in the previous year.

That got a ripple of laughter.

'Easily shortened to Lucy,' muttered Caplan, provoking another giggle. 'But from that to murdering five people? It's a bit of a leap, and to execute them with such' – she struggled for the word – 'efficiency? There're brains behind this. Is there any connection between Adam and Bainsy?'

'That's why I'm glad DI Caplan is here,' Kinsella said to the assembled personnel, looking more confident. 'She's looking for something akin to the Manson family, but tidier.'

Another ripple of laughter.

'No direct link between Bainsy and Adam McGregor so far, but DS Gourlay is on it. DI Caplan?' Kinsella invited her to address the group.

Caplan got to her feet. 'Did somebody orchestrate this? This crime scene' – she pointed at the picture labelled 'Capulet' – 'is perfect. Planned. Accurate. Precise. The victims' heads are in line. There's an awareness of forensics. And to do that' – she tapped at the picture – 'while keeping a cool head shows a degree of maturity, education and nerve. And it all fits together beautifully, apart from this.' She tapped the picture of the slashed portrait. 'Almost two crime scenes.'

'I just thought, looking at it, the way the painting's so high on the wall, that it looked a bit angelic. Could that have upset our Deilmen?' said Gourlay, his dark eyes scanned the room. There was a murmur of assent.

Caplan was undeterred. 'Mr McBain was in a state of shock when he left the scene, as if it was new to him. Not behaving as if he had left it that way three weeks before.'

'Maybe he didn't think they would smell or look like that,' Gourlay said. 'Look how quickly he pulled himself together – cool as a cucumber at interview.'

'Okay, but we also look at Adam. No forced entry, somebody they trusted, somebody who knew the plans of the family, who knew the one time they would all be together. Motive? Would his inheritance be affected by the forthcoming wedding? The slashes in the portrait could easily point to him. All that satanic stuff to put us off the scent, but he couldn't quite resist that wee spiteful act at the end,' said Caplan.

Kinsella nodded thoughtfully. 'There's no way Bainsy's an inspiring, charismatic leader. He wouldn't be able to control others, incite them to commit a crime like that, but . . . and it's a big "but", he might be a follower. And Adam's not hung around to be questioned, has he?'

'And there's power,' agreed Gourlay, rubbing his upper arms, thinking out loud. 'The old dear might have been eighty, but she was still doing her roses and could manage the stairs. The other four were capable of defending themselves. There was muscle power or some coercive control taking place.'

'One other thing to keep in mind.' Kinsella pointed to a photograph of something that resembled an ostrich egg. 'The Deilstane is missing, the bleeding stone. Gordon's wearing a Patek Philippe watch worth at least ten grand, Charlotte's rings have real diamonds, but they took the stone. Their purpose was quite different. I've put a link on the system for you to read. It freaked me out. God knows what it'd do to a brain like McBain's. What he might believe that it was capable of. McBain is being psychologically assessed to see if it's possible that, maybe, the stone made him do it.'

'*The stone made him do it?*' Caplan repeated slowly, echoing the ripple of disbelief going round the room.

Kinsella smiled. 'Thank you for not bursting out laughing. But I've seen people kill for a tenner. I'm sure McBain is the answer to this in some way. He waited until his cousin came up from Glasgow before he revisited the scene. Why? Did the world need to know that the family were dead, and Bainsy waited until there was corroboration?' He shrugged. 'That doesn't rule out Adam of course.'

'Was there some reason they had to be discovered before the family was due home on the ninth of July?' asked Caplan. 'But I can't see why.'

'Good point. Harris?' said Kinsella.

'Frew was up here on the twelfth, thirteenth and fourteenth of June, the latter being the day of the McGregors' last seen, as far as we know. Jackson said there had been a big party in the woods near Otterburn House on the Monday. That takes us to the night before the murders. Jackson's getting the list of who was there.'

'I was bloody there! Ten drunk teenagers, most of them naked. Naked with those midges, braver than me,' said Gourlay, laughing.

'Thanks. It was Oswald's belief that the Deilmen were behind it, so bear that in mind. He was an experienced murder investigator – we need to follow that up carefully.'

Caplan winced. 'Do we have any sign of Adam yet?'

Gourlay continued: 'Still not come to light. We searched the island and nothing. His phone had been on and off over the last few hours, making its way down south. It's not proof of life but it's a start. He could be off the grid because that's the life he lives. A contact on Skone said that Adam was heading to a commune in Wales; Gwent police are monitoring that for us.' Gourlay turned back to Kinsella. 'Jack Innes says he brought Adam back from Skone on *Wavedancer*' – he tapped the photo of the white speedboat – 'on the thirteenth of June. We've searched Skone; he's not there.'

'So, Adam McGregor was on the mainland at the time of the party and at the time of the murders?' Caplan confirmed.

'Yes. DI Caplan is going to interview Sandra Leivesley to get a feel for Adam's recent mood. And if he mentioned where he was going.'

'Of course,' said Caplan. 'Can I have a look at the interview with McBain – before I speak to Frew?'

'Please do. Toni, can you set that up? The DI is partnering Craig.' Craigo nodded, pleased.

'I'd like at least one of the local boys to look good. And your—'

'Reputation's already in the gutter?' Caplan suggested, laughing. The rest joined in. It was a bonding moment, and for an instant Caplan felt herself relax.

'I'll be masterminding the forensic boys at the house with the Eviscan machine. Should be there by eleven. We're hoping for finger-prints from the skin.'

'From the forensically aware satanists?' Caplan asked, keeping her voice light.

Kinsella smiled. 'Yes, I know. They'd be wearing gloves, but we're ticking boxes.'

'Sir, Sandra was a friend with benefits,' said Mackie, 'but I suspect there were other women around. Blossom, who lives on Skone, and another I've not traced yet, described as mid-twenties, dyed dark hair, with a tattoo of a peacock on her left upper arm. Called Devi when on Skone, but that's not her real name, obviously.'

'I spoke to Blossom yesterday during the search. She's not seen or heard from Adam since he left. She sounded legit,' said Gourlay.

'Right, we look for Devi, we keep looking for him. Adam was a handsome, rich young man – girls would be easy.' Kinsella nodded. 'Craigo can direct you to Sandra's house, Christine. He doesn't drive. Iain, about the family dynamics?'

Gourlay walked to the board. Caplan happened to look at Mackie, who was gazing admiringly at his bottom, pulling a long piece of chewing gum from her mouth. 'The other two kids, Gordon and Catriona, did everything they were supposed to do as a McGregor. The dad, Stanley, went to Sandhurst and then into the family business. And married Barbara, who had a life of making jam and doing good things for charity while sharing a kitchen with the old dear. She went to church every week and popped out three children including the lovely Adam, who left uni without a degree and has been an eco-warrior ever since. Gordon was about to get married to Finola Stewart-Parry, who's on a hen fortnight in Dubai. I've checked she's still there. Not even left the resort.'

'I bet it's cooler there,' said Mackie, fanning herself.

Another ripple of laughter.

The meeting broke up. Mackie gestured Caplan over to her desk, and her podgy fingers flew over the keyboard, quickly finding the video file of Bainsy's interview and pressing play.

'You can watch the whole thing. He's silent all the way through, but look at the bit from one minute to one minute ten.' She got up and gave Caplan the seat, but still stood too close for comfort.

Caplan watched carefully, her attention fixed on the young man. McBain was thin, short, much smaller than she had expected. A weird-looking bloke with eyes too big for his head and a nose, broken twice, that spread over his pockmarked face. His hair was cropped so close to his skull it was almost invisible. The sleeves of his black hoodie were pushed up above his elbows, revealing tattoos on both forearms. Caplan thought she recognised the shape and googled it on her phone. She was right: Aleister Crowley, the unicursal hexagram, the symbol of Thelema. She'd bet Bainsy didn't even know what it meant. From her point of view, it seemed he was deliberately displaying them, making a statement. He pushed the chair away from the table when the police officers entered, the plastic feet grating noisily on the floor.

Caplan watched the introductions. Kinsella asked if Mr McBain needed anything. McBain rocked back in his seat a little, raised his right fist, lowered his left and extended the first finger and the small finger of each hand, slowly sticking out his thumbs, just as Jackson had described. Keeping that pose, he stared up at the camera with eyes as dark as the pits of hell.

CAPLAN WAS STILL DISTURBED by the image of McBain, the intensity of his stare, as she walked into the sunshine to find Craigo standing beside the Duster. The DC gave her directions to Lower Bardo, then sat quietly. Caplan suspected that Kinsella was right. The older detective was out of his depth and out of touch for a case of this magnitude. He had been rather reticent when she'd asked him for more details about the McGregor family, and she suspected he'd been warned about talking out of turn. He was in the habit of walking four or five feet behind her, like a creeping Jesus, silent but listening. It was easy to forget he was there, and then he'd say something that disturbed her chain of thought.

Sandra Leivesley lived in a small white cottage on the shore at Lower Bardo, a tiny village ten miles to the north of Cronchie. It had a picturesque harbour with tourist boats bobbing on the water, ready to load visitors for a trip to see the whirlpool, common seals and bottlenose dolphins.

The warm breeze blowing did little to disperse the heat, and Caplan was glad to walk into the darkened hall with the cold tiled floor. She could see the kitchen opened out to the garden that ran down to the shore with its dried seagrass. A chestnut Border Collie lay in the sun. It looked up when they came in then went back to sleep.

Sandra was a twenty-five-year-old classroom assistant off work for the summer. She'd just returned from walking the dog, hence the butterfly of sweat on the back of her vest top. She chatted nervously about the atrocity which had taken place along the coast from her idyllic little home. Sandra made Craigo a cup of tea, asking him about his dad and his cousin. They were not mentioned by name, but there was some situation that Mr Craigo senior was doing well with, that was good news. Sandra and Caplan had a glass of tap water, the latter wondering if there was a Mrs Craigo by marriage, but she couldn't see it. Surely no woman would let a man go to his work looking like that.

Seated in the compact living room with all the windows and doors open, the sea breeze flowing through the cottage, all Caplan could hear outside was the chirping of songbirds and the thrum of a tractor in the distance. It was nearly midday, and the heat was building.

Legs tucked neatly beneath her, sitting on the sofa, Sandra Leivesley was happy to talk about growing up with Adam, her best friend for years, and warmed to her theme. It was 'my Adam' this and 'my Adam' that, and how he'd always been different from the rest of the McGregors. He didn't like his family, she said. He detested everything they stood for.

'They made their fortune from slaves, you know. They were one of those Edinburgh families who made their money that way.'

'Tea and slaves,' added Craigo helpfully.

'Maybe they did,' said Caplan, recalling having the same argument with Kenny: the morals of yesterday being looked through the prism of the present. Life wasn't like that.

'The family rode with the hunt when it was legal, shot everything that moved, yet refused Adam the freedom to go to sea and stop dolphins being caught in tuna nets. The McGregors were always hunting, shooting, fishing. The estate made a lot of money from it all, while Adam was a vegan. And a socialist.'

'Was he now?' asked Caplan, holding her smile back, recognising a privileged young man's anger. It could be Kenny talking about his mother being an instrument of the capitalist state in her role to oppress the masses, then asking that she spend her police salary buying him a new car.

'Did he have a faith? The family were Church of Scotland.'

'Yes.' A flick of a look from one detective to the other, she was about to test a lie.

'Satanism?' asked Craigo, causing Caplan to swear inwardly.

'Oh, yes,' Sandra agreed, then shook her head. 'Well, no. He's always been a bit of a Pagan, living with the rhythm of the moon and the sun, the seasons. But I think he was drifting towards darkness. At first, I thought he was winding me up. There was a big fight with the family, them saying he was wrong to turn to Satan and worship the God of excess when . . . well, you've seen the house. I mean, who lives the excessive life? Not him, was it? It was them. All that argument about the omniscient power of the Lord of Light but not so good at admitting there might be a greater power of the Lord of Darkness. If you look at the way the world is going now, with the big corporations, the way everybody hates everybody, how can you deny that there's evil out there? Adam was struggling with all that. Chris Allanach, who runs the Foundation, inherited wealth, inherited Rune in fact, on the south of Skone He lives a lovely life, very rich. It's not mutually exclusive. Do you see?'

Caplan nodded, wondering what Craigo, sitting behind her, was making of all this. Probably chewing on his lip.

Then she heard him speak. 'There's always been rumours around Otterburn that the family were into satanism back in old Edward McGregor's times. They'd summon up evil spirits after the whisky had been passed around and the ladies had retired for the evening. Aleister Crowley, Conan Doyle and fairies. It was the way of many families in those days. Crowley was called the wickedest man in the world; he started his own branch of the occult,' Craigo said to nobody in particular.

'Indeed,' said Caplan shortly and turned back to Sandra. 'How long were you two together?'

'Were? We still are,' bristled Sandra. 'This was his place, this was where he stayed when he was home.'

'Rather than at Otterburn House, you mean.'

'Yes.'

'Even before he was kicked out?'

'Yes.' She looked a little more wary now.

'Can we see his room?'

'I've only got the one room,' she said sharply, uncomfortable.

'Can we see that? His things?'

'He travelled light. There's nothing here . . .'

'When was he disowned by the family?'

She shrugged. 'More of a drift than a severance, two years maybe.'

'And when you were together, was the relationship exclusive?'

'Yes, of course. It still is.' Sandra was on the back foot, not able to see where the conversation was going.

'Yeah. He was a good-looking young man, living in sandals, worshipping the god of excess. Rich.' Caplan raised an eyebrow, thinking of Adam's monastic bedroom in Otterburn House. 'Sandra, do you think Adam was capable of murdering his family?'

She went slightly pale, taking a long time to answer. 'I don't know what happened there, I've only heard rumours.'

Caplan spoke slowly. 'Would Adam be capable of strangling his sister, looking into her eyes as she breathed her last? Was Adam capable of doing that? To her?'

Sandra took a sip from her water, backhanding the drips from her chin. Her voice, when she eventually spoke, was that of a much younger girl. 'He would get so angry with his dad or Gordon. He really had issues with them.'

'But Catriona?'

She shook her head. 'He'd never do anything to her.'

'When did you last speak to him?'

'Not for a month. Early June maybe, the Wednesday? The eighth, I think.' Sandra's eyes drifted over to a pile of brochures on the floor, holidays and summerhouses.

Caplan noticed it. 'Seems a long time. Do you suspect there's somebody else significant in his life, romantically?'

'There wasn't anybody else.' The pain in her eyes when she said it suggested otherwise. 'I'd made a decision to stand on my own two feet.' She nodded, approving the idea that had just entered her head. 'Everybody wanted Adam's money – I wasn't one of those people.'

'Apples don't fall far from the tree,' said Caplan. 'They might roll away, but they tend to roll back again. Did you see any sign of him and his parents making up?'

'No. And it's too late now.'

'Yes, it is.' Caplan closed her tablet. 'Did he know Billy McBain?'

'That wee weirdo from Otterburn, always on the wacky baccy? Yes, I think so. He's weird full stop.'

'Scott Frew?'

A slight pause while she took the time to look out at the dog in the garden. 'Never heard of him. Er . . . I do have a lot to do, so . . .'

Caplan nodded; Sandra had been too slow to answer that. 'We're putting an incident room together. We might ask you to come down and look at some photographs, answer a few more questions.'

She nodded, trying to stop the flicker of uncertainty from showing on her face. 'Yes, of course. Happy to help. It's a big shock for us all.'

'It was a terrible thing to happen,' agreed Caplan. 'How well do you know Otterburn House?'

'I've never been—'

'Sandra?' interrupted Craigo. 'As far as you know, how often was Adam on the island?'

If Caplan had been sitting looking at Craigo, she would have missed the expression that flitted across Sandra's face. She couldn't quite find the word to describe it, but panic was close.

She shrugged, acting nonchalant. 'He liked being at Rune—'

'Rune?' asked Caplan.

'Yes, the village on the south of Skone, ma'am. Where Allanach lives, where the Foundation—'

'Yes, I know,' she snapped at her DC. 'But Adam was there?'

'He liked the community. He'd spent all his childhood holidays there. What's not to like?'

'Was he there recently? Since the eighth?' asked Craigo, ready with the question.

Again, the pause was a moment too long. 'I'm not sure.' The tears fell again. Sandra looked from Craigo to Caplan but said nothing. The sound of a car engine broke the silence. It stopped; a car door opened.

'Sorry, I need to get the dog in otherwise he'll bark at the neighbours.'

CAPLAN WAS IN THE Duster, out of earshot, before she turned to her companion. 'How much of that did you believe?'

'Not as much as I was supposed to believe, ma'am. She cared for him, and he dumped her. He'd stopped paying her rent. And she was behind. Then the dog gets a kennel cough injection, so must be going to kennels. Sandra can now enjoy a holiday.'

'How do you know that?'

'Everybody knows that, ma'am. Adam had another woman some-where, maybe the one with the tattoos that Toni was talking about. What kind of relationship was it when she was never invited home? She was speaking the truth there.' He made a note in his notebook. 'I was just thinking, ma'am.'

'Well, don't strain yourself.' Caplan tapped her fingers on the hot steering wheel.

'Adam was still getting his allowance from the family. It's in the bank; he's not spending it.'

'Yes. Hard to square that with Adam being a satanist.'

'Toni says that Adam was a yoghurt-knitting eco-warrior who eats lentils and wears alpaca socks. Paganism, maybe. Satanism, I doubt it. The Allanachs and satanism? The Devil Stone and the Foundation out at Rune? Polar opposites I'd say,' said Craigo thoughtfully. 'The problem is that my head gets a wee bit busy. Sometimes I have theories, and they just come tumbling out. My ideas aren't appreciated, so I've learned to keep them to myself. Sorry, ma'am, I didn't mean to derail your chain of thought. But, usually, nobody's listening.'

'Sorry, what were you saying?'

'Oh, I see, ma'am. That was a joke. Very good.' He nodded, smiling. 'Very good indeed.'

THEY WALKED ALONG THE hospital corridor, warrant cards in hand. They were greeted by the nurse on duty, who introduced herself as Sonja Ferries. She looked at them and guessed correctly who they were in to see, then immediately got on the phone again.

'The nurse wants to speak to you before you go in to see Scott,' she said.

'Why? I thought he only had an infected hand,' said Caplan.

'And the rest,' the nurse said obliquely. 'I discharged his friend this morning. I think he was taken straight to the police station. We've no beds in the psych unit at the moment for Scott, we're juggling.'

'We know the feeling,' said Caplan, bristling at the word 'psych'. That was a can of worms as far as she was concerned. It could form a wall of protection round a suspect. She looked around for somewhere to wait, then the door opened and the nurse at the station pointed to them. A woman, bedecked by lanyards and security devices, her long grey hair crinkled like steel wool, in blue linen capri pants showing four inches of white ankle and bright red sandals, walked towards them. She had a laptop under her arm.

'You looking to speak to Scott? I'm a nurse down on the psych ward. Angela Petrie.' They shook hands. She looked down the corridor expectantly, then the nurse at the station came to her rescue.

'Room three's about to be cleaned, you can go in there. The family room and the doctors' office are both occupied at the moment.'

Petrie nodded, and strode off at a clip. Caplan glanced at Craigo; his podgy white face was expressionless.

In the room, the nurse closed the door behind her and placed the laptop on the vacant examination bed. 'One thing to understand before you go in: he's been hallucinating and he believes that he saw the Devil staring at him. Please don't confront him on that. Here's a video clip that will give you an indication of what he's going through, his frame of mind.'

'Does this not breach his confidentiality?'

'You think he's guilty of murder? That's the end of that argument.' She pressed play. The laptop started screaming like a banshee. The screen showed a bed, on which Frew was curled into a ball, an arm thrashing out at something only he could see. One hand shielded his eyes. Terrified, he scrambled from the mattress, slithered to the floor and scuttled into the corner of the room, pulling the bedside cabinet over him with a terrible clatter. Two uniformed figures appeared on the screen: one reassuringly calm, the other ready with a syringe.

'I've seen enough,' said Caplan. 'That's heartbreaking. Would it help to tell him what he actually saw in the house? It was just a clock.'

The nurse shook her head. 'He's too conflicted. Let his foster mum tell him when she feels he's ready.'

'But he should know. It might calm him down. It's ridiculous.'

'Well, whether it's ridiculous or not depends very much on your belief system and how you see the world,' said Craigo in his singsong voice.

Caplan caught the alarm on Petrie's face. 'Shame you're short of beds on the psych wards, otherwise I could send you more patients – one in particular.'

There was no police presence outside Scott Frew's room, just an ordinary woman sitting on a single chair, staring at the door, white hands clasped on her lap. She stood up when she heard them approach, smoothing her linen skirt behind her and lifting her jacket from the back of her seat.

Caplan recognised the type.

'Hello,' she said, now standing in front of them. 'Are you from the social?'

'Police,' said Caplan, showing her warrant card. 'Are you Scott's foster mum?'

'Yes, yes, I am.' She looked relieved, then wary. 'Alice Keane.'

'I'm DCI, sorry, DI Christine Caplan, and this is DC Craigo.'

A nervous laugh. 'This is all so awful. I'd like to think that I've made some difference in his life, but looking at where we are now, maybe not.' She welled up.

'You're here, Mrs Keane. That's what matters.'

'Alice. They won't let me see him as I'm not family, not officially, but I'm all he's really known.'

Craigo coughed lightly. 'Ma'am, will I get a coffee? Would you like anything, Alice?'

A tear fell, a response to sudden kindness. 'A white coffee would be lovely.'

'We might even push the boat out to a biscuit.' Caplan sat down on the vacant seat, both of them watching as Craigo made his way out of the ward, his odd little walk making it appear as if he was holding something precious between his knees.

'Scott would never kill anybody.'

'What if he was under the influence of alcohol, drugs or a dominant personality?'

Alice shifted in her seat. 'That's why I sent him up here, to get him away from his old neighbourhood, the street gang he'd been hanging around with since he was thirteen. But he had changed recently, said something about how he was going to be rich. There was something going on that he wouldn't tell me. He was slipping away from me. I thought I'd done the right thing, letting him come up here. I was wrong.'

'You were doing the best you could. But he gave you no more information on how he was going to get rich?'

Alice shook her head.

'And when was he last in Cronchie?'

'About three weeks ago, I think. He came up on the Saturday coach. The eleventh? I had to give him his fare.' She blew out a long slow breath. 'He thinks he saw the Devil.' She turned to Caplan. 'Were there bodies on the floor? I read it in the newspaper.'

'Something like that,' she replied vaguely. 'But the red eyes coming at him out of the darkness . . . that was just a digital clock, battery-operated. The electricity was off, but it kept time. The red digits were reflected in a tilted mirror. When the time is right, you can reassure him on that front.'

All Alice could manage was 'oh'.

'Why not come in with us? He's under suspicion of murder, but I'll try not to upset him. We get into all kinds of trouble when we do that. It would be helpful if you could persuade Scott to tell us exactly why he was in that house. Where he thought this money was coming from? Even if not now, maybe later. Here's my card. Call me if he says anything.'

Alice nodded. 'I know him – he'd be nicking stuff, money for drink and cigarettes.'

'And that's the one thing he did not do.' Caplan opened the door.

Scott Frew lay on a bed, his hospital gown tied loosely around his scrawny neck, eyes closed. He looked about twelve. His blond hair was now flattened on his skull, instead of gelled up into spikes. All the bravado from the mugshots taken back in Glasgow was gone, unlike McBain. It struck Caplan how small he was, like his cousin, possibly growth-stunted in utero, a pregnancy hampered by substance abuse.

Caplan stood back at the door, letting Alice go forward and take the small white hand lying on the blanket cover.

'Scott? Scott? What have you been up to, darlin'?' She placed the back of her hand on the side of his cheek and his eyes opened, fluttering a little at the light, dulled by medication. She looked at the bandages on his hand and the stitches on his face.

He started to cry and whispered, 'I'm scared.'

'There's nothing to be scared of now.'

'It wis awful. There wis like dead bodies everywhere and . . .' His eyes drifted from Alice's face to Caplan, standing at the door, rucksack over her shoulder, looking very official in her smart suit.

'She polis?' His eyes were wary now.

'Yes. Scott? You've got to listen to me,' said Alice. 'You're in big trouble, and the only way out of it is to tell the police, this lady, the truth about what happened. You broke into a house where people died. What were you doing in there, son?'

He closed his eyes. 'It wis bloody awful.'

'Scott,' said Caplan, 'we just want to know what happened and what you did, that's all.'

'You need to do it, Scott, you need to tell them,' urged Alice.

He took a deep breath and started to talk. 'We went up tae the house. Bainsy wis really keen on getting this old stone. We broke a back windae, climbed through, and then we smelt it. A horrible stink, up the stairs tae the top, and then a' they bodies. Bainsy says the stane wis important, so we goes tae get it, but this thing came oot, like it wis protecting it. We ran away intae a hoose doon the road and the woman wis puttin' a thing oan ma haun. Ah wis bleedin'. Ah dunno whit went on in between. But it wis there, Ah swear, red eyes in the dark and horns . . . it had horns . . .' He moaned and looked at the ceiling.

'Talk me through it, Scott. I need to know the details, up to the point before the thing appeared,' said Caplan.

He closed his eyes. 'They wir lying there in a row, dead bodies, wrapped up, Ah think. We didnae see the faces at first, we wir larking around, looking at the . . . wis there a piano?' He looked at Caplan, checking for a sign that his memory was accurate.

She nodded.

Craigo came in the door carrying two plastic cups and a bottle of water. The water in the jug on the bedside table looked warm and slightly cloudy. Caplan wondered how long it had been sitting in the full glare of the sun. She placed the bottle of fresh water beside it and unscrewed the cap for Scott, noting again how small his hands were when he reached for it.

He had noticed things that Caplan, who always thought of herself as observant, had missed. He had noticed exactly how many gold and how many silver trinket boxes were on top of the piano. She hadn't.

'Ah didnae think they wir real, like . . . no' even dolls . . . they were white, all white and puffy, eyes all cloudy. They looked weird.'

'They'd been dead for some time.'

Craigo slurped noisily from his cup, disturbing the silence, then coughed. 'I grew up round here, you know. I grew up with the stories about the bleeding Devil Stone. You're right, Scott. It wards off evil spirits. It gave the McGregors their fortune – all those big cars, horses and fancy clothes. I thought it was the stone doing it. But in the wrong hands, it can summon evil.' He took another slurp and sat down.

Caplan wanted to punch him. 'It's all about coercion, Scott . . . what you were made to believe. What did your cousin believe?' She didn't look round, scared she'd strangle Craigo, but Scott was thinking it through.

'He's ma pal, he's okay, is Bainsy.'

'He's not your pal, Scott,' said Alice.

'Who told him to get the stone?'

'The Devil.'

'No, Scott. Somebody told him that and he believed it. That's not the same thing.'

Scott looked very young and vulnerable, and his voice began to quiver as he said, 'Naw, it wis the Devil.'

'You know, that makes sense if you ask me,' said Craigo, casually, ready to pontificate.

'Well, it's a good job that we aren't asking you,' Caplan hissed, dragging Craigo out the room.

EIGHT

Caplan's phone bleeped; the message gave her the address of the old school building in Otterburn, now being converted into an incident room. Craigo directed her, not saying much on the way, but looking out the window, deep in thought, only speaking to warn her when there was a bad bend approaching.

In the old school hall, the practice mats were stacked against the far wall to clear the floor for office furniture. Kinsella was looking more relaxed, deep in conversation with Gourlay; the latter winked when he saw Caplan, then rolled his eyes at the chaos around them. She wondered what she'd need to do to get partnered with him, an ambitious go-getter rather than the secretive little gossip twister that was Constable I've-never-been-promoted-in-my-puff Craigo. Two uniforms she didn't know were moving tables and unstacking seats. A woman dressed in jeans and a long T-shirt emerged from under a desk with a screwdriver between her teeth; every so often PC Whyte would hand her another piece of duct tape.

DC Mackie was making her presence felt and heard, making tea then staggering back and forth with files, dumping them on a desk before lifting them off again when they decided that the desk was to be moved as the computer cables were too short to reach. Caplan saw the plan up on the bare wall. Incident rooms were the same the world over, she guessed; the most important things were the kettle and the fridge.

She caught Kinsella's eye and they walked to a part of the room already sectioned off by boards. They had a quick chat about Sandra Leivesley and decided that she might be worth questioning again.

Caplan suggested that somebody research the stone, to quash the rumours, if nothing else.

'The locals are a superstitious lot. Witches, kelpies, Devil Stones, standing stones and satanism – you name it. But Sandra said she hadn't seen Adam since the eighth? Adam's been living on the island for a while but he's not there now. We've been all over that place,' Kinsella said. 'And that's the only place Sandra thought he might be?' He pointed at the map that showed the islands of Skone, Mull and Lismore. 'Skone, home of the Allanach Foundation. It's down here at Rune. On day one, Gourlay and the guys had a good wander around, even spoke to Allanach himself – "the Magus" as he's known. Some think he's a wise man, others think he's a total prick. I agree with the latter.

'They also spoke to the two guys who run the place for him: Callum, who does much of the day-to-day maintenance, and Roddy, who's the money man. They said Adam was there on the thirteenth of June but they haven't seen him since. That fits with Jack Innes bringing him back to the mainland the day before the murders. There's no clocks or phones at Rune. It's a technological black hole that makes precision impossible. But Roddy said Adam was his normal, happy self, doing his chores. There was nothing to suggest he was planning on slaughtering his entire family, and I think he'd know. He keeps the place ticking over while the Magus and Callum sit cross-legged and contemplate their navels. Adam mentioned going to the commune in Wales, and that ties up with his mobile flicking on and off. He regarded them as evil big tech, so he's not as mobile-friendly as your average millennial. Obviously, we're desperate to trace him to tell him about his family.'

'Avoiding news takes some effort in the world today.'

Kinsella rubbed his beard and said quietly, 'Oh, and we have a trace on McBain and Frew's phones authorised, tracking them where they were on Tuesday, fourteenth of June. That'll be very telling as they have their mobiles glued to them.' He filled her in on the Eviscan examination; a few prints had been lifted and they were being processed at the lab. He sidestepped her further into the corner. 'We got the authorisation for the phone traces because, and keep this to yourself, when using the Eviscan we found a piece of jewellery in with the bodies. It's a small prong with a silver skull on it.' He indicated with his finger how long it was.

'Like the post for a tongue piercing? More McBain than McGregor, I would have thought,' said Caplan.

'Do me a favour in the meantime?' She nodded. 'Have a quiet chat with Craig and find out exactly what he knows about Rune, Honeybogg Hill and Christopher Allanach. Craig has been here all his life; the rest of us have been away and come back. It's amazing how small his world might be. If you ask, it'll be out of curiosity. If I ask, he'll know he's being questioned.'

'Questioned?'

'Just find out what he knows. He's local and may have split loyalties. Or stupidity. And stubbornness. He doesn't do it deliberately, but sometimes he needs to have information pulled from him.'

'I've noticed.'

'He's not savvy enough to judge if what he knows is important. But he does know everybody. See if there's anything useful.'

'Honeybogg Hill and the Magus – really?'

'Bunch of nutters and accountants. But more importantly,' said Kinsella, 'we know that the last handshake of the phones at the house on the fourteenth of June was Catriona phoning the farm to make sure they'd received a supply of tripe for the dogs at half past three. Gordon called his fiancée in Dubai at ten past two, but nothing after that.'

'I've contacted their lawyer to see if the wedding would affect any inheritance. He wants a face to face,' said Caplan.

'Good thinking. Follow the money.' Kinsella walked along the wall, pointing. 'Mackie's fleshed out what they were doing a bit more.

Charlotte was left in the greenhouse by the housekeeper at eleven on Tuesday. Ina goes on holiday herself; they'd booked to coincide. Stan and Barbara were in Cronchie, had morning coffee at the garden centre, from the till receipt and credit card record. We presume they came straight home. Also, Barbara had just had an op on her knee, so she often got dropped at the front door and he'd drive the car round the back. The other two—'

'Gordon and Catriona . . .'

'Came back separately. The time stamped on the Polaroids could be the exact time of death. Charlotte was four minutes to twelve, Barbara ten past twelve, Stan twenty-two minutes past twelve, then Gordon and Catriona at twenty past two and five past four respectively.'

'There must have been more than one perpetrator there, surely. And in the house for how long? And they left no forensics?'

'Five hours. I would imagine they could "dispatch", for want of a better word, Charlotte quickly. But Barbara and Stan were killed within twelve minutes of each other?'

'And it can take, what, five minutes to strangle somebody. Anything from the McGregor family's contacts? Business enemies?'

'Nothing coming down the line, nothing obvious. I think it's personal. Somebody knew their movements very well.'

Caplan traced her hand around the photograph of the old lady, as she was in life. She tapped her finger on the image of young Gordon, the ex-soldier. 'Do you think you could take him down in a straight fight?'

'No way. Gordon's ex-army, a clear mind. I doubt a drug-addled devil-worshipper is going to get the better of him.'

'With no signs of a struggle, no scuff marks, no blood spatter. Do you think they had a gun pointed at them? Or a knife at his mother's neck?'

'I think she's dead by the time Barbara walks in the front door. There's only a small window of time between Faulds leaving Charlotte in the greenhouse and Barbara arriving. The timing on the Polaroids suggests that they were killed one by one.'

'Nobody passed Faulds on the road, so they must have been waiting somewhere. Well planned, like I keep saying.' She turned to look at him; his eyes were dark and tired. 'How did the press conference go?'

'Not as good as I hoped. I suggested to those upstairs that you take over, but they want you to stay below the radar. Bob usually—'

'Still no word?' One look at his face told her the answer to that one.

'Some gossiping bastards are saying that he must've been involved in some way, but that's shit. If you hear that from anyone, you let me know.' He placed his hands on his hips and let out a long, slow breath.

'How are you playing that with the media?'

'HQ are keeping a lid on it.'

'Okay,' said Caplan slowly.

Kinsella shook his head. 'It's a bloody nightmare. What would you do?'

Caplan folded her arms, looking at the frantic activity in the incident room, mindful of her colleague's lack of experience. 'It might not feel like it, but you're doing a great job.'

'Thanks. I keep thinking that Bob'll turn up in a hospital or . . . Christ, I don't know.'

'Was there any sense of him being unhappy at home?'

'No. He was looking forward to his retirement. Lorna and the girls mean everything to him, but that crime scene did upset him.'

'Okay. Well, fingers crossed we see him soon, eh? You know you can ask me for any advice you need,' she said. 'For instance, media liaison are great, up to a point, but better at telling you when to put your specs on and when to take them off rather than "this is how to answer a question that you don't want to". A case this size, a high-ranking officer should be the media face, might be better with ACC Sarah Linden,' she suggested. 'Do you mind if I head back to Otterburn House? I want to have another look at that satanic stuff now that the bodies are away. Do you have any experts in that kind of thing who might be worth talking to?'

'Yes. Harris is on that. The dried leaves on the floor at the scene were a type of parsley, something to do with satanic ritual, I heard. Might be why the flies kept away. Dr Felix McGarrick, he's at—'

'Sorry, I wasn't implying that you weren't on the ball.'

'No, please talk to him. All that stuff gives me the creeps.'

'I wanted to know what that weird thing was that Bainsy did with his fingers at the interview.'

'Oh, this.' Kinsella made a fist and pointed his fingers and thumbs out. 'I thought at first it was a rap thing, boys in the hood and all that.'

'Young people today?' mocked Caplan.

'Yeah, I'm showing my age.' He tapped at his iPhone intently, pulling a face then tapping again. He turned the screen to show his colleague. 'Then I googled it. It's a two-fingered satanic salute, the Horned Hand.'

'I could think of another two-fingered salute I'd give Billy McBain.'

'When you go to Otterburn House, take Craigo with you and keep him on a short lead.'

'You know, I just can't see that this carnage was because of a stone, bleeding or otherwise.' Caplan let her disbelief show in her face.

Kinsella said, 'Killing that family was very important to somebody. Maybe the stone was also important to that person, so they took it with them.'

'All we need to do is find out who.'

CAPLAN TOOK A PILE of files marked for her attention in what she now knew was DC Mackie's loopy handwriting; the dots over the 'I's were circles. She sat quietly at an empty desk in the corner of the incident room, sipping a glass of mineral water and shutting out the noise in the rest of the room, a talent she'd mastered when needing solitude in a busy dance rehearsal studio, to hear only her own music. She flicked through the photographs of Lady Charlotte. Fragments of her life, smiling with a dog at her side, a stick at her feet. Caplan recognised the back of Otterburn House. Charlotte had moved there when she married and then had her child, who had grown and left, to return in their own time. She checked her notes. This was the last holiday as a family unit. The tickets proved that Finola had not been invited. Neither had Adam, a slight maybe, but hardly enough to warrant a massacre.

Caplan keyed her ID into the computer and tried to track Adam on social media. He had no individual presence but the Allanach Foundation did. Lots of photographs of people swimming, gardening, diving, planting, weaving, making aromatherapy oils, collecting honey from the beehives up on Honeybogg Hill. Shiny happy people. She found a few pictures of Adam, often in the company of a rather attractive young woman with a heart-shaped face and honey-blonde hair. Adam had a bee tattoo on his wrist, his female friend none. She searched through the tags on the photographs to get her name. Blossom, the one Gourlay had spoken to on the day of the search. There was a connection between them in the pictures, heads touching, smiling at each other, closer than Sandra ever knew, Caplan suspected. She looked through a few links that Toni had left her for Facebook, Instagram and other social media following McBain and Frew. Frew kept a very low profile; anything posted was years old. McBain was different. His profile picture was recent: him in a baseball cap holding a panting black Staffie on a tight lead. Skull piercings in his eyebrow, nose and tongue, the one he may have lost at the time of the murders, which she felt was rather convenient. She had a good look through the friends and their photographs – lots of him and his mates with pouting girls, typical teenage behaviour. She uploaded the pictures showing the tongue pin onto the system, in case it helped with its provenance, and while she was there she clicked on the link to the history of the Deilstane. It had been found when the foundations of the house had been dug up, and was thought to be the recovery of a clan stone of the old chief of that land from the 1400s. Its history was well documented: in 1645, Donal McGregor had lost it in a bet and promptly been killed by a bolt of lightning. In 1782, a servant had stolen it and tried to make his escape across the water. All on the boat had drowned and the stone had 'floated' back to shore at Galveston. The McGregors vowed to look after it – and it appeared to look after them.

Caplan wondered how old fake news was.

She quickly closed the file and picked up her pen, setting to work on Adam and the timeline of his disappearance until Kinsella tapped her on the shoulder. Craigo wanted a run back to the station in Cronchie.

She looked at the clock, shocked at how late it was, at how empty and quiet the incident room had become. Her head was pounding after staring at the screen for so long; even Craigo wittering would be preferable to the sudden outbursts of filthy laughter from Mackie, now that she was aware of it. Caplan nodded thankfully. She needed to phone home first.

The call was a short one. Emma's work on her dissertation had gone well. Her dad wasn't really making any progress but wasn't going backwards. Both took that as a good sign. Kenny had got extremely drunk and come home with a girl who'd spent twenty minutes in the shower and used all Emma's fancy shower gel. But the complaining was upbeat, Emma sounded cheery; the novelty of being home, mothering her wee brother, hadn't worn off yet. Emma asked how the case was going. Caplan replied that it was like wading through treacle with her ankles tied together.

She was thinking how unlike her daughter it was, to ask about the progress of her work – a result of her own maxim to keep her kids distanced from the horrors she faced every day. Okay, they were nineteen and twenty-two now, but they were still her children.

'Mum?'

She knew that tone; her daughter was about to ask a favour.

'You're up in Cronchie, aren't you? Near Skone?'

'What do you know about Skone?' asked Caplan, intrigued.

'Well, Mum, the Allanach Foundation at Rune is one of the best examples of an ecological and economic system on the face of the planet. It's self-sufficient and carbon neutral. They do trailblazing work on keeping the planet clean.' She sounded very excited.

'Really?' she answered cautiously.

'Yes, ask around if you have the chance. I know they do day trips, but Allanach keeps himself to himself, never gives interviews. He has Roddy to do all that kind of thing for him, but I'm not interested in him.'

'Christopher Allanach, the Magus?'

'Oh my God, yes. Have you met him?'

'No. Not yet.' All she needed was her own daughter to get her nose in this investigation. 'I'll see what I can do.' She cut the call with the noise of Emma squealing in delight at the end of the phone. Bloody kids never grew up.

CRAIGO SUGGESTED THEY TAKE the quickest way back to Otterburn House if Caplan wanted to revisit it. The Duster was soon on the single road that hugged the side of the loch, winding, dangerous, at times perilously close to the water. It was one of the few short cuts from Otterburn to the house, but nobody was really sure if Oswald had taken that route home, or the safer, longer inland road on the night he had disappeared.

Caplan drove carefully. The sun was setting, but the darkness of night had not yet arrived. The lack of streetlamps, the last glint of daylight on the rippling loch and the low clouds made visibility difficult, especially for a woman more accustomed to driving round a busy city. In front of them, the sky was streaked with red and orange, an oil painting of heavy colour, solid. Behind them, determined-looking clouds bore down on the horizon. A full bright moon was glowing through the clouds. It would be easy to be beguiled by the beauty and colours of the composition. She thought about the stone and shivered.

'You read the report on the deaths?' asked Craigo. It was the first time he had spoken since they had left the incident room for the house, suddenly voicing something that had been churning in his mind.

'The initial forensics? Yes, but I've not seen anything back from the Eviscan yet,' said Caplan, keeping her eyes on the narrow strip of cracked tarmac in front of her.

She didn't want to speak. She needed to concentrate. She'd had either Craigo, Kinsella or Linden in her ear all day. She'd been working for eleven hours straight and needed to get some space in her head. Kinsella's words about not trusting Craigo, that he was a confidentiality sieve, were still reverberating. Craigo knew too many people in the area. For a case that needed to keep the intelligence ultra-tight and well controlled, the chatty little detective was a nightmare.

'What are you thinking about the deaths, ma'am? The way they were done?'

'The strangulation, you mean?'

'Yes. Three by hand: her ladyship, Barbara and Catriona. The other two by ligature. It takes a long time to do that, ma'am. Minutes. There were knives there, sharp ones, but they preferred strangulation.'

Caplan remained tight-lipped. 'Well, that means we might get something from the Eviscan. What does that mean to you? Satanism suggests stabbing and a lot of blood to me, maybe removal of organs, maybe from a goat or while wearing a goat's head. But strangulation looks, well, non-ritual.'

'It's much less personal to kill somebody with a ligature, isn't it? But why the men by ligature and the women by hand? Is there a sexual thing we're missing here?'

'Are we?' She was genuinely intrigued by the nature of his question; it was something he'd been thinking about.

'Not easy squeezing the life out of somebody while you're looking them in the eye, although some guys get a sexual thrill from that. Are we looking at the wrong type of ritual here? Did somebody enjoy killing the women but merely dispatch the men? Women killed face to face, the men from the back – just thinking it through, ma'am.'

Within the field of her vision, she saw him demonstrate with his hands. 'DC Craigo, you look like you're talking from personal experience,' she joked.

'Been in the force a long time, ma'am. Just because I'm still a DC, doesn't mean that I can't figure it out for myself.' He stuck his chin up, turned to look out the window which might have been an interest in the dramatic sky, or petulance. 'Doesn't mean that I've not been involved in murder cases . . . accidents, suicides, whole manner of things.'

'Sorry,' she apologised, 'I didn't mean that.'

'You need local knowledge. I think more than one suspect, don't you? A group who knew what the family's movements would be that day? If you think about it, they knew that Granny would be in the greenhouse. They knew about Barbara's knee, and if they wanted a time gap between her and Stan – he had to park the car. They knew about the dogs going to the farm, knew Ina was stopping at lunchtime that day, knew about her COVID and loss of smell. And then killed in the order they returned to the house? And the alarm is a problem too, ma'am. Linked to the station at Cronchie but it's either switched on or switched off. Who was doing that? It's on when Ina goes in but off for Bainsy and Frew. That doesn't make sense. I mean, it can't be anybody but Adam. And if the boss is right about when the phones went off the grid, lunchtime on the Tuesday, who put the alarm back on so that Ina had to switch it off when she came in for the mail after her holidays? Adam also explains why he waited for them all to be in one place. The two kids in London would soon sound the alarm if the parents up here went silent.' He sighed. 'Adam's a complex character.'

'The keys were on a rack at the back door. Easy for somebody to lift them and keep them for access any time they wanted, to put the alarms on and off. Turn the electricity off once they had persuaded the boys to go in. Or back in. I agree: it all points to somebody local, it all points to Adam,' said Caplan.

'He's still missing,' said Craigo, almost regretfully.

Caplan said nothing. Kinsella had said that DC Craigo might harbour an agenda; as far as she knew, they both had access to the same information, but Craigo seemed to have thought it through. Well, he'd had more time to think about it than she'd had.

She changed tack, slowing down on the road slightly. 'You remind me of somebody I used to know at primary school. She used to stand at the side of the playground, watching – nothing ever went by her. But when a wee girl from the school was reported missing, that lassie gave a good description of the woman who had waited at the gates and taken the girl.'

'And was that wee girl you, ma'am? Did you want to grow up to become a detective?'

'No. Her name was Vivien Green. She's a marine biologist and lives somewhere near the Great Barrier Reef. One of those people you track on Facebook.'

He shivered. 'Uh, Australia. I couldn't be doing with all those spiders. Plus, the heat. We don't do sunshine like that, not up here. It's August before I take my vest off.'

She laughed. He'd not annoyed her for a few minutes; maybe she'd gain his trust and get him to open up a little, get him to say something that he shouldn't know. He wasn't as daft as he made out. 'You do notice things though, don't you? Like Frew noticing things I missed.'

'I am a detective, ma'am. I noticed that the satanic stuff was too staged to be right. If they were sacrificing anything, there'd have been blood, and nobody can clean up every spot of blood in a house with wooden floors like that. That was a crime with not one drop of blood spilled. They tend to remove the hearts and viscera, these satanists . . .' He raised his hand. 'From what I've read, you understand. We don't do devil-worship in Otterburn . . . well, not much.

That McGarrick bloke spoke a lot about Baphomet and the caduceus.'

'And in English?'

'He said he'd looked at the photographs we sent him. His impression was that it was a set dressing for a play on satanism. Nothing about it was genuine. Just like we thought, ma'am.'

'But why was Oswald convinced that it was significant?' asked Caplan.

'He wasn't. I heard him say that he . . . Oh! Did you see that?' He pointed over the water.

'What?'

'There was something in the water, right there!'

'What? I didn't see anything.'

His hand flapped beside her. 'Pull over. Now.'

It wasn't a question; it was an order.

She stopped, pulling on the handbrake. 'Why, what is it?'

'There's something in the water there.' He got out the car.

Caplan, aware they were on their own on a remote stretch of road, watched him jogging back down the narrow track of tarmac, then he stood, shielding his eyes. Caplan tucked the Duster in a little more, pulled her jacket from the back seat and followed.

When she approached him, he was walking away from the lochside. She stood beside him as he dipped and bent over, trying to get an eyeline on the water, looking for something submerged. She walked across the grass verge, going further down the shore, putting some space between them; the brightness of the moon's glare from the undulating shallows of the loch was blinding here. Like her colleague, she cupped her hand round her eyes. She saw it, a glimmer of something that did not move with the surface of the water, something that stayed still while diamonds of light danced around it. She closed her eyes slightly, trying to take the visual noise out of what she was looking at, sensing Craigo at her shoulder.

'What do you think that is?' she asked.

'It's big. A car?'

'Really?'

'Common place for them to come off the road, wouldn't be the first time.'

'Shit.' She looked down at her feet, judged the distance to the shadow in the water that was forming into a recognisable shape. There was no way she was calling this in without being sure. Her confidence in herself to make decisions was rock-bottom, only slightly more than the confidence that Police Scotland had left in her. 'Okay, only one thing for it. Hold my jacket.' She kicked off her shoes and rolled up her trousers.

'No, ma'am, don't . . .'

'And the options are?'

He didn't volunteer. Instead, he took her jacket. 'Be careful, ma'am. It's very slippy – you might fall.'

Caplan knew she wouldn't fall. For much of her life she had balanced on her toes on a block of wood two inches by an inch; a few rocks didn't faze her. Her body was used to the cold. She stepped into the loch, knowing her feet would go numb. She kept her arms out, her balance perfect as she focused on the glinting mass in the water, the submerged shape whose outline was too regular to be of nature. She waded slightly to the side, the water creeping above her knees, when the pattern of what she was looking at suddenly became clear. A door handle, the white billowing of an air bag, a pattern of squashed features, white and light blue blotches, marshmallow lumps of skin flattened and crimped against the glass, an arch of hair over a closed eye, a white protruding tongue from grey lips.

CAPLAN WAS SITTING IN the Duster, engine running, letting her trousers dry. She had largely ignored the circus going on in the rear-view mirror except when a mechanic stuck his head in and asked if she could move her vehicle up to the next passing place so they could get a bit more room. She watched as the Audi was winched, inch by inch, from the loch, the spotlights shining on the curtain of water that poured from the door seals, the boot and the bonnet. Slowly, it emerged, and the corpse inside shifted, pinned by the seatbelt, as the vehicle rose, giving a fleeting impression of life. The body was then inspected in situ before being removed and placed in a bag, and lifted onto a stretcher. The onlookers stood still and silent, in two rows as an informal guard of honour for the body bag as it was taken from the shore to the back of the waiting private ambulance for transportation. Once the rear doors were closed, and the red lights had disappeared round the corner, the hub of activity commenced. The Audi was lined up to go on the back of the low loader, the ramps of which were down and ready to receive. Caplan had no idea who was guiding the operation, some traffic incident unit she guessed, before she recognised Kinsella, looking distressed, and Gourlay standing in the road looking grim-faced and even more tired than she was. Happy Harris was there too, the expression on his face suiting the sombre occasion. As she watched, Gourlay turned and placed a hand on Kinsella's shoulder, said a few comforting words in his ear, but Kinsella shrugged him off and walked away, wanting to be on his own with his grief.

Caplan considered getting out to show some respect, but they had known him, she had not. She'd be intruding on their grief just to score a few points of being inclusive.

Within hours of the crime being discovered, the senior investigating officer was dead and she was, vaguely, next in line. She realised that she and Craigo were being kept apart, which was interesting but not that unusual as they were witnesses.

She jumped at a knock on the passenger window of the Duster. The door opened and Kinsella slid into the seat, a plastic cup of coffee in his hand. He handed it to her. 'Don't ask where it came from. It's hot, just drink it.' He looked terrible, even a little red-eyed.

'It's Bob, isn't it?' She placed her hand over his.

He nodded, staring ahead, not trusting himself to look at her. 'I knew it, I bloody knew something had happened to him.' He looked as if he was going to cry: tears of anger, she suspected, of sheer frustration. 'He shouldn't have been here, shouldn't have been on this case.'

'You can't think like that.'

'I shouldn't have let him drive away. It was late. He was knackered. I keep thinking of that haar rolling in, the visibility on the road, how uneasy he was with the crime scene.' He shook his head. 'Why didn't he take the main road? Why did he turn his phone off after making the calls?'

'Would it have made any difference? The phone ended up in the water.' Caplan glanced at her dashcam, wondering how robust it was. 'He was a grown man. It was an accident . . . hard to accept, but you know . . .' She didn't want to add 'these things happen', but it was on the tip of her tongue. 'You said yourself he was tired. He'd just landed this case. Imagine that crime scene, driving home thinking about that. No wonder he lost concentration. Maybe, with his faith, it shook him more than it might shake someone else. If you live your life with the belief that a man walked on water, you might also believe that the Devil walks amongst us.'

'Do you think so?'

'What's the alternative?' She sipped the coffee; it really was awful. 'Are you thinking that it's a bit convenient that Bob was looking at a mass murder and then dead in the loch less than twenty minutes after leaving the house?'

'But it was an accident. He swerved to avoid a sheep, a deer, surely?' He turned to look at her. 'And he was tired, it was late, and it's a dangerous road.' He looked behind him, making sure that the other vehicles and their personnel were well out of earshot. 'Christine, how did you end up here . . . now?'

'What do you mean? We were going up to look at the house. I wanted to—'

'Who suggested this road? You're not a local. You wouldn't know about this route to get to the house. Who sent you along here?'

'Craigo said that—'

'Said what? That at this time of night and in this darkness, he saw something shining in the water? He asked you to stop. He got out the car but doesn't go near the water, but you do and, hey presto, you discover Oswald's body. Am I even close?' His voice was tight with emotion.

Caplan looked out the back window. Craigo was standing on the shore observing everything that was going on, just like the girl in the playground. A local cop who had not been promoted in his twenty-five years of service.

'That was exactly how it happened,' she admitted, realising the emotion under the grief.

Kinsella was scared.

'We'll catch whoever did this, Garry, we will.' Caplan's eyes were still on Craigo, but the car door slammed and she was left sitting on her own.

NINE

Caplan had eventually driven back to the hotel at three in the morning, ignoring a beguiling notion in her head that she should keep on the A85 until she was home. The road was quiet, she was making good time, the clouds had cleared, and it was a moonlit night. As she turned a sharp bend a stag dashed across the road in front of her, then scrambled up the bank on the far side. She jerked the wheel to avoid it, and the back of the Duster swung out as she braked. She swore as she regained control of the vehicle then pulled it to a stop.

She sat for a few minutes, hazard lights flashing, trying to calm herself. The idea of driving home grew even more attractive; the road round Loch Lomond would be free of tourist coaches and the occasional jackknifed caravan that would cause hours of delay. She could be home in two hours. See how Aklen was doing. Had Kenny managed to get out his bed yet? And Emma, trying to juggle it all in the juggler's absence, how was she?

On opening the hotel bedroom door on her return, she immediately sensed something wasn't right. There was a trace of a scent in the air, not the cleaner's just-been-vacuumed kind of smell of a room after the door had been closed on a hot summer day. The duvet cover wasn't as smooth as it should have been. She opened the wardrobe. Her clothes were still there, but pushed slightly off to the side. Closing the door, she checked the lock. Nothing was amiss. A quick call down to reception gave her no reassurance.

But . . . there was a but.

She had a shower, stretching in the hot water, then letting it run cold, refreshing her. She was there for a long time, turning thoughts over in her mind, mentally throwing the pieces in the air and seeing where they landed. If it didn't suit, she'd throw them up again. As an investigative exercise she had used it often. It had never got her anywhere, but she lived in hope. There was Craigo, a strange wee guy, not dangerous she thought – he wasn't smart enough for that – but parochial, a local man. It wouldn't be the first time a discontented cop had been persuaded to turn a blind eye or guide an investigation in return for financial rewards. She could see Craigo doing that, but she couldn't see him guilty of the murder of a senior police officer.

Had he known where Oswald's car would be found?

He had been on his own at Otterburn House. Then there was the figure in the woods and Craigo appearing out of nowhere. He didn't like Kinsella, and the feeling was mutual. Kinsella was a modern cop, Craigo, a dinosaur. The DI wasn't wrong about that, and the wee guy was weighing down the entire team, but it didn't make him dirty. She'd need to think where her loyalties lay, and the answer to that would be back in the mortuary in Glasgow. Repacking her rucksack, she only left out her notebook and favourite pen and laid them on the bedside table, now unable to sleep despite the overwhelming tiredness gnawing at her bones.

Somebody had been in this room. She lay back and checked her phone for messages. Two from Emma. She'd make sure to call her later in the morning, and then type up some notes for herself, save them, date-stamped, on her computer so she could prove anything that she had thought, mentioned in a meeting and had been discarded, could not be used later and claimed to be somebody else's insightful suggestion. Linden had advised her to do that years ago. She had never thought it necessary until now.

There was nothing new on the unfurling drama of the Cambridge Street incident. Maybe no news was good news, or there was a lot going on that nobody dared tell her.

Her mind had been taken up by somebody else's problem. She wondered what Lorna Oswald was going through right now. It was bad enough losing someone, the father of your children, to illness, but to lose them so totally, so suddenly and completely to the water, that must be hard.

Her sleep was short and deep; in no time at all, it was six thirty. Time for another long cold shower, then some stretching to warm up her muscles. When she came out the bathroom, somebody had slipped an envelope under her door. Her name was on the front: DCI Caplan. DCI? She ripped it open. A handwritten note from the lovely Erika informed her that there was somebody waiting to see her in the breakfast room.

Craigo? Kinsella? Some higher-ranking officer wanting to talk to her about the passing of Oswald?

Caplan dressed quickly. Thought about going downstairs in her shirt and trousers, but given the events of the last few days reconsidered and pulled her hair back into a chignon, slipped on her jacket and took the tablet from its charger. Just in case whoever it was wanted to make this official. She placed the charger in her rucksack, then removed a beige file and took a long strand of hair from her hairbrush, unclipped the contents from the file and laid the empty file on the bedside table, squaring it up to the corner of the tabletop. She placed the hair across it. She replaced her cup back at the kettle so there was less chance of housekeeping moving the file. On leaving, she looked around the room then closed the door behind her, making sure it was locked. She checked for security cameras in the short corridor and saw none. Who would have a master keycard? A reward for overlooking outside-hours drinking? Who had booked her into this godforsaken place anyway? She'd need to check that. She texted Emma while walking to the stairs, saying she'd call as soon as she could, but she could see no quick resolution to the case.

It was just after seven in the morning, but Emma texted back a thumbs-up immediately. She had no doubt that whatever she was going through up here, Emma would be having it as bad down there.

The dining room was almost empty, but there sat ACC Sarah Linden, a daily broadsheet folded up neatly beside a plate of scrambled eggs on toast. To the untrained eye, she was just wearing a neat white shirt and dark skirt, but there would be a jacket in keeping with her rank secure in a suit bag in the car.

'Hello. Imagine meeting you here.'

'Good morning, Christine. How are you?'

'Christine, is it? Then I'm fine, *Sarah*. As good as can be expected. What brings you here?'

'Don't worry, you can order your breakfast first. I'm catching up, thinking of the best way to move this situation forward.'

Before Caplan could ask which situation, the lovely Erika appeared, with slightly less enthusiasm than last time, if that was possible.

'You want yoghurt and fruit? Tea from the table? Apple and cinnamon?'

'Yes, please,' she said, surprised that the girl had remembered; smarter than she looked. She wondered, by connection, where Craigo was that morning.

'Robert Oswald?' Linden lifted her coffee cup so it was in front of her mouth, her voice low. 'Sent a shiver through the whole force. What do you think? Any instinct?'

'I'm not sure what to think.' Caplan shook her head. 'The locals say the haar can come in quickly. Oswald knew the road, but he was tired. He might have been driving too fast, maybe not concentrating, and lost control. I think it could be as simple as that – it nearly happened to me last night.'

Linden let out a long sigh and looked round to check that their table was out of earshot of the few other guests. 'That was an attempt at explaining it. Do you suspect something more sinister?'

'Why did you drive all this way in order to ask?'

'I've no reason to suspect foul play. Easy on the paranoia. I'm here to do the pep talk at Otterburn, then the press conference. This situation needs to be controlled.' She took a sip of her coffee.

'Well, cheers for that. Good to know I've no reason to be paranoid.'

Linden ignored her sarcasm. 'If you feel better being paranoid, go ahead, but that's all I'm telling you.'

'I've hardly had time to digest it. But somebody's been in my room. Is that paranoia?'

'No, that's housekeeping.'

Caplan noted the easy dismissal and wondered how long Linden had actually been up here, then immediately dismissed the notion as definitely paranoia. Maybe Linden had a point. 'Just tell me if you have any reason to suspect that there might have been something sinister going on? He seemed a popular police officer, but with a long and successful career, there'll always be enemies.' To her surprise, Linden didn't discount it. The way her boss, her colleague, kept her eyes down, balancing a tiny lump of scrambled egg on top of her toast, was rather unnerving.

'Is the job getting too much for you? I'll understand.'

'What?' Caplan snapped.

'It's just that the only experienced DCI we have available, in inverted commas, is DCI John Fergusson.'

'Oh, please, no . . .'

'Yes, The Bastard. Lizzie's ex and your extramarital.'

Caplan shook her head. 'Please tell me you didn't put him in charge of this?'

'DCI Fergusson was reported to be winding up Operation Jackdaw, with the drug squad and HM Customs, but it's not as resolved as he thought it might be . . . prudent if, instead of bringing him up here, we officially promote you back up to acting DCI.'

'What is it he's winding up with Jackdaw?'

'Sorry, I'd have to kill you if I told you.'

Caplan squeezed her apple and cinnamon teabag with more

strength than she intended, nearly toppling her cup over. 'Acting DCI?' she asked.

'Yes. Kinsella hasn't the experience. I've been contacted by those higher up the chain, the regional service here in Cronchie and Otterburn. They want you to take command of both cases.'

'Both?'

'McGregor and Oswald. There will be the official road traffic incident enquiry, of course, but they'll keep to their own expertise. From major incident's point of view, I'm not ignoring the possibility that somebody didn't want a highly experienced officer investigating the McGregor case. It was the first thing that went through my head when I heard he was missing.'

'You thought that even before his body was found?' asked Caplan, her mouth suddenly going dry.

'He was an unusual police officer, a practising Christian. He said he was eleven years old, as that was when he was reborn. So pure he couldn't be bribed. Who did it suit to get him out the way? He was never supposed to be on this case. It should have been Kinsella. Maybe somebody didn't want such a professional eye on the situation. You need to get Garry Kinsella to track down the McGregor boy. Pull that together with the Devil Stone or whatever those wee buggers were after. But neither of those leads feels like killing five people for.'

'I keep thinking of the Manson Family, don't ask me why.'

'Home invasion that ends in the death of all present on the premises? Not too far off. God help them. You work on the Oswald case, quietly if you can. For any ears that are listening, it was an accidental death until proven otherwise.' Linden looked hard at Caplan, considering her lack of reaction. 'You don't seem overly surprised I'm asking you to do that.'

'I'm not,' Caplan said, peeling the skin off an apple with a knife, making a long strip. 'You're not the first one.'

'Do you want to expand on that?'

'No. I'll keep you updated. Like you said, there's a road incident team who'll be thorough. They'll check out the mechanicals of the Audi, check the vehicle forensically in the true sense of the word. Do you think we can link Adam and Oswald?'

'Let's keep things fluid. And if you find anything else, you need to pass that back up to me and only to me.'

'What do you mean by *anything else*?'

Before Sarah could answer, Erica appeared with the yoghurt, Greek from the look of it, in a small bowl, and a plateful of fruit that included blueberries and other summer fruits.

'God, no wonder you stay stick-thin,' said Linden.

'What do you mean by *anything else*?' Caplan repeated.

'I mean something worth getting out my bed at half three in the morning for, not that I don't like your company. How are things at home? How's Aklen?'

'Does it ever change? I'm about to call Emma. She needs a break. Kenny can be a tad trying.'

'Good. Maybe you should go home and see him, keep an eye on the situation. Oh, and one more thing, Acting DCI Caplan.'

'Back to that, are we, ACC Linden?'

'Gillian Alexander has made a formal complaint, basically blaming you for the death of her boyfriend.'

'Who?'

'Daniel Doran. We need to take a complete statement again. No pressure. The PM hasn't taken place yet. The Fiscal's very keen to know if you had apprehended him at the time; their lawyers are saying that you did. If you apprehended him, it could be interpreted that he was in police custody when he died. Did you identify yourself as a police officer?'

Caplan could feel the fury rise. 'I could really do without this crap,' she hissed.

'We could all do without it. We could also do without allegations of a cop killing a drug abuser on the streets.'

'I'll tell you what, next time I'll just let him mug anybody he wants and wait until the media find out that a member of Police Scotland didn't lift a finger to help a disabled old woman being attacked by a thug.'

'That's pejorative language,' Linden said easily.

'Daniel Doran was a piece of shit.'

'That's even more pejorative.'

'Well, honestly, what's the old woman saying?'

'She's still in high dependency. The stress of it all seems to have given her a cardiovascular incident that's taking time to settle.'

Caplan placed her cup back into the saucer with a loud clatter. 'What about the daughter? She saw what happened. She'll agree with me.'

Linden was looking down at her coffee, avoiding Caplan's eyeline.

'Okay, what's she saying? She saw it all.'

'The daughter, Kate Miller, says that you appeared to kick him in the head, or in the stomach. Or something.'

'I beg your pardon?'

'She was vague at first but getting more precise now. She was in a terrible state with her mother being ill, but now things have calmed down, her memory of it all has clarified.'

'Pish.'

'Her memory's very clear. When they tell you that, don't forget to look outraged.'

'I presume they're talking to Emma as well.'

'She's your daughter.'

'She's a witness.'

'The CCTV was facing the wrong way. We see the attempted mugging. We see him cycle away. You need to be in Glasgow tomorrow twelve noon for a chat with professional standards. Just to keep it all above board.'

'Sarah, what's going on here?' Caplan folded her napkin, rearranged her cup and saucer. 'Tell me, are you hanging me out to dry over this? It would seem that there's been an escalation of crap being flung my way. Things that would be no issue are suddenly an issue and . . .'

She didn't get to finish her sentence before Linden averted her gaze.

'Oh, I see. It's like that, is it.' Caplan stabbed her apple with a fork. 'Is The Bastard trying to drive me off the force?'

'He's an adulterer, not an evil genius.' Linden frowned. 'I'll deny that I said this, but I share your concern. Speak to the pathologist: make sure that you know you're right.'

'I can see how that would look in the report. The acting demoted acting promoted DCI nips home to see the family and while there she pops in to make sure the pathologist was going to say the right things. I'm sure that'll go down like a—'

'You're a genuinely interested party in how the young man died. Nobody knows we discussed it here, do they? I'm only here to address the team after Oswald's passing.'

'Right. Okay. Thanks, Sarah.'

'But give us a minute and we'll probably find a way to pin Oswald's death on you as well.' She smiled. 'You do have friends watching your back, you know.'

'So did Caesar, so they knew where to stick the knife in.'

Linden stood up. 'Phone home. I'm going to check out the incident room. If you need anything, let me know. Meanwhile, I'll instruct the squad about how you and Kinsella are going to work this together.'

'Who's your contact?'

'DC Toni Mackie. I've not met him yet.'

'She – lovely girl, quiet. Doubt you'll get much out of her.'

Linden rolled her eyes, recognising the sarcasm. She stood up and said goodbye, leaving Caplan with her own thoughts for five minutes until her own mobile rang. She glanced at the number. Emma. She went outside to take the call, leaving the coil of apple skin on her plate.

THE ROOM WAS TRANSFORMED. Desks, computers, tables, cabling, phones, boards for timelines and photographs, graphics, immediate actions to be taken. Also, she was glad to see, a list of operational protocols to keep people right, with her name at the top left, Kinsella's, top right. Equal billing.

The atmosphere in the Otterburn incident room felt heavy with emotion. Caplan went in the back door, a nod of acknowledgment to both Kinsella and Craigo as she made her way to the front. Be visible; they needed leadership. Toni Mackie was red-nosed and sniffling. Soon more personnel appeared, downcast and tired, standing at the back, finding desks, searching out old colleagues for comfort. Some had notes ready to prompt a stressed memory, a few were furiously typing, and others were reading what the overnight team had added to the investigation. They were still on duty, their desks surrounded by empty coffee cups and scrunched-up sandwich packets.

ACC Linden, now resplendent in her uniform, very confident and very much in control, was deep in conversation with Gourlay, leaving Caplan to wonder if the DS was one of her new bright shining stars. They broke off, a respectful nod, then Linden walked to the front, like the lead mourner at the funeral, and waited for silence. She said a few appropriate words, perfectly judging the mood. She talked about Oswald and how respected he was by the rest of the team, assured them that she had spoken to his wife and that she was being supported, and that family welfare were in touch with her. Lorna was thankful for all the prayers and good wishes of his colleagues. Caplan was sitting behind her, watching the expressions on the faces of those who were listening intently. Kinsella, jacket on even in the heat, was slumped, eyes downcast; Mackie was dabbing her face with a paper tissue. Gourlay looked at the overhead lights, deep in thought. Harris just listened, neutral. Craigo was focused on some point in the middle of the room, blinking slowly. Most of the others were looking down or staring into a personal void, no doubt thinking that it could all too easily have been them. Linden was now talking about the McGregor case, the hand-picked team that Oswald had built around him before retiring, a team that he'd want to carry on and get the job done.

Anybody who was needing help could contact her directly and she'd make sure they got the support needed. The only one who looked up was DC Craigo. Caplan felt his pale eyes rest on her, drift over to Linden, then back to her, perhaps trying to assess the relationship between them.

After Linden left, the incident room remained quiet as Kinsella got to his feet and nervously cleared his throat. He stood in front of the five whiteboards, the photograph of Charlotte peering over his shoulder as he started speaking, the room now silent.

He started by saying how good Bob was at his job, how they would all miss his leadership and that he himself had big shoes to fill. They'd have a few drams in his honour once this was all over. He himself would go out and see Lorna to make sure that she was being looked after. He was godfather to their youngest child and had lost a close family friend as well as a colleague and mentor. He said they were fortunate that DC Craigo had once fallen off his bike on that road as a kid and so knew it was an accident black spot. Now they knew what had happened, he hoped they would have a degree of closure.

Caplan listened. Kinsella turned to glance at her; he was telling her something.

Bob had been looking forward to a retirement he would never see, but in the meantime, they had a killer to catch, so they should stay focused.

He walked over to the whiteboard that showed the images of the scene at the top of the stairs. 'Bob thought that the satanic angle was an important lead. The boys, Frew and McBain, were at a satanic gathering at the Bodie Neuk the day before the mass murder. They call themselves the—'

'Deilmen,' offered Gourlay from the side.

'Well known to the local police, but there's been an increase in their activity over the last few months. They've escalated from minor anti-social behaviour to Class A drugs, incanting, trying to communicate with Beelzebub himself – generally making a serious nuisance of themselves. But it could be being used as a way to control the young-sters. As DI Caplan said, there's an intelligence behind this.'

'The Devil didn't make Oswald drive his car off the road though, did he?' muttered Happy Harris.

'Well, no, but being a Christian man, it might have concerned him, distracted him more than a non-believer.'

Caplan's eyes floated over towards Craigo. He seemed to be paying a lot of attention, his mouth set firm, eyes narrowed slightly as he absorbed what DI Gourlay was saying, maybe thinking that his recol-lections differed somewhat.

'Shite.' It was Gourlay, sweeping back his long brown hair, managing to get two syllables out of the word.

'Well, speak your mind, Iain, why don't you?' said Kinsella with a smile, breaking the tension.

'You can't deny the way the crime scene was set up. These people were sacrificed – carefully chosen and sacrificed,' said Harris.

'Do we think the stone important? Why?' asked Gourlay. 'Where is it? Why did they take it? Sorry, I'm playing Devil's advocate here.' A high-flying sandwich wrapper veered away from the bin and was caught by Gourlay. More laughter, relief rather than humour.

'Well, find out why that stone's important.'

'I'll get onto it, I fancy a day on the phone,' Gourlay said. 'I'm not sure it'll be safe out there for the likes of me.'

'Yeah, the Devil only sacrifices virgins, no wonder you're worried,' said Toni Mackie, her filthy laugh echoing round the room.

Everybody joined in, letting off steam, and Kinsella was skilful enough to let them. Any time Caplan had seen this squad, they had been stretched and stressed. Now the worst had happened, what else was there to worry about?

'And, just in case, please everybody keep in the company of your partner. Don't go off on your own because you've had a bright idea. And that brings us to the two lads themselves. Scott Frew's still in hospital, had a chat with DI Caplan yesterday. Bainsy's out and about but not leading us anywhere. We've charged him with housebreaking – still a long way from a murder charge. The Eviscan will be important evidence there. We at Otterburn, assisted by DI Caplan, will be overseeing Operation Capulet. For obvious reasons I'll be stepping down from the lead role but will be here, helping and hindering. There'll be increased security.' The assembled squad nodded acknowledgement at this statement. Caplan had had to show her ID twice to get into the car park, which she took as a good sign.

The meeting was over.

Ranged along the top of the board were the five now familiar photographs of the deceased found at Otterburn House. There were also four photographs of young Adam, on the board as a person of interest along with Billy McBain and Scott Frew. Adam appeared to be a young, healthy handsome man with the entire world at his feet; one picture showed him after a hill climb, exhausted and weather-beaten but happy. Nothing to her eye suggested long-term substance abuse or too much of the good life. By stark contrast, the arrest pictures of McBain and Frew showed them dull-eyed, in need of a shave and hollow-cheeked, the effects of their drug lifestyle writ large on their faces. Caplan had seen it a thousand times before; the features may vary, the names change, but the dead-eyed stare was the same.

Bainsy's card was marked the day he was born. He was too stupid to know how much trouble he was in, but she felt that Scott was still trying to figure it out; it was just that nobody had ever really shown him how to find his way in the world.

Caplan looked sideways to the aerial photograph of the island of Skone, in large and small scale, covered with stickers and lines drawn by a ruler, names against them with the ID numbers of each officer involved in the full search for Adam the day after the bodies had been found. Kinsella had made it sound as if it had been the odd question here and there, but it looked much more than that. The DI had taken the idea that Adam was on the island very seriously.

Without his phone, not using his bank account, a cash-free commune would be a great place to hide.

She held up the curling edges of the paper, scanning the buildings, the natural features marked out: the hills, the river, the lochs and beaches. The peanut-shaped island was cut by a narrow band in the middle shown by a thick black marker. Rune was written in italics on the south, Skone in the same hand in the north. The narrow waist seemed to be important. Was it a division of the haves and have-nots? From the contour lines it would seem that it was bordered by two hills on either side, two natural bays with white sand and some cliffs, and a promontory on the southwest edge. It looked beautiful. Her eyes drifted up to the pictures of Frew and McBain and Adam McGregor again. The white noise of Kinsella talking droned in the background, swirling around her head in a cloud of nothingness.

She felt a familiar feeling at her shoulder.

Craigo.

'The island of Skone, not far from the coast here' – he pointed it out on a smaller-scaled map – 'searched it for Adam on day one. Even those who knew him well said they hadn't seen him. We know that *Wavedancer* brought him over on the thirteenth.'

'Gone to a commune in Wales?'

'Aye, some purists get disenchanted that Allanach runs the Foundation at a profit, ma'am.'

'My daughter is very interested in it, she wants to go and visit.'

'Didn't know you had a daughter, ma'am.'

'Yes, I do. She's at uni, doing a dissertation on future-proofing the planet and all that. Emma's very keen.' Caplan looked at the board again. 'How the hell can a commune run at a profit?'

'It does. He's clever, the Magus of Honeybogg Hill, or Christopher Allanach as we older guys recall him. Now he has Roddy Taylor and Callum running it all. Allanach was born here in the bit below the waist.' He pointed with his finger. 'Village of Rune. The McGregors own the upper half. It's rumoured that the commune want their hands on that really badly,' he whispered, giving her a sly little glance.

'The Magus of Honeybogg Hill? It sounds like a kiddie's story book: *The Bees of Honeybogg Hill, The Tax Avoiders of Honeybogg Hill.*'

He looked at her as if she had spoken Dutch. 'Oh, you're making a joke, ma'am. Very good. The Foundation on the island, especially on Honeybogg Hill, is an authentic way of life for some people – vegetarians, those who live off the land – or a load of lazy, lentil-eating druggies, if you ask Toni. The McGregors were very anti the settlement there, being their neighbours.'

'Adam defected to the enemy?' Caplan looked at the map. 'The family own the northern half and the Foundation the lower half. This Allanach guy?'

'Christopher inherited the land, set the place up and the rest is history. They do lots of natural remedies, treatments, yoga, wild swimming, and they make lovely honey.' He pointed at the drawing of the honeybee on the leaflet.

'Oh, I've seen that logo. So, Roddy Taylor and Callum . . .?'

'McMaster.'

'Callum McMaster. That name means something to me.' Caplan thought for a moment, but she couldn't place it.

'In ancient history, the McGregors and the Allanachs were inter-married, and they divided the island up between them. The waist of the island, the Narrowing, has a fence with one cattle grid. That's the split. The north got the ferry terminal and the shops. The south got the marina and Tamarin beach. One of the best beaches in Europe, very clean.'

'Does the Foundation go for devil-worship? Because that would be really convenient,' said Caplan, half-serious.

Craigo shrugged. 'They believe in all sorts on Rune. We tend not to approve but we live and let live, ma'am. DC Mackie has prepared a workstation over here for you. We can get the desk turned round if you'd rather be facing the room.'

'Where's your desk?' she asked.

'Oh, I don't warrant a desk, ma'am. I park my arse where I can. Can I get you a cup of tea? I got Toni to buy some of your tea bags. Apple and cinnamon, isn't it?'

'Yes, thank you. That would be very kind.'

'And I'd like to bring to your attention, again, that I'm not sure Oswald was that keen to pursue the Deilmen as a focus of the investigation. When he spoke to me about it, he saw issues. He said exactly that.'

'Explain?'

'He told me that he was of the opinion that it was too perfect. He said that he thought it was overdone, slightly staged, and he commented on the lack of blood.'

'Maybe it's just an angle that Kinsella wants covered, thought it might carry more weight if he said it was Oswald's idea. We have to disprove as much as prove sometimes. Especially if we have to close down arguments that could be part of any prospective defence.' She nodded at him. Then said, 'You were going to get me a cup of tea?'

For a long moment the light brown eyes looked into hers. He raised his finger as if he'd heard a penny drop. 'Oh, righty-ho.'

Caplan took her seat, hanging her jacket neatly on the back of the chair, placing her bag in the lower drawer and locking it after she had removed her tablet. There were two files on her desk and a folded note from Mackie, with her passwords, to be changed as soon as she had logged in. The first contained copies of the Polaroid pictures that had been taken from the mouths of the victims. She flicked back and forth, looking for the time of the post-mortems. It would be interesting to see what they had died of, if they had all indeed been strangled, and if one or any of them had been tortured in any way.

There was a large file on McBain, too large a file for one so young and another slimmer one on Frew, there'd be nothing in there that she hadn't already seen.

The fourth file was all about Robert Andrew Oswald, the DCI of Highland Division. There was a sign on the wall, a JustGiving page had been set up. The ubiquitous Mackie was organising that. The road traffic incident unit were still looking at the car. The skid marks on the road showed he had veered violently while travelling at speed; a deer was the logical conclusion. His mother and sister-in-law had moved in to help Lorna with the children. Caplan looked at the file and kept reading, then noticed the case he'd been working before he was put onto the McGregor case, a sudden death in Fort William. Mark Sutton had run off the end of the pier into the water and drowned in Loch Linnhe. Why would a DCI be investigating an incident like that? She didn't notice the mug of tea, the water still steaming and the string of the teabag hanging over the side, being placed in front of her. She studied the photograph of the boss she had never met. Bob Oswald looked like he was ready to have a heart attack at any moment. She checked that he wasn't retiring on health grounds, but it was simply that he wanted out. He had a bit of hypertension, but it was well controlled. He was only fifty-three. To make sure, she called his GP and insisted that she be put through to speak to him. Oswald was as likely to suffer a sudden cardiovascular incident as anybody else, which was contrary to rumours. He was an experienced driver in a new car on a road that he knew well. If he was in good health and the post-mortem found no pathological changes, was it an accident or had he been forced off the road?

It begged the question: who had he pissed off?

THE DOOR OF THE rather posh detached bungalow in Taynuilt opened. A middle-aged woman, fresh-faced and clear eyed, stood there. Not the widow, thought Caplan.

She held up her warrant card. 'Can I speak to Lorna Oswald, please? I know it's a bad time but I'd appreciate a quick word with her.'

The woman looked behind her, then closed the door a little. 'Can

I ask why? She's incredibly upset. I'm her sister. Perhaps I might be able to help you.'

'I do have a few questions for her. If it could wait, I would, but I do need five minutes of her time.'

'She's praying at the moment, finding solace in the Lord.'

Caplan didn't move, so the sister opened the door further, inviting her through to a living room that suggested it was occupied by an older couple, with its large dark furniture, rose-patterned wallpaper. There were already several bouquets of flowers on the coffee table, next to a large wedding photograph, the groom much older than the bride. Bob's graduation picture sat next to his wife's. So, she'd been a cop as well. Lorna was sitting on the settee, pale-faced, red-eyed, a closed King James Bible in her lap. She looked exhausted, her hair scraped back into a ponytail, a half-drunk mug of tea on the floor beside her, a biscuit nibbled, nearly finished.

'I brought you some flowers, Mrs Oswald. They're from the team Bob was working with on this latest enquiry,' she lied, placing the flowers with the others and leaving the card upright beside them.

'That's very kind.'

'I'm sorry. I didn't know your husband, I never even met him, but I've lost a colleague on duty, so I know what the rest of the team are going through . . . what you must be going through. I need a little minute of your time and then I'll be on my way. This must be incredibly hard.'

'Hard for everybody. Who are you?'

'DCI Christine Caplan.' She held out her warrant card again. 'I'm working the same case as your husband.'

'Are you?' Lorna closed her eyes, numb to the conversation. 'I thought Garry was taking over.'

First name? Of course, he was godfather to the eldest daughter. Caplan's eyes flicked over the photograph display on the wall. Kinsella was in one, his arms round two young girls at a barbecue, maybe in the back garden of this house.

'Yes, Garry, but he hasn't been in the post long. I'm a little more experienced in a situation as serious as this.'

'DCI? So you're Bob's replacement?' Lorna said, her fingers clasped round the Bible, her voice wavering with emotion.

'No, I was sent up before . . .' She let her words drift off. 'I doubt I could ever fill his shoes.'

'You're not from round here, are you?'

'No, I'm from Glasgow.'

'And what's your name again?'

'Caplan, DCI Christine Caplan.' She sensed a slight change in Lorna's attitude and saw a look pass between Lorna and her sister.

'What can I help you with?'

'Basically, I'm looking into the case your husband was working on before he headed up the McGregor case.'

'Sorry?'

It wasn't the answer she was expecting. 'I was going to ask you if he'd said anything about the death in Fort William.'

'What are you really trying to say?'

'With the death of a police officer, we need to look at what they were working on. We need to see if there's any reason why a man, with an advanced police drivers' course behind him, driving a mechanically solid car, would leave the road. Was he worrying about something? I know he was tired but . . .'

Lorna started crying again. Her sister joined her on the sofa, placing a comforting arm on her shoulder.

'We were told you might do this,' said the sister, suddenly hostile.

'Do what?'

'Try to get your rank back by pulling down the reputation of a man better than yourself.'

'Nothing is further from my mind,' Caplan said quietly, feeling suddenly very tired.

'You, you just see all this, my Bob, as a stepping stone to get your reputation back. Why do you want to make out that it was his fault? Get out, just get out now.'

Caplan stood up: angry at the situation, angry at Lorna and most of all angry at herself. She walked to the door, then turned and said, 'Okay, Lorna, let's cut to the chase. Your husband's car didn't leave that road because he was a bad driver. Something happened. And if anything like that happened to my husband, I'd leave no stone unturned to find out who was responsible. I'll do the same for yours. With or without your help.'

The two sisters exchanged a glance, but Caplan couldn't read the expression.

She went back to her car, drove it round the corner and pulled over. She'd messed that up badly. Who said she might be appearing? The obvious answer was Garry Kinsella.

TEN

Caplan sat on a wall looking at the water, her eyes shielded by the designer sunglasses she had bought on holiday with Aklen in Montreal. Most of all, they cut out the glare from the water, and if she concentrated hard enough, she could cut out the chatter of the tourists milling around behind her. She was aware of the police presence, the cars coming and going. She had a briefing at five o'clock today when a group of detectives she hardly knew were changed for another group of detectives she hardly knew.

She was watching the incident room; a few officers were popping out to the car park to use their mobiles. She recognised Craigo, shirt hanging out the back of his trousers, leaning against the roof of a vehicle to make notes while talking with his phone tucked between his cheek and his shoulder. She wondered why he was in the car park: better signal or so that the others couldn't hear? Gourlay came out and waited until the call was finished. They had a chat, quite animated. Then they both quickly went back inside, Gourlay striding ahead and Craigo jogging to keep up with him. It had looked like an intimate conversation; they'd certainly seemed closer than they ever did inside the station. It unsettled her.

How soon after Caplan leaving had Oswald's widow picked up the phone and moaned to Garry? She had been unsettled by the exchange; it wasn't what she had intended to happen. Going through the conversation in her mind, she couldn't work out how it had gone so badly off course. She had been asked to look into the incident by Linden, and Linden had maybe not told Kinsella. Or was she just being paranoid? She was trapped in so many situations at the moment, none of them of her making. She wondered if she was losing her judgement. People kept telling her that the stress at home would affect her, sooner or later.

It had been seven years.

She took a deep breath, enjoying the heat and the scent of the sea, and realised that she was feeling hungry for the first time in a long while. She'd pick up a sandwich somewhere and take it in for the later briefing, then stay on and think about what needed done tomorrow while she was away. Much depended on how Kinsella's search for Adam McGregor was going and whether the extensive press coverage today would bog down the phone lines.

A shadow fell over her. A young woman, dark hair in pleats that hung neatly behind her ears, a large tattoo of a bird decorating her shoulder and upper arm. 'Are you working on the McGregor murders?'

Caplan stood up and removed her sunglasses. The woman had sharp cheekbones, bright blue eyes and a rucksack over her shoulder, the jacket over the other shoulder suggesting that she had travelled to get here. Her legs were muscled, tanned; she enjoyed the outdoor life. More than that, she looked Adam's age – and Adam's type. She had the tattoo that Mackie had mentioned.

'Can I help you?' Caplan asked.

'You working with the McGregor murders?' she repeated.

'Yes, I am, but if you've got any information, we should go over to the incident room.'

'No, I'm not doing that.' She turned to go.

'Wait.'

She spoke out the corner of her mouth while walking away: 'I don't really want to be seen talking to you.'

'Okay, what is it about?'

'Adam. Galveston, in half an hour, see you there.' And she walked away.

The way she said his name, it was obvious that she knew him. And had been close to him.

Caplan pulled out her phone and tried to find a shadow so she could see the screen. She ended up crouching down behind the stone steps, leaning against the harbour wall, cold and rough against her bare arm. Pulling up Google maps and looking for Galveston, she saw it was along the coast just a few miles. And it would be her lead, something that Kinsella wouldn't know about until she told him.

Another shadow, short and squat, drifted over her. 'You all right down there?'

The voice belonged to an old man, lilting accent, a deep baritone.

'Yes, I'm fine. I'm just looking something up on my phone. Difficult to see in the sun. I'm looking for Galveston. Is that a boat? Did I hear the name right?' she lied. She had recognised the name as where the Devil Stone had 'floated' ashore.

'That's it over there beyond that outcrop of rocks, perfect place for wind and kite surfers. You're not dressed for that though. As Joni Mitchell would say, they paved paradise – and they made a right mess of it.' He turned to look out to sea, folding his arms, looking as if he was staying for the duration before closing his eyes against the sun. 'The weather's going to stay nice, but the pressure's on the drop.'

'You're a local?'

'Aye. You're not from round here. Glasgow, I think.'

'Yes.'

'You found Adam yet?'

He had been listening to the conversation. She too closed her eyes, facing the sun, not answering, waiting to hear what he had to say.

'Can't think of any other reason why a woman from Glasgow in a suit would be hiding behind the harbour wall and looking for Galveston.' He stood to one side, revealing a large blue wooden boat with a white cabin. 'The *Julia-Phillippe*. If you ever need to get to Skone.'

'Never been one for the ocean waves.'

'Well, if you do, my boat's for hire. You just remember that – Wullie Dodds.'

She thought the offer might be of use to Emma. 'Are you always around here?'

'Finnan Craigo will always know where to find me. I knew Stan McGregor man and boy. All the McGregors have been on the *Julia-Phillippe* at one time or another. I wish you well in catching the bastards who did that. They're scum.' He nodded, smiled, his mouth wizened from a lifetime at sea. He could have been the same age as her, or twenty, thirty years older.

'You know Adam?'

He snorted. 'Who doesn't know Adam? Nice lad. Still needing to find his feet. You know, he was caught in that family and couldn't quite find his way out. Used to love sitting on the boat, telling the tourists about the dolphins around here.'

Caplan swiped her phone closed and dropped it into her rucksack. 'Mr Dodds . . .'

'Wullie,' he insisted.

'I'm hearing conflicting reports about Adam. I understand that he's not a bad lad.'

'He wouldn't have done that to his family, no way.'

'We need to find him.'

'Who's we? Them?' He nodded towards the incident room. Kinsella was now outside tapping at his mobile as he walked towards his Merc; a quick call then he put the phone back in his jacket. They watched in silence as he drummed his fingers on the roof of the car, thinking hard.

'Any reason why you wouldn't tell us anything that might help us?'

'You got kids?'

She nodded. 'A boy not that much younger than Adam. He has his issues. My husband was, is, a hard act to follow, so I know what successful parents can do to a child.'

'Adam was never interested in making money. He liked to feel the sand between his toes. He spent a few summer holidays here taking the tourists out to Corryvreckan, spotting seal and porpoise. He was a good guide, folk loved him – just a nice guy. A bit of an eco-warrior but there's always room for them on the planet.'

'And lately, where's he been?'

'Well, not strangling his family – that was a total shock to everybody.'

'But where's he been? He's around but he wasn't staying at the house. He wasn't staying with Sandra Leivesley.'

The old man looked at her as if she was daft. 'No, he was through with her. He was with that wee blonde at Rune.'

'Do you have a name?'

'Oh, it'd be something daft. They're all called daft names out there. Daisy, Rosie, Pepper – sounds like the seven dwarfs.'

'Blossom? When was Adam last on the island?'

Wullie looked around, then made a noise as if he was sucking a pipe. 'Couple of days before the family were killed, if what it says in the paper's right. I took him over myself.'

'Did you bring him back?'

'Nope. Jack brought him back on *Wavedancer*, which is unusual.'

'Why?'

'Well, look at it.' He nodded to the low-slung white boat, orange flames painted along the sides, just a windscreen at the front for shelter. 'It's a petrolhead's boat, for speed merchants who like a lot of noise and a lot of spray, not a nice steady old girl like *Julia* here. And I don't know who took him out again but somebody did. You lot think he's still there from the way you're going on.'

'She looks nice.' Caplan pointed to a sturdy, red-hulled boat, pink and white flowers painted all round her. 'Pretty. Does she have anything to do with the Foundation at Rune?'

'The *Bettina Mae*? She looks it, but no. She's a lovely wee craft for sightseeing, as steady as they come.'

'You like the old boats, I guess.'

'I hate those plastic things. If you ever need to get to Skone, and you don't fancy the ferry, you know where to come. I tell you, I'm not sure how well Mr Kinsella's conducting this enquiry. Finnan's not impressed.'

She nodded, trying to gauge if she was being told something, or if this was the usual locals versus incomers conflict. She handed over her card. 'Give me a shout if you hear anything that you think would help Adam. I just want to talk to him.'

'Nicely phrased. But some of us are not too keen to speak to cops, not since Bob was found dead.' His faded blue eyes met hers.

'You knew Bob?'

'Aye, man and boy. A good lad. Too many cops in good suits these days' – his eyes crinkled – 'unless they're pretty like your good self.' He looked back onto the road. 'Always happy to have a pint with Finnan. Fine man. Anyway, you'd better get going to meet yer pal. Her bus has just left.'

IT WAS NEARLY HALF five when she walked back into the incident room at Otterburn. She had taken her time visiting Galveston, treating herself to some peace, some sea air and a strawberry ice cream. Kinsella immediately summoned her to the old changing room, which he was using as an office. The team were quiet, heads down, working. He turned on her as soon as the door was closed, trying to keep his voice as quiet as possible while he berated her for visiting Lorna. Her sister was very upset and, most of all, so were the girls, and what the hell did she think she was doing?

She listened until he was finished. That she was not defending herself slowly dawned on him. She just waited.

'I was following orders,' she said with no rancour whatsoever. 'She'd been spoken to before I got there. That's something of interest in itself.' She placed her hand on the handle of the door. 'Maybe that's something we both should think about. And I'm going to ask Mackie to look into Galveston Sands and where the money went from that project.'

'What? Come back here. What the hell has that got to do with anything? Is this a new line of enquiry?'

'I'm here as a DCI of many years' experience. Always good to follow the money. Just an idea I have; if it has legs, I'll let you know.'

Kinsella sighed in exasperation. 'Did Craigo put you up to it?'

'Put me up to what?'

'Visiting Lorna?'

'No. An officer died on duty. There are procedures.' She spoke as if she was talking to Kenny in one of his moods.

He crumpled back in the seat, exhausted. 'Look, I'm sorry. I'm stressed out my brain.' He sighed. 'I've an email here saying it was only three nights you had in the hotel, wasn't it? Where are you now?'

Caplan noted how keen he was to change the conversation. 'At the Empire in Cronchie. The bed is comfy, the room is very boutique, it looks lovely, but you can't work in it. If you try to use the desk, you get impaled on the TV rack. It'll take my eye out if I'm not careful.'

Kinsella nodded, stroking his beard, smiling. 'You know, I think I remember a pal doing exactly that at somebody's wedding, had to go through the whole ceremony with an eye patch.'

'Not the groom I hope.'

'It was the bride, actually.' He winked.

'For a moment there I believed you.'

'The whole set-up in that hotel was designed by an idiot, probably a relation of Craigo's. They're all inbred, you know,' he added quietly. 'Why don't you try the wee lodges on the coast road, Lismore View. The English kids aren't on holiday yet so they might have a space – give them a call.' He got out his phone and found her the website. 'You'd have to make your own breakfast, but the rooms are spotless, they have a desk and good Wi-Fi. If you ask, they won't come in and clean. You could leave all sorts lying around without frightening anybody. Better to go somewhere quiet as I don't think this case is going to be closed quickly.' He held his phone out. 'Give me your number and I'll send you the link.'

'Is my number not on the contact sheet?'

'Not yet, we were testing you out first. If you were a pain in the bum, we were going to send you back. But, well, I'm very glad you're here, now that Oswald is . . . gone.' He smiled sadly. 'Mackie's organising a wee drink after work. Why not join us? It's always good if the team that works together plays together.'

Caplan smiled back, getting the strangest sensation that he was flirting with her. Was he? Or was this his way of being friendly? 'And there we differ. I believe in divide and rule, and I need my beauty sleep.' She smiled to remove any offence caused.

'Believe me, you don't.' He grinned. 'Or is that sexual harassment?'

She closed the door on him and walked away. That wasn't sexual harassment, that was a test to see what she'd do. The answer was nothing.

Not yet.

She sat down behind a large monitor and flicked through her phone, studying the photographs she'd taken of Galveston and reading the notes from her chat with Devi. It had been a pleasant drive to the small cove just southeast of Cronchie, sparkling waves to her left, large Victorian houses, now Airbnbs or hotels, to her right. As she parked she was immediately pulled back to her childhood: the old-fashioned promenade, the ice cream van and, staggering up the beach, a couple of old blokes, trousers rolled up, having just gone for a paddle.

The view at the water's edge was lovely, but behind her was the most monstrous development borne of an architect's nightmare.

She kept swiping through, thinking about Devi's words. Adam was gone, and she didn't think he was coming back. They had been very close until Blossom had come along. She'd pursued Adam, and in the end had got him. But Devi was sure that Adam had left on *Wavedancer* despite hating Jack Innes and his boat. He must have been desperate to get away to do that. Devi was worried, Caplan could see that. She had asked about the holiday. Adam hadn't been invited on the cruise. He had wanted to go for his gran's sake, but he hated the way his dad and brother had spoken to the crew last time they were away. Caplan had given her a card, then appealed to Devi to tell Adam that he'd be safe. But Devi was adamant that Adam wouldn't call. He didn't like the police; they were all friends of his family.

But she gave a name, Pop Durant. She gave a place, Rune. She gave advice: don't go with any other cops. Although she used the word assholes.

The photographs moved on to a view of the bay. There was a low seawall, a beach of golden sand, and at the western end, colossal blocks of flats. She'd smelled the hotdogs and burgers. Dodds was spot on. It was as if a little bit of hell had escaped to take control of heaven. The flats were all glass-fronted to get the best of the view, with tiny gardens, well maintained and all replicas of each other. The balconies faced up the sound, looking out to Lismore and beyond.

The final photograph was of the plaque on the wall. The development was: *Gifted by the McGregor family of Otterburn for the enjoyment of all citizens of the surrounding areas and our welcome summertime visitors.*

How did Adam feel about it? Her reluctant informant was keen that she should see it. Was this a project that had ruptured the family?

She looked up to see Mackie marching across the office towards her.

'Have you upset Garry?' she whispered.

'Went to see Lorna Oswald without permission.'

'You cheeky wee monkey.'

'Was Kinsella married?'

'Why? He's a potatohead.'

'I'm enquiring after his marital status, Toni, that's all.'

'Well, the wife hopped off with another bloke, took the boy with her.'

'How old was he?'

'Four, five, something like that. Kinsella was working too many hours, not bringing in enough money. The usual stuff. He took it hard. So the rumours go.'

Caplan nodded, which Mackie took as empathy but was actually speculation about bribery and corruption.

'Does the name Pop Durant mean anything to you?'

'Nope.'

'Mark Sutton?'

'Nope. You been on Tinder?'

'I've been to Galveston. Any gossip?'

'Anything you want to know in particular? They do great ice cream.'

'The locals? The development? Seems a mismatch.'

'Oh God, aye. We were all wondering who was getting the back-handers, jammy bastards.' Mackie pulled her phone from her bra strap, pressed a button, then scrolled through until she found the map of the local area. She held her hand out so that Caplan could see it. 'There's Cronchie. There's Galveston Sands. Otterburn House's much further inland, but it's all owned by the McGregors.'

'Yes, I know.'

'Galveston, like in the song.' Mackie opened her mouth and sang some lyric about sea winds blowing. Badly.

'Yes, I know the song. What about it?'

'Rumours are Stan sold the planning permission but kept the land. Something very dodgy about a beauty spot like that being wrecked by those ugly holiday flats. Bet you're shocked.'

'I was.'

'But, aye, there's a load of money there.' Mackie chewed noisily on the end of her pen. 'Ma'am, you're dead brainy, so you are. Was this all about money? Nothing to do with the Devil at all?'

'More about the evil that men do. The development at Galveston's finished. And Gordon McGregor's about to get married. I'm thinking about inheritance.' She tapped at the picture of Adam on the monitor. 'The lovely Adam, last seen on Honeybogg Hill around the thirteenth of June? Reported to have been brought back over to the mainland on *Wavedancer* but has vanished . . .'

'If Adam did it, he'd have needed to move fast. As soon as the new missus pushed out a couple of inbred crotch monkeys, especially if they were boys. The inheritance would look very different: eldest son of the eldest son and all that.'

'Is that still the way it works out here?'

'Keeps the land in the family.'

'What do you think Adam would have inherited if they'd all stayed alive?'

'I think he'd have been disinherited once Gordon was in charge,' Mackie said. 'He wasn't that type. My gran used to tell the story of another McGregor who shot himself rather than live in that big house with the rest of them. They were hardheaded when it came to money. A lot of locals detested them for the Galveston development. The protectors of the lands betrayed the rest of us. They didn't need the money. It was pure greed.'

Caplan looked round at the whiteboard. 'We're supposed to be reducing the suspect list, not adding more. The development was five years ago; it's a long wait to get revenge.'

'Waiting for the family to be in the same place? People are people, ma'am, and greedy wee bastards will always be greedy wee bastards. Why don't we go out to the island tomorrow?'

'I've got to go home tomorrow.'

'Oh, that's something to look forward to. You'll enjoy that.'

At this point she thought that getting her teeth pulled out might be more enjoyable. 'Sunday?'

Mackie nodded.

Caplan wanted to say 'good work' and well done. She looked at Toni Mackie, spilling out her top, chomping at a cheese sandwich, her dirty big feet up on the desk. Easy to mistake her for being stupid, easy to dismiss her. Like Craigo, she realised. The two of them were telling her things that they didn't tell the rest of the team. And there must be a reason for that. Was the dislike between the local cops and Kinsella mutual? 'Well done, Toni. That's all been very helpful.' She cast her eyes over the board again, landing on the map. Honeybogg Hill. 'Do you fancy a bit of overtime?'

'As long as it doesnae interfere with ma sex life.' She laughed. 'Aye, so any bloody time really.'

'I'll let you know as soon as I've thought a few things through, but I'd like it, really like it, if you kept this to yourself.'

Mackie looked at her and opened her eyes wide, her mouth stopped mid-chew, distrust written all over her face. 'It's just that it's not easy right now. I'm a dog with two masters. And you're under suspicion of killing that wee druggie—'

'Well, I didn't touch him, but yes, I am. Let's keep this between us. Can you do a bit of digging on the McGregor family? Money. Anything that might shed a bit of light on their darker side.'

'Wealthy landowners, how many people did they piss off? Is that the kind of thing you're after?' Mackie nodded slowly, biting her lip. She looked at Kinsella, then quickly looked away.

'Do you feel uneasy doing that for me? Do you want me to square it with Kinsella first?'

Mackie shook her head. 'No, it's fine.'

'Do you ever feel threatened by them – the others? Sometimes you seem a little ill at ease.'

'I am that.'

'Why?'

'Nothing much.'

'But there's something.'

'Just a joke. But it's only a joke if both parties find it funny. It can be hurtful and cruel.' She crunched up the sandwich wrapper with a degree of ferocity.

'Tell me, I'm listening.' She looked straight at her, right into those brown eyes. 'I heard you were organising the squad going for a drink. Is that an olive branch?'

'No, it's because Garry Kinsella thinks it's all I'm good for. I'm not bloody going.' Mackie shook her head.

Caplan was shocked to see how close to tears she was. 'No harm in telling me then, is there?' She kept her voice soft.

'Wee things . . . it's always Finnan.'

'Finnan? Oh, Craigo.'

'Always. They told him the wrong place to turn up for the Christmas night out. He went all the way to Fort William. We were in Inverness. They didn't invite either of us after that.'

'Really?' She wondered if Craigo had just got it wrong. He didn't seem like the sharpest tool in the box at times.

Toni continued: 'They put shite in his locker – human shite, not dog shite. Maggots in his dinner – you notice he never eats in the office? He takes his dinner out his bag. And they set him up on a date with a woman who didn't exist. They let him turn up to meet her and they all appeared in the pub, laughing at him. They say it's all in good fun and that it made him one of the boys, but I never see anybody else being treated that way. And there's more, much more, that I won't bore you with.'

Caplan stood up and fastened her jacket. 'Make me a promise, please, DC Mackie. If anything, no matter how small, ever happens to him again while I'm on this case, you come to me – instantly – or send DC Craigo to me. And I'll make a point of knocking seven shades of shite out of the perpetrators. I say that because I can do that.' She smiled at her. 'And I will.'

Mackie nodded, slightly hesitant – almost bored – and Caplan wondered how many others had said that to her. Then she smiled. 'Okay. I believe you, ma'am. Craigo has a lot of time for you. Maybe you'd like to look at this first, before anybody else.' She placed a USB stick in her hand. 'It's not up on the system yet; it will be first thing tomorrow.'

'Okay, thanks.' Caplan curled her fingers round the memory stick, watching Mackie stomp her way between the desks.

She looked at Craigo, the wee kid in the playground, the last one to be picked for the football team. The police had changed a lot over the years, but in these small rural backwaters, it would still be a who-can-piss-the-highest competition. Craigo, an unremarkable man by any measure, had been a target from the minute he had signed up for the police service.

Was he now kicking back? Out-thinking them all? What was going on behind those cold, pale eyes?

CAPLAN INTENDED TO TIME the drive from Otterburn back to the crash site; it would help her to examine the dashcam footage on the USB stick. The road seemed to bounce off the shoreline and return, as if the narrow strip of tarmac wanted to head for the hills but was drawn back to the water's edge. A couple of bedraggled sheep eyed her from the narrow grass verges on both sides. They were Scottish Blackface, not dangerous per se, but she knew they could do a lot of damage if they felt threatened, especially when they had their lambs with them. Had one of them caused Oswald to swerve? There were enough warning signs along the road, including one about feral goats.

Seeing the disturbance to the vegetation made by the recovery vehicles, she pulled the Duster into a passing place, then rolled forward a little so another vehicle could get in behind her, though three cars in an hour along this road would be regarded as rush hour. She killed the engine and sat for a moment before pulling out her tablet and flicking through the scene photographs of Oswald's car, and his body, as it was wrenched up from the water.

She tucked it under her arm, got out and walked round the back of the vehicle, across the grass towards the shoreline, trying not to disturb anything that was left of the scene. She looked at the tablet again, gauging distances. She had reached the bit where Oswald's car had left the tarmac and become airborne. Here was the crumpled grass. Four tracks in the small embankment, each wheel leaving its own scar and indentation as it crashed over onto the stone shore. There was no evidence of any impact on the stony beach; all the bits of plastic had been picked up by the RTI unit, and any shale moved by the crash had settled again in the movement of the tide. The story round the station was that Oswald had hit his head on the side stanchion of the car, a sideways impact. The air bag had deployed. He had probably been unconscious at that point. If he had been able to, surely he would have made some effort to unclip his seatbelt, open the car door and get out. He'd know, as any cop did, to stay calm and allow the car to sink to equalise the pressure; the door would then open easily. It would have been a couple of strokes before the water was shallow enough to stand up in. He was local, he'd know what these sea lochs were like. Caplan liked to think that she would not have panicked, but you never knew. It was interesting that the car went in here and was distant enough from the shore that, even at low tide, the vehicle was hidden. Or was that just chance? She could imagine Linden talking about that in a meeting, flicking through the photographs and thinking that there was more to it.

There was now a general acceptance that this was an accident. She didn't think the dashcam would show any different. A sheep or a deer had wandered onto the road and Oswald had swerved to avoid it. The locals drove about like idiots at high speed, gambling that there was nothing coming in the opposite direction, even sensible folk like Oswald.

But there were no injured or dead animals, no carcasses burst open and pulled apart by predation lying at the side of the road, and God knows she had seen plenty of them on the way up.

He had turned his phone off after the last call home, so they didn't know exactly when the incident happened, but she guessed her timed journey from the gates of Otterburn House to this point would be pretty accurate.

Caplan gazed over the open water to the hills on the opposite side of the loch, alone with her thoughts, the tablet closed and tucked back under her arm, thinking about the relationships within the squad. Of course, they would have known each other well, Craigo and Oswald. She thought about the bullying that Mackie had spoken about. Was that the old boys' network just up to a few harmless pranks? Kinsella, Gourlay and Harris seemed very close.

Caplan wondered why Craigo's career had never got going. Not the 'if' but the 'why'. Craigo, while irritating, was bright, hardworking, maybe a little scatty, maybe not good at coming forward, hiding behind his glasses and his creased shirts and ironed trousers. Quiet and thoughtful: when did that become a barrier to having a good career? Maybe he just didn't have the drive that was needed these days. No arrogance. Or was there some other factor – an illness, a bad break like growing too tall, a twist on an ankle – one of those small things that can alter the direction of an entire life?

Kinsella was pleasant, he seemed to have a good human touch. Gourlay had something of the charismatic bastard about him. He was ambitious and maybe not too choosey about how he got where he wanted to be.

She needed to get her career back on track with this case. She needed to get back to DCI, she deserved that.

She walked along the tarmac, following the skid marks to their inception. She looked around, thinking about Oswald's line of sight, what would have been clear and what might have surprised him. The initial exam by the RTI team had suggested that all the damage to the car was a result of the impact with the ground, not any impact with a large animal. Further forensics were needed and were underway.

He had a large powerful car and he liked to drive it hard. He could simply have lost control of the vehicle . . . except, except . . .

She was now level with the four markers on the grass verge, one for each tyre, surrounded by flattened flowers with broken stems. The road here was one of the few straight stretches before it swerved towards the water. A few gorse bushes with dying flowers and some thick rhododendrons past their bloom lined the roadside.

Craigo knew this was an accident blackspot and had a good idea where a car might go. Caplan walked on slowly up the middle of the tarmac, looking for anything: cigarette butts, a footprint, a sign that somebody had jumped out, a sign of human activity. Checking the battery on her phone, she put the video on and walked up to the cluster of bushes, the one hiding place on this stretch of road.

She imagined herself driving, slowing down. She could see well ahead, so why the sudden swerve? She crossed the road, away from the water, and walked along, thinking where she'd jump out and scare a driver. It would be along here, close enough to be dangerous, but if they knew their victim, they'd know he had good reflexes.

She stepped into the undergrowth, switching on her phone torch, seeing evidence of sapling snap. Leaning forward, she placed the back of her hand behind the broken twigs so the video got a good image of them. A little flattened undergrowth.

Somebody had stood here, watching and waiting.

Her heart began to thump. Her theory was gaining traction. Given how remote this place was, they must have had a car. She scanned the grass, the vegetation, seeing an area of stones on the landward side of the road big enough for a car to be parked there. Looking at the bigger boundary stones, she saw a fleck, two flecks, of what might be white paint, recent, hanging on the rough rock. She allowed herself a wry smile as she pulled an evidence bag from her pocket. Somebody had scraped their bumper while trying to hide their car.

For only the second time in her career, DCI Christine Caplan made a decision to withhold evidence.

BACK AT THE HOTEL, no one was on reception. She rang the bell, offering to settle her bill as she'd be leaving early in the morning. Her credit card was declined. She apologised, embarrassed, and tried her debit card to see if there were any funds left in the joint account. Again, declined.

The girl at the desk, badge name Mona, said sorry, again.

Caplan opened the small pocket on the side of her rucksack and dug around for the emergency credit card she kept secreted away.

It was gone.

A look passed between her and the receptionist.

'Problem?' Mona asked, tired of hotel guests doing this and wondering what story this chancer was going to come up with.

'If I get somebody to call you and give you their card details to pay the bill over the phone, would that work? I do need to be here. I can't go home and strangle my family who have just maxed out my credit card.'

'Hang on, and I'll ask my supervisor,' said Mona, glad that a solution was in sight.

Five minutes later, the room was paid for and Caplan was texting Lizzie her sincere thanks. She steadied her nerve as she went into her hotel room and called home, despite the time. She was going to sort it out right now.

Aklen answered, sleepy. 'Hi, how are you doing?'

'Have you taken any money out of our account?'

'No, love, I haven't. Why, what's going on?'

'Can you check that your card is where it should be? Can you remember where it should be?' She heard the snap in her voice; she was being cruel.

'Yes, I've not got dementia, you know,' he said, and she heard his footfall as he went upstairs and opened a drawer. Time passed. She could imagine him moving his things around. 'I can't seem to find it.'

'Do you think it might be in your jacket pocket rather than your wallet?'

'No. No, I don't think so.' She could hear that little distance in his voice, the uncertainty that things were not as they should be. The fear of the brain fog.

'Okay, could you have a look around and see if you can find it?' A thought struck her. 'Did you give it to Emma to nip to the supermarket?'

'No. No, I didn't do that.'

'And obviously you didn't give it to Kenny?'

The pause was just a beat too long.

'Please tell me that you didn't give it to him?'

'Christine, I can't remember, but I might have . . . but he'd be sure to give me it back.'

She was sure that Aklen would get it back when it was maxed out and further credit had been refused.

There was no point. 'Okay, I've got to go now. I'll phone the bank and cancel the card.'

'Is that necessary?'

'Yes, Aklen, it is. Kenny didn't come home last night, so, yes, it absolutely is.'

There was a long pause. 'Did he not?'

She rang off and dialled the credit card company. It wasn't the first time, and every time she promised herself that it'd be the last.

Only then did she look round the room, at the empty file that was still sitting on her bedside table but tilted slightly to the right, the hair she had carefully placed gone.

Not her imagination.

She wasn't going to be distracted from this mess by somebody who wanted the investigation derailed. She was leaving here today. She wouldn't go to the lodges Kinsella recommended; in fact, she'd not tell anybody where she was going.

She sat down, opened her laptop and plugged in the USB stick with the dashcam footage, now thinking that she might see something, probably a white vehicle parked at the side, a vehicle they could recognise.

The strip of driveway rolled on the screen as the Audi left Otterburn. Caplan watched it all the way: fast, moving left and right in front of the camera, a slightly distorted view, the road being eaten up by the headlights. She let it run, knowing she wasn't interested in anything before the twenty-minute marker. After making herself a cup of green tea, with one eye on the screen, she settled back on the bed, checking her phone messages. The haar gave an eerie stillness to the image. Caplan was watching, thinking, paying little attention, when something flashed across the screen.

Green. Then darkness. The timer stopped.

It happened so quickly that Caplan nearly missed it.

Pause, go back and pause.

It was something, something black. And upright. With horns. It wasn't a sheep unless they'd taken to running around on their hind legs. Caplan stared at it for a long time, thinking she was seeing a forked tail.

The light and the distortion made it hard to see, but her brain was filling in the details.

Just as Oswald's had.

This is why he had swerved. His mind had been full of devil-worship and then he saw this? Who knew he was going to be there? The drive was in easy view of anybody on the top landing of Otterburn House.

Caplan made a note to check the log of who had been there. Tomorrow, this bit of footage would be subject to intense scrutiny, but she had proof. She made a copy of the footage, mentally placing it with the little evidence bag containing the flecks of white paint.

She lay down, smoothing out the map of Skone on top of her bed, and googled it on her phone. Kinsella and a whole specialist search team had been out there searching for Adam the day after the bodies had been found, which suggested he was in receipt of convincing intelligence. He had been very keen to follow the idea about the satanists, while, according to Craigo, Oswald had been less convinced about that as an avenue of investigation. And she could see why: McBain had the IQ of a teapot. The boys had gone into that house thinking of the Devil Stone; it was no surprise that the interpretation of what they saw would be framed by that mindset.

The work of the Devil.

That fitted with Frew being spooked, while McBain had regained his bravado so quickly.

She scrolled through her tablet, going back to the McGregors. Caplan thought she had the measure of Charlotte. She had kept her family about her. How had Barbara really felt about bringing her family up in her mother-in-law's house, sharing a kitchen with the old woman, always having another woman's opinion, however welcome, on how to bring up the kids. Caplan knew she'd have left Aklen the minute he suggested that they move in with his mum.

Did Stan feel emasculated by his mother, the matriarch of the family? What stresses and strains were pulled there? Gordon had dutifully followed the career path of his father, who had followed the path of his father: Sandhurst, same regiment, then into the family business. How many generations had that gone back for? She had an appointment to speak to their family lawyer about who controlled the purse strings. Who said who was being disinherited? According to Toni Mackie, the entire village knew that Adam had been written out of the will. Yet whose photograph was closest to the pillow the old woman slept on every night.

Maybe because Adam was the only one who was any bloody fun.

She swiped through the pictures of Gordon. Way too big for Frew and McBain to overpower. He looked back at her, posed with his foot up on the tailgate of a Land Rover, dressed in a green Barbour and flat cap, ready to kill some woodland creatures. A smile that wasn't warm, more businesslike. She could imagine the ligature being looped round his neck from behind, the killer leaning back, pulling, constricting. She swiped again to a picture of him and his fiancée, flicked over her paper notes. Finola Stewart-Parry. She was moving into Otterburn after the wedding; the whole family would advance a step as soon as Lady McGregor died. With that advancement would come Galveston, the planning permission, the estate, the northern part of Skone – that amount of money might be worth killing a whole family for.

And who had disliked them that much, apart from the young man they couldn't find?

Caplan lay back on the bed, her head on the pillow, thinking about the wedding that had been due to take place later that year.

It was the last time Lady McGregor was going to go on the family holiday; she was getting too frail. That meeting was the last time they would be together, predictably together.

She stared at the ceiling. A lot of people knew that.

The mobile rang. She glanced at the clock; it was gone midnight.

'Ma'am?' the voice said. It was Craigo. 'We need to get going. McBain's on the move.'

ELEVEN

Saturday, 9 July, five days before

Such was her paranoia that she immediately called Kinsella to confirm where the meet-up was. He replied, in a vehicle from the sound of it, that Craigo knew and was coming to collect her. She closed off that message and turned on the locating device on her phone before texting Lizzie, the one person who had the connecting app. She phoned Mrs Keane, expecting voicemail, but the call was answered, with Alice saying immediately that Scott wasn't there.

'Is he out of hospital?' asked Caplan, curious.

'Yes, he was discharged this morning. I've got to make sure he takes his medication. He was doing well, more like his normal self, and then, a couple of hours ago, a friend of his phoned and he went out.' There was a pause. 'I thought it was a good sign, you know, that he felt well enough to go out.' Another pause. 'Should I be worried?'

Caplan, tired and stressed, had no answer for her.

The street outside was empty except for a battered old Hilux pick-up. She looked up and down for Craigo. A horn peeped at her, and the pick-up's door opened a little. It was Craigo, looking like a child in a man's car.

She climbed in.

'Is this yours? I thought you didn't drive?'

'And you believe that from a man who never gets my name right? Of course I can drive. Just don't like bringing this into town – that's all, ma'am. It's bad for the environment.'

On their way into the darkness, Craigo said, 'Bainsy's not been

163

doing much, just hanging around, getting drunk. Seems to have a lot of young, very young lady friends. He's certainly not been hiding – either too confident or too stupid to think we're not keeping tabs on him. Yesterday he got together with his mates – the core of the Deilmen, we think – got drunk on the beach, lit a fire, smoked some weed, did some dancing. But this evening is different. He's stayed sober for a start. He got the bus out of town, then back in again. Acting like somebody trying to lose a tail.' He crunched the gears and took a corner fast; Caplan grabbed her seatbelt.

'He wouldn't have worked that out for himself?'

'Doubt it. He then travelled by coach to Glencoe village, cut through the caravan park at the top of the glen. He was carrying a rucksack, moving quickly, which is unheard of. He's up along the path that goes to the fairy pools.'

'I've no idea where you're talking about,' said Caplan, noting a change in Craigo. He was handling the big vehicle easily, and the information he was giving was precise and ordered. He could be efficient when he wanted to be. It unsettled her.

'We need a dog. It's not the terrain for a man on the run, too easy to hide.'

'But for a daft boy like McBain? Surely, he's more likely to get lost and die of exposure.'

'Unless he's meeting somebody.'

'Craigo, did you see anything on the system about Scott Frew and his whereabouts at the moment?' Caplan watched his response.

He didn't flinch. 'He's still in the hospital, ma'am.'

She nodded, 'How long until we get there?'

He handed her a crumpled old map from the glove compartment. 'About forty-five minutes, less if we're lucky.'

AT THE HEAD OF the glen, they drove past the holiday park, chock-a-block with campervans and caravans. Some people were paddle boarding in the dark, head torches bobbing and beaming out across the water through the darkness. Craigo indicated and bumped the 4x4 up on the grass verge as she looked ahead, seeing no other vehicles. She was reluctant to get out, not happy at walking into that unknown ebony that was so total, so absolute.

'Don't worry. The others will be up the road there, ma'am,' he said as if reading her mind. 'I hope you've got decent shoes.' He got out and opened the back door, pulling on a pair of wellies, then took two torches. 'One for you, ma'am. Stick close to me. For the purposes of the search, we'll need to stay within sight of each other.'

She followed him across the road and up a lane that passed a nursing home. The track started to climb, and the quality of surface deteriorated, although it was still passable by a normal car driven carefully.

'There's a big house here, been used for all sorts over the years,' he said, hardly out of breath. Caplan kept up with him easily. A familiar melancholic voice shouted hello, and Happy Harris stepped out of the darkness of the tall fir trees, holding a tablet which he was using as a map.

'He's gone up here. Kinsella and Gourlay have gone after him. Mattie Jackson and Whyte have gone further along on the parallel path to cut him off. We're going to follow from here. He's easily tracked as far as the fairy pools, then we need a bit more manpower as there're so many paths after that. Though, to be honest, I don't see him climbing the Ben.'

They decided that Caplan would go up the track with Craigo and Harris, each ten metres apart on the wooded contour line. It wasn't a steep incline, but it was a good test of the calf muscles.

They walked in silence, the only noise the hollow thud of their footfall on the forest floor, the odd rattle of a stone on the path as Caplan's shoes kicked one free, sending it rolling and bouncing down the hillside.

Through the trees, there was a shout. They heard running, sensed movement. Caplan immediately took off, leaving the path, weaving her way between the trees, moving uphill. On a sprint she was much faster than Craigo and had a more direct route than Harris. She crossed another path on the contour line and bounded up the next incline.

'Who's that?' shouted a voice.

She recognised Gourlay. 'Caplan.'

'I'm here to your left.'

There was a quick flash of torchlight, then another, enough for her to get her bearings. She headed towards it, away from Craigo, with Harris catching up behind her. The four of them advanced as a line, hearing activity somewhere ahead of them, and above them, in the darkness. A cry, a splash, a muffled scream. A shout from Gourlay who ran off at full-tilt towards the direction of the noise, to his left, away from the others, moving slower as he hit another ascending path. As they ran up the hill, Caplan lost sight of them, but she could still hear their footfall.

She heard splashing and swearing, confused shouting, three or four voices echoing through the hot dark air that clung to the trees. Kinsella shouted out, calling to Gourlay, who answered, 'I'm here, guv. Caplan and Craigo are right behind me.'

When she got to the side of the pond, Gourlay was knee-deep in the water of the first fairy pool, the lilies and short reeds camouflaging the border between land and water. He was bending and dipping, frantically looking for something amongst the lily pads and the rushes.

Kinsella's voice echoed out: 'Iain, come on!' His voice was lost in the trees as he ran off to the left, into the darkness in pursuit of somebody.

Gourlay climbed out of the water. Caplan reached out to help steady him on his feet. He levered himself up, smiling at her in thanks, his hand gripping hard on hers.

'Thanks.' He was panting. He bent over to catch his breath, hands on thighs. 'Christ, I'm fucked. We've lost Bainsy . . . I heard a splash.' He grinned at her and ran off after his DI, Harris, after a moment's indecision, following a long way behind.

Caplan and Craigo looked at each other. Suddenly it was calm as the men receded into the trees. Caplan scanned her torch across the water, across the giant lily pads, some of which were already in flower. The moonlight glinted off the surface, highlighting the green algae and the blood-red flowers.

'What was Gourlay doing in here?' asked Caplan, aware of the water creeping up over the tops of her trainers.

'Don't think he could stop,' Craigo said, shining his torch around the edge of the pond to the start of another path. 'That's where they went, the other three. Shall we go after them?'

'No. Gourlay said he thought Bainsy went in there. Or was it through there? This is the fairy pool, right?' She stood stock-still, listening, hearing nothing but her own breathing and the odd shout from the deep woods to her left.

Craigo was back to being his vague self again, distracted, looking at the sky, scanning his torch beam around the trees. 'Pipistrelles, ma'am, there's loads of them. I was thinking that . . .'

Caplan never got to hear what else he was thinking as her own torch had settled on something white in the water. At first, it appeared to be a lily bloom, but the contours didn't look right. Something white was underneath the lily pads, trapped, prevented from returning to the surface. She did not hesitate. She was already in the water, wading towards it, as her mind tried to make sense of what she was seeing, and, as with the Audi in the loch, the patterns were beginning to make sense. Craigo's wellies were sloshing behind her. She saw the toe of a trainer caught under a stem and reached forward, pulling, and pulling again. The body, released from its anchor, bobbed to the surface. The white T-shirt, the jeans, the face and the open gash across the front of the throat. Something black was pouring out into the murkiness of the pond. She thought she saw the neck pulse, but it was probably the movement of the disturbed water. The skin was gaping, the curve of the cut following that of his jaw. It was already too late.

She heard Craigo curse quietly.

Wading closer, she placed her fingertips on his carotid artery; she knew it was hopeless. How much of his blood was she standing in?

Craigo helped her get the body to the bank, where they stood, soaking wet, checking their phones for a signal. None. Craigo offered to go back down the hill, then quickly rescinded the offer, saying that he would rather they stayed together.

'Kinsella must have seen it happen and gone after the perp. I hope to God they catch him.'

'So do I. Oh, bloody hell.' Caplan groaned as she looked at the face below her on a bed of pine needles. The moon came through the cloudless sky again, the light passing over his face; with the trees, the lilies on the pond, it felt weirdly romantic. He was at peace now. His small face looked like that of a wee boy, maybe nine or ten years old. She didn't want to think about the life he had led, the adverse childhood events that had brought him to this point.

Again, Craigo seemed to be reading her thoughts. 'It's a beautiful night to die, isn't it, ma'am?' he said, blinking hard while looking at her.

She regarded the body of Billy McBain beneath her. How thin and puny he looked. She glanced at his trainers. And wondered where Frew was going when he had got that call. 'Craigo, what size are your shoes?' She walked across the woodland floor to the marks of the running feet, pulling her phone from her pocket. She looked down at the disturbance in the pine needles, took pictures of each and placed her own foot against the one she thought was the smallest.

She heard Craigo shout from the side of the fairy pool, 'What are you doing?'

Alone on the hillside with a DC she hardly knew, and hardly trusted, she decided to say nothing.

BACK IN THE HILUX, Caplan dried off as she waited. Another soul who had no need to be dead. She was trying to work out the significance of this latest development when Kinsella knocked on the driver's door and Craigo got out to let him sit in the seat.

The DI was out of breath and looked exhausted. 'Scene of crime are on their way. I've left Gourlay and Harris up there, looking after the . . . looking after him. You moved the body?'

'Of course. I pulled him from the water. I had to make sure he was dead. What was I supposed to do, leave him floating in there? He'd been alive minutes before.'

'Just make sure you write it up properly. Don't want another scandal at your door.'

'How did they get away? Make sure you write *that* up properly,' snapped Caplan.

'Sorry. I'm getting paranoid about all this. He was so fast. Much faster than us. Even with us right on his tail, this still happened. A clear head, well planned. It echoes the McGregors in execution, if you pardon the expression.'

'But who?' asked Caplan.

'I have no idea.'

'Frew was discharged this morning into his foster mum's care? I wonder where he is right now.'

Kinsella was silent. For a while they watched the crime scene officers go back and forth, organising their equipment for the long walk up the hill.

'They didn't do any of it. Bainsy's thick as mince, Frew's not much better. They were scared and they were used. Why can't you see that? Who are the big people pulling the strings here?' said Caplan. 'Do you really believe that a couple of muppets could do a quintuple murder like that?'

'To tell you the truth, Christine, I do find it hard to believe. But the evidence is there. I need to find out where Frew was tonight. I'd like to find Adam McGregor and ask him what he thinks. If you have another theory, I'd like to hear it.'

'I don't.'

'Let's see what the fabric sample brings, the tongue pin. I know it's Bainsy's; I saw one just like it on his Facebook page, and he doesn't have one now. If it has his DNA on it, then he was there when the family died. With Frew? With others? We don't know . . . yet.'

'But where is Adam? He's due to inherit in excess of five million and he's not exactly coming forward, is he? That must mean something.'

'Sorry, Christine, I'm just tired. Of course the Fiscal is going to say that this picture is not complete until Adam is interviewed under caution.'

'He hasn't responded to any of the press reports so far, has he?' Caplan was aware of getting very cold. Her body temperature was dropping fast.

'Do you think he's safe?' asked Kinsella. 'Adam?'

'No. I think he's in serious trouble. We know his phone's being used intermittently, but that's not proof of life.'

Kinsella said, 'It's all so tragic.' He looked out the front window at the Ben, dark and glowering. 'What chance did wee Bainsy ever have?'

Caplan, weary with the night, said, 'None whatsoever.'

LIKE EVERY POST-MORTEM SUITE Caplan had ever been in, the room at the Queen Elizabeth Hospital was bright and shiny, with a constant buzz of harsh overhead lights and every noise echoing off the walls. Multiple hoses and wires hung down from runners in the ceiling. One of them held the microphone that pathologist Jennifer Ryce was now talking through.

It was still early in the morning. Caplan had been up at dawn, then driven two hours to get back to Glasgow after one hour's sleep. Clearing the McBain crime scene had been arduous; the hill seemed steeper each time she'd had to climb it. She'd stopped counting after three.

She was in no fit state to face the noon meeting at professional standards, and her brain was telling her that a black coffee and an almond croissant might help. She was starting to see why Lizzie, with a full-time job, two kids and no husband, fuelled herself like that. And she owed Lizzie the hotel money. And she needed to borrow her credit card.

'Can you describe the events that immediately preceded this young man's death?' Dr Ryce's tinny voice echoed through the mic. She was standing under the viewing gallery, two assistants moving around her silently. On a slab between them lay the body of Daniel Douglas Doran.

Caplan related the story again, from when they left the ballet to the stealing of the handbag and the young man falling off his bike.

'Fell off?'

'Yes, he kind of jerked. A bit weird. I thought he'd tried to bump the bike up onto the kerb and misjudged it. He flew off the saddle and then he was on the ground, screaming and roaring. I thought he was having a fit of some sort. I was scared he was going to batter his head off the pavement, so I knelt down beside him and was going to put my jacket under his head when he was violently sick and started bleeding. Actually, I think he was bleeding before he reached me.'

'Was he cycling uphill towards you?'

'Yes, we were at the top of the street.'

'And did you restrain him in any way?

'No, he fell off the bike before he got to me.'

'Did you check to see if he was injured?

'Not until after he passed out. Up until that point he was ranting, threatening to kill me, so I didn't bother. Emma was with me, and she went to the aid of the woman in the wheelchair who was having a cardiac arrest. I had enough on my plate without assaulting the young man who was already on the ground.'

'Did he appear to be under the influence?'

'Absolutely. Don't know what, though. There was no smell of alcohol from him.'

A look passed between Dr Ryce and one of her assistants. Caplan thought she heard him say, 'Another one?'

'There are metabolites of cocaine in his blood, plus Valium. We're starting to see this combination. He was haemorrhaging through his eyes and nose, his ears also, and his BP rocketed at some point, probably with the excitement and the effort of cycling up that hill. It's a new drug combination – a great high for some, deadly for others. It's Russian roulette out on the streets.'

Caplan sighed. 'Did he have a history?'

'Of just about everything. He was a well-educated young man, a life ruined. I think this is the sixth death we've seen from this same drug combination.'

A synapse connected in Caplan's brain. 'Was one of them called Mark Sutton?'

Dr Ryce pulled a face that said she couldn't possibly say, but yes. 'There've been a few deaths in Sweden, Germany, a couple in Holland. It looks like it's arrived here. There's a good stream of supply that's causing a tragic loss of life.'

'I think our DI mentioned it. Any ideas how it's getting into the country?'

'You should ask Operation Jackdaw.'

'So people keep saying,' answered Caplan dryly.

'This drug combination is highly toxic. The folk using it for their entertainment will use it properly: be lying down when it hits, relaxed. If you're upright or moving when it "snaps", then you could be in trouble. So far, all the deceased have been male, with a visible degree of irritation beneath the tongue. We're hypothesising that the method of ingestion might be a tablet placed in the mouth, then the outer coating dissolves quickly and releases a vasodilator, and after the delayed release coating dissolves, the cocaine kicks in, in one almighty surge. That's the snap I referred to. Or snapping the dragon. The effect's like going through the sound barrier. Their eyeballs will hit the back of their head. If you're fit, your heart will take it – the first time – but—'

'Street name?' asked Caplan.

'Snapdragon. The second wave is concentrated cocaine. The first drug absorbed under the tongue is a benzodiazepine . . . mostly,' she added.

'How common is it?'

'Getting exponentially more so. The Drug Squad might want to talk to you. I've already reported back to professional standards that Doran died of a drug interaction and that there was nothing you could have done to save him.'

'Thanks.'

'But the girlfriend's still insisting that you assaulted him.'

'What's the matter with these people?'

Dr Ryce moved over to the sink and began washing her hands, still talking through the microphone in the centre of the room.

'Two more things: they're testing the tongue post this morning. Did DI Kinsella tell you or had you already left?'

'Sorry?'

'The tongue post, in the duvet wrapped round the sister.'

'Oh yes, of course. Sorry, my head's a bit scrambled. Did you find DNA?'

'Yes, results ASAP, same with the sample of fabric. I've got something else for you, might be of some interest. Thomas has done Robert Oswald's PM. He drowned. Marks on his body of seat-belt and air-bag impact, and a nasty blow on the temple, linear, which suggests he whacked his head on the car as it went in the water. His seat belt was on, but that impact can happen to tall men.'

'Yes, that's why he didn't try to escape from the vehicle.'

'We've had a wallet and a notebook in the dehumidifier. I think they need to go back to the widow – pictures of the kids, you know. I trust you won't lose them, DI Caplan.'

'Oh, don't you start.'

★   ★   ★

THE MEETING WAS EXACTLY as she'd expected it to be, she thought as she sat in front of two of her colleagues, at least one rank above. The office was smarter than any other she had ever worked out of, which was another thing that pissed her off. The man, shiny-faced in a very good suit and totally humourless, asked her to make a statement again, which she did. When she was finished, he told her that her statement was exactly what she said last time. As you would expect if it's the truth, Caplan answered. Not really feeling the love.

The woman was worse; same breed as Sarah Linden, tight-mouthed, blonde bobbed hair, pretending to be nice but would stick the knife in her best friend if she thought it was good for her career. At the moment she was looking at Caplan as if she had found half a wasp in an apple she had just bitten into.

Caplan related what Dr Ryce had said and opened her diary, pointing out that both versions tallied. The woman retorted that both versions were not mutually exclusive, and that they needed to make further enquiries. A young man had died.

Caplan was about to say she hoped he really was dead as she'd just seen him lying on a slab a little more than an hour ago, but she had already noted the lack of humour in the room.

'Your daughter's version matches yours. However, Kate Miller, Mary Prior and Gillian Alexander all tell a different story. All three of them are in agreement.' The man nodded. 'It seems to us that they all saw . . . something.'

Caplan shrugged. 'As a working detective, with my rank – whatever that may be today – and my record on major crime, I'd question that. They were at the far end of the street. Mrs Prior was on the ground, having a cardiac incident. How could she possibly testify accurately to anything? She wasn't even looking in our direction when the young lad went over; she was clutching her chest. I saw that. I was standing up, not kicking lumps out the deceased, or whatever it is I'm supposed to have done.' She leaned forward. 'You need to sort that out. Sometimes you need to put on the big pants and do the difficult stuff, interview her without her daughter around, establish what she actually saw and what she was told to say.'

'One, we do know how to do our job. And second, she's just had heart surgery.'

'My point exactly,' said Caplan. 'You don't think having a coronary might affect the memory? Same argument goes for the daughter, who I ran to the hospital. She never mentioned anything at that point. Please, give me a call if you need any help, but my case, seven dead, has just broken so that remains my priority.' She stood up and put her bag over her shoulder. 'Just to be clear, that's *seven* dead, including one of ours, a married man with two small children.' She pulled a small polythene bag and a water-stained leather wallet from her bag. 'There's a photo of his wee kids. I'm returning it to his widow later today. With a total lack of explanation as to why he died. He was a good cop. End of. I'd like to say it was nice meeting you, but you depress me. Any future meeting will be with my Federation rep. I'm not doing your job for you and I'm not accepting inaccuracy and laziness as fact. You're supposed to get to the truth, so get on with it.' And she walked out, wishing she could bang the door behind her, but it swung back, painfully slowly, on a self-closing arm, depriving her of the pleasure.

Caplan had never spoken to another officer like that. Certainly, never a senior one. The caffeine and sugar rush had done its job. She should do it more often.

Linden was standing behind the Duster, having a quick cigarette in the sun and trying to look as if she was merely on a casual break.

'If you're going to tell me that it's not looking good about the death of Daniel Doran, you're too late. Even the pathologist saying that he died of some new street drug wasn't enough. Somebody is pissing on my parade and enjoying every minute of it.'

'Yes, but three witnesses have said that you hit him. They're all in agreement. Their stories match,' said Linden, blowing out a long plume of smoke.

'But I didn't.'

Linden put her hand up, to stop her mid-flow. 'You say you didn't. The media doesn't care that the drug caused his death – what they care about is that you lied to your colleagues, lied to the family of the deceased and now you're lying to me. Three witnesses say different to you. *Three.*'

'Ma'am, I'll put my hand on any holy book that you wish me to, any book at all, and repeat that there was no physical contact between me and that young man until after he was on the ground, and at that point I'd already requested medical help and was trying to do what I could to keep him alive. I failed, and I'm sorry that a human being lost his life, but as to the rest of it, it's a bloody pantomime.'

'That's not what the witnesses say,' Linden repeated, making Caplan wonder if she was winding her up.

'My witness and my memory say different.'

'Your daughter can't be expected to be impartial.'

'And Kate Miller's mother can?' Caplan shook her head. 'What a load of crap. Is somebody out to get me?'

'Heat of the moment, Christine, who knows what you might have done? But it's all going forward to the enquiry. Keep away from any of those witnesses. And what the hell happened with Billy McBain? If you're not losing muggers and evidence, you're losing suspects. You signed off on him getting out? You only have Frew now to take the brunt of the McGregor massacre, while McBain was probably killed by some drug dealer he owed money to.'

'*I* signed off on him getting out?' asked Caplan, confused. 'That's rubbish. Is that what Kinsella said?'

Linden shrugged.

'Look, I don't want to fall out with you, but just fuck off out my way. If you don't believe me, you'll have to excuse me if I get it sorted myself.'

Linden stomped her cigarette out with her high-heeled shoe. 'Good.' She smiled slyly. 'I'm pushing your buttons, Christine. You need to get

proactive here. Because you're right about one thing: somebody is out
to get you.'

THE OFFICES OF RADCLIFFE & Tate were plush, all dark cherrywood
and thick racing-green carpets. There was only a skeleton staff
present, it being two o'clock on a Saturday afternoon, and not the
usual throng of lawyers and paralegals sitting behind huge desks as
they would have been on that Tuesday when their clients were
slaughtered. It was a calm environment. The odd unseen door clicking
open and shut, the faint smell of fresh coffee brewing, the subtle
notes of a phone ringing, a traditional dial phone, not the shrill,
tinny ringtone of a mobile. Caplan closed her eyes as she sat in the
reception area, a paper cup of water from the chiller held against
her throat. She was still frustrated by the interaction with Linden,
while trying to think of what on earth she was going to say to Lorna
Oswald. The young widow was in Glasgow with one of the girls
and, strangely, had seemed happy to meet.

She heard a door open, then gentle footsteps approaching, and tried
to fix a polite smile on her face.

'DCI Caplan. You called me?' A warm hand held out in greeting.
Jonathan Tate was much younger and more casually dressed than she
had imagined. Maybe he'd come in just to see her, because of the
clients they were discussing.

He ushered her into a large office where they chatted through the
basics of the case. Caplan went through her list of questions about
the wills, the inheritance and the forthcoming marriage of the eldest
son as she enjoyed a refreshing cup of green tea and being spoken to
as if her opinion mattered.

'It's important who died first,' said Tate.

'We're in possession of pictures taken at the time of death of each
victim, date-and-time-stamped Polaroids that show us the order in
which they died.'

'Oh, that's rather convenient,' he said, making a steeple of his fingers and looking over his knuckles at her. 'And could you tell me what order they were killed in a way that might stand up to robust cross-examination in court.'

'I'm not sure we're at that stage yet, but we've surmised it from the order the family returned to the house, the sequence of the Polaroids and the fact that those pictures seem to have been taken immediately post-mortem. I suspect they were killed in the order of Charlotte, Barbara, Stan, Gordon and, finally, Catriona, so from the oldest to the youngest of the McGregor family present. Which I would imagine is the way the will would have gone. So, yes, we do have a very precise order and time of death.'

'In a very narrow time frame, and then it's weeks until the bodies are found. Gordon was down a few weeks ago, talking about the terms of the new will which comes into effect when he marries Finola. They are a traditional family, and they do things in a very specific way.'

Silence dropped on the room like a blanket. A phone rang in the distance; she could hear the deep comforting tick-tock of a Grandfather clock somewhere behind her. The lawyer still had his hands like a steeple; maybe he'd open them up and let her see all the people. He wasn't a man to be hurried.

'Meaning?'

'Meaning that the majority of the money would be settled on the eldest son on his marriage, not so that they get the money per se, but more that they have the wherewithal to keep the house and estate going and to support the rest of the family. Gordon would have been trained for that role all his life. If the eldest son seems to be lacking in morality or fails the family in some way, then we would make capacity for an allowance in fiscal terms for them, and another member of the family would be chosen to be the keeper of the legacy. The estate would be placed into their stewardship. This is not done lightly as it changes the fortunes of any future generations, but it didn't matter in this case. With Finola and Gordon at the helm, the good ship

McGregor would have set sail in good hands. They needed somebody who would never let the estate go on his watch.'

'Except they're dead,' said Caplan. 'What happens if they divorced?'

'She would not have been able to claim half if they divorced; there is an old version of a prenuptial agreement in place. The money goes with the house and the estate, the land and properties, Skone, Middar, Bardo and Galveston Sands. There is a fiscal allowance to keep that together as that funds the rest of the family.' Tate took his time opening a leather binder, taking out a piece of paper and sliding it over to her. 'With a view to this discussion and the time of the demise of the family, I think you should be aware of the money deposited in the estate from the final payment on the Galveston Sands development.'

Caplan looked at the document and felt her heart skip a few beats.

'That's for your eyes only just now. We shall release it formally on warrant.' His bony fingers reached out and retrieved the single sheet of paper.

'So the final payment on the Galveston development has *just* been made.'

'Financially, a very shrewd family, and since May the payments for Galveston have been made in full. But the family still retain ownership of the land. The development merely rents. An income in perpetuity.' He looked at her, his expression inscrutable.

'Who inherits it all now?'

'Adam Stanley Rupert McGregor, now that he's over twenty-one. All the McGregors were required to have a will when they turned of age for obvious reasons.'

Again, there was a long pause.

'Did you draw up Adam's will?'

'Yes.' The steepled fingers fell, the first sign of discomfort she had noticed.

'And it's legal?'

'Yes.'

'And who inherits it all when he dies?'

'But he's not dead. It would take seven years for him to be presumed dead, as I assume you know.'

'And if we find his body in the next few days, what happens then? Presuming that the five in the house predeceased him.'

At this point the lawyer looked uncomfortable. 'It was an interim document, as he wanted to do something that was totally against my advice and the wishes of his family.'

'Something that nobody foresaw coming to pass has now come to pass?'

'Yes.'

'Can the contents of that will be made known? Is it a breach of confidence to release that information if we have no evidence that the subject of that will is deceased?'

Tate thought for a moment.

'Could you give me a vague idea of how much that would be?'

The lawyer sighed.

'Just a rough guess.'

'The house and that land would be four or five million. Then there's the business interests and Galveston. There are also two London properties. I think the total would be in excess of ten million, and that's a very conservative estimate.'

Caplan tried to sound calm as she said, 'I could get a warrant, as you suggested, or you could just tell me who would benefit from Adam's death?'

'Adam McGregor left everything, absolutely everything, to the Allanach Foundation.'

CAPLAN WAS VERY PLEASED that Lorna Oswald was on her own in the café. She had thought the choice of venue was a little odd, in the basement of a guitar shop on Sauchiehall Street, but Lorna quickly explained that Jenny, the eldest daughter, was at the dental school across the road. She patted her mobile phone. 'They'll call when they need me.'

'Thank you for agreeing to chat. I have this for you.' Caplan handed over the wallet.

'I bought that for his fortieth. We went to Edinburgh for the weekend. The weather was awful, the hotel had an issue with the fire alarm, and the whole thing was a disaster.' Lorna smiled wryly, running a bitten nail round the edge of the wallet.

There was a pause.

'Lorna, as I mentioned before, I'm taking a close look at the incident where your husband died and—'

Lorna interrupted her, her voice strong and bitter. 'It was what you said about Bob being worried. He was, you know, he really was.'

'In what way?' Caplan asked, as casually as she could.

'He never said exactly, but it was just that . . . Well, I know the name John Fergusson has got something to do with it. Do you know him?'

'Very well,' said Caplan.

'Is he a good guy?'

'Why?'

'It's just that Bob stopped hanging out with the guys at work. He started finding excuses for Garry not to come to the house. He was Sophie's godfather, and Bob wouldn't invite him round for her birthday. I thought at first he was kind of preparing for his retirement, you know, putting some distance between work and home? But there was something more to it than that.'

'But he never said what?'

Lorna shook her head.

'There's a note in the wallet, torn from his notebook, that says *TA 2012 5s*. Any ideas? Was he ever in the territorial army?'

'No.'

'Does that mean anything at all?'

'No, sorry.' Lorna pursed her lips. 'You were right: he was killed, wasn't he?'

The image of the black horned beast dashing across the road flashed across Caplan's mind. 'I don't doubt it.'

LIZZIE ARRIVED, SAT DOWN, looking harassed as usual. 'God, I need a coffee. Got the boys out playing with the neighbour's kids, she's keeping an eye on them.' She looked at her friend. 'If I didn't know you were driving, I'd take you for a drink. You look like shit.'

'If I wasn't driving, I'd take one, believe me. Thanks for the use of the credit card. Can I take it for a few days? I need to sort out Aklen and Kenny.'

Lizzie laughed. 'Well, good luck with that. What do you want? Green tea and toast?'

'I'll have an espresso, two shots, and an almond croissant.'

'Bloody hell, you are in a bad way.' Lizzie went in to order. When she returned, Caplan had not moved; she was deep in concentration, eyes fixed on the back of her hands.

'Lizzie, before I go mad, I need to run something past you. I was thinking about the way things have gone in this case, and I was going to pick your brains about . . . well, about bent coppers.'

'What kind of thing do you mean? Dipping the coffee can for a few quid, or turning a blind eye to lock-ins, letting the local woman of the night earn a dishonest crust? Down here, there's scope for that kind of thing, but up there? What would they do?'

'How would you know if I was taking backhanders? Or if The Bastard was,' Caplan said flatly. 'I mean, how would anybody know? The Bastard works in the Serious Crime Unit, the Drug Squad. He's the ultimate two-timing lying little shite of a human being. As a copper I'd accept anything he said. What if I'm surrounded by coppers just like that? How would I know if a colleague was bent?'

'This whole bloody thing about the McGregor family, the death of

Bob Oswald, then McBain within two days of being released stinks. Somebody on the inside knows the movements we're making. Somebody on that team is watching everything I do. And somebody's been in my hotel room, looking for God knows what. Think how good an actor The Bastard was: he convinced you he was faithful and convinced me he was single. And that's in an intimate relationship. How much easier is it to do that in the workplace, acting nine to five?'

'I couldn't think that of any of my colleagues.' Lizzie closed her eyes slightly, and then looked up at her friend.

'I just don't have a trusted colleague. And I've just realised how bloody miserable I am, Lizzie. There's such pleasure in walking on the sand, feeling the sun on the skin, just the silence. Even the rain's nice up there.'

'You'd see it differently in the middle of winter, when you can't stand up because of the wind and it chucks it down for six months solid.'

'It would be a hell of a lot warmer than my house at the moment.'

'Look, you've a good nose on you. You'd smell a bent cop a mile away. I'm sure of it.'

Caplan nodded. 'I hoped you'd say that. It's like I can smell it but can't tell where it's coming from.'

'Unless there was a team of them. Synchronised. One might stick out because of their behaviour, but if it was a whole team, then you'd be out of step and they'd be normalised. Or . . .'

'What do you mean?'

'Is there somebody who's been bribed? Somebody with a lifestyle that makes them vulnerable. Illicit affair? A bad habit? But you just have to be careful – those guys won't mess around.'

'Okay. So, an incorruptible cop dies, is killed, within thirty minutes of leaving the scene where five people died. In his wallet is a note that says *TA 2012 5s.*' Caplan held out the brittle piece of paper.

Lizzie made a grunting noise and pulled out her mobile. 'I bet that's Tulliallan Training Academy five-a-side football tournament.'

She swiped a few times then showed her colleague the image. 'There you go.'

Caplan looked at the photograph, then took the phone from her friend. 'Two of those guys are on this enquiry. That's Gourlay, and I'm sure that's Whyte in his young days, with a decent haircut.' She frowned, looking carefully at the rest of them; it was a small image but she committed it to memory, especially the broad-shouldered squat man in the middle of the back row.

'What was Oswald thinking? Does all this link back to those days? It's more than a coincidence. I know two of the five and I'm sure I've seen a third one. What's behind all this?' said Lizzie, also looking closely at the picture.

'Money, I'm bloody sure of it. Adam gets it all and he leaves it to the nutters on Rune. And it's millions, Lizzie, it's *millions*. We're not talking about bleeding stones and devils, all that crap. Oh, and that was confidential.'

'You lost me at millions. I'll send you the link to the Tulliallan site.' Lizzie sat back in her seat as the waitress arrived.

'And when I find Kenny, I might be under arrest for strangling the wee shite. There's nothing on the credit card left, there's nothing at home, and I need somewhere to stay. I don't feel safe in the hotel. All my stuff is in the car.'

'Did you ask at reception if they saw anything?'

'They're useless. It's a tiny place so no one's there half the time. Might have been one guy, a man draped round a woman, but the girl didn't get a good look at his face. They walked straight past the reception desk, got out a key, so they looked as if they belonged.'

'Security cameras?'

'Focused on the bar and on the tills. And Toni Mackie booked it.'

'Is that suspicious?'

'On Iain Gourlay's recommendation. He's the good-looking one who wears Bleu de Chanel. I could smell it in my hotel room, but it's pretty common. But then he's on that five-a-side team.'

Lizzie looked pale. 'Oh my God. What are you going to do?'

'I'm not quite sure.' They sipped their coffee in silence.

'You need to go to higher up.'

Caplan thought for a long time, eyes closed. 'I've no idea how far up the tree it goes. I was even doubting talking to you about it.'

'Hang on! What do you mean? So you only thought I was okay because I'm too far down the food chain to be of any use?'

'Your ex-husband's not. I'm starting to come across his name in this investigation.'

'He's a lying bastard but he's not a bad human being, if you know what I mean. Could it be professional, drug-related?'

'Could be.'

'Sarah? Do you think she's bent? She'd be a boon to any organised crime, she's an ACC.'

'I was looking at her earlier and asking myself the same thing – if I could believe anything she says, you know? She said I was to pass anything dodgy straight back to her. I thought she meant so it goes to internal investigations but I'm not so sure now.'

'Have you withheld anything?'

'Don't ask.'

'Right.' Lizzie screwed her eyes up, thinking. 'But it's odd they're after an inheritance. Any McGregor involvement there, or anything in Otterburn? Why not prostitution or drugs, extortion? The usual things they go for?'

'The five million plus the estate plus the entire island. Ten million in all?'

Lizzie nodded. 'Yes, I guess there's always that.'

THE HOUSE WAS THE same. Airless. Emotionless. Lifeless.

Aklen was wrapped in a duvet, on the settee in the front room, watching an old re-run of *Columbo*. He looked up and smiled at her but didn't say hello.

'How's Kenny doing?'

'He'll never get a job. He's useless, and his mood swings are out of control.'

She didn't want to say the words that jumped into her head; since he was twelve, his role model has been you lying around the house. Instead, she said that she was going to have a shower and put the kettle on. Did he fancy having a look in the freezer to see what there was for tea?

'Emma said you'd see to that when you got back. She left a note for you.'

'Okay.' She took a deep breath, found the note on the corkboard, and gave it a quick read. It was Emma with a quote from her supervisor regarding her dissertation and how good it would be to visit the island, how valuable for her education. Guilt tripping par excellence.

Caplan closed her eyes and leaned her forehead against the bathroom tiles. Her family life was a series of disasters, a slow drip of one malfunction after another. Aklen in his dark tunnel, receding rather than moving into the light. Kenny drifting further from a normal life, becoming less engaged with every week that went past. Emma, the golden lion in the den of black sheep. At least that was how Kenny saw it, and how far was he from the truth? The truth was that Kenny had always been her favourite. Emma had never needed a mother from the moment she was born; she was always the first on the swings, the first up the chute. Emma had a life plan and nothing was going to get in her way. She was ambitious, self-contained. She wasn't entitled, she just knew where she was going. She'd help out, but she'd do nothing that would derail her career or her life.

Caplan knew her daughter was more like her than she liked to think. And Aklen – sensitive beautiful fragile Aklen – was probably too good for this world. Burned, used-up and spat out by a profession when the younger fitter and less principled colleagues tried to take over, he had no fight left in him. He had walked before he was pushed, and Caplan had advised him that it was the correct thing to do for them all.

She'd meant it then. Now she thought it might have been one of the worst decisions she had ever made.

His spiral into depression had developed into a full-blown nervous breakdown, and it was the physical impairment that had shocked them both. Seven years on, he could still sleep eighteen hours out of twenty-four.

She put the kettle on and placed her laptop on the kitchen table, clearing the dirty dishes with a swipe of her arm. After checking her emails and messages, she googled the Allanach Foundation and watched a few rare videos. The Magus was there, dark-eyed and handsome, a little older than she'd presumed. There were young women picking lavender, a few lads tending to the horses, and a large man with heavily inked arms, the familiar honeybee symbol tattooed on his wrist, who appeared in almost all the clips but seemed to be shy, always moving away from the camera. Another man, slightly younger, broadly built, also turned his back when the focus was on him, rejecting the scrutiny of the lens with a cheery wave. They all looked genuinely happy in their pseudo uniform. She thought the second man looked familiar, but she couldn't place him.

TWELVE

Sunday, 10 July, four days before

Toni Mackie looked like she was going off on a hen night to Glasgow, in her canary-yellow capri pants and a low-cut vest that revealed two grubby bra straps, the left one of which she had to keep pulling up as it succumbed to the weight of her chest. DCI Christine Caplan was dressed in straight navy-blue trousers and a pristine white T-shirt, her work rucksack over her shoulder.

On the ferry, the *Sound of Skone*, there were a dozen locals, a handful of tourists and a few from the Allanach Foundation, Caplan guessed, who sat together, very happy and smiley.

She and Mackie looked like ill-matched companions, Caplan with her severe hair and Mackie with her dyed blonde frizz, held back by a head band which she'd exchange every five minutes with her sunglasses. One of them looked as cool as a cucumber, the other was sweating copiously, bare feet spilling out of her sandals and showing glossy tomato-red nails. Caplan always kept hers covered. There was nothing worse than having to look at the bony distorted feet she had, but when she moved, it was with an elegance that drew the eye.

Mackie was keen that their first stop should be the Skone Coffee Shop. Caplan was determined to get out to the Foundation, on the opposite side of the island, as quickly as possible, but her companion advised caution and that they should go with the flow; arriving too early as tourists might give rise to some suspicion. They should go later, amongst a group, and the coffee shop was the best place to wait and watch.

The café was furnished Quaker-style with sanded floors and neatly ironed red-and-white checked tablecloths. The smell of baking was fantastic: vanilla and strawberry muffins were the day's specials. There was a display of cakes and fresh bread, as well as a counter of herbal potions and natural face creams, lavender and honey oils, all with the Allanach honeybee logo. There were few free seats even at this early hour of the morning. It opened early, Mackie explained, because of the ferry; the place made a fortune simply because of its location in the village square, at the top of the slipway. With nowhere else to go, everybody who got on and off the ferry had to walk past this café; in winter, it became a cosy waiting room.

Caplan ordered her usual fruit tea, Mackie a latté with caramel syrup and a slab of carrot cake. They chatted as they waited. Apart from her volume, Mackie was good company, full of daft stories about the trials of the island and the Foundation's first attempt at home-brewed beer that gave the entire community a case of 'the squits', as she called them.

The café door was wedged open to let in the fresh air. Someone dressed in a light blue T-shirt, jeans and a long white starched apron, all with the honeybee logo, was putting more tables and chairs outside. Then people started moving, picking up bags, scooping up their last bit of cake and finishing their drinks. The easy atmosphere was infectious; nothing was a bother – just sunshine, and banter.

'I think our transport's arrived, but don't worry, there's plenty of time,' said Mackie, unconcerned. She was muttering something about the Honeybogg Express approaching when Caplan heard a noise, a steady clatter getting louder, that she recognised eventually as horses' hooves on the road outside.

'Here's our taxi.' Mackie winked, and they joined the queue of customers at the door as everyone tried to get out at once.

It was a blisteringly hot day with a cornflower-blue sky. Caplan felt the sweat running down her back as she looked around, trying to get her bearings. She looked south to the dumpling that was Honeybogg Hill. In the sun it looked verdant, enticing, almost alive.

She had read about the natural inlet that had been exaggerated by the quarry down on the promontory, leaving two arms to form a perfect marina for visiting yachts. And within the Tamarin Lagoon as it was called, the water was the strangest colour of azure at certain times of the year.

Caplan had enjoyed the tea. Its pure taste was quite unlike any herbal tea she had had before. She took a deep breath and realised that she had not thought about Daniel Doran all morning. It was obvious why Adam enjoyed the island so much, so light and airy, free-flowing rather than Otterburn House, awaiting a grim portrait in oil of the youngest child.

This was a million miles away.

Toni Mackie was well known and well liked. Like Craigo, she had lived here all her life, the families intertwined by generations. Caplan was starting to think that she could tell the locals just by looking at them. Her companion was now acting like a tour guide to the small throng who had, as British people do, formed a queue merely because there was a queue to join. She was explaining that the café was run by the Allanach Foundation, how everything was organic and freshly made, to enthusiastic nods and smiles.

Caplan saw a rough timetable on the wall. A picture of a bus, and a picture of a pony's head. Mackie was now explaining that in the summer months the Foundation ran a horse and cart for those who wished to go on a guided tour. Most of the time, there were no combustion engines allowed beyond the point of the cattle grid – The Narrowing – the flat land between the two Munros that halved the island.

Along the road came two open carts, each pulled by two horses. Caplan recognised the Clydesdales pulling the large charabanc and two Shetland ponies pulling the small cart behind. The horses, Victor and Hugo written on their headbands, stood proud, huge beasts groomed to a high sheen, their russet coats iridescent in the sunshine. Their feathered hooves stamped the ground as they stood, posing for photographs and eating apples and polo mints from the outstretched palms of small children.

Mackie pulled her up onto the cart, where she sat sideways, legs dangling over the side. She sat beside a tattooed young man from Liverpool, who was returning after being away from the Foundation to go on holiday. He was one of the carpenters there. He said he loved working there, out of the rat race, living the good life. He smiled as he spoke, swaying with the gentle roll of the charabanc, and closed his eyes and raised his face to the sun. Caplan put on her sunglasses and let her body relax to the hypnotic clip of the horses' shoes on the tarmac, the wind in her hair and the chatter and laughter of her fellow passengers.

Suddenly, they felt the hard rattle of the cattle grid at the Narrowing as they crossed to the Allanach Foundation. Boards were laid for Victor and Hugo to walk over. A sign requested that mobiles be turned off; they were now entering an area of calm and tranquillity. They had travelled a fair distance, six miles, and the Foundation now opened up to them in the flat area between Honeybogg Hill, the sea and the cliffs beyond. It was much bigger than she had thought. There was no real need to worry about being noticed here as there were so many people about.

She recognised the Pagoda, the house of the Magus, sitting high on the hill, from the brochure in the hotel. The view must be spectacular from there: the king looking down on his subjects, the little people. So much for socialism and the equality of the common man. She suspected that all this controlled loveliness was merely a cover for a cult. And maybe the cult was a cover for something much worse. It reminded her of the Stepford Wives.

The Magus – even the name was pretentious – would be sitting up there on the hill, planning for power, cutting the young and the dispossessed from their families, robbing them of their identities, stripping them of their names. The casualness of the logoed uniform was the acceptable end of the wedge – a control that would lead to domination of their lives, their sexuality, their money. She was looking forward to meeting the esteemed leader. He'd be a charmer – they always were.

'They say he's a really good-looking bloke, the Magus.' Mackie cut into her thoughts.

Caplan whispered, 'Have you never met him?'

'No. He keeps himself to himself. Do you think he takes young women up there to, y'know, initiate them?'

'Oh, probably. It's one of the things that cult leaders do,' she said.

'Where's the queue?' Mackie nudged her with a pointy elbow and laughed so heartily that even Caplan had to smile.

ONCE THEY CLIMBED OFF the charabanc, Caplan hung her camera round her neck, hopefully looking like somebody interested in the Foundation, but not too interested. They joined a small group at the signpost with directions to the marina, to Tamarin Lagoon, Tamarin Beach, the wreck, the dive pier, the beehives, the shops, the stables, the distillery and the café. Mackie was keen to check out the therapy centre and the spa pools. Caplan decided to take a walk around and go onto the beach, have a look at the yachts in the marina. A pretty woman had met them off the charabanc, wearing the regulation light blue T-shirt and baggy jeans that didn't quite manage to disguise the contours of her body. If Caplan had picked a person to lead the greeting party, it would be somebody like this woman – attractive, young, wholesome and engaging – and, to Caplan, familiar. It was Blossom. The new woman in Adam's life.

Or was she bait? Charles Manson floated through her mind again as Blossom looked at them both, then back at her, her expression unreadable. Caplan guessed she knew who they were.

Blossom introduced herself to the group and offered a tour of all the Foundation's facilities including a final stop at the farm and tea shop. And on the way there, there might be a wee stop-off at the distillery, which had a selection of their own organic gins and the infamous beer – the new improved recipe, she reassured everyone. The farm had two Clydesdale foals that were proving hugely popular, but they were very young, so please ask before giving them any treats. With a quick 'just follow me' and a flick of her honey-blonde hair, she set off on the grassy path that led to the giant wooden vats used as plunge pools, with the visitors trotting along obediently after her.

Caplan was amazed at how big it was. How many officers had Kinsella sent over to search for Adam the day after the bodies were found at Otterburn House? It must have been a quick chat and a look here and there; this area needed a big operation, a co-ordinated search team. She'd read the reports, the interviews, and they all said the same thing: Adam had left on *Wavedancer* on the thirteenth. He had spoken about going to Wales but had not said anything about coming back. She was losing faith in the Wales idea; there were brains behind this operation. They only had vague word of mouth of Adam's intent to leave, and a mobile-phone signal did not prove where the owner was. She was growing concerned about Adam. He was a very wealthy young man, and his family had been murdered.

Caplan scanned the beehive-lined paths that bordered the fields, but none went up to the Pagoda. She leaned on the fence, enjoying the sights and the sounds of the central square, devoid of the backing track of engines. Colours seemed brighter here. People were moving around, busy and engaged, but nobody looked stressed. She looked at the signpost, wondering where to go next, and saw a broad, squat man, dressed in the Foundation uniform, halfway up Honeybogg Hill. His hand was shading his eyes as he looked down onto the square. He was standing very still, watching. There was something about him that looked familiar – or maybe it was his type that was familiar. Stocky, thick-necked, a light beard: she was confident she'd recognise him if their paths crossed again. Was he watching her? She headed down to the marina, feeling his eyes on her, or was it just her paranoia? But when she turned, pretending to follow the path of a bird soaring overhead, he was still there: standing, watching.

At the Tamarin Marina was a modern development with a small café, a grocer shop and a shower block. There were six yachts out on the false bay created by the outreaching arms of the old quarry, something she had seen in other coastal areas of the West of Scotland. The southwestern arm was the natural tall cliff of the promontory, the northern arm rock debris covered with wire mesh to protect it from the battering waves.

This area had been quarried, but the land to the northwest was a completely different geology. There was a fine sandy beach with grassy dunes that sloped down to the sea. She could see the skeleton of an old boat, the flat grass of a campsite, the tents islands of orange in the green.

Along the path there were carved seats every ten metres or so, all facing out to sea; most were occupied by people enjoying the view. None of them had on the T-shirt and jeans combo; she guessed they were visitors as well.

Caplan sat at the first vacant seat, gathering her thoughts. She watched a yacht line up to sail into the marina, taking its time about it, nudging its way slowly into the mouth of the lagoon. A quick look at her watch and she was shocked at how late it was. It was already time for her to go down to the beach and catch up with Mackie.

As she got ready to leave, she became aware of voices, more formal than day-to-day chatter or tourists' exclamations. Blossom and the visitors were coming back along the path. She was deep in conversation with an older woman, and her eyes met Caplan's as they passed, quickly flitting away as if Caplan had disgusted her. It seemed personal somehow. She got to her feet and tagged along with the tour party, keeping her distance and wondering about Blossom's strong reaction to her. The party were heading back to the village. Caplan turned to walk along the sand and looked up to the hill. Mackie was looking down at her, watching. Caplan waved at her and got a wave back.

As she walked along, her feet sliding in the sand, she heard music, quiet music, caught on the wind and recognisable. An older man in the same denim and T-shirt uniform, individualised by a gaudy bandana round his head, was strumming a guitar, sitting on one of the tree trunks placed around a fire pit on the beach. He was playing a Beatles classic. The tanned face, the longish hair, everything about him, suggested he was a resident of the Foundation. His sunglasses were so dark it was difficult to tell if he was looking at her or not. He was concentrating on his playing, as if the music was taking all his attention, but Caplan suspected he was sizing her up. That was what she was doing to him. She had intended to keep walking down to the water's edge, to have some time for herself. She kept thinking about 27 Abington Drive. Aklen wasting his days. Staying indoors, curtains closed, under the duvet, hiding from life in general and from her in particular. And Kenny in his virtual universe because he was more comfortable there. What had happened to the wee boy who used to build sandcastles on the beach? What happened to the dad who used to love helping him? She heard a cry and a foghorn voice shouting, 'Hiya.'

She knew it was Mackie before she turned round.

ONE OF THE GREAT things about Mackie was that she talked to anybody, and everybody; conversation came easily to her.

'Do you mind if I take a pew? I'm gasping,' she said, plonking herself down on the trunk near the guitar man.

'Make yourself comfortable,' he said, in a voice that was deep and resonant, well educated.

'Ma bum's like the start of *Bonanza*. That was a rough ride on that horsey thing,' she moaned.

'Sit as long as you want. Put a penny in the hat and I'll sing you a song.'

Caplan recognised the type. He liked to talk, and he didn't seem like the sort to stay at a cult.

'Oh, go on,' said Mackie. '"Blackbird"? Haven't heard that in ages.'

'You're showing your age, or did your mum sing it to you when you were a bairn.'

'I just enjoy a good song.' Mackie doffed her head; the man did the same.

The word 'bairn' hadn't slid off his tongue easily, thought Caplan. Something or nothing.

'Sit and relax a while,' he said. Caplan could see blackened sand under the driftwood bonfire and wondered if they ever sacrificed people here. God, she was being ridiculous.

As they listened to the music Mackie took off her shoes and emptied the sand from her sandals. She asked the man if it was safe to paddle here.

'Safe?'

'Jellyfish?'

'Not usually on this beach. You're local?' he said to Mackie, then nodded to Caplan. 'But you're not?'

'I am,' said Mackie. 'She's not. You can tell by looking at her, can't you? A gust of wind would blow her over. That's why I'm fat, cannae get blown away in a northeasterly. I'm the ideal woman.'

The man laughed heartily and patted the beer gut that was visible over the top of his guitar. 'Well, I've been working on my anchor for a wee while and I can't say it attracts the ladies. Or it might be my singing putting them off.'

'In that case you're looking for the wrong ladies.'

They both laughed.

'The paddling's okay, though?'

'It's bloody freezing. The Arctic Ocean's just round the corner. The divers here wear wetsuits. It's snorkelling for the hardy.'

'Well, I'll not bother then. I'll just sit and get my vitamin D.'

'What brings you here?' The man turned to Caplan.

'My daughter's doing a dissertation on the sustainable green lifestyle, and I was roped in as the advance party.'

'I've always wondered about this place,' said Mackie. 'I'm from Cronchie, but you know how you never visit the places you stay near? Takes a tourist like her to make me get off ma arse and come across. It's bloody nice, though. Glad I made the effort.'

'Yeah, I've been here for a year. You should see it in winter. Siberia with honey,' said the music man.

'It's truly lovely. You live here now?' Caplan asked politely.

'Mostly. And I'm Pop, Pop Durant.'

Caplan smiled. 'I think I met a friend of yours out at Galveston.'

'Oh, I have friends everywhere – most of them in low places,' was the only answer she got, and the conversation died. She was sure he was watching her through the dark glasses as he strummed away, moving onto an Oasis number now.

Caplan felt the tension ease from her shoulders as the warmth in the sun penetrated her T-shirt; her eyes began to close. Mackie chatted aimlessly to Durant about some people they both either knew or had heard of, with local gossip going in both directions.

Caplan kept waiting for her to push the conversation towards Adam McGregor but she never did. She gleaned from the discussion that this wasn't a cult where the main aim was to isolate people from their loved ones, friends and family, and remould them into something they were not. From the way Pop spoke, this was more like a retreat. He complained a little about how busy it got with day trippers in the summer months and that the council had decided there might be times of the week when it was closed at the Narrowing.

'There's a council?' asked Caplan.

'We're run by our own council, led by the Magus and Calm. Roddy's the one who brings the money in. It can be a stressful union, but it works. They pull in different directions, but it keeps the Foundation on course. They decide what's right for us all, but we have voiced our concerns, like the peace and quiet being ruined by—'

'People like us?'

Pop turned his head towards her. 'You're very polite and enquiring, but lots of folk just come over from the mainland to go to the distillery and see how fast they can get drunk.'

'Is it not difficult, the council telling you what to do?'

'Not really. Our community is made up of those with the same values. It's not that hard.'

Caplan slipped her feet out of her trainers and buried them in the soft gold sand, thinking about the grilling she'd endured from people who were supposed to be like-minded. She dismissed it from her train of thought and looked out to the waves: brilliant diamonds glistening in azure blue, white horses chasing each other up the beach before falling and dying. She was hypnotised by the water. She looked down at her feet and remembered stepping into the icy cold of the fairy pool, wading towards McBain's body, the cruel gash on his throat. On Honeybogg Hill, someone was checking the honey in the hives, and in the distance a yacht manoeuvred lazily, sails billowing, to catch as much wind as it could on the still air.

No wonder they wanted to protect all this.

She realised that she liked it here. Emma would love it. It might help Aklen. The Foundation was renowned for having a therapeutic retreat, with traditional and ayurvedic medicine, plus all kinds of complementary therapies. Caplan recalled how helpful acupuncture had been in her dancing days.

Mackie and Pop were talking about somebody called Jake. He was here on the island now after going to uni in Edinburgh and having a nervous breakdown. His second. Pop said that his family should stop banging a square peg in a round hole and maybe let Jake find his place. He was staying here for now, happy as a sand boy.

Despite having no idea who they were talking about, Caplan knew exactly *what* they were talking about and was comforted to hear it. She wished she could speak about her husband in those terms. It struck her how unhappy Aklen was: every day too awful to face, every day the same, a life that was black and unyielding. A life wasted. Guilt crushed her heart.

Then there was Adam, making his way here, trying to find himself, only to be lost again.

Her thoughts were echoed by Pop saying that the issue wasn't with Jake but with his parents. Now the lad was here, and happy, they weren't talking to him, dismissing him as a dropout, a failure and worse.

All things that had been through Caplan's head, if the words had not actually come out her mouth.

'It should be different strokes for different folks,' said Pop. 'I've never been able to do a nine-to-five, and there's no reason why I should be forced to.'

Caplan was intrigued. 'You sounded a bit bitter there, Mr Durant. Did you turn out okay, as far as your parents were concerned?'

'Eleanor Rigby' stopped mid-melody.

'She's a nosy cow, my friend,' piped up Mackie. 'They're like that in Glasgow, do you not think?' Mackie gave her a gentle dunt with her elbow.

'I recognise a Glaswegian when I hear one. I'm from Edinburgh myself. I think your friend wants to ask what an old man like me is doing here?'

Pop Durant was smiling again, the sweat not caught by the bandana streaming down his face. 'I used to perform, and then I stopped. I decided I didn't like it any more. What made you stop performing, my Glaswegian friend? What happened to you?'

'I never made it to the top and that's where I wanted to be,' Caplan said half-honestly.

'I can always tell a dancer by their posture, and I can see those feet have battered the boards a few times. Did you dance because you loved it, or because you were paid? Here, you'd dance because you'd rediscover your love for it. You could grand plié and arabesque out on the sand at five in the morning and nobody would bat an eyelid.'

'How lovely that would be,' she said earnestly.

'You should come over for an overnight stay in one of the cabins.

Come for the beach party. Friday nights are the best. I play, and every-body sings. The food is good, and there's a fair bit of drink.'

'Then the skinny-dipping and the shagging?' said Mackie.

Pop shook his head. 'Not for me. I'm in bed by ten.'

They laughed.

'The tourists all go eventually. It takes a wee bit of grit to stay. Some think they have a duty to go back, but maybe it's their duty to remain here – let the others gain confidence fending for themselves.'

It was so close to home that Caplan bit her lip, her toes curling in the sand. She wished that Mackie would say something, anything. She closed her eyes, willing herself not to be seduced by this. She could be. But not quite.

'Jesus,' said Mackie, 'where's the loos? I'm bursting for a pee.'

BLOSSOM WAS BEAUTIFUL. IT was the only word that fitted those huge blue eyes, the honey-blonde streaks in her long hair that was the colour of autumn bracken. Maybe she was growing out her highlights after joining the Foundation, mused Caplan, but Blossom was not as young as she had first thought. She spoke well, engaging her small audience with a warm goodbye as she finished her tour. Showing people what they were doing here was one of the assignments the council had given her, she told Mackie.

'What if you get given something you don't like?'

'We like what we do. I like talking to people. I like company – not everybody here does. I get to show people round and I help out in the coffee shop in town. When the sea's calm, I do some diving at the wreck. The tours are a lot more controlled than they look. There's only one path of ingress by land, one by the sea, and that's it. We really know everybody who's coming and going.'

'Who cleans the toilets, though? Is there a queue for that job?' said Mackie.

'Jess does the toilets. She loves it. I give her a hand if we've been busy. I'm addicted to the smell of sodium bicarb, but folk here don't make the mess they do elsewhere. We all own this, so we're all responsible.'

'With rights comes responsibility . . .' said Caplan, thinking that she wasn't buying a word of this crap.

'Absolutely,' said Blossom, giving Caplan her best British Airways faux smile, with teeth that were a bit too white, a bit too perfect.

'The gardeners do the green. I'm hopeless at that, but I'd like to learn how to bake. I love eating the stuff but I'm a hopeless baker.'

'That carrot cake was lovely,' said Mackie.

'What does Pop do?' asked Caplan. 'We met him down on the beach.'

Blossom looked around for a moment. 'I think he was a musician, then in music promotion, but maybe got into a bad way. Not unusual in that industry. Now he strums his guitar and does a bit of social media, Facebook and stuff, for us. He has a bad back so he likes the therapy centre and the heated spa pools.' She nodded at the giant wooden vats nearby.

'And the Magus – what does he do?'

'Are you a journalist?' Blossom narrowed her blue eyes.

'No, no, nothing like that. Just curious. I want to tell my daughter about this place. She's a bit of an eco-warrior.'

'We see him maybe twice a month. He doesn't come down from the house too often.'

'Oh, does he dictate from afar?' Caplan couldn't stop the sarcasm.

Blossom looked irritated. 'No, he has a bad knee and the walk up the hill makes it worse. The Foundation really organises itself; there's no powerful and powerless. I come from the corporate world, so this is lovely. I want to stay here for ever. It's magical.'

'Right. So how long have you been here?'

'Not long enough.' She smiled her best sunny-days smile.

'Can you leave?'

'Of course I can leave. I can leave anytime I want to. Loads of us do. I go on holidays like everybody else. This year I was up in Shetland, Paris, Barcelona. Lots of people stay here to recharge their batteries and go. There'll come a time when a mortgage and the city will appeal to me, but until then I'm staying right here. I want to do more diving and wild swimming, but maybe somewhere warmer.'

'I bet you do,' said Caplan, looking for the bus stop on the far side of the cattle grid.

THIRTEEN

The atmosphere at the Fáilte campsite was much quieter than the hotel. Caplan had chosen an older pod with decking, a hot shower, a slightly saggy sofa bed and good Wi-Fi. The air freshener almost hid the smell of dampness, but she opened the window wide, preferring the scents of nature. There was hardly anybody here; all the holidaymakers were on the other side, in the cabins. Most people had already gone to bed.

The pod was palatial compared to Adam's room at Otterburn House. She could see the attraction of this simplicity: one knife, one fork, a couple of spoons, a cup and a plate. It was enough. The campsite was inland, close to the main road, the Lobster Restaurant and the standing stones at Kentilloch Castle, and nowhere near the one that Kinsella had recommended.

She had chosen one up at the quiet end of the woods and left the Duster near the road. She didn't get changed for bed, didn't put any lights on and didn't draw the curtains. She decided to sleep on the sofa with the window open. She hadn't told anybody where she was staying, and she wasn't going to.

Her feet were aching, her back tight after walking in the soft sand. But she was calmer in her mind. She was beginning to see the clarity of the case and that the answer, she was sure, was out on Rune. Adam was there somewhere in the background, protected by the Foundation. And that Blossom, whatever else she may pretend to be, was, or had been, a police officer.

The shower was hot and very strong.

She turned the lever to cold and closed her eyes until the ice-like jets hit her face, letting her mind wander. It seemed to her that the 'cult' was a commune of some of the sanest people she'd ever met, much nicer than any of her colleagues, who were all steeped in cynicism. They seemed good people, genuinely good. But as soon as that thought entered her head, she'd think of the ten million inheritance. People had become cynical over a lot less.

She slipped on her black leggings and a jumper, did a half-hour of stretching while her muscles were still warm, then sat on her bed. She arranged her tablet and notebook, then emptied her rucksack, scattering the contents before settling down to organise her thoughts and her paperwork. Opening her purse, she pulled the receipts from the café and unfolded them, remembering the cake, the lovely herb tea. There were three bits of paper: the card-machine receipt and the receipt for what they had ordered, but there was also a small card tucked inside. Something written on it by hand, a name: *Alan Rooney*.

She flicked the card over, thinking about the friendly girl in the café, the customers in the queue. Was this a message for somebody else? A note for the waitress about somebody's order? But the receipts had been folded round the card and handed to her specifically.

She slipped it into an evidence bag and pulled her tablet towards her. She googled the name: one American surgeon, the other a country and western singer. She scrolled down and kept reading. Alan Dominic Rooney, found dead in Nairn, eighteen months before. It was an appeal for any witnesses to his death. He had been seen running over the dunes, along the beach and straight into the sea. She googled the local paper, then spent an hour on the phone, pulling rank and getting over the hurdle of 'the case she was working on being close to closure and was this connected in any way?' And yes, she did know how late it was. She asked why the Nairn office thought the McGregor case was near closure. The answer was simple. It was rumoured that Kinsella would have the case written up, done and dusted within the fortnight; in fact they were having bets on it. It took a huge effort for her not to say that it was news to her. She ended the call and took a deep breath. She was being stupid; that was all lads' talk. Kinsella was probably lying awake right now, thinking that the case that had been set to make his career was slowly drifting away from him. How much of that was down to Gourlay?

She read the initial crime report on Rooney, still recent enough not to be zipped and filed away in deep storage. The full report from the Fiscal went through the basics of the unexpected death of Alan Rooney. She read it quickly, trying to connect the death of an apprentice electrician with two convictions for drunk driving, and one for possession of a Class B substance, with her case. The convictions were all from years earlier. He was older, engaged to be married, straightening his life out. Then he was dead. The story in the official report was a little different to that in the newspaper. He and some mates had been larking about on the golf course at midnight, then Rooney had taken off, running through the dunes and into the waves. One friend, not as drunk as the rest, had called an ambulance. Rooney's blood revealed a high circulating level of the metabolites of Diazepam and cocaine. She put a request through for the full file and sent an email to Dr Jennifer Ryce asking if she was aware of the Rooney case. He hadn't drowned. He'd died of what the drug had done to him.

She read it again, that line about him running faster than anybody else. It was the same as Doran pelting up the hill on his bike. Then she realised the significance: somebody on Skone knew she was a police officer, knew about Daniel Doran and the way he died. Why tell her like this? Why not just call up the incident room? Why had Devi wanted her to talk to Pop Durant? He hadn't taken the bait earlier. Because Mackie was there?

Why tell her, the outsider?

Or was that the point?

Mark Sutton's name entered her head from nowhere. The case that Bob Oswald had noted in his file, the boy who had run off the pier in Fort William. Then she reminded herself Oswald had died. A cold chill crept over her. She left the bed and made herself comfortable on the sofa, pulling her thick jumper over her despite the heat, then she got up and made sure the door was locked. She looked out the window to check the quickest way to the car and noted where the car keys were. Lying back down with her notebook, she drew lines around names, making patterns.

She made a list of those she could trust, those she could tell about this new lead. Her trusted friends? She got to Lizzie Fergusson, who owed her everything, and Sarah Linden, who would probably throw her under a bus if it would further her career. She wasn't sure about Linden. Was that friendship on shaky ground?

She googled 'Pop Durant', tried different spellings and got nothing. After ten minutes on Facebook she found him. Peter Durant had been a music journalist for a London paper. He'd written a column about his heartbreak over the senseless death of a family friend, how devastated the family had been: substance abuse destroying the closest of families was the message. It didn't take her long to work out that the deceased, Rooney, was Durant's nephew. He was sniffing around the island after the death of his relative.

From snapdragon.

She could see steps and stones along the way. The same drug, Oswald's suspicions about Sutton, Pop, a retired journalist on Skone.

The drugs were far away from here when they wreaked their havoc, but Oswald and Durant had ended up here.

As indeed had she.

She called home. Nobody answered. She tried Emma's mobile and it went to voicemail. Maybe she was studying or had gone to bed, which was where most normal people would be at this time.

She'd leave it until morning.

She could hear the late ferry. A light breeze entered the room – scents of seaweed and diesel. She took a bottle of water from her bag, opened her tablet and switched it to night mode so that nobody outside would see the glow. The signal failed, so she used her phone as a mobile hotspot and waited.

She typed in 'snapdragon' and pressed search. Images of the flower she remembered as a kid in her parents' garden and a game that involved setting brandy alight and trying to pluck raisins from the flames. There was no mention of snapdragon, or snap as the drug was sometimes called, but much more about chasing the dragon. She typed in 'drug deaths', then 'dragon'. She found a link to an academic paper about street drugs, listed by their street names, and there was the name she was looking for. Snap. It was the young executive's drug of choice, placed under the tongue before partying. When taken in that way, by the fit and healthy, it was relatively safe. The issues came when youngsters whose body chemistry was already altered by other drugs and alcohol used it. The result was a massive overdose that rapidly swamped the bloodstream, causing blood pressure to rocket, and then a burst of intense energy before bleeding from every orifice. More or less what Dr Ryce had described.

She re-opened the email informing her that she was being given formal notice that Doran's girlfriend was accusing her of assault that resulted in his fatal injury. His mother found it difficult to believe that her darling boy could still have been on drugs and was joining in the chase to blame Caplan for the loss of her son. She guessed she could understand that. She saw Kenny for what he was. If he had tried to mug an old woman, then died of the drug he had taken, she hoped she'd take it as a sign that she had failed as a mother and not as a way of getting compensation from the police service that had intervened.

Further down the complaint was a note that said both Kate Miller and her mother had witnessed the assault.

Caplan lay back on the sofa bed, still in her trainers, hands behind her head, the thoughts looping through her brain precluding sleep.

At three thirty in the morning, her mobile rang.

TWO EMPTY POLICE CARS sat, abandoned, lights still on, in the car park beside the souvenir shop at Kentilloch Castle. Beside one, highlighted by the Duster's headlights, was a man with padded bags over his shoulder, holding a tripod and talking to a female officer – the photographer who found the victim, Caplan presumed. She got out and looked up to the castle, magically appearing and disappearing in the haar. It was cold now, the water still and glassy. Only the bleating of sheep from somewhere on the hill. Down near the sea loomed the standing stones, eerie and shape-shifting in the encroaching mist. Caplan could appreciate the mystical beauty that the photographer had been trying to capture.

PC McPhee emerged from the darkness of the trees and showed her the path, quickly filling her in on the details. Two photographers had been out to capture the sunrise through the standing stones. They had separated, one walking into the circle of stones in the dim light. He had been aware of some commotion – two people, a raised voice – but when he came across them, one had run away, the other had fallen to the ground.

'You're here before the ambulance,' commented McPhee. 'That was quick! He's still alive but only just.'

'Do you recognise him?' Caplan asked as McPhee helped her scramble down the slope.

'Facial similarity, hair's different – he's over here.'

Together they jogged across the field, past a wrought-iron bench, the back of it sculpted to form four soldiers in various stages of alert, keeping the headland safe from any invading army. It looked like death had sauntered in, unseen and unheard. She felt a chill run through her, one much more to do with emotion, sadness and the sheer waste of a human life than the dropping temperature. Two officers were leaning over the figure on the ground: one of them was talking, repeating that the ambulance was on its way, and she realised that she was the only detective here. Not even Craigo was present to annoy her. Staying at the campsite, she had been much closer to the locus than anybody else.

The victim was lying on his side, crouched into a ball.

'How long since he was found?'

'Thirty-two minutes. We picked it up, and I called you and DI Kinsella,' said McPhee.

Caplan knelt down, looking at the young man, imagining the brown hair a much lighter tone. He was so still, lying on his left side, his hand almost underneath him. She felt along his right arm, turning it over at the wrist. The honeybee tattoo. His fingers were clasped around something hard and rectangular. 'It's Adam, isn't it? Poor guy.'

'It looks like him, but there's no ID we can find. When the photographer came through the standing stones, somebody ran off up the path. The guy said there was no other car parked here when he drove in. We're taking a statement.'

Caplan leaned forward and pressed her head to his chest, then her cheek to his mouth. 'How far away is that ambulance? Can you find out?' she asked, and as McPhee turned round, she slid her right hand along the victim's forearm. Adam had thought he was going to die, but his attacker had been interrupted by the approach of the photographer. Before he passed out, he had tried to reach for something important. Her fingers found hard plastic, a small phone.

'This is partial strangulation. It can still be fatal after the event through vascular damage. But he's young, so fingers crossed.' As she spoke, she moved her body between Adam and the officers. 'Where has he been since he came off Skone?' Looking as if she was in the process of removing her jacket to give the young man some warmth, she took a deep breath and stuck her hand in her trouser pocket.

The victim was only four years older than her son, four years older than the dead boy who had cycled into her, rabid from the effects of snapdragon, she was sure, and then there was Mark Sutton and Alan Rooney. And a hell of a lot of money.

It looked like the plan was going wrong now. Adam had to stay alive.

There was a bigger picture here and she was not being allowed to see it. Her blindness had nothing to do with the rolling haar and everything to do with the clever bastard who was manipulating this investigation.

She looked at Adam. They wanted him dead, yet they'd walked away a moment too soon when disturbed. It was the first mistake they had made; she wondered how difficult it would be to keep this quiet. Useless in a place like Cronchie. He'd be in even more danger if he pulled through.

They needed to be careful.

She needed to be careful.

A figure appeared as a shadow through the mist, clambering his way down the path. She didn't recognise Kinsella at first with his hat and bulky jacket distorting his body shape, but she could recognise his haste. She looked at her watch – he'd got here sharpish.

Craigo was walking behind him, easily recognisable from his gait, but he veered off towards the castle, looking at the standing stones, regarding each one carefully before walking up to the next one, taking his glasses on and off as he peered at them closely.

'Did the guy get a good look at the perp?' asked Kinsella.

'No. He ran off back to the car park,' said McPhee. 'But he'd no vehicle.'

'Okay, this is a game changer.' Kinsella wiped his mouth with the back of his trembling hand.

Caplan said, 'Are you okay?'

'Yeah, yeah, I'm fine. He's alive, that's the main thing. The ambulance is less than five minutes away.' He knelt down beside the victim.

Caplan told McPhee to stay with Adam and walked back to Craigo, who looked as if he was talking to one of the standing stones. What was wrong with that man?

'You got here before us, ma'am?'

'Yes, I'm staying nearby. Why are you here? You're going to tell me that he's been laid out in some weird way that lines up with the stones.'

'Yes, ma'am, that's exactly what I'm telling you.'

'Well, keep that under your hat for the moment. Let that be our wee secret.'

'I say, ma'am, you'll be picking up all my bad habits.'

'Yes, I've noticed how you play your vagueness to your advantage.'

'We've been looking for him for so long, and here he is, right under our nose. Makes you think, ma'am, doesn't it?'

FOURTEEN

Monday, 11 July, three days before

The atmosphere in the incident room at Otterburn was electric. The team was recharged with the big break.

Adam could tell them what happened. If he lived.

Kinsella looked terrible; the hours he was putting into the case, possible trouble at home and nervous exhaustion were all taking their toll. Only adrenaline was keeping him going.

Gourlay and Harris were at the front of the room, on either side of Kinsella. Craigo and Mackie were sitting together, talking quietly. Caplan went to sit at the back; the rest ignored her. She watched Gourlay, aftershave above his paygrade. Maybe Kinsella's car was above his.

'Okay, we all know that Adam McGregor was found last night.' Kinsella tapped the photograph. 'He's still alive, and we hope he stays that way. The update from the hospital is not good concerning the hypoxic brain damage, though. Caplan has arranged a police guard for him in the QE in Glasgow, coordinating with ACC Linden. He's safe for now. Gourlay is trying to establish where Adam has been.'

People nodded, started taking notes.

Caplan watched him carefully. So Gourlay was on the case regarding the attack on Adam. Interesting. This was Kinsella's move. She had to wait her turn.

'Better news. The results of the cell site analysis by our good friends in Edinburgh have come through and the phone used by Billy McBain was either "very close" or "at" Otterburn House on Tuesday the fourteenth.' There was a small cheer. 'And guess what? Scott Frew's phone was there as well. Both phones on site when we think the murders were taking place.' There was a bigger cheer. 'Okay, okay, then Scott's goes back to Glasgow. Also' – he held up two photographs: one of a triangular piece of dark blue fabric, the other of the fabric, with a matching hole – 'the sample from the top of the gate at Otterburn. The lining of a jacket we found at McBain's flat. The fabric in the sample has been exposed to the elements. It wasn't there from them climbing over the night we found it. It was there from an event weeks or months earlier.'

A smattering of applause went round the room.

'The case is being pulled together for the Fiscal. Scott Frew will stand trial alone. There's a warrant out for his arrest. As well as the cell site, we have the DNA on the tongue piercing. It does, as we expected, belong to Billy McBain. DI Caplan found pictures of him on social media with exactly that piercing. One picture, dated twelfth of June, tongue post in place. Then he's snogging some bird on the twentieth of June, tongue post gone.'

Kinsella paused to let that sink in.

'We'll get the pictures blown up to confirm it. We can only speculate why Charlotte, why any of the McGregors, let them into the house. But that mistake led to their deaths. Also, we're trying to find out where Scott Frew was at the time McBain was killed. He was out of hospital. Alice Keane had booked them into a Holiday Inn. But watch this . . .' He clicked the remote and a screen came to life behind him: CCTV footage of a car park at night, a slim solitary figure swaggering towards the main road, hood up, his bandage looking like a sleeve on his right hand and wrist. 'Whyte is going to look at other CCTV from further along the road.'

'Cheers, pal,' said Whyte in sarcastic good humour.

Kinsella continued. 'We'll know if they move. Gourlay and I were right there when McBain was murdered. The assailant ran down the hill in front of us, at high speed. He was young, fast and nimble. It could easily have been Frew, but we can't swear to it. We can't establish where else he was, and he hasn't come forward to help us with our enquiries.'

'Why did they go back to Otterburn House that second time?' asked Caplan.

'To get the stone? To steal valuables they saw the first time? It takes a strong stomach to look at five bodies that have been dead for three weeks. And they do have some very odd beliefs about Satan and so on, but you can't ignore the physical evidence at the scene just because it doesn't suit your theory.'

'And it would have looked bloody odd if they had scarpered,' said Gourlay.

Kinsella went on. 'Our position with the media is that we are looking for a young man to help us with our enquiries. It'll get out soon enough who he is but not from this office, understand. The papers will be full of it tomorrow – "significant breakthrough" – but that's as far as it gets.'

There was a murmur of consent.

'Good work, guys. We're not quite there yet but we're on the home straight.'

There was a round of applause. Kinsella nodded thanks and retreated into his office.

Caplan dialled a number on her own phone, looking round for the answering ring. It was no surprise to her that Kinsella closed the door of his office firmly before pulling his ringing phone from his shirt pocket. She followed him, knowing that Gourlay, Craigo, Harris and Mackie were all watching her, sensing that all was not as it seemed.

Kinsella didn't look up. She didn't say a word. She just put Adam's phone, still in its evidence bag, signed and dated, on the desk and slid it over to him.

He saw it, and his face flushed as he got up to make sure he had closed the door properly, putting them in a bubble from the outer office.

'You know, I've always wondered why you wear a jacket when it's so hot. Who leaves their phone in their jacket pocket rather than put it on the working desk? It's because you have two phones, isn't it? The number I've just called was on the phone Adam was carrying, one of only two numbers it has. It rang on your second phone, the one you keep in your jacket, rather than the official one you have in your back pocket.' She spoke quietly, her composure hiding her fury. 'You knew where Adam was all along. You've known from day one. You even spoke to him yesterday. At about quarter past five. I'm letting you explain it to me first before I go over your head.'

He slumped in the seat, head in hands. 'I'm sorry.'

'What the hell did you think you were doing?'

He sighed and leaned back in his chair. 'To be brutally honest, I didn't think it was going to go this way.'

'To be brutally honest, you weren't thinking at all.'

'Adam got in touch with me, right at the start. The phone record will prove that. I wanted to bring him in, but he was terrified, didn't trust the police, so he left Skone and went into hiding.'

'And he convinced you of his innocence so much that you accepted two young lads out their heads on drugs and alcohol killed five people and only left two pieces of isolated evidence?'

'Christine, they knew the house, they knew the family, McBain's a petty criminal, and we have the tongue piercing. Look who was at the party Monday night, at the Bodie Neuk. It includes McBain and Frew. Gourlay and Whyte split them up. Whyte knows both boys by sight. Anything could have gone on that night, those boys were high as a kite.'

'To whose benefit? Who benefits from these murders? Adam McGregor. The Allanach Foundation benefits from his death. I think your first hunch was correct: the answer is out there.'

He smiled sadly. 'And I thought I was doing so well. I thought I was protecting Adam. I was telling him yesterday about the DNA. I thought we were home and dry. He thought he was safe. He was wrong. And so was I.'

'I'm glad you see that. But he can tell us himself when he wakes up.'

'The hospital aren't positive about a full recovery.'

'Yes. But it takes a long time to strangle somebody. Why is your knowledge of Adam's whereabouts not on record? Why did you not tell me, if nobody else?'

'Because Bob suspected we had a bent copper on the squad. Adam thought it too. Then you were flown in with all this nonsense going on in the background, witnesses telling lies, evidence going missing. If I'm being really honest, I wanted to get one over on you. I wanted this investigation to be mine. I made a point of getting to know Adam. I thought if I kept it between the two of us, he'd be more likely to engage, respond to me, have some confidence in me. Thought I'd get more out of him. That was at the start, when he was more suspect than victim. Then things changed, and I realised it was up to me to keep him safe.'

'How do you know he didn't do it?'

'Too scared. He was terrified they were coming after him. I protected him.'

'Did you write any of this up?'

'I have it diarised and dated on my own laptop.'

Caplan sat back and folded her arms. 'I should report you. But if I ask myself what I would have done in that situation . . . if I was sure I was right . . .'

Kinsella looked over Caplan's shoulder to the incident room and lowered his voice. 'If we are being honest . . .'

'We are.'

'I think there's somebody in this team who's dirty.'

She was interested now. 'Go on.'

'Not with this case specifically but I know there are concerns . . .'

'John Fergusson?'

It was Kinsella's turn to be interested. 'I think he's part of the team. They have concerns that there's a network of bent cops in the West of Scotland. There's a huge increase in drugs in all the coastal villages. Just small fry that the big boys weren't interested in, but now it's a different story. There's money to be made and the problem is spiralling outwards from the cities.'

'That's common knowledge,' agreed Caplan.

'And' – he looked over her shoulder again – 'if we do have a leak in the service, I think I know who it is.'

Caplan turned to follow the line of his vision. Her eyes rested on Craigo, sitting hunched like a little goblin, scribbling something in his notebook rather than typing it into the system like a normal person.

'Remember the night you found him alone at Otterburn House? I hadn't let the other two officers go; he had.'

'Why was there only three on the rota? I saw it afterwards.'

'Bob was gone. I knew Craigo had been up to something. What else could I do but change it? I've my own version, date-stamped on my laptop. Something Bob always told me to do. And do you want to know the other reason why I kept Adam to myself? I thought the dirty cop might be you.'

She had to smile at that. 'Well, thanks for the compliment.' She tapped the phone. 'Let's keep this to ourselves and take a look at this second number. Twelve hundred text messages in the last eight weeks.'

'Did you phone it?'

'I did, gloved, from Adam's phone. It turned off before it was connected. I suspect that person thought he was dead. Who would be thinking that? We might get the tech boys to track it, but I think the other phone will be in a ditch by now.'

'That's a lot of texting, that's harassment.'

'They go both ways; there's a conversation. There's lots of sexy chat. They're close physically at times, from what they say. Do you think we can get the movements of that number over the last few weeks tracked?'

'Have you seen our budget? Can we work it out for ourselves?'

'Maybe. The known party is called Adam. Guess what the other is called?'

'Eve?' guessed Kinsella. 'Adam's heterosexual, so I'm guessing Eve is female.'

'I'd also bet that this phone never left this area. I don't think it ever needed to.' Caplan looked out the window again. Craigo and Mackie were still sitting together, talking closely. 'Are those two involved with each other?'

'Hope not – they're cousins, twice over.'

He watched them. 'Interesting. I think we both need to be very careful here.'

'Yes,' said Caplan, watching Kinsella. He'd had all night to think up this story as to why he kept Adam to himself. But she could ride with it for now. She had some empathy with him. She trusted him about as much as he trusted her. 'This discussion was between the two of us, okay? It'll stay that way.'

'I THOUGHT YOU MIGHT be interested in this, ma'am.' Craigo carefully swiped a few pictures on his phone as if it was a novel experience.

Caplan was trying to keep calm. Her conversation with Kinsella had made her head spin. 'What is it, DC Craigo? I'm busy and I'm stressed, so whatever I'm going to be looking at, it had better be good.'

'It's 52 Holmview Place, ma'am. In the driveway is a lovely Weinsberg motorhome.'

'What?' She closed her eyes. What was he bumbling on about now? Then she realised that the address was familiar; it had been mentioned at the hospital, with Mary Prior. She opened her eyes, looking deep into those pale brown irises that appeared so inhuman close-up. 'Where the Millers live?'

'Yes, ma'am. Kate lives there with her three kids. The woman who claims that you hit that guy in Cambridge Street.' He was looking closely at the image on his phone.

'DC Craigo, what are you doing with that picture?'

'Trying to figure out how she could afford an eighty grand motorhome.' He sat down and looked at the ceiling. 'You don't seem to me to be the type of cop who'd strike somebody and not admit it. Why would the witness say something so obviously untrue? And now they have a motorhome over eighty grand. I thought it was a wee bit' – he scanned the ceiling as he searched for the right word – 'interesting.'

Caplan felt her heart sink. 'Have you been looking into their finances?'

'Me, ma'am? No, ma'am.'

'Thank God for that. ACC Linden warned me to stay clear of the witnesses.'

'It was Toni.'

'Okay.' Caplan took a deep breath. This was the last straw; this was an unofficial, personal look into somebody's private data. This would be the end of her career. Was that part of Craigo's plan? Or were they genuinely trying to help? Had they done it for her, knowing that she couldn't prove they'd acted off their own bat, especially if they said she had asked them to investigate. The truth would look different to the powers that be, this subtle malevolence that was following her around, sitting on her shoulder and taking her air, suffocating her career.

'You have been investigating that family?'

'Well, yes. They lied about you. And no, we're not. We're looking at Galveston Sands and the holiday park. They put in an insurance claim about a missing Weinsberg CaraLoft, stolen from their site. And one turns up on the Millers' driveway. Her new boyfriend lost his beloved motorhome in the divorce, and both he and the Millers are hardly wealthy. The plates on that vehicle are false. There's no money out their account. Toni and I have to be a little honest with you, ma'am.'

'Please.'

'The timing's convenient. It happened after it became known there was no CCTV to prove your version of events was correct. And Sandra Leivesley is behind on her rent. Very. She's poorly paid. Then she pays off her arrears, her credit card debt, books a holiday in Gran Canaria, hence the dog visiting the vet, and she's getting a three-grand summer house in her garden judging from the catalogue, according to a wee chat I had with Maxwell the joiner. It's all very interesting.'

'Interesting?'

'They're being paid to lie, ma'am.'

'Have you told anybody else?'

He shook his head.

'Okay, what do we do now?'

'Well, I have a suggestion, ma'am.' A slow blink. 'We do nothing. We have the knowledge, and that's all we need – for now. The motorhome would be stolen again very quickly. I mean, who's she going to complain to?'

'Okay,' she said, glad for the distraction of her ringing phone. She walked outside to the sunshine, immediately invigorated by the fresh air.

'Hi, Mum. Have you been arrested?'

'No, Emma. Are you having a laugh? Of course not.' Her sixth sense was telling her that something had happened. 'What's going on?'

'Two cops came to the door late last night. I was in bed. They were looking for you. I had to tell them you weren't here. That you were up north, working.'

'Plain clothes or uniform?'

'Plain.'

'Did they show you a warrant card?'

'Yes, Mum. I'm not daft. They were really nice but they said a strange thing that you should . . . no, that wasn't how they phrased it, they said . . .' Emma's voice began to stutter as she realised what she had heard in the light of a new day and a new interpretation.

'What did they say, Emma?'

'They said they were surprised that you left us alone in the house. Why were you away?'

'Did they ask who else was at home?'

'They knew. I thought they must know you or know of you.'

'Okay. Emma, I want you to stay there. And don't go anywhere for now.'

'Okay,' said Emma slowly, 'and what about Dad? Kenny isn't back yet.' Silence. 'I'm scared, Mum.'

'So am I. I'm on my way home. While it's fresh in your mind, tell me what they looked like . . .'

IT TOOK FIVE MINUTES to get hold of Dawn McIntyre, a sergeant working on the Cambridge Street incident, who was surprised to hear of the visit and confirmed that nothing had been actioned by her team. She questioned Caplan about what was actually said to Emma. Caplan said nothing, but persuaded the sergeant to look at the CCTV to get a good image of the two callers. In the meantime, McIntyre said, it would be noted as a threat to the family.

Thanks for nothing, muttered Caplan. She hung up, then called Sarah Linden.

Linden listened to her for five minutes without comment. The story sounded increasingly bizarre to Caplan as she recounted the sequence of events from Oswald's fatal crash, the demonic spectre that caused his car to swerve, the white paint that might have belonged to a car that had no reason to be parked where it was, then back to the staging of the scene at Otterburn House and the rather convenient finding of the tongue post with its DNA, and now the stolen motorhome and the police visit. Linden was quiet while Caplan texted her an image from her phone, with instructions to delete it immediately.

Linden's voice shook a little as she said, 'That's bloody terrifying.'

'I bet they laughed when they did that. Yet Garry Kinsella will just not listen. He's not experienced enough to send a balanced report to the Fiscal, and that could cause all sorts of issues down the line. He's closing the biggest case of his career. But I'm not sure he's right. He's being diverted by a trail of evidence that's convincing but planted.'

Linden asked who had done the sampling of the tongue post.

'Owen Fraser's team, I think. I'm not criticising him. I just keep thinking that the placement of it is very convenient . . .' Caplan ran out of steam.

Linden replied, speaking very quietly and emphatically, 'Christine, I'll tell you what I'm hearing. I have a very stressed detective who, off the record, is in danger of losing her job. Maybe you ought to think about applying for a package. The service would give you a good deal. You'd have to pull your horns in, but it might give Aklen space to mend properly.'

Another flash of doubt crossed Caplan's mind: was Sarah trying to warn her off? 'Nobody's taking this job away from me. And I want to know what those two coppers were doing chapping my door and asking where I was. I want to know who they are.'

'Okay, I understand, but do you think you might be overreacting? You have a lot going on in your life.'

'I saw Oswald's body when they pulled him from that car. What do you think is on that video? A kelpie? I saw the bodies of the McGregor family laid out on the floor and the chief suspect with his throat cut. Adam McGregor was nearly murdered yesterday. And now somebody comes to my door, scaring Emma. I thought you might be able to piece it together, but I was clearly wrong.' She cut the call and looked out across the water, noticing the *Julia-Philippe* bobbing in the current, a bit like herself. She turned to walk back into the station, passing Craigo and Whyte, the taller man stooping down to speak to Craigo. They were so deep in conversation they didn't even notice her passing. Whyte, who was at the Bodie Neuk with Gourlay. She pulled herself up. They were part of the same team; of course they'd speak to each other.

Maybe she should call Mattie Jackson herself and find out exactly who had been at the Bodie Neuk that night.

NUMBER 27 ABINGTON DRIVE was dark in the shadows of the overgrown trees. The bottom of the lawn was covered with moss, damp and dull, a place where sunlight never intruded. It seemed so gloomy and oppressive after the fresh air and sunshine of the coast.

When she unlocked the door, she found Aklen asleep on the sofa, the drawn blinds cloaking the room in further darkness. He didn't wake when she called his name. She went back into the hall wearily and noticed that Emma had gathered a neat pile of mail for her. Aklen was not better in the sense that he could cope with opening the post. She found a note from Emma stuck to the kitchen door; she was going to stay with a friend, she'd feel safer there. Moving quietly, like a thief in her own house, Caplan climbed the stairs to her son's bedroom. She called through the closed door. No answer. No change there. For a moment she leaned against the wall and swore quietly. She had so much to think about and no space in her head. Her career was on the line. Where was their stability after this? She was running out of friends fast.

She knocked on Kenny's door, then again, louder. There was no noise from within, no noise at all. She opened the door and looked in, surprised that the room was bright and light. He'd opened the curtains before he left. She noticed that his bed had not been slept in.

Okay, so her nineteen-year-old son had stayed out overnight, and in normal circumstances she would be happy that he might actually have a social life, but with all that was going on, it made her feel very uneasy. She bent down and placed her palm on the pillow, lifting it up and smelling her son's scent, remembering picking him up as a small baby. There always was that smell in his hair. It was still there, but Kenny had gone. And Emma, unable to stand being in the house, had left a note with an excuse to leave.

*　*　*

OWEN FRASER WAS BUSTLING about his chaotic office, trying to find his mobile phone. It was half past three and he was due to give a lecture at Strathclyde University, but as far as Caplan was concerned, he was the god of Eviscan and she needed to speak to him.

'Sarah Linden said that you and your DI are slightly at odds with the lab's findings on the tongue post found at Otterburn House.'

'Not yours. I'm at odds with his interpretation of the entire situation and I'm trying to find one bit of evidence that might halt him in his tracks.'

Fraser looked unimpressed.

'There's a forensically aware crime scene way beyond those two lads. No other suspects. The tongue ring is just too neat. McBain's dead, Frew's young and gullible, and Adam's in a coma. Somebody's clearing up the mess behind them. I was thinking that I might be able to compare your results to the crime scene pictures?'

Fraser opened a case, laid the photographs out on the only clear surface in the room, then glanced at his watch. 'What is it you want to know? We didn't get good prints. You can see the deep bruising on the neck.' He checked the pictures' reference numbers and placed five separate pieces of paper on top of each one. 'That's what the Eviscan picked up. Not much, too blurred to see, too much time had passed, and the underlying tissue had become bloated and then hydrated. I'm sorry.'

'Is there anything else?'

'Like what?'

'Anything? I just find it difficult to believe that those two young men did this all on their own. I need to find something to put them at the scene or put somebody else there.'

'You can't bend forensics. Sometimes things are exactly as they appear. Why do you dismiss the tongue pin?'

Caplan sat down on his office chair and sighed. 'Because if I was trying to frame someone for this crime, that's exactly what I would do. Get those two boys so pissed and high that they don't know if it's

New York or New Year, maybe get some lassie to get jiggy with them – all, *oh, take that thing out.* When they pass out, take their phones off them, take a jacket off them, take the phones to the crime scene, stage it with satanic nonsense, plant the tongue pin, kill the victims, rip the jacket lining on the top of the gate, then take the phones back to the comatose babes in the wood. Using my knowledge of their interest in satanism, I'd send them back to the house for the stone, so they discover the bodies. Then wait and watch. Ending up dead in McBain's case. I've no doubt Frew's not under arrest so that he can end up bobbing in the harbour at some future date.'

Fraser raised an eyebrow. 'My, my – that's quite a story.'

'Yes, I know it sounds crazy. But the scan results are the only thing I've not seen.'

'Because there's nothing else to see.' But he was intrigued. 'So what're you thinking?'

'Oh, I don't know.' She rubbed her eyes then looked at the printouts.

'And one of those boys has been murdered, hasn't he?'

'Yes. Billy McBain had his throat cut, supposedly by the other one. There're hands all over this, and I'm not seeing who's pulling the strings, but there's enough that I think any conviction is going to be unsafe.'

'Yet there's nothing else pointing in any other direction.'

'I know, and that's what I find bloody odd.'

'I wish all the detectives were as thorough as you are.' He smiled. 'I have a lecture to go to, but I'd really like to help you. There's a lot more stuff on my computer if you promise to behave. I'll set you up here with the file and only the file. You have two hours. If you haven't found anything after that, it's not there.'

'I'd be very grateful. Oh, and can you do me a favour? Just run a basic check on something?'

'Why do I get worried when I'm handed an evidence bag with no paperwork? We do need to bill somebody for it.'

'Send the bill to ACC Linden. It has to stay away from Operation Capulet. Just a basic check, please, for the kind of car that paint came from.'

Fraser nodded, still unsure. 'Leave it on the desk.'

He logged her in, found the files relating to the case, copied them, set her up with limited permissions and left her to it.

She stared at the largest picture, with the wide focus of all the bodies in situ, then progressed through the individual images. They showed the bodies under the duvet, their clothes looking filthy in parts, pristine in others, faces bloated and sunken eyes clouded.

Catriona's blouse was open, a couple of buttons undone. It had been a hot summer day when she had returned to the house. Both men had collared shirts; then there was Lady Charlotte with a frilly, high-necked blouse, and Barbara in a simple, round-necked linen top.

The men had been strangled by ligature, the three women by manual strangulation, so the Eviscan machine had concentrated on the latter. Caplan minimised the files to look at the machine printouts, marked on graph paper for scale. She enlarged the image, then closed it back down so the scale of the graph matched the actual size. She looked at the marks where the fingers could be. A two-dimensional representation of a three-dimensional situation was never easy, but she could see that there was not enough detail to even suggest whose fingerprints they might be.

She felt deflated and a little silly. She was never going to find a definitive print that the experts had missed; cases were never solved that way.

She looked at the backs of her hands on the desk, the slim fingers and thin skin making them appear veiny and skeletal. She thought of Craigo's hands, smaller than hers, then she held her own hand up to the image on the screen, a ghostly shape on the white background. The perpetrator's hand was much bigger than hers, much more substantial. A man's hand.

She checked Barbara and Charlotte's scans. She couldn't tell if it was the same hands, but still, they were bigger than hers. She tested the span as if she was strangling somebody, looked at the distance between her thumb and her fingertips. The one on the screen was much wider.

Her heart started thumping. She looked again. And again.

It wasn't what she saw, it was what she couldn't see.

She cleared a space for the evidence bag with the white paint in the centre of Fraser's desk, hands shaking, then left.

BY NINE THAT NIGHT she was back in her cabin. She'd had a shower, and was dressed in a black top and leggings, looking like a ninja. She ran through the case in her mind, slowly filling in details now that she had the knowledge that Kinsella had known all along that Adam was alive. Now that she knew about the murders. She made herself comfortable on the bed.

They had presumed it was a power thing that the two men were strangled by ligature. But was it simply that somebody was disguising the fact that small hands could not have achieved fatal strangulation without leaving evidence of such on the skin of the two men with their well-muscled necks? Charlotte, Barbara and Catriona were all slim, fine-boned women. Caplan had noticed how small Scott Frew's hands were as he reached out for the water from his hospital bed. A killer with small hands would leave indents of their squeezing fingertips on a large neck simply because there's not enough hand span to reach right round. Was that why the two men had been killed by ligature? Because the fingermarks left by small hands would be a giveaway? The boys would never have known that. A more forensic mind was at work here.

The image of McBain floating amongst the lilies, his slender frame, childlike hands and feet. She made a mental note to check the photographs of Frew's alleged footprints as he fled the scene in the forest. If she was correct, they'd never come to light. She phoned Alice Keane, as she had several times, but this time Alice was reluctant to talk. She only spoke freely when Caplan said she only wanted to know what Scott had done the night McBain was killed. Caplan was hoping for a provable alibi. Scott had received a text, gone out and then come back feeling ill with a raging temperature. His turning back had forced them, whoever they were, to change their plans. She doubted that Frew would have got off that hillside alive. She advised Alice to keep Frew close, ideally move him elsewhere, and not to go back to an address where he was known.

Caplan needed to go back to the island, confirm her thoughts about Blossom, and try to have a chat with Pop Durant, on her own. She googled the Foundation, looking to see if there were any new videos, but there were no more uploads. The few she'd seen must have been taken before such electronic wizardry had been banned.

She was still considering who the main players in the game were, thinking about Allanach and snapdragon, when she must have fallen asleep. She was woken by a noise, or some intuition of an interruption in the peace. The cabin window was wide open to allow the warm air to circulate, and a familiar smell was drifting in, carried on the breeze. She looked out to see whirling smoke coming from the cabin across the way. As she watched, some accelerant caught, and a ball of flame exploded. She heard somebody yelling and saw a figure moving away through the trees as the doors to the neighbouring cabins were flung open. Somebody shouted to call the Fire Brigade as they ran over to the fire point to get the hose. Guests began to appear in doorways, bleary-eyed, in their nightwear, to watch or offer help. The flames caught quickly, and within a minute the cabin was a blazing inferno. She heard a loud voice saying no, there was nobody staying there, and then someone else asking whose car that was. They were pointing to her Duster, the car parked closest to the fire.

But Caplan's eyes were focused on the woods.

FIFTEEN

The Magus was sitting, one leg crossed on his lap, the other stretched out in front of him, supported by a cushion on a bamboo stool. He was dressed in the same casual uniform of jeans and T-shirt. He looked world-weary.

'I don't think we should be disturbing him,' said the man who had introduced himself as Calm. 'He's meditating.' He was in the statutory blue T-shirt, jeans and sandals, but the lemon-coloured scarf was at odds with his muscles and the mosaic of tattoos that decorated his arms. Caplan noted his hands: rough, gnarled and strong. His accent was broad Glaswegian, from the wrong side of the city.

Chris Allanach opened his eyes in a single movement and registered no surprise whatsoever at the two people standing in front of him.

'DI Caplan, unless I'm very much mistaken,' he said, slowly pulling one ankle up and tucking it underneath his knee.

'Fancy a cup of tea?' asked Calm, turning to Caplan.

'No, thanks. How do you know who I am?'

'It's all over the island. Everybody's talking about Adam. How is he?' said Calm.

'No progress,' she said, leaving him to make of that what he wanted. 'Was he here?'

'Not since we said he was. The thirteenth or so. Like everybody else, he comes and goes. We don't keep a register. But the work rota might tell you precisely – ask Roddy or Blossom.'

'Are they close, Roddy and Blossom?'

Calm seemed to think about it. 'Not really. She wasn't around this morning for her dive. She was called away, Roddy did it instead. He's still down at the pontoon if you want him.'

'Not like her to miss her assignments.' Allanach climbed down off his plinth, stepping round the yoga mats on the wooden floor, wincing and holding his knee as if it was troubling him. He was taller than Caplan had expected, and a handsome man, fine-featured with almond-shaped eyes.

'Do you know the contents of Adam McGregor's will?' Caplan asked.

'His will? No.' He was either genuine or a very good actor. 'He'll be okay, won't he?'

Again, his concern seemed genuine.

'He's in a coma, and it could go either way. So, the will?'

'I've honestly no idea what would be in his will. Why would I?' Allanach shook his head, more in disbelief than negation. 'I've had this place for a long time. I know folk. It's easy to be here in the summer when the weather's sunny, work is easy, and life's good. Adam was one who stayed here all year round. He was the kind of person that this place was made for. He should have walked through our doors and found the purpose in his life.'

'Because he was rich?'

'Because he was lost. And I thought he'd found himself. I was mistaken.'

Caplan raised an eyebrow. 'You must have a neat line in inheritance, or how could you keep going?'

'What's with the death obsession?' He smiled, blue eyes crinkling. 'You know, when the world ends and we have wasted the planet, folk will go back to using horses for transport, sheep for wool, wood for heat and building. We'll need skill to work the land, to grow food. We own a few businesses, we pay our way. I might be acclaimed as a guru, but I've also got a degree in economics. I'm not an airy-fairy greenie – well, I hope not. Things can be sustainable without profiteering. Roddy makes sure we break even; we don't need dead men's money.'

The trio walked down to the pontoon together. It was going to be another blistering hot day. Caplan noticed how badly Allanach was limping.

'You wouldn't have all this if your dad hadn't left the land to you.'

'What do you suggest I do? Dig him up and hand it back?'

Caplan ignored him. 'And Adam, you thought he was better?'

'I thought he'd come to terms with himself. I hope he recovers. When the time comes, he can come back here to recuperate.' He stopped walking and turned to look at her. 'But I see where you're coming from. I thought he was the real deal. He reminded me of myself. Born into wealth. It can be hard to get out of bed in the morning when you have no reason to. It's an easy life when your family has the wherewithal to buy you out of any trouble you find yourself in.'

'I've never suffered from being too rich, so I wouldn't know.'

'It's a curse rather than a gift. In Adam's case the money was always used to bring him back to the fold. He had no self-confidence at all. The last straw was when his dad offered him twenty thousand to keep him away from here. It was all about control.'

'Was he on drugs?'

'Adam? I didn't think so.'

'Do you have a substance abuse issue in the Foundation?'

'Not again,' he said, his irritation showing. 'Calm, would you mind talking to this lady, please? It's a story you'll be familiar with, DI Caplan. Hopefully, you'll see that we, as a community, are moving in the right direction.'

Calm turned round. He unwound his scarf to reveal a huge tattoo on his neck.

'Oh, one of that lot, were you?' said Caplan dryly, recognising the symbol of a gang active in Glasgow some years before. 'Callum McMaster? Yes, I thought the name meant something to me.'

'Well, you'll know I've got a criminal record. I'd tried everything to get off the drugs, then I came here. I've never left. I can't really handle life on the mainland. Too many people who know who I am, too many scores to settle, people who want to drag me back. But not here. Haven't touched a thing. I do cold-water swimming every day, even in the middle of winter, and that takes the anger from me. It might sound shite, but Callum the hard man has gone, and Calm is here now. I helped the mare give birth to a wee foal a few weeks ago. Never experienced anything like that in my life – I was greetin' like a wean. That cycle of poverty, abuse, violence – all those gateways to drugs are missing here. It takes time, but you do realise that life can be magic. There might be a bit of weed smoked here, in the summer on the beach at midnight, but I've never taken any of it. I'd just get lost to it again, and everything would spiral out of control.' He looked around him, his eyes resting on the black colt standing on long spindly legs, a worm of a tail flicking, grazing contentedly beside its mother. 'Chris has done a lot for me. I was in jail for over fifteen years in all and I was this close to killing somebody. Why would I allow anyone to destroy all this?' He gave a little laugh, almost childlike. 'Christ, I've even got a girlfriend, one with all her own teeth!'

Caplan looked round to Honeybogg Hill, at the slow pace of life and nodded. She had to agree with him.

'People here are not repressed. Do you feel safe walking around?' Calm asked.

'Yes, I do.'

'Good. This place is full of people who are frustrated and angry because they think they haven't lived up to their expectations. In reality, they've not lived up to other people's expectations,' said Calm. 'And that's not the same thing.'

'The square-peg-in-a-round-hole scenario. What about Adam? Can you tell me about him?'

'He was a thoughtful young man. I think he visited once, then decided to stay. Folk are attracted by the same thing, but they stay or leave for different reasons.'

'Free food and free booze? I wonder why? Calm, while you're here and we're speaking in confidence, I've heard the name Rooney in connection to the island. Do you know anything about that?'

Allanach had returned with a gourd of cold water. He sighed with a long slow outbreath when he heard the name. 'We're onto that again, are we?' He sounded disappointed.

It was Calm who replied, with the dull weariness of an old story being retold. 'Yes, he was here for a while, trying to find himself. He died of an overdose. That's what you'll have heard, I guess. The police investigated it. I think he died in Inverness.'

'Nairn,' corrected Allanach.

'Thanks, that was the only thing I was concerned about. If I hadn't seen you, I wouldn't have bothered asking.'

'But you walked up the hill looking for me?'

'Yes, I did.'

'So you did intend to ask me that question?'

'No. Nobody knows I'm here.' She looked out across the fields. 'I have a son, nineteen, and he's not choosing the best path in life. I liked what I saw when I was here last. Hugo and Victor. He used to love horses when he was a wee boy. Even the fresh air would do him good.'

'I've never known it do anybody any harm. Why not bring him out? Maybe he'll rediscover his fondness for horses. He'd be very welcome,' said Allanach warmly. 'As a mother you need to make sure your children are safe, no matter what bloody age they are.'

She walked down to the field, watched the Clydesdales pulling the charabanc along the path. More visitors, more workers dressed in that uniform. She looked at the yurts, their canvas doors folded back, the therapy centre with its oils and potions in pots and jars, floors being brushed, carpets being beaten over clothes lines – that sense of shared activity, of industry. The beehives up behind Honeybogg Hill where the Magus sat in cross-legged contemplation attended to by an ex-con.

She wasn't quite sure what she made of it all.

By the time she reached the pontoon, Roddy Taylor was nowhere to be seen.

There was something too controlled about this place, about Allanach himself. The fact that he knew who she was for one thing. Maybe it had been foolish to come out. Maybe she and Mackie had stood out like sore thumbs. Of course they'd know Mackie already, what she did for a living.

She shouldn't have come. Adam was in a coma. He wouldn't be talking anytime soon, and there were other more fruitful leads to explore.

'Hello,' said a voice, making her jump.

'Sorry?' She couldn't see anybody.

'I'm over here. Just walk to your left and have a seat on the dunes.'

She recognised the voice now: Pop Durant. 'All very cloak-and-dagger. I suppose this is one of the few places on the island you can't be seen. Are we being watched?' she joked.

'Are you looking into Alan's death?'

'Was it you who gave me the name?'

'A friend who works in the café. I recognised you as a cop the minute I saw you walking around with Toni. Didn't take long for the gossip to get back that you're a police officer, DI Christine Caplan.'

'Was Alan Rooney your nephew? A close relative? There's a family likeness.'

'You've done your homework. Alan was a much-loved boy, not a bad boy, not going off the rails. He was away on a golfing weekend and, well, he never came back. It's the kind of tragedy that a family never gets over – just awful. My sister died not long after. She just gave up, and that was all my family gone.'

'And you were a journalist, not a musician. When Alan died you came out here. I find that interesting. They come here to get away from the drug culture, but it's easy to get sucked back in.'

'Or, equally, a good place to send those you wish to turn into traffickers.'

Caplan nodded thoughtfully. It was the first time she'd heard the idea voiced. 'What does snapdragon – or "the snap" – mean to you?'

'A flower we used to play with when we were wee, a game and a drug that's way too unpredictable to be on the street.'

Caplan looked out at the gentle ebb and flow of the tide, the blue sky, the golden sand. The sadness of the man next to her was palpable.

'When the flaming dragon of the Hesperides was killed by Hercules, he cut the dragon up and ate the hot, flaming meat. He called it snapdragon. And it's here,' he said. 'But I can't find it. I don't know where it's coming from.' He shook his head and turned away, so she wouldn't see his tears.

SIXTEEN

Wednesday, 13 July, the day before

The case was on the front of every newspaper. Adam McGregor had been found, barely alive, and a nineteen-year-old male was being asked to come forward and help with enquiries.

ACC Sarah Linden held a press conference in Glasgow, keeping a tight rein on what she said no matter how much they pressured her.

Caplan walked into the incident room at half eight the next morning after a night of tossing and turning in an anonymous B&B. She was on the lookout for anybody who thought she should have been burnt to a crisp, but there was no reaction. She wanted to update Kinsella about Adam, snapdragon and the Eviscan results before the daily briefing. It was exculpatory but it would help. And she wanted to see exactly how he would react. Lizzie had texted her with the names of the guys in the five-a-side team. Iain Gourlay, Neil Whyte, James Wilson, Alistair McDade and Jimmy Armstrong. Two out of five. Not really such a coincidence. If Oswald had found any stronger link, it had died with him.

As she walked through the incident room, she was aware of more computers being set up, new phone lines being put in. There was a palpable sense of urgency. Something had happened. Her phone beeped; it was a brief text from Aklen to say that Kenny was still not home.

Before she could say anything, Kinsella came out and hurried her into his office.

'What's going on out there?' she asked, shrugging her jacket from her shoulders. 'Has something happened?'

'Bloody right something's happened. And it's going to have nothing, absolutely nothing, to do with you! I'm bloody lucky I'm still on the case.' He was incandescent. 'What the fuck did you think you were doing out on Skone? Talking to McMaster? You've no idea what's going on here, do you? No wonder you were asked to step down a rank. Where's your professionalism? You're bringing this team down, *my* team down. Compared to Bob, you're nothing. You're a failure as a cop, a wife and a mother. Are you even competent to do this job? I've made a formal complaint, so kindly get out and leave us to do our work properly.' He regained his composure and sighed. 'Just get out.'

There was a terrible silence in the incident room. DI Christine Caplan stood up and put her jacket back on, lifted her bag with the USB stick of the dashcam footage, and slung it over her shoulder.

'I'll leave you to calm down.' She walked towards the door, paused and turned, watching him. 'Leave you to think about your management of Adam McGregor. Did you play football with the Tulliallan five-a-side football team?'

The shock crossed his face before he could stop it. As a shot from left field, it had hit home. Oswald had indeed been onto something. She nodded at him, said goodbye to the squad in an upbeat way, and walked out the door. She climbed into her car and began reversing slowly out of the car park when there was a knock at the window. It was that wee shite Craigo, his face all innocence. He knocked again, and she lowered the window.

'Fuck off, Craig, or Craigo, or whatever your bloody name is.'

'Can I join you, ma'am?' he said, climbing into the passenger seat as if she had said nothing.

'It looks like you already have.' If she was going to get angry, he was easy to get angry at.

'He shouldn't have said that, ma'am.'

'Why not? It's true, it's what you're all thinking.'

'Well, actually, it's not, ma'am.'

She glared at him.

'I think it's all rather interesting,' He scratched his scalp, then inspected his fingernail for dandruff.

'*Interesting?* He just ripped my career apart in a single minute. What respect am I going to have in there now? Jesus Christ!' She dropped her head onto the arch of the steering wheel, accidently banging the horn, which blared, startling a teenager out walking her pug. 'I need to go back home. I came up here for all the wrong reasons. My husband's not well, my son is God knows where – I'm just going to head back.'

'Oh, I don't think you should be doing that.' Craigo was very firm.

'You don't?'

He shook his head. 'It was interesting what was going on in that room. So, who has respect for you now? What respect do you think we have for him after that? He left the door open so we could all hear. He wants you to walk off the case, ma'am.'

She took a deep breath. 'Craigo, I told you and only you where I was staying.'

'Yes, ma'am. Kinsella asked me at the standing stones how you got there before him, so I told him you were staying close. Anybody could work out where. They just needed to find your car. Now they're doing their damnedest to get you away from here because, whatever is going on, they think you're getting too close.'

'Why don't they get rid of you if you know so much?'

'Because they think I'm thick, that I don't notice anything, ma'am, which is fine as I notice quite a lot. And they ignore me. Nobody has ever taken notice of me before, and you did, and I respect you for that. I really do. You're not paranoid, ma'am. They are out to get you.'

'Who?'

'No idea. Well, not much, and even if I did, nobody would listen to me anyway. I'm the bloody invisible man, me, pardon my language.' He got out the car and walked away in the huff. She looked at the horizon. Clouds seemed to be rolling in, a darkening sky over her head.

Craigo was right: Kinsella's outburst was unprofessional. He'd been caught completely off guard. Maybe he hadn't expected her to turn up today, after the fire. She felt very lonely but, strangely, in control. Somebody was lying, and it wouldn't be long before she'd find out who it was. Kinsella was an emotional type; he got upset and angry when stressed. She made some notes and checked a few details on her tablet, then drove away. She was determined to speak to Kinsella about the Eviscan results. Let him argue his way out of that.

As she passed the usually quiet harbour, she noticed a lot of commotion: HM Customs boats, personnel in protective gear, sniffer dogs and their handlers. She parked and got out the car, and watched the activity by the pier for a while, enjoying the sun. Her brain was telling her that she was seeing something but that she wasn't recognising what. Kinsella's Merc was there, the Mini she thought was Mackie's too, and then she saw a brand-new black Audi glistening in the sun. It was the reg plate that caught her eye. It ended *JFF*. John Fergusson was here.

So, it was all coming home to roost now.

PC Whyte was at the door of the incident room. She said hello, but he blocked her from entering. He said he was sorry but he had orders to refuse her entry. He didn't try to hide his pleasure. There was 'an operation underway', he said, and glanced across to the island. She crossed the road and looked down to the harbour; a flotilla of boats was making its way across the sound. The ferry was tied up, going nowhere.

SEVENTEEN

Thursday, 14 July, the day

He was lying on the ground, bleeding. His head felt heavy, and every breath sent searing pain through him.

He thought he was going to die. He was slipping away, but somehow his body felt that he was still running. His heart was racing. Blood was seeping from him onto the grass.

He was aware of a man beside him, placing a comforting hand on his shoulder. The Good Samaritan asked for the code to unlock his phone, said he'd get help, that everything was going to be okay.

He pursed his lips together, tasted blood, and muttered his PIN number, thinking that there was no air in his breath, no breath in his lungs. Through the blades of grass in his eyeline, he saw the middle-aged man squatting beside him, now on his phone and asking for help. He sounded as if he was at the end of a tunnel. He was saying there'd been an accident. His head felt fuzzy and warm. He couldn't quite put the ideas together, but something told him that it wasn't 999 that had been called. The man said where he was and then something like 'less than five'. The man repeated it: 'Less than five, I'll see you.'

The phone was returned to his pocket, a hand rested on his shoulder. The voice spoke to a few people, telling them to give him space, there was an ambulance on its way. There was no need to panic and nothing to see.

He felt himself drifting in and out of consciousness, like waves on a beach. His heart went on beating for an eternity, stuttering then restarting. He heard an engine, a car stop. A door opened and slammed closed.

A voice he knew said, 'Oh my God, what's happened to him?'

He heard running footsteps, could feel them through the earth. The man who had taken his phone had gone. He saw feet in familiar trainers run towards him and a black car being driven at speed. There was the sound of people moving. He saw the shoes leave the ground as if their owner had been scooped up and tossed away. The noise of flesh on metal, a dull thud, and people were screaming, the noise of the engine ever louder.

The car kept coming towards him. He braced himself, trying to gather his strength to move out the way as the tyres came closer.

Then nothing.

IT WAS A LARGE room with a very clean dark blue carpet, the track marks of its recent vacuum still visible in the pile. The long wooden table was polished to within an inch of its existence, the chairs tucked in neatly, ready. A uniformed cop who had introduced herself as Helen was placing biscuits and coffee on the table, chatting in an inane way that suggested the shit was about to hit the fan and she knew it, but didn't want any questions as she was in no position to give any answers.

They came in one by one: four men, one woman, all good suits and decent haircuts. There was a lot of handshaking despite the fact they had probably already met elsewhere in the building. Their chatter was light, and it excluded her. Helen threw DI Caplan a look of empathy as she went out the door. There was silence except for the rustling of papers and the sniffing of superiority.

The Bastard walked in.

She hoped her face hadn't betrayed her when he smiled at her, the same easy smile.

'Hello, Christine. How are you?'

She was sure that if the table had not been between them, he would have reached over to kiss her. Instead, she stood up to accept his handshake; it would look as though they were friends and colleagues from way back. This man was a chameleon: her own lover, a husband to Lizzie, father to the boys, career cop, head of a drug squad and boss to most of the people in this room.

But not, as far as she knew, her. She gave him her death stare.

'Do you two know each other?' asked the other female, slightly confused.

'Intimately,' replied Caplan, deadpan.

Their colleagues would be thinking nights spent on surveillance, eating chips in comfortable silence with nothing else to say. But she and The Bastard knew differently.

Fergusson grinned. 'Yes, Rona. Christine and I did some work together earlier in our careers, when we were much younger. How are you doing?'

'I'm fine,' she said as the suit with the buzz cut unfurled a map of Skone and placed four glasses on the corners to stop them from rolling up.

'IT issues. We're going back to paper,' Fergusson explained. He was still wearing his wedding ring, the disguise of a happy family man.

Buzz Cut said nothing.

'This is DI Christine Caplan, SIO Major Investigation.'

'Who's getting the feeling of being kept in the dark *re* intelligence that may have been of use.'

'The old need-to-know basis. My hands were tied.'

A memory flitted between them, and he had the good grace to blush slightly.

'We'll get to that in a minute.'

Buzz Cut intervened. 'DI Caplan, you're addressing one of the heads of the new OCI, Organised Crime Initiative. We have some questions for you. Please keep your answers concise and on point.'

Caplan blinked. 'All this would be a tad easier if I had some vague idea of what this is about. As far as I'm concerned, there have been seven murders in Operation Capulet. One family, a police officer and a suspect. I'm getting a little tired trying to do my job with one hand tied behind my back, and I've been saddled with a DI who can't draw a conclusion and an idiot for a DC, so I'm—'

'It's delicate. I was hoping to have dealt with you directly but after last night . . .' Fergusson shrugged.

'The massive raid on Rune that failed to uncover anything at all?' she asked.

'You know Skone?'

'Yes.'

'You visited it?'

'Yes.'

'Well, you shouldn't have.' And there it was, the change in the voice. The ball was at his feet now.

'I went on my day off. I was seeing if Chris Allanach would talk to my daughter for her dissertation.'

He looked amused. 'Frankly, I don't believe you.'

'I don't care,' said Caplan airily.

'The SIO in the McGregor case said that you went there to pursue a lead that was not an active part of the enquiry and then returned to follow up that lead.'

'By SIO, do you mean DI Kinsella?' Caplan took her time to look at each person in the room. She placed her mobile on the desk in full view and pressed record. 'Good. Can you just confirm that this meeting is being minuted accurately, without anybody else putting a spin on it to further their careers, sir?' she added with a hint of sarcasm.

'So, you know nothing about snapdragon?' he asked, matching her sarcasm with his own.

'I know it killed Daniel Doran and' – she allowed some poison to drip into her voice – 'of all the people in this room, I have a right to know that. I also know of two others I've found . . . so far.'

Caplan enjoyed the ripple of unease round the table. 'Sorry, are we not investigating sudden deaths any more?'

'Daniel Doran was a young man who died after DI Caplan

apprehended him. She witnessed him mugging an elderly victim. His PM reports that he died of snapdragon,' Fergusson informed the rest of them.

'Who told you I was on Skone?'

'We are not at liberty to say. Why were you there?'

'If I had been advised of an ongoing operation, I would have steered clear or sought further permission. I was not advised. As I said, my daughter is doing a dissertation on commercially viable ecology, and the Allanach Foundation is a prime example of that. DC Toni Mackie offered to take me across on our day off. Feel free to contact my daughter's lecturer if you don't believe me. It was he who suggested it.'

'Really?'

'Yes. I have an interest in my children's education.' She emphasised the 'I'. That hit home. Caplan realised that, in fact, she had no idea where Kenny was. What kind of mother was she? 'Did I cause a problem?'

'We think there's a connection between snapdragon, Skone and the McGregor family.'

'I think you're correct.'

'We're keen to trace it back to its manufacture and cut the supply line totally.'

She said, 'A highly public raid was hardly the best way to go about it. I might have information that is useful to you.'

'I doubt that,' said Buzz Cut.

'I'm certain I do,' she replied, straight to Fergusson.

But Buzz Cut spoke again: 'Your interference on Skone cost us a lot of money.'

'Well, I had some lovely herbal tea and listened to a nice man playing guitar on a beach, so there's something very wrong with your intelligence. And if I did interfere in some way, then your team should have informed Capulet.'

'We did.'

'Well, please note it did not come through to me. Somebody else is responsible for that. Somebody not at this meeting.' She lifted her phone. But did not stop recording.

Buzz Cut ignored her. She was confused by the way Fergusson seemed to defer to him. He spoke with an English accent, and there was something here that she wasn't quite getting. Buzz Cut nodded at Ferguson, giving him the go-ahead.

'The Allanach cult—'

'Foundation,' corrected Caplan. 'It doesn't fit any criteria of a cult.'

Fergusson started talking. 'Within the Foundation is a cult, and within that is a drug distribution network. Snapdragon is making its way to Skone and then to the mainland. As you know, the cities are pretty much sewn up in terms of drug distribution, but the Highlands is a relatively new market. The price of the drug is dropping due to an increased supply, and as the price drops, snapdragon moves from a high-end recreational drug to a lethal street drug. We have traced it back to Skone, and Chris Allanach, and Callum McMaster. The yachts, those folk who come ashore to use the facilities, that's the start of it. We don't know where it goes. We don't know where it comes from. We carried out an operation that has taken three months of planning – and you ruined it.'

'Really?'

'You went out a second time to speak to Allanach personally?'

'Yes, I did, and that conversation is written up in my notes if you want to check. I also spoke to Callum. He has a past of substance abuse with the Carlton Elite, if his tattoo is anything to go by. I didn't ask for any information; they offered it.'

Buzz Cut shook his head. 'Does it surprise you that Allanach is using the Foundation to launder money?'

'It would disappoint me.'

'The accounts of the businesses on Rune have been forensically audited.'

'Might explain how an ecological foundation like that makes a profit,' Caplan said. 'Does this have any link with the Galveston development?' There was another ruffle around the table, a mix of annoyance and respect.

'Told you she was good.' Fergusson sighed and pressed a number on his phone.

Even before she came into the room, Caplan knew who it was going to be.

'Hi, DS Annette Evans. I'm sorry I'm late.'

'Hello, Blossom. You weren't late. He just texted you so you could make an entrance.' Caplan was bored with it now.

The guide from Skone stared back with youthful insolence.

'Let's cut the crap. Somebody killed the McGregor family because they knew the entire fortune would fall to the Allanach Foundation.'

'I think Garry Kinsella had got that far,' said Buzz Cut dryly.

'And he knew where Adam McGregor was all along but kept it to himself. You might like to calculate the money *that* has cost.' Caplan watched Evans' face as she shot a sideways glance at Fergusson. She wanted his back up but Buzz Cut was in control now. She saw the way Fergusson looked back at Evans. She knew that look; she'd been on the end of it often enough.

How much did pillow talk cost?

Caplan's mind was reeling. Everybody around this table had training in interview body language, and they suspected she had an ace up her sleeve. They just had no idea what it was.

'But it's not about money, is it? It's not about the money launder-ing, it's about the drug itself.' She looked round the table. 'You didn't find anything, did you? All that effort and you got nothing – must have caused a few red faces.'

Buzz Cut recovered himself. 'I see from your record that you are no longer operating as an efficient police officer, to say nothing of your inability to work at the level of your rank. You leave me no option but to recommend that you're placed—'

'Where, sir? While I'm talking out of turn, just have a think about Bob Oswald. He was my rank. He was murdered—'

'You have no evidence of that.'

'Actually, I do. And you might like to ask Cronchie Fire Service what they were doing last night. Oswald was killed because somebody, probably somebody who sits behind a desk like yours, is manipulating this situation for their own ends. This entire investigation has leaked like a colander from day one. That's why he's dead.'

'Don't lecture me on operational matters, DCI Caplan.'

'It's DI Caplan, actually.' She stood up and walked slowly towards the door. 'And if my visit to the island caused your raid to fail, what did the search for Adam do? That was on the sixth. How much warning did that give them? How many officers went out to look for Adam? Who signed off on that? The one person who may have known where he was all along! I'll leave you to mull over that.' She checked her phone was still recording.

Fergusson stood up and opened the door for her.

'You're one bitch,' he said under his breath.

'Bastard,' she muttered back sweetly.

'You don't fancy doing a Brindley on this one and losing some evidence, do you?'

'Bastard,' she repeated and walked away.

CAPLAN WAS STILL STANDING at her car checking her phone when The Bastard jogged over to her.

'Hey, hey! Chris?'

'Oh, piss off and leave me alone. What was all that about in there?'

'Chris, come on. We've just spent tens of thousands on a drug raid and got fuck all. Allanach's probably going to sue us. Those guys round that table need a fall guy, a fall woman.' He grinned.

'Well, pick somebody else.'

'Chris, come here.' He took her by the elbow. She shrugged him off. He grabbed her again and frogmarched her to a shadowy corner behind a police transit van. 'Look, I didn't know you were on Capulet until I saw it in the memo yesterday. And in there, when you mentioned Galveston, I had to have a quick change of plan. I'd be really stupid to give away an asset like you. I've got you up there and right at the scene.'

'You're so full of crap. Who told you I was there?'

'Intel from an undercover officer. We were told that two cops from the mainland had come over, two women. After three words of description, I knew who it was. We were going to ask you to back off before, but now you could be the best chance we have of nailing these bastards.'

She remained unconvinced.

'My neck is on the line here.'

Caplan said nothing.

'You deserve a better life than a DI in the middle of nowhere. You're a great cop.'

She still said nothing.

'This is going to be a difficult case for us.'

'Us?'

'You and me?'

'Is it?'

'You know what I mean.' He put his hand out to caress her jacket sleeve.

She glared at him, at his fingers, then back at him. He removed them quickly. 'No, I don't know what you mean.'

'We have a history.'

'Yes, we do. It's history for a reason. You told me you were single: you weren't. I've always been good friends with your ex-wife and you can't be bothered paying for your children. You're so full of shit.'

He smiled. He had a very disarming smile, and he knew it. 'But I never said I was single – you presumed that.'

'Oh, come on. You took your wedding ring off.'

'How is Lizzie?'

'She's good.'

'I'm in a bit of a mess with money at the moment, just a temporary thing, you know? She's in the house, and I'm paying the mortgage on it as well as my own rent.'

'Taking Blossom to Paris must have been hard.'

'She paid for that, actually.'

'So, you admit it? Maybe she can chip in for your kids' school uniforms as well. Oh, and maybe a new Audi while she's at it.'

'I'm not a total bastard, Chris. Why don't we go out for dinner, catch up? It's been a while.'

'No, let's not.'

'It'd be fun. I never thought badly of you, Chris. I did love you in my own way. Jesus Christ, I'm being serious. I always respected how you coped with all that's going on at home and, well, I think you deserve better. If going out for a curry while we're up here, no strings, makes it all a little easier, you only have to give me a call.'

She nodded. 'Okay, I'll remember that.' Again, the hand came up to stroke her upper arm. 'But, just to let you know, it wasn't me who messed up the raid you had on Skone.'

'You didn't mean to, but I do believe you did.'

Caplan dropped her voice very low. 'I don't really give a shit if you believe it or not, but maybe you should be careful about the company you keep. Little whispers on the pillow – I'd think about what she knew if I were you. How easily she might have been turned by the island? She's not a very good undercover cop. The minute she opened her mouth I knew. Who uses the word "ingress" except a cop or a plumber? She may be feeding you false info. Why not test her and see what happens? At least you can distance yourself from her. Because when she goes down, she'll take you with her. You have two children to support, and you can't do that from a prison cell.'

His eyes narrowed. 'Has Lizzie put you up to this?'

'No. I'm telling you to be careful for the sake of your boys, and

I'm asking you because you're too good a cop to be taken in by this. But, believe me, if you believe nothing else, somebody is fucking with your case and your intelligence.'

He walked away, and although she knew he was an arrogant prick, she couldn't help thinking how nice it would be to have some decent food in a restaurant, some company, relax and have a laugh. She and The Bastard had always shared the same sense of humour. Rolling their eyes at each other over the other officers' heads in a chaotic incident room when some ridiculous suggestion had been made. That was what had bonded them in the first place.

He was one of the few people who understood what was going on at home. They could talk, they'd always talked. But could she trust him? Probably not. And she couldn't trust herself.

Her phone beeped. A voice identified herself as DC Sharon Ayres and asked that she confirm who she was talking to and if she had anybody with her at the moment. Caplan's blood ran cold; she knew what those words meant.

One minute later, she was leaning against her car, trying not to be sick, trying to think of what she needed to do now. A hand took the phone off her and Fergusson started talking. 'Yes, I've got that. I've got a car.' He cut the call. 'Chris, we have a driver, we'll blue and two it.'

'No, I can . . .'

He was on his own phone, and she saw the patrol car pull up, lights flashing, ready.

She nodded and got in the car.

'What happened?'

'I don't know. Kenny's in the hospital, badly hurt – a fall, I think. He's unconscious.'

They were soon out of Cronchie and on the way back to Glasgow. She tried to push from her mind that somebody had given her a warning and she hadn't heeded it and now she was paying the price. The countryside rolled past, cows grazing, lambs enjoying the sunshine, tractors trundling across green fields. Life was going on as usual. She felt tears fall.

NINETY MINUTES LATER, SHE was banging her way through hospital doors, jogging along corridors. At the ward, she saw Lizzie's head peer round a doorway. Inside, Kenny lay in a bed, his bruised and bloodied face unrecognisable, his arm in plaster, neck in a brace and with two IV drips hanging beside him.

'What the hell happened?'

Kenny looked at Lizzie through the narrow slits of his swollen eyes.

Lizzie said quietly, 'Christine, don't panic. We didn't want to tell you until you got here, but they've taken Emma to theatre.'

'Emma? Why? What's going on?' She saw the expression on her friend's face and turned to look at Kenny.

'I'm so sorry, Mum.'

It was Lizzie who spoke next. 'Emma was hit by a car and she's down in surgery.'

'Surgery?'

'Neurosurgery. Fractured skull, two broken legs.'

'What's wrong with her? Sorry, I don't understand what's happened.'

'They got to her really quickly. She's safe now, and I'm sure she'll be fine.'

'Was it you Kenny?'

'He had a fall.' Lizzie walked her out of the room, out of earshot. 'Kenny was off his head on something. He climbed up the war memorial in the park and jumped off. He's broken his arm, his cheekbone, and he's badly concussed. But while he was on the ground, somebody took his phone and phoned Emma. He sounded young, like a friend of Kenny's. When she got there, she was hit by a car as she ran across the road. She was thrown to the side, then the car drove over the grass and tried to run Kenny over, but he managed to roll out the way. Two witnesses say the car went straight for her, then straight for him.

They think it was a black Ford Focus. Plenty people saw it. They thought the guy who took his phone was a friend of Kenny.'

'So Emma was lured out? She wouldn't ignore a message like that.'

'It looks like it.'

'Because of me.' Caplan sidestepped Lizzie to get back into the room, wiping the tears from her eyes. She stroked her son's hair, took his good hand and squeezed it gently.

'I'm so sorry, Mum.'

'It's not your fault – it's my fault.' She dropped her head, her face in his hair; he still smelled like her boy. 'Where's your dad?'

'He collapsed. He was in shock.'

'At least he's safe at home,' said Lizzie.

'They're never going to stop, are they?'

'Well, I'm not sure they wanted to kill your children. I think they're just proving that they can. How big is this thing? Could you walk away?'

'That's what they want, but somebody else would step in.'

'They couldn't get rid of you professionally, so they tried to get rid of you personally.'

'So what do I do? They're never going to—'

The door opened and John Fergusson walked in. Lizzie automatically stiffened.

They all said hello in awkward unison.

'We were just asking how big this thing was,' said Lizzie.

'You'd be better coming back up and finishing it off, Chris,' said Fergusson. 'You've got us closer than anybody.'

'How do you make that out?'

'Because they're taking huge risks to stop you.'

'Lizzie? Can you get hold of Kenny's phone, look for a fingerprint?' Caplan said. 'Then find out who did it.'

Her phone beeped. Sarah Linden.

'I've just heard. Anything you need, you have it. Keep John F. with you. He might be a bastard but he's good in a crisis.'

*   *   *

THEY TALKED A LOT on the drive back up to Otterburn. Caplan was angry, too angry to sit about at the hospital waiting. Lizzie was going to stay there to look after Kenny. She'd just texted to confirm that Emma was still in surgery but a good outcome was likely. She was young and healthy. Caplan had no regrets about driving away. She regretted not seeing her daughter the last time she was in Glasgow. She regretted not finding Kenny when he hadn't made it home. But she was going to catch the bastards who were bringing snapdragon into this country. From the way witnesses spoke of Kenny's mania when he climbed the statue, her son may well have taken it. He'd survived but there'd be many more who would not.

Caplan and Fergusson knew they had the ability to stop this, and that was what they intended to do. They didn't quite have the big picture yet, but the incident with Kenny and Emma had shown they were close. The intimidation of Caplan's family had demonstrated that. During the drive they talked about the search on Skone, trying to identify individuals or a location that had slipped through the net.

They parked outside the incident room in Otterburn. They had set up a meeting with Mackie, Craigo, Kinsella, Gourlay and Harris en route. Fergusson was adept at people watching; he wanted to observe them during the discussion, see if anyone slipped up. He nipped across the road to get a can of something cold and fizzy. Caplan said she'd phone the hospital and join him inside.

Lizzie sounded upbeat. The reports from Emma's consultant were positive. Kenny came on the phone briefly, sounding like her little boy again. But she wondered for how long he had been under the influence of drugs. Why had she not been aware of it? Had she ignored it? Was that where all the money was going?

She was just about to get out the car when her phone rang. A landline number she didn't recognise. She swiped tentatively to accept and had to put her finger in her other ear to drown out the noise of the diesel engine of the tourist coach that had pulled up at the harbour. The voice was breathless, female. She introduced herself as Mary, and asked if she was the police officer who had worn the yellow dress. Caplan confirmed that she was and put the name to the voice.

'Mrs Prior? How are you doing?'

'I'm getting there – slow progress. Was that your daughter who was hit by a car? The girl who helped me? It was in the news.'

Caplan was going to cut her off – she had no time for this – but Mrs Prior persisted. 'I just wanted you to know that something's not right. It's just that Kate, my daughter . . .' Caplan started listening very carefully.

She caught Fergusson as he came back across the road, two cans in his hand, and told him that Kate Miller had been offered a motorhome if she changed her story to match that of Daniel Doran's girlfriend. That fitted in with what Craigo had suspected. Did that encompass Sandra Leivesley as well, feeding them the satanism idea? It was important to somebody that Caplan was discredited, that they bought the idea of devil-worship being involved. Following that lead wouldn't take them to the mastermind of this, though. The guys at the top were clever – nothing would get back to them. Fergusson made a phone call to get Leivesley and Miller picked up for their own good.

When they walked into the incident room, all conversation stopped. Caplan took a look around the room; it all seemed different now. The faces of the McGregor family on the wall were someone else's problem. A wave of anger came over her. Her daughter was under the surgeon's knife, and there was Happy Harris fiddling with a jammed printer. Kinsella came out from his office. Craigo and Mackie were both sitting at their computers, heads down. The latter immediately came over to Caplan and gave her a hug.

'Please don't,' she said. 'If anybody's nice to me, I'll cry and I don't have time for that.'

Fergusson spoke: 'As you know, DI Caplan's daughter Emma was involved in a traffic incident today. I'm DCI John Fergusson of SCD, and I hope I can count on your support to get on with the job in hand.'

There was a murmur of consent.

'We still believe that there's a sizeable quantity of snapdragon at Rune, but we haven't yet located it. Two senior members of this team have now been targeted, so we must be close. There's been a drone monitoring movement on the island since the search, but nothing obvious has been moved. We need to look at this with fresh eyes.'

'I'm up for that,' said Mackie, as cheery as ever.

'DI Kinsella has been doing a competent job, but inexperience has, let's say, left you with an inability to share,' said Fergusson.

Kinsella was about to protest but he nodded; he knew the superior officer had a fair point.

'DI Caplan has been privy to intel she felt necessary to keep to herself, and I'll be coming to this, with SCD, from a more operational angle. Somewhere within these four walls is the answer. They were forewarned we were coming . . .'

'You have a spy in the camp,' interrupted Caplan, 'like I said.'

Fergusson ignored her. 'Please. Let's get round the table and speak freely regardless of rank.'

'The drugs will be somewhere you didn't search,' said Craigo, provoking an exasperated eye roll from Kinsella, 'somewhere the dogs could not follow the scent. They track through air and shallow water.'

'What if a stronger scent is used to mask the scent they're looking for? Not my aftershave, though – I wasn't there,' quipped Gourlay.

'Maybe the lentil curry?' joked Harris, something Caplan had never witnessed before. It was odd. But then, when had she ever really noticed him?

They pulled chairs round as Fergusson rolled out a map of the island and, alongside it, another covered with times and directional arrows. It was the plan for the raid on Rune, the raid that had achieved nothing. Fergusson summarised where they had searched and what their aim had been. They had blamed her for their failure, but she listened intently, knowing there was something there. The fury of what had happened to Emma was twisting in her stomach; she wanted the people who had done that to her girl caught and punished. Now she could understand why Pop Durant had left his life behind to pursue justice.

Caplan looked round the table, monitoring them all, hypersensitive to every nuance, every word. The Bastard, her ex-lover, was looking for a way to re-establish his name and reputation after the disaster of his operation. Kinsella, she had always had doubts about, but she could see that she might be being unfair. He had behaved like a drowning man trying to keep himself afloat in a situation where he was way over his head. Maybe he was guilty of nothing more than pride. A man whose wife had left him and now had nothing to go home to.

Gourlay, smart in every sense of the word, was another Fergusson in the making.

And there was Craigo, holding all his cards close to his chest and saying nothing when he should have been volunteering information. After years of being overlooked for promotion, stuck in this one-horse town and being bullied by the in-crowd, he was saying nothing but listening to everything.

Fergusson was still talking. '. . . so the yachts that bounce around the coasts of the UK are probably doing the trafficking. It's less than two hundred miles from here to the coast south of Dublin. On Skone, the Tamarin Marina is totally legitimate. All paperwork and computer records in order, craft registered and logged. The drug is brought in, then what? We had some intel that the drug was being moved in those little pots of cream or jam, or the boxes of lavender oil, the jars of honey, but they're exactly what they appear to be. However it's being transported, it's small enough, ubiquitous enough, for it to come over by the ferry to the mainland without us seeing it. We thought it was Allanach up in his pagoda – very few people go there. Just the two guys who run the place with him, Roddy the accountant and McMaster the ex-dealer. We're faced with a legitimate business that posts things all over the world. We ripped his place apart, found nothing.' He rubbed his eyes, frustrated and tired of it all. 'We have no idea of the scale of this operation.'

He tapped the desk with a gold pen that Caplan recognised. 'Snapdragon's flooding the market, the amount coming in is increasing, and this deluge is a ploy to increase dependency before the supply is cut to force the price up. It's very tightly controlled. We've had an undercover officer on this case for a year, but they didn't get enough intel to pull it together accurately, it turned out.'

'Or she's crap at her job?' Caplan sighed again.

'If they're a tight gang, they'll be impossible to infiltrate,' said Gourlay. 'I've been undercover – it's hell.'

The four of them brainstormed for forty minutes while Craigo sat quietly, studying the maps and scribbling details here and there. Then he'd shake his head and rip the page from his notebook, only to start again. Every time a page hit the wastepaper bucket, the discussion round the table would stop and they would look at him. Totally unaware, he'd go back to his scribbling. At one point he got out a magnifying glass to look at the picture of the island, then went over to the wall to the large Ordnance Survey map and stood there, deep in thought for a few minutes.

Kinsella spoke up. 'What about the rubbish? The ingredients they order in? What about animal feed? And there's—'

Craigo talked over him. 'When you were on the island, ma'am, did you see a signpost for the caves?'

Caplan shook her head. 'No, don't think so – wrecks and the marina but no caves.'

'The dogs would have taken us right there if there had been drugs in any cave,' said Fergusson automatically, still looking at the map, drawing his finger around the therapy centre and the health food shop, thinking of all the little things that people buy and take back to the mainland, in a bag with the honeybee logo. Nobody would think twice about it. 'One dog did alert, but it was a mid-air alert, not usually reliable.'

'It must have been recent, though, to be caught in the air on an island with a constant breeze,' said Mackie.

'Yes, I know that!' snapped Fergusson.

'The dogs wouldn't alert if the cave was below water level,' said Craigo, placing a stubby finger on the map, causing everybody to look at each other in confusion. 'There'd be no scent left. The cave on the other side would be above sea level. For storage. And not getting wet. Obviously.'

'There are no caves on Skone,' said Gourlay.

'Yes, there are. I remember stories of kids getting caught in them and drowning,' said Mackie.

'Underwater? There's a diving school,' said Caplan, thinking about Blossom the diving instructor and getting a dirty look from Fergusson, which evaporated when the same thought crossed his mind.

'There's caves on the old map here,' added Craigo, blinking slowly as he looked at his cousin. 'There was a rockfall, years ago, that closed the quarry. It collapsed the cave. That's why it's not on the recent maps.'

'Was that before Allanach inherited it?' asked Fergusson.

'During his dad's time,' said Mackie.

Fergusson shook his head. 'How was this missed from our intelligence?'

'Much depends on who was giving you that intel,' said Caplan sharply. 'The caves might still be accessible to a qualified diver.' She was thinking about Blossom, the pretty young thing who was close to Adam and had never cleaned a toilet in her life if she thought sodium bicarb smelled.

Kinsella had paused his perusal of the photographs and was listening intently until Harris broke the silence.

'Why no signpost for the cave? Why are they keeping that quiet? They abseil off the top of the cliff, so you'd think they'd mention that there were caves there.'

'For all his scarves and yoga poses, Allanach has a very good business brain, good enough to run a drug-smuggling operation. Callum

McMaster, his right-hand man, has previous for similar, and every cartel needs an accountant like Roddy Taylor,' said Fergusson.

'But why Allanach?' asked Caplan. 'To what end? So he can afford an island and a few goats, a yacht and a fancy lifestyle? He has all that already.'

'Power,' said Gourlay quietly. 'He wants power.'

'I think he has that as well; he just uses it differently.'

Fergusson spoke in low tones. 'Are we agreed that it comes in on a yacht, is stored somewhere and then carried by the foot soldiers in small amounts to Rune and on the ferry and away? There are good currents and prevailing winds, the Tamarin lagoon at Rune is sheltered, and the marina has great food, showers and so on.'

'Not difficult to notice the boats that do that journey frequently,' said Mackie.

'Very many do. And while we could stop and search the lot, there'd be little return. Shut down this supply and another would open up. What we want to know is the big picture. It's stored on the island, and nothing has come or gone since the raid. The drones have picked nothing up. They're not subtle but they're efficient.'

'What about the ongoing undercover operation? Why are they not here?' asked Kinsella.

Fergusson paused before replying. 'They're back on the island. They were uncooperative during the raid, so their cover wasn't blown and—'

Kinsella interrupted: 'You must have had some good intelligence before your raid.'

Fergusson nodded and looked at the map again. 'If the caves are open at all, how do you get access? We've been watching that island for months and this is the first I'm hearing about caves.'

'I wonder why,' muttered Caplan.

'Well, they're underwater so who would know? If the rockfall was twenty, thirty years ago, it'd be slipping from memory,' said Kinsella.

'Allanach would know. So would a diver.' Caplan drew a glare from Fergusson.

'Leave it with me,' said Mackie, wandering off with her mobile, causing Fergusson and Caplan to exchange a glance.

Caplan pointed out where Adam had been found at the standing stones, then quietly asked Kinsella how he managed to get there just after her, as she knew he lived some distance away.

'I wasn't at home. I was at Lorna's. She was asking about the post-mortem and the funeral.'

'Really?'

Lorna hadn't said anything about their meeting. Caplan was desperate to solve this case but was she now seeing connections where there were none? She had a thought that Kinsella and Lorna might be closer than she'd thought; they were of a similar age. Maybe Oswald suspected something and that's why he was keen to keep his DI away from the family. It was the middle of the night when Kinsella had arrived at the standing stones.

The door burst open, and Toni Mackie entered the room like a Spanish galleon in full sail. 'Looks like a no-go with the cave theory. There's only a very narrow entrance left and it's probably filled up now as the cliff face is unstable. And there was a cage put over it to stop anybody going in. There was an internet challenge a few years back to get into the Tamarin cave system, so the Coastal Commission got the Foundation to close it off completely. It's still inaccessible, totally vandal-proof.'

Again, Fergusson and Caplan exchanged a glance.

'Is the gap too small for a diver with scuba gear?' asked Caplan.

'It's fenced off, ma'am.'

'Yes, but a slim diver skilled enough to take their tank off and put it back on again could maybe get through the grating?'

Fergusson muttered to Caplan, 'You're obsessed with it being Blossom, aren't you? Why? Is it because of me?'

'Don't flatter yourself.'

'Adam used to dive,' said Kinsella. 'It's in the report about him going out to the Galapagos. Something else he fought with his parents about.'

EIGHTEEN

Caplan was lying on the sofa in yet another B&B. This time, she was in a separate building, with an en-suite and excellent Wi-Fi. She had made a cup of strong black coffee and eaten a plate of shortbread, fuelling up for a long night ahead. Fergusson had organised a boat, they were going to scout for the cave and appear to find nothing, but try to put in place a plan to track the drug's movements. And they were not going to set foot in Rune; they'd be as covert as was possible. Fergusson was determined to play the long game of bluff and double bluff.

While waiting, she had called Lorna. Kinsella had left her much earlier than he had said on the night that the attempt had been made on Adam's life. Kinsella hadn't said where he was going, but Lorna had thought he might be going out to meet a woman. She said he'd been on edge, nervy.

And somewhere in all this, they were losing sight of the family who had lost their lives, the family who had lost their father. The woman that Emma should become was now in jeopardy. And maybe somebody somewhere was missing Billy McBain, but she couldn't think who.

Caplan decided to go back to the start. She read the Knoxes' statements about the boys turning up at their house after they had discovered the bodies, while the video of McBain's interview was paused on her laptop. McBain and Frew had been in emotional distress at that point, then, at the interview just hours later, McBain was back to his usual arrogant self. Frew had remained badly shaken. She checked the log. Officially Frew had not been seen or heard of since McBain had been murdered. Caplan hoped Alice Keane had him hidden in a hotel room somewhere, with Netflix, pizza and a good lock on the door.

Caplan phoned the hospital, trying to remember the name of the nurse at the desk on Frew's ward. The one on duty knew who she meant by her description; it sounded like Sonja Ferries, she said, but she refused to give out her colleague's contact details, no matter how much pressure Caplan applied. She had to be content with leaving her number and asking that Sonja get in touch. Now. Not once she came back on shift. It was important. Somebody had calmed McBain down, somebody with influence over him. Sonja had said that he had been picked up during her last shift, which suggested a gap of at least twelve hours when he had been in Gourlay's company.

She had a lot of questions written down, plucking them from the air as they crossed her mind. Kinsella – always so keen to push Frew and McBain forward, dismissing the evidence that might point to an alternative solution, while ignoring the Eviscan results. Whyte and Gourlay – on the same five-a-side football team, and Harris in the same year. Oswald had thought he was onto something there. Whyte – the local man, the one who'd know the routines of the McGregors' lives. From what Lorna had said, Oswald might have had his doubts about Kinsella but was there an ulterior motive? She had known early on that it was either Kinsella or Craigo who had engineered the latter to be alone at Otterburn House, to plant the convenient evidence. Was Craigo's reasoning of finding Oswald's body true? Or had he helped put it there? Why was it not Kinsella who had retraced his friend's drive out on the lochside, on that lonely road, trying to find out what happened? She recalled a conversation she'd had with Kinsella during which he'd made a passing remark about Bob 'resurfacing'.

She put down her coffee cup. A chill fluttered through her bones. A Freudian slip or a figure of speech? She had played with the idea of Kinsella being a bad cop, but she had refused to truly accept it. He was bad only in the sense of not being strong enough to manage the team.

It was Craigo who knew she had a daughter, and knew her name, but Kinsella had researched her background when she had joined the squad. It wouldn't have been difficult for him to find out. But why was she thinking that it was one or the other? This was organised crime they were talking about. They could be two of a whole team.

Wullie Dodds and Mackie had both expressed issues with Kinsella, but was that the locals resenting the incomers? That was a conflict as old as time itself.

Twice Kinsella had asked her to find out what Craigo knew. And Sarah Linden had asked Caplan to report back to her and only her. Why? Was she involved? And all along Kinsella had known the whereabouts of Adam. The DI had explained it well but he had kept her out of meetings, kept her out of the loop; not admirable and not procedure, but perhaps it was understandable for a man in his position thinking that Bob Oswald was coming back.

It all went round in circles.

An image of Craigo and Kinsella coming down the path towards Adam at the standing stones at Kentilloch Castle struck her. Kinsella had not only got there quickly, but he had also arrived dressed for the conditions, not the usual wellies and thin waterproof they carried in the boot of the car.

Maybe Kinsella was just a nice guy, looking after his friend's widow and Adam, who was now floating somewhere between life and death. Emma was closer to the former than the latter. Kenny was on the mend. She herself felt incredibly alive. It was Aklen who was stuck.

Caplan leaned back and drained her coffee, closing her eyes and replaying the night McBain was killed. Craigo couldn't have slashed the boy's throat as he was behind her. It wasn't Frew as the footprints in the pine needles on the forest floor were too big. It was Kinsella who raced after the perpetrator who nobody else saw. If she remembered right, Gourlay had held her back slightly when she'd helped him out the water. He had actually shouted to Kinsella, warning him that she and Craigo were right behind him. She cast her mind over it again. Had Harris tried to hold them back as well? God, she was seeing enemies everywhere.

Toni Mackie, who seemed to get on with everybody, was guarded around Kinsella, and there were her stories of Craigo being bullied. But were they true? If so, it might drive him to get one over on his bosses, a small wedge that could widen into being an informant. Craigo could be so helpful and charismatic at times, just bloody awkward at others.

Neither Kinsella nor Gourlay had been present that first night she had visited Otterburn. Whyte had, though; he'd been on the phone as she walked down the drive to the house. Warning Craigo she was coming? Or talking to the person who was stalking her through the trees?

Her phone rang, the number unrecognised. It was Sonja Ferries calling back. She didn't know the name of the man who had picked up Billy McBain in the small hours of the morning but she remembered what he looked like and described him as handsome, average height, longish brown hair, late thirties or early forties. Oh, and he smelled really nice.

'Bleu de Chanel,' muttered Caplan as she rang off. It had taken him eight hours to do the thirty-minute journey from hospital to police station. What had come to pass in the car? *Just hold your nerve, son.* Gourlay, who had suggested that Mackie book the hotel, the one who had been in her room. Gourlay, the pretty one. The one who had held her up at the fairy pool where McBain had died, who had shouted a warning to Kinsella.

She ran through the sequence of events again. The two boys had gone on a bender on the Monday evening. The McGregor killings were carried out on the Tuesday – immediately after the housekeeper left, which left the longest possible period of time before her return and before the bodies would be discovered, so it was somebody who knew Ina Faulds well enough to know that she'd not go upstairs and that COVID had left her with no sense of smell. That pointed to somebody local – not Gourlay. The scene at Otterburn House was not the chaos of a drug-induced frenzy; it was meticulous and planned.

The phones, the snip of material and the tongue post were too neat for her liking. None of it proved that McBain was there. They could have had the phones taken from them, the scrap of lining could have been cut from the jacket. McBain and Frew wouldn't have known. Somebody with a clear mind had lifted a key to gain access to the house and the electricity; otherwise the alarm would have sounded at the police station when the boys went in. A local cop would know that. The alarm was off when the boys broke in but had been on in the intervening days when Ina entered the house. If the alarm had been off, she would have been suspicious. To keep up the illusion that the family were away, the alarm had been reset.

The local boy whose mum worked in the GP's surgery? Whyte. Whyte who played in the five-a-side team with Gourlay. Oswald had been right.

Her mobile rang. Sarah Linden.

'Has something happened?' A surge of panic.

'No, all is good. Emma's doing well so you've not to worry about her.'

'Has she regained consciousness?'

'Not yet, and they don't want her to. Meanwhile I've put a review team on your evidence – well, two from cold case are having a quick look at it. We're under pressure for you and Fergusson to get something out of this mess. I'm sure you've already worked out that none of the forensics sit right. The good news is that the fibres on the fabric sample are contra . . . They go the wrong way, equal stress on all three sides, whereas if it had been caught on the spike as the perp was moving forward, the tear in the fibres would be unidirectional.'

'Is that a really convoluted way of saying it was planted?'

'It's not clear cut. Or, rather, the sample was very clear cut – *cut* not torn. Which is the problem. And as you keep pointing out, the rest is so forensically clean and suddenly two lovely pieces of evidence are put right in front of us. And I had a nice chat with Owen Fraser from the university. Plus a bill. You're looking for a white Renault. He was very keen I should know that.'

'Thanks, I'll look out for it. But who's doing it? Gourlay, I'm sure, and Whyte's in the frame. We're keeping them out the loop from here on in.'

'Be careful, Christine. There's more than two of them. Keep John with you – he has experience in this kind of thing.'

'Don't worry, I will.' She rang off, checking the time. She had to trust somebody, and it may as well be The Bastard; at least she knew for certain he was a devious liar.

She was dressed and ready. As she looked in the mirror she thought about the game Murder in the Dark. Then remembered something her mother had said: *Beware the anger of a quiet woman.*

MICK MCCANN WELCOMED CAPLAN and Fergusson aboard the *Blue Buoyo*, just as darkness was falling. McCann wasn't introduced to Caplan, merely giving her a brisk nod of greeting before calling Fergusson 'Johnny', leaving her to suspect he was either SCD or HM Customs. They had passed Jack Innes working under a spotlight on *Wavedancer* as they had walked down to the harbour. They had exchanged a friendly wave but nothing more. It was going to be just the three of them. Nobody else knew.

McCann was taking them out to the cliff on the west side of Skone and had suggested the rigid inflatable, as it was quicker and the sea was calm.

As they chugged out of Cronchie harbour, wrapping their jackets around them, Fergusson nudged her and nodded to a small rotund figure on a blue-and-white boat, the *Julia-Philippe*. Their observer was on his phone, blatantly watching them.

'Wullie Dodds. He's had a boat here for a hundred years,' said Caplan to Fergusson, holding onto her Crewsaver as the RIB left the shelter of the harbour and started to bounce over the swell of the open sea. In the darkness they could see the lights of Skone, the northern tip where the ferry terminal was, before they headed round to the west side of the island to the walls of the marina where they motored into the calmer waters of the Tamarin lagoon. It was empty of the yachts and small motor cruisers that had been there the day before. They had been boarded and searched during the raid, then they had all left.

It was eerily quiet over the steady thrum of the engine, the dull beat of the waves hitting the side of the *Blue Buoyo*. McCann cut the power to a low thrum, a heartbeat throbbing across the dark water. The RIB passed the sands of Tamarin beach to the northeast and headed to the foreboding black cliff face, which looked so much more hospitable on a summer day when it was a playground for abseilers and puffin spotters.

McCann pointed to a large white buoy, easily visible in the dark churning water. 'I'll set the boat there – good place to see the entire cliff. The cave must be here somewhere, but God only knows. They've been closed off for as long as I can remember.'

Caplan and Fergusson searched with their torches, occasionally checking the reference maps they had on their phones and scanning the cliff formation for any evidence of rock fall. They could see a pattern – vertical crags that looked cleaner, less weather-worn than the others.

Caplan turned to ask McCann to reposition the boat, but he was looking out to sea, out to the darkness. She tapped Fergusson on the shoulder, thinking she heard another engine approaching. There was a faint drone across the water, steadily getting louder. Trying to focus her eyes in the poor light, she saw a bigger craft appear through the night air, motoring towards them. Caplan paused for a moment, wondering who could be out at this time. She expected the boat to pass them, but as it neared, she heard the engine increase in pitch. It was speeding up, heading straight for them. McCann was standing with one foot on the side of the RIB, easily absorbing the rise and fall of the boat with the increasing impact of the bow waves. He was on his radio, requesting help, reading something in the situation that caused him alarm. She looked up, a tiny moment of recognition – the flowers on the hull of the *Bettina Mae*.

Coming ever closer.

And closer.

Caplan felt a punch in the back. She went high into the air, her hand losing her grip on the phone, and she saw clouds, the moon, black waves on the horizon and the clifftop before she plunged into the freezing water, total darkness over her head. Something hit her in the face as she went under. There was an almighty crack, then a splash.

The shock of the cold water squeezed the breath out of her. The Crewsaver was lifting her up towards the surface where somebody was shouting, *there, she's there*. The engine changed tone again. A bright circle of light was panning the surface above her. They were picking up speed, trying to run her over. She unclipped the life jacket and dived down, aiming for the protection afforded by the shadow of what she presumed was the upturned RIB. She swam instinctively, pulling herself through the water, getting her bearings when she surfaced under the *Blue Buoyo*, holding onto the top of a seat. She shook the water from her eyes, gasping for breath, trying to think. The way Wullie Dodds had phoned the minute they left the harbour. The way Jack Innes had been working on *Wavedancer*. The sea around her began to churn, awash with bubbles. The RIB over her head was being pushed sideways. She held on for as long as she could, filling her lungs with air before swimming down, getting as much depth as possible, kicking her shoes off and unzipping her jacket, their wet bulk impeding her movement.

She felt the water roll past her, around her, over her. As the propellers got going again, she held her nose, trying to keep her depth as the water clouded with bubbles. She saw something large float up to the surface. It was there and gone before she could recognise it. Or them?

Where was John? What had happened to McCann?

She had to think. Her brain was dancing around with ridiculous thoughts about her nice jacket while her lungs were screaming at her to breathe. Every survival instinct she had was telling her to stay below the surface. The bright beam of the torch crossed above her again.

John Fergusson. His two wee boys. Lizzie. How can this be happening? She remembered the white buoy. Where there was a buoy there would be a rope, something she could hold on to. It might be nothing, but any action was better than waiting here to drown. She started a horizontal swim. The huge shadows above, *Blue Buoyo* and *Bettina Mae*, were doing their little waltz in the water under the moonlight. She struck out upwards, keeping away from the propellers, difficult to see now that they had fallen silent; they were listening for her as much as she was listening for them. She carefully resurfaced at the red hull, one hand on the side to steady herself as she opened her mouth to let the air out silently, regulating her breathing, something that she had learned as a dancer. She could hear male voices above, thinking that she could recognise some of them, homing in to hear what they were saying. The propellers started churning the water, nearly catching her out as the boat moved. She dived again, jackknifing, striking her way down, ignoring the sharp pain that rattled through her foot as the propeller struck her.

She swam as far as she could, ignoring the cold, ignoring the numbness. Her arms were weakening when she caught sight of the torch beam swiping its way through the water, the light catching something. It was the chained rope of the buoy. She headed for it, waiting for the beam to move back across before she surfaced and took a deep breath, keeping the buoy between her and the boat.

Two men were aboard, waving and pointing. They were looking for bodies in the water.

She heard a shout, but the light did not come her way. Something closer to the shore had caught their attention – John Fergusson's frantic front crawl splashing in the gunmetal seawater. He wasn't far away but he was closer to the boat than she was. The *Bettina Mae* moved into gear, the propellers starting to turn again. She could see, clearly, Gourlay at the bow, waving his arm, orchestrating the movements as the two boats tried to disengage. The upturned hull of *Blue Buoyo* was pushed out the way, the difficulty of getting untangled causing *Bettina Mae* to turn and swing her stern towards Fergusson. Caplan swam towards him, under the water with a perfect dolphin kick, feeling the pulsing pain in her ankle. She reached out and grabbed Fergusson by the leg. He kicked her hard. She let go. He realised that she was trying to tell him something. He curled into a ball and dived, flicking over in the water. She grabbed him and pulled him down, their combined muscular effort sinking them easily. As their faces met, she pointed towards the chained rope, let go of him and swam up for more air. It was up to him now.

Once she reached the chain, she ascended on it and released a long slow breath through pursed lips, too small for the bubbles to be heard or seen, her head behind the buoy, hopefully out of sight as those on the boat scanned the surface, looking for them. Caplan dived again, lungs full, getting more used to holding the breath as deep as she could, filling every space with air. She felt Fergusson grab the chain, kicking her in the back in his desperation to get to the top. He had seen her, followed her example, only exposing his head for the breath in. He pulled himself back down the chain, where the two of them hung suspended in the freezing water, their hair waving like halos, unable to do anything but wait.

She noticed a tag on the line at one metre and could feel the outline of another at two. Dive markers, but they didn't dive from here to the wreck. That was on the other side of the marina wall. She looked down to another line, fixed and heading where? The cliffs? Inland? She'd bet it went towards the cliff. After another breath, she pointed to Fergusson, then to the transverse line, catching his attention, and started to swim along its length. Holding onto the rope made it much easier as she didn't have to fight to keep any depth. She made her way along, resurfacing every eighth arm stroke. She emerged, keeping her eyes on where she was going, knowing she was now moving towards the cliff. The rhythm gave her something to concentrate on, allowed her to ignore the weight of numbness that was creeping along her limbs, her fingers losing their grip on the chain she could no longer feel.

At the cliff face, they both surfaced, seeing *Bettina Mae* in the middle of the marina. She could see who was at the helm now. Even without his yellow T-shirt and jeans, she still recognised the squat bulk of Roddy Taylor. All the players were on the stage now, for next to Gourlay was Whyte, sweeping the beams of the boat's lights across the water, but they were concentrating on the shore. The buoy was behind the *Bettina Mae*; they were focused on the wrong direction; she had bought them some time. They gulped in fresh air, clinging onto the cliff.

Caplan needed to know if they had been right. She felt her way down, sinking below the water, letting the air trickle from her lips. She found a broken metal grate over a narrow vertical fissure in the rock, solid black with a sign, dull with age, that read: *Do Not Enter. Danger of Death*. She held onto the grate with one hand, trying to feel the ends of the spars with her numb fingers. She had enough feeling to know they had been cut through, rather than rusted away.

As slim as she was, Caplan could have swum through it with a few inches of clearance, but Fergusson wouldn't make it. Just as she'd thought, it was only wide enough for a slim, experienced diver who could remove their tank under water then replace it. Blossom.

She surfaced again, keeping close to the side of the cliff. The upturned hull of *Blue Buoyo* was still swirling in the water. *Bettina Mae* had pulled herself free. Fergusson, beside her, allowed himself the luxury of a violent cough to clear his lungs, then he looked up, trying to assess how to get out of here. Swim for the shore? Swim for the netted boulders that formed the edge of the marina? They'd be sitting ducks when *Bettina Mae* turned their way. There followed what seemed a very long time, but was probably only minutes, when neither party moved: stalemate. They heard the ring of a mobile, and again the tone of *Bettina Mae*'s engines changed and she headed out of the marina, her red stern lights fading into the night air.

Teeth chattering, Caplan and Fergusson edged their way along the cliff face. The only sound was their gasping breath and the slap of the waves on the rocks. They heard another engine in the distance, saw a figure at the bow of the faster new arrival shining a torch in the water, scanning, looking for them, calling out 'Christine'. White with distinctive flames along the side, Caplan recognised the sleek lines of *Wavedancer*. She could see Kinsella, Harris and Innes from the marina, bouncing quickly across the surface of the waves. Another familiar voice, female, rolled over the water, saying, 'They must be somewhere. What the hell happened? That RIB's destroyed.'

Fergusson shouted back, 'Over here.' But he was so weak his voice had no power.

A mixture of voices answered. *Wavedancer* turned in an elegant arc, sending spray high into the night, coming ever closer, the white water peeling away as her bow sliced through it. The disruption sent pulses of waves over their faces, but Caplan could feel the stress leaving her – they were safe. All they had to do was hold on; they were being rescued. Then home. A hot bath. Back to the hospital tomorrow. See Emma. This nightmare would be behind them.

She could feel tears of relief on her face. *Wavedancer* was slowing, and she saw Harris reaching for them over the bow rail, Kinsella and somebody else at the side. Harris held out a coiled rope in one hand, in the other, a lifebuoy. Fergusson was closer. With one hand reaching for Harris, holding onto Caplan with the other, he was pulling her ever closer to the bow of the speedboat.

Harris seemed to take an age to throw the buoy.

As Fergusson reached to grab it, there was a flash. A crack.

Harris somersaulted into the water. Caplan was forced backwards towards the cliff face, diving down and to the side. Harris moved with the pull of the water, his life jacket puffed above the surface, before he was dragged downwards. He floated past her, drifting sideways into the darkness, a cloud of dark blood across his face.

Caplan jammed her fist into her mouth, fighting shock and nausea. They had killed Harris.

She surfaced, trying to breathe, and watched as *Wavedancer* sped up and started frantic circling, her bow high above the waves. Caplan heard a scream and saw somebody splash as they entered the water. The screaming went on – a female. *Wavedancer* swung in a huge arc and accelerated towards the figure in the waves. The bow light caught the honey-blonde hair and a single hand waving in the darkness.

There was one final shriek of terror as the boat went over her, the propeller only stuttering a little as it hit flesh and bone.

Wavedancer circled and left for the open sea.

They were never going to get out of this nightmare. She had lost sight of Fergusson. Where was McCann? She was sure she'd seen Kinsella on the boat. She had no fight against a firearm. They knew she was here – all they had to do was wait.

She'd either drown or succumb to hypothermia.

At that moment she knew she was going to die. She thought, as she floated in the water, how peaceful it would be to relax and simply fall through the depths, to stop fighting and let it take her. Just let her breath out, let it bubble away. She extended her arms above her head and sank deeper into the sea.

But wait, not yet, she had a final breath to take.

Caplan could feel the vibration of another engine with a deeper tone, a bigger boat? Somebody shouting. She swam, too exhausted to hold position in the water, and a wave picked her up and battered her against the cliff face, hitting her head on a jutting sharp edge.

She surfaced again, now dizzy through lack of oxygen and the blow to her head, not able to make sense of the noises in the water. A glaring bright light pinned her against the rock.

She felt dead inside. Her ears were picking up nothing but the roar of water. Shouting. The engine moving away.

The light left her.

She was alone.

It was very quiet now.

She was chilled to the core and had no sense of where her body was. Her head was going under the water and she was swallowing brine.

There was a splash at her hand, then another and another. Something was hitting the water beside her. She reached out and felt the warm contours of smooth wood, the oar of a rowing boat.

She heard a familiar voice saying, 'There's a pole right in front of you. You might like to grab it, ma'am.'

NINETEEN

Ten days later

When her mobile rang, Caplan pulled onto the grass verge at the old farmhouse and turned the Duster so it faced out to sea. She didn't care – there were no neighbours to annoy.

It was Kenny with his daily update from the hospital. Everything was good. Emma had been awake most of the afternoon, her speech was coming along, and they'd played Scrabble. Kenny told his mum that he loved her, then threw in a request for a tenner just to soften the sentiment.

'No chance,' she replied.

She knew her son had had a fright. He had made a bad choice, but he was getting another chance – more than Billy McBain, more than Daniel Doran ever had. She hoped Scott Frew would make better choices now that he was out on the island. He'd thought that his streetwise pal was making inroads to play with the big guys; in reality he was being groomed as any vulnerable individual is by a Machiavellian mind. He'd been lucky that Alice Keane had taken the initiative and kept him out of harm's way after McBain had been found dead. That night, Scott had received a text, luring him to a car park, but the walk had been too much for him after the infection. He'd sat on a bench, feeling sick and dizzy, and missed the rendezvous. He turned back to his foster mum. That decision had saved his life.

Calm said the lad seemed to be enjoying being on Skone, the fresh air on his face. He was learning to swim and had bonded with the narky wee Shetland pony. He was keeping a close eye on Scott, having walked that path himself.

Caplan sighed. It wasn't over yet, but every day that passed brought another bit of closure. Her team had stopped the supply of a very dangerous and addictive drug. They had saved many lives, but it would all be lost in statistics. The ringleader, as far as Fergusson could make out, was Roddy the accountant. He was an ex-cop who had changed his name, and much of his face, but his posture remained the same. In his days at Tulliallan training college, he was James Wilson – the man at the back in the photo of the football team. His prints were on file, a match for the one on Kenny's phone. He had removed his glove to enter the PIN. Whyte had run the operation from the Otterburn side, feeding back the intelligence from Gourlay and Kinsella.

Oswald had been close, so close they had had to get rid of him when he was given this case. He had looked back at the careers of those he had suspected, friendships and loyalties bonded on the playing field many years before.

Chris Allanach, his mind on higher spiritual matters, had never noticed the money laundering and drug trafficking going on under his nose. He was heartbroken at the way his dream had been broken and corrupted.

In the dark confusion of the marina, when Caplan threw her phone, it had landed onboard the *Bettina Mae*, pinging a location signal back to Lizzie's phone in Glasgow, so they were not as invisible as they presumed. When the *Bettina Mae* was finally picked up, she was unmanned and adrift. They knew who had been aboard that night from the evidence on the abandoned vessel: Gourlay, Whyte and Taylor. The big three.

Wavedancer had also been found abandoned. Jack Innes was suspected of being a large part of the operation but hadn't stuck around to be questioned.

The *Julia-Philippe* had chugged round the island, spotted the upturned RIB in the water, and alerted Craigo and Calm, who were waiting on the shore. Wullie Dodds had tried to follow the other two boats out to sea, but they were too fast for his old vessel.

Caplan was still annoyed she hadn't spotted Taylor, or Wilson, in that photograph: Roddy, before his broken nose and two stone lighter, was in the middle at the back, thick-necked, arms folded. The posture was recognisable. SCD had tracked their phones retrospectively, and there had been no signal from Taylor's phone for the day of the murders or the days before and after. They were too clever to make a mistake like that. Two well-dressed police officers, Gourlay and Taylor, had approached Charlotte McGregor in her greenhouse at Otterburn, the reason for their visit the McGregors' complaint about the antisocial behaviour at the Bodie Neuk. Gourlay's charm would have done the rest.

Gourlay and Whyte were the two men at the front of the photo-graph. Fergusson was examining the careers of the other two, Alistair McDade and Jimmy Armstrong, with forensic scrutiny. God help them if they were innocent cops who had fancied a wee game of fives when the photo was taken.

Organised crime was a patient and long-lived beast. This had been a career move. The money to be made, the hold they'd have over the operation of both drug distribution and money laundering was staggering, well worth the investment in time and planning. The ten million for the inheritance was nothing; it was that gateway they had wanted. How long had this operation been going on? Where did it start? Was it the TV programme about the Devil Stone that sparked the whole thing? Who decided to groom McBain as a patsy? Gourlay and Whyte? Taylor had made his move on Skone, seeing the island and the Magus as ripe for his purposes.

Caplan looked out across the water; today the island looked smaller and darker than it had before, as if the sunshine had been turned off.

Had Whyte recruited McBain? *Keep your head down, son. Stop drawing attention to yourself, you're playing with the big boys now.* There had been an eight-month period when he had not come to the attention of the authorities before the incident at Otterburn. Promises of drink, girls, satanic power, money – a life of crime – must have been seductive to a boy who'd never had anything. After the murders, they had needed the boys to go back; stealing the stone was just an excuse. They needed the boys back on site to be 'guilty' of the murders, the plan being that neither of them would live long enough to stand trial. They had got that half right.

It was complicated, but it fitted. This was all set up to be the perfect drug route into the UK and into Europe beyond, with the McGregor millions and the ownership of Skone. They had needed control at every level, and almost achieved it – until Oswald, then herself.

How long would Chris Allanach have lasted before everything passed to Taylor? The idyllic life on the island would have continued, the dark underbelly unseen.

Tate, the lawyer, was taking control of Adam's money until the young man recovered. The will would stand; Adam was now a multi-millionaire. Caplan could see the Foundation playing a big part in his life, especially as early signs indicated he was going to be left with a degree of physical impairment. Recently, however, Adam had regained consciousness, and his progress had been almost miraculous. Blossom had been his shoulder to cry on, his confidante after he'd heard the news of his family's fate. Under Taylor's guidance, she had scared him into the police protection of Kinsella that had led him into the spider's web. Their main concern had been that Adam had to die last, and it had to be proven so. The mistake they made was tasking Kinsella with disposing of Adam.

In the end, Kinsella couldn't quite do it. He wasn't a cold-blooded killer like those who had committed the atrocity at Otterburn House. He had been genuinely shocked, and scared, at Oswald's death, and he should have confessed when he had sat in the car with her. He couldn't bring himself to strangle another human being and had paid for that with his life. His body was washed up on Galveston beach three days after the *Wavedancer* had motored out of the marina.

Was it the downward spiral of Kinsella's personal life that had made him vulnerable to manipulation and temptation? Caplan was convinced that he had never been in the inner circle; like Blossom, he had been used, then dispatched.

Adam was still under the impression that Kinsella had been on his side, having no memory of the incident at the standing stones. And Fergusson would let him believe that until he was stronger. His specialist was keeping him sedated, allowing him to rest and build the strength he would need for the emotional pain that lay ahead. Allanach had taken the three McGregor dogs out with him to the island, to await Adam's return.

For the moment, out in the bay, Skone sat in the glistening water, Honeybogg Hill a carbuncle on its face, the ridge of cliffs on the far side just visible.

Police divers had found a huge stash of snapdragon, ready for market, sealed and stored in a part of the cave that always remained above the high-tide mark, packages hanging from the roof like giant bats.

They were lozenges of coated benzodiazepine with a core of pure cocaine. They hadn't come close to finding out where it was being manufactured. That would be the task of another operation. Fergusson admitted that no matter what they did, they would always be one step behind, even on a good day.

While on Skone he stumbled across the two vehicles that the Allanach Foundation kept up in the village, both white Renaults. But they had no proof who the demonic figure that caused Oswald's death was. They suspected Taylor.

Caplan hoped that those traumatised by all these events would find peace at Rune and, eventually, heal. But it wasn't the end of the story. Journalists were lining up to tell the tale of the orphaned little rich boy, the mysterious Magus, the Devil Stone and the satanists – and the pretty, double-dealing undercover cop who had died so violently. Tourists now visited the marina to gawp.

Skone would forever have that tragic association.

Caplan wound down the window, letting the cool breeze into the car. There were a few seals out on the water, their doglike heads above the waves, bobbing around like they were having a conversation. They dropped below the surface, one after the other, then popped up a little further out.

She looked over the water beyond the islands to where they had found the body parts of Annette Evans. Her death had deprived Caplan of the pleasure of arresting her; still, she was somebody's daughter.

Pop Durant had left the island and gone back to Edinburgh. He had sent Caplan flowers, saying he hoped she understood. Wullie Dodds was still tinkering away with the *Julia-Philippe* in Cronchie harbour, sucking his pipe and saying absolutely nothing on the subject.

Caplan was still vague on some of the details. She had no recollection of Harris being pulled ashore or of Fergusson hanging on the back. She had no recall of McCann helping them to dry land. Calm had gone back out and found Harris holding onto the cliff face barely alive. The bullet had hit his shoulder, and the momentum had pushed him into the water, but the freezing temperature had shocked him back to consciousness.

She knew she would be spending a lot of time writing up reports. The images of the family at Otterburn House were the ones that stayed with her, their faces, and the cold, cold water, the feeling that death was close and how comfortable she had felt about it. It frightened her.

She opened the car door and got out, walking down to the shore where she stood enjoying the sun on her face, the birdsong and the quiet lap of the water.

Right on time, a black Audi drew up beside her car.

John Fergusson got out. 'Hi, just checking how you're doing.'

'I'm okay, thanks. Well, my face's better. I've still got stitches in my foot. Half an inch further and the propeller would have sliced it off.'

'You were lucky there. It's so lovely today, it's hard to imagine how cold it was that night. I don't know how you stood it.'

'I'm used to it. I spent years sitting in cold baths.'

'Is that a dancer's thing?'

'Yes. Good for the muscles. So, what are you doing here?'

'I wanted to see the house you were talking about.'

'No, you didn't. You want to know how I'm going to write this up. I could make you look very stupid.'

'You could, but I don't think you will. You're not one to score off people – you're better than that.'

'Such flattery.'

'Seriously, you know the emphasis that you could put on certain things.'

'Like Blossom? Annette shagging you to get information on what SCD was doing? Yeah, they'll love that back at HQ.' She allowed herself a wee smile when one of the seals started doing acrobatics in the water. 'I'll do what I can.'

'I know you will. You put your career on the line for Lizzie.'

'You shouldn't listen to crap. Lizzie needs to work. Her ex-husband never gives her any money.'

'You and I know that isn't true. If I get bumped here, there'll be even less money to go round.'

They watched the seals for a moment.

'Have you heard I've decided to step back up to DCI?' she said.

'Good. You'd be welcome over at SCD if you ever want a change of scene – we could do with you.'

'Not for me, I don't think.' Caplan sighed. 'Where would we be if Bob Oswald had rejected the case? He'd be alive, wouldn't he? Kinsella actually said, "He shouldn't have been there."'

'I'd say they were banking on Kinsella getting it. But when Oswald accepted it, he signed his death warrant. They thought they were home and dry, then you turned up. I'm advising the European operation about snapdragon now. As I said, you'd be welcome to join us, but it's very hush-hush . . .'

'I've been offered another post, up here at Cronchie, with Craigo and Mackie, God help me. They might be crap detectives, but they know how to row a boat. Never been so glad to see another human being as when I saw Mackie on the shore at the marina, with a big tartan blanket!'

Fergusson laughed. There was a sense of relief at the night they had lived through, a shared horror that was not quite a mere memory.

'Oh, and two bizarre things have come to light. One is that the Devil Stone is just some iron compound that seeps red when it's wet. It's chemical, not supernatural, so we're safe from the Devil after all. And, even more bizarre, the stone stolen from the house was a fake.'

'A fake?' said Caplan.

'Yes, when the *Antiques Roadshow* came to Cronchie a few years ago, they did a wee bit on Otterburn House and the stone. Because the stone is rare, it went off to the Natural History Museum to be examined. It was a replica they had in the glass case at Otterburn House. Adam has the original back now, kind of a fitting end to the story. It was probably the stone, the connection with the Foundation, that was the seed of the whole thing.'

'A replica stone? Bloody hell.'

'The weird thing is that as soon Adam knew the stone was back, his recovery was remarkable, almost overnight,' said Fergusson.

'I might get one for Aklen.'

'How's he doing now?'

'He's doing okay, going to move up here too. Emma's taking a year out of uni and might go over to Rune when she's well enough. In fact, Allanach's falling over himself to employ her. I think he'll be very happy to have her there, with her eco-marketing brain and the fact that she can be trusted.'

'And that her mother is terrifying.'

'There might be that,' agreed Caplan.

'And Kenny?'

'Kenny's still Kenny, not too sure what he's doing, but we're selling the house.'

'And this is the new one?'

They walked across the road and looked at the house, her house. There was a gap in the wall and two hinges on a loose frame made out of old wood. A gate had been attached here at some point, but the opening itself was enchanting and inviting. The garden was more of a meadow, and the tree line was angled in front of the house so that the view across the bay to the larger islands was uninterrupted.

'No neighbours for miles.'

'You already own it? You don't mess about,' he said.

'I did once and look where it got me.'

He smiled, hovering at the gate, sensing that she wanted this moment on her own, and then said his goodbyes.

How good it would be to come home and be welcomed. She thought she was beginning to understand this place, this benign wildness that it was not safe to challenge.

Mother Nature would always win.

She intended to get a dog when she moved up. It would do Aklen the world of good, having something to be responsible for. There was a cat roaming around here, a queen tabby who looked as if she had kittens tucked away somewhere. Caplan had some cat food in the car; she'd leave it in the outbuilding and replenish it in a couple of days.

The seals were closer to the shore now, enjoying themselves cavorting around together. And where was the rest of the team? Oswald was in a drawer in the mortuary; his girls would grow up without a dad. Assistant Chief Constable Linden would be in her penthouse flat with its floor-to-ceiling windows, working. Lizzie would be kissing her boys goodnight and tucking them up in bed, opening a bottle of cheap red and settling down to read a crime novel.

She tasted the salty air on her lips. She was starting to feel different, to embrace a sense of comfort with the clouds and the islands, the hills and the sand. She was missing Toni Mackie and her constant chatter, Craigo and his weird logic.

And Aklen, the man she loved, her best friend, the father of her children. He was still in there, still alive in that husk of a skeleton lying in his bed. That bright flame had been snuffed out. Would this place heal him? He was born up here. Maybe they would come back and leave the rest behind.

Just as she was taking her mobile from her pocket to take some pictures of the house, she heard a mewling. The cat appeared through the rhododendron bushes, tail in the air, carrying a tiny kitten in her mouth.

It was time to move on.